BLUE FLAME

BLUE FLAME

BOOK TWO IN THE DAEMON COLLECTING SERIES

ALISON LEVY

Published by SparkPress, a BookSparks imprint,
A division of SparkPoint Studio, LLC
Phoenix, Arizona, USA, 85007
www.gosparkpress.com

Published 2022
Printed in the United States of America
Print ISBN: 978-1-68463-171-1
E-ISBN: 978-1-68463-172-8 (e-bk)

Library of Congress Control Number: 2022904937

Book design by Stacey Aaronson

FOR MATT AND ERIC.

PROLOGUE

Flame undulated over his skin.

Smokeless fire covered him,
consuming nothing.

Crimson and gold blazed and flickered
from the points of his ears
along his long arms and wings
and down to the claws of his feet.

He was always burning,
never hot.

He was angry.

Ripped from his home and cast adrift,
he was now perpetually in strange surroundings.

Humans.
Humans everywhere.

They invaded his senses.
The smell of them—
a pungent odor of wet shit—
infested his nostrils.

The noise they made—
those punchy, vibrating voices—
was a poison to his ears.

Everywhere he looked he saw their
cold, artless constructions,
hill after hill of hideous termite mounds
squirming with maggoty flesh.

He loathed everything in this world.

He despised the one who had
snatched him away by force
and dropped into this cesspool.

This offense could not stand.

To be abducted by a human was an affront
to him, his family, his race.

He could return home at any time
but how could he face his people
if they learned that he'd let this insult slide?

His family's flames would dim
from the shame of his failure

and they would be shunned by the community.
No.

The slight must be repaid before he went home.

But avenging himself was proving challenging.
His abductor seemed to sense his approach every time and,
using enormous power, sent him reeling
into distant lands before he could get close enough to strike.

Again and again, he drew near,
sneaking through shadows
or charging toward his target at a breakneck speed,
only to be knocked away.

The blasted human even had the audacity
to look annoyed at his continued efforts.

After weeks of failure and frustration,
he finally understood:
vengeance would require a different tactic.

Tucked into a less visible layer of reality,
imperceptible to human eyes,
he stared across the room at his new target.

The woman sat at a dressing table,
braiding her hair and humming a little tune.

She was unguarded, unmindful,
and, from his observations,

devoid of power.
More importantly, she was much loved by his abductor.

He hooked one long, pointed finger
into a lock of her hair and flipped it loose—
and drew no response from her but a soft *tsk!*
woven into the flow of her song.

She tucked the loose strand back into the braid,
stood up, and walked within inches of him,
never noticing that she was not alone.

A low rumble rippled through his chest.

Here was vengeance within reach.

He would be home again by nightfall.

He swept a wing over her,
encasing her head in its cloth-like folds.

Though she did not see him, she felt his touch.
She put a hand to her face,
swayed, and grabbed the edge of her dresser for support.

He drew his wing tighter around her,
letting his flames consume the air
until she gasped for breath.

Choking, she fell to her knees
and clawed wildly at the air,

but her hands passed through him with no effect.
His lipless mouth drew back from his sharp teeth
in a pleased grin.

How simple it was!

The death of this one
would sufficiently wound
his human nemesis
to uphold his honor
and maintain his family's pride.

With her death, he thought joyfully,
he could finally go home.

The bedroom door flew open with a bang;
he whipped his head around
and roared at the sight of the intruder.

He dropped the woman and jumped away,
teeth bared.

The woman collapsed in a heap,
heaving deep breaths,
hands on her chest.

An orange glow filled the human's eyes
and danced over his fingers as he raised his hands.

Knowing what this meant,
he tried to escape,

but his body would not produce the speed he needed.
Orange lightning forked through the room,
and ripped a hole in the world
that sucked him in like water down a drain.

On the far side, he saw nothing
but a vast expanse of ice and snow under a gray sky.

Frustration punched him in the gut.

Wherever this was, it would take him time to find his way back.

Anger and misery devoured him in equal measure.

Another failure!

Another missed chance to return to his home,
to his family,
and to everything that mattered.

As he fell through the passage
he heard the patter of his enemy's feet,
hurrying to the woman's side.

"Mama!" cried the little boy. "Mama!"

PART

I

1
THE MORLEYS

"**B**ach! Hey, Bach!"

The young man popped out of his room and stood at the top of the staircase, looking down at Rachel, who stood at the entrance to the living room.

"What's up?"

"Get your *tulira* dog out of here!" she yelled. "It's jumping all over the Morleys!"

Bach had lived in her house for barely a week and despite the fact that she found herself using the word "*tulira*" about ten times each day, it had only occurred to her yesterday that he didn't know what it meant. Still, since he didn't ask, she opted not to volunteer the information. Given her tone of voice every time she used it, as well as his prompt response, she suspected he understood the spirit in which it was spoken.

"I'll take him outside and run him around until he's tired," he said, hurrying down the stairs. "Sorry about the jumping. He's just a puppy."

"*Tulira*," Rachel grumbled.

Bach opened the front door and whistled. The puppy immediately bounded out of the living room and trotted out of the house past him, his tail wagging madly.

As soon as Bach closed the door behind him and his overexcited pet, Rachel returned to the living room.

"Sorry about that dog," she said, sitting back down in the armchair opposite the sofa, where the Morleys were seated side by side—Mrs. Morley between her daughter, Leda, and son, Simon. "My, uh, visitor lured it out from under the house and now it won't leave."

"Don't worry about it," Leda said.

"Mrs. Morley," Rachel said to the older woman, "has Leda told you everything?"

"Um, she's told me a lot of things," the older woman hesitantly replied. Her full lips pursed and her lightly-wrinkled face tightened. Eyes-tight, she shifted her matronly form in the cushions as if searching for a comfort in her body that her heart did not share. "She told me about being abducted by a strange man and being locked up and beaten in his basement. She also told me," she said, sweeping an accusatory glare between Rachel and Leda, "I'm not supposed to call the police, even though this man somehow escaped custody. She showed me some of the things on the flash drive that you gave her, and said they were written by our ancestors hundreds of years ago." She clasped her long fingers together, the gentle clicks of her many gold rings and bracelets filling the brief silence. "She's told me about something called 'gatekeeper' that I don't quite understand, though apparently it's a thing the women in our family have had for a very long time."

Rachel nodded. "Did she tell you about daemons?"

"Yes," Mrs. Morley said quietly.

"And you had a look at the daemon in the coat?"

Mrs. Morley's dark, dark eyes darted fearfully to the crumpled coat at the far end of the sofa. Simon was currently staring at it through Rachel's glasses, the lenses of which allowed the wearer to see beings, like daemons, that existed out of phase with reality. "I did," she said slowly, "although I don't know what, exactly, I saw."

"Looks like something out of *Lord of the Rings*," said Simon, poking the oblivious daemon with his pen. "Weird."

"Simon, don't touch that thing!" exclaimed his mother. "It might bite you!"

"It won't," Rachel said. "I told it to sit there and behave itself."

"But you said it was defective," Mrs. Morley countered. "Why would it listen to you if it's defective?"

"It listens *because* it's defective. It's kinda messed up that way."

"And it lives with you?"

"Until the Central Office takes it back, yes. And believe me," she added, her jaw clenched, "I ask them to take it back at least once a day." *And I get the same reply each time*, she thought bitterly. *"We have insufficient resources at this time."* She narrowed her eyes at the coat. "It won't be here forever." *It better not be here forever.*

Mrs. Morley shot her son one more warning look and, despite being a twenty-something grown man, he obediently pocketed the pen.

Eyes still glued to the old coat, Simon removed the glasses from his face. "The demon that's connected to our family," he said. "Does it look like this one?"

"No," said Rachel. "This is a riot daemon. Apep is a chaos daemon. I've only ever seen one chaos daemon, but it was huge. It looked like a . . ." She held up her hands, as if waiting for the right words fall into her fingers. "A big, dark snake with a million swirly coils, and a skinny head with big, target-like eyes on it. It was hard to look at, too, because light kept bending around it."

"Is that why it was busted?" Simon asked. "Is that why it got sent to the—whatcha call it—the wasteland?"

"No, that's what a chaos daemon is supposed to do. Apep was sent to the wastes because it developed a defect that caused it to swallow light instead of bending it. Apparently, it was swallowing so much sunlight that it was withering crops and significantly lowering the temperature of multiple countries. It was captured and brought in for correction, but once it was released, its defect returned and kept getting worse and worse, until the sunrise was barely visible in the areas affected. My people sent it to the wastes because leaving it alone would have eventually wiped out entire civilizations. Sending it to the wastes and creating the first gatekeeper of your bloodline was the best solution."

"So . . ." Mrs. Morley said, slowly spinning one of her bracelets. "Our family is important?"

"Extremely. Without the women of your family, Apep might escape and eat the sun."

"I see," she whispered thoughtfully.

"Only the women," said Simon. Rachel saw with surprise that his jaw was set and his nostrils were flaring like an agitated bull's. "The men in this family don't count, right?"

"Uh . . ." Rachel said, "they aren't gatekeepers, if that's what you mean."

"Why?"

"It just happened that way," she said, shrugging. "Some gatekeeper responsibilities pass from father to son, some pass only to the firstborn child, some skip a generation. During my training, I learned about a family where the gatekeeper title only passed to children born with the same birthmark as the original gatekeeper. There's really no consistency about it at all. Your family's mantle just happens to pass from mother to daughter. We don't know why."

"Shut out of an inheritance without explanation," Simon grumbled. "That's just great. That's fucking awesome."

"Simon!" Mrs. Morley said.

"I don't need to be here, do I?" he said curtly. "None of this shit applies to me."

"Shut the hell up!" Leda shouted. "Aren't you paying attention? This is our family!"

"How is it 'our' anything? This whole damn thing's got nothing to do with me."

"Shut your mouth, Simon," Mrs. Morley said, straightening her back. "Your sister is right. This is our family and we're heaven blessed to have our history returned to us." She swept her arm in a commanding arc and pointed toward the front door. "If you can't take an interest, then leave."

With a grunt, Simon stood up, edged his way around the three women, and headed for the front door. "I'm out."

Rachel watched him go: one part perplexed, and one part annoyed. While she didn't understand Simon's negative reaction to this situation in particular, this sort of over-the-top reaction wasn't foreign to her. Rachel's older brother, Grigor, was the sort of man to act out like this if he felt slighted. Seeing Simon storm out of the house was just like seeing Grigor stomp off when he was offended.

"I apologize for him," Mrs. Morley said as her son left the room. "Now, what is it that we're expected to do?"

Rachel shrugged. "Nothing."

Mrs. Morley's brow furrowed. "Nothing at all?"

"The part of you that keeps the daemon where it is," Rachel said, "doesn't need to be maintained or anything like that. It was with you when you were born and it'll be with you until you die. All your family has to do is let my people keep a running record of your family tree until the daemon has completely broken down."

"How long will that take?"

"Unclear. To date it's been about five thousand years."

"Five thousand?" said Mrs. Morley, putting one hand to her chest. "So long? My God, is that normal?"

"Chaos daemons are bigger and denser than most," Rachel said. "Something like that riot daemon there would probably break down in less than one hundred years but a big one like Apep is sure to take more time. Still, five thousand years is pretty impressive. It's probably its defect that makes it so tough. And it's hard to gauge how it will happen. It might break down tomorrow or it might take another thousand years."

"And if it got out? If that horrible man had done what he meant to do"—Mrs. Morley put a hand on Leda's knee—"what would have happened?"

Rachel felt her skin grow cold, as if all her warmth was retreating deep within, afraid to touch the light. That man. She'd spent a lot of time revisiting her interactions with him. Some of the things he'd said had left deep, sticky imprints on her mind. Whenever she remembered those moments, she always seemed to get bogged down. And the thought of that guy freeing Apep— that was the stickiest of all.

"It, uh, it wouldn't be good," she said carefully. "That's why it's in the wastes. Until it's gone, we'll watch over your family tree to be sure it doesn't die out. To do that, we'll take DNA samples from you and Leda for our records and we'll keep track of birth certificates, death certificates, anything else that affects your lives and the lives of your daughters and granddaughters in the years to come."

"Just for the sake of argument," Mrs. Morley said with a sidelong glance at her daughter. "Tell me what happens if Leda never has a daughter."

"Then at some point the decision will be made to transfer the gatekeeper mantle to another family. Of course, we'd rather it not come to that. It's not like we can just pass around gate-keepership like a hand-me-down shirt; it's an intensive process. We'd be a lot happier if Leda has at least one daughter."

Mrs. Morley chuckled, her lips drawn into a tight, humorless line. "From your lips to God's ears."

"Mama, stop it," Leda murmured.

"At least one daughter, baby. You heard what she said."

"Mama," Leda said through her teeth, "don't start this here."

"You're not gettin' younger," Mrs. Morley replied, now directly looking her daughter up and down. "What are you waiting for?"

"Anyway," Rachel interrupted in as polite a tone of voice as she could muster, "I need to get as much information as you can give me about the last few generations of your family."

"For your people's files?"

"Yes, but also so we can get a starting point for digging through Notan records to see if you might have a long-lost rela-tive—a third cousin or something—who's also a gatekeeper."

"I see." Mrs. Morley turned one of her rings around her fin-ger thoughtfully. "I'll tell you what I can, but it may not be as much you'd like. You might have your work cut out for you."

Glad it's not my department to follow up on it, Rachel thought. "Whatever you can offer would be appreciated. Aside from documenting your genealogy, there are some basic things about the Arcana and the things my people do that you should know. Most gatekeepers never need to get involved with us, but if ever you do, you'll have to know how to get in touch and what resources are available. I'll give you the relevant information and I'll try to answer any questions you might have."

Mrs. Morley gave a brisk nod. "Thank you."

Straining to remember her recent meeting at the Skiptrace office, Rachel ran down her mental checklist of everything her superiors had told her. *Daemons, Apep, gatekeepership . . . what else? I should have written this crap down . . . Oh, right. The liaison thing.* She let out a quiet sigh.

"In a case like this, it's standard procedure for someone from the family to shadow a collector on the job—someone who can serve as a sort of liaison for the gatekeeper. I go back to work tomorrow; if Leda's interested, she could tag along with me, see what it is that I do."

"That's not a bad idea," Mrs. Morley said. "Leda?"

Rachel saw Leda's eyes light up. The sight of that eagerness made her uneasy. In the short time since they'd met, Leda had shown an intense fascination with all things Arcanan. She was full of questions—to a degree that Rachel had never experienced before and didn't quite know how to process.

"For sure," Leda said. "I want to learn all about it. I have work, but I am taking a lot of half-days because of my leg."

The eyes now gazing at the crutches leaning against the arm of the sofa were full of resentment. Rachel sympathized. Leda's knee was still immobilized and would continue to be so for several more weeks. So far, the doctor was sufficiently impressed with her progress that no surgery had been scheduled, but that didn't mean her life was any easier right now.

"I'll work around your schedule," Rachel said. "They'll start me off with a light caseload anyway, since I'm coming off an injury, so I'll try to get assigned cases that won't pose a problem for your crutches."

"We'll figure it out," Leda said. Her lips curled slightly, as if she tasted something tart, she pointed a long, bandaged finger at the coat at the end of the sofa. "I won't actually have to touch one of those things, will I?"

"No." Rachel shook her head. "That's my job. All you'll have to do is watch." She took a deep breath and, despite feeling a bit overwhelmed, managed to smile. "The weekly assignment is tonight. Why don't you come with me, meet the collectors, and see the local office?"

Leda grinned. "All right."

COLLECTION PLATE

Muttering under his breath, Simon Morley took a seat on the crooked front steps. A cold wind blew through his coat and sent a chill through his bones, but he ignored it. He was too irritated to be bothered. Thoughts of his father popped into his mind; he felt a primal longing for non-feminine commiseration. He had felt this sensation so many times over the course of his life that, after the initial sting of pain, it mostly left him numb.

His eyes wandered upward to the clear sky. When he'd driven his mother and sister to the alley that served as an entrance to this weird place, the sky had been a solid screen of gray. He'd wondered about this inconsistency but had not had a chance to ask about it before the talk of "gatekeepers" began.

Despite what his mother and Leda thought, he was both grateful and fascinated to have their missing history returned; he was just disappointed that the history was more theirs than his. Those diaries had been kept and passed down to preserve this thing to which he had only an indirect claim. Everything good about the situation was soured by his distance from it.

How many times had he heard about the women of their family and how "important" they were? Generation after generation had passed that message down. He had heard it from his mother and grandmother since before he could walk, and now he got to hear it from a stranger. The family's centuries-old verbal history had been confirmed wholesale, and it didn't include him. It might bring a smile to Leda's face, but it gave him nothing. Nothing but another pebble tossed into the gaping hole left by his father's death.

A brown and black puppy with gangly white legs, enormous ears, and oversized feet bounded into view from around the side of the house. A barefoot, blond guy in baggy clothes followed close behind. Simon cocked his head at the sight of them. Both were lanky, all bones and sinews, hardly a scrap of meat on their frames, as if both were in the process of growing into themselves. The owner grabbed the stick clamped between the dog's teeth and the two playfully tugged on it from either end, the puppy growling anew each time the man praised him. After a moment, the puppy released the stick and dropped the front half of his body to the ground, his back-end high in the air and his tail wagging so hard that his legs wiggled. The man flung the stick to the far end of the yard and the puppy gleefully bolted after it.

As he waited for the dog to return, the man noticed Simon on the steps.

"What's up?" he called out.

"Just waitin' for them to finish," Simon answered, gesturing toward the house.

"How long do you think they'll be?"

"Fuck if I know." Simon glanced down. "Aren't your feet cold?"

"Huh?" The guy glanced down at his feet as if noticing for the first time that he had no shoes on. "Oh. Not really. I've been barefoot in colder weather than this. I guess my skin's a little tougher for it."

The puppy returned with the stick, but instead of surrendering it, he ran to the house and ducked under the porch. Simon leaned over and saw the dog's ever-wagging tail protruding from his hiding place and heard him making low, loving growls as he chewed.

The dog's companion took a seat on the far side of the front steps. Seeing him close-up, Simon was struck by how pallid and sickly his face looked, as if he had been seriously ill for an extended period.

"Man"—the guy expelled a lengthy sigh—"I am outta shape." He turned his head and stuck out a hand. "I'm Bach."

Startled by Bach's eyes—electric blue, weirdly penetrating—Simon shook his hand. "Simon Morley."

"Nice to meet you."

"Yeah." Dropping his hand, Simon inclined his head toward the house. "So, how'd you end up in this freakshow?"

Bach laughed. "I wandered into it. I wandered into it, I had nowhere else to go, and now I'm living here on Ra's charity."

What he said might have piqued Simon's curiosity at another time but in this moment, after the day's many disappointments, he wasn't willing to delve into it uninvited.

Fortunately, Bach didn't wait for him to ask questions.

"I was homeless," he said. "Ra kinda brought me in from the cold, and so I tried to help her out a bit. I may have done more harm than good, but I tried. I told her where to find your sister."

"How'd you know about Leda?"

"I didn't. I'm what Ra calls an oracle—I have a 'sight-beyond' that lets me sometimes know things without knowing how I know them."

"What, like a psychic?"

"No. I don't talk to dead people and I don't know what anyone's thinking. I just suddenly know things about people, places, events—stuff I have no logical way of knowing."

Simon held a stony expression, but internally, he rolled his eyes. This guy Bach sounded suspiciously like a woman that his loony ex-girlfriend had taken him to see, a woman who talked a lot about vague events that might or might not happen in the future and who claimed to have a direct line to his dead father's spirit. He'd walked out in the middle of that "reading" (and out of that relationship), and he'd never regretted his decision. Suddenly, he felt a deep distrust for this person sitting next to him.

Despite his unchanged appearance, Bach seemed to pick up on the shift in Simon's opinion. "I don't read people's fortunes or any of that bullshit," he said. "I don't even talk about it much. I'm not sure why I'm telling you now, honestly, except that you and your family are Ra's guests and I figure if she trusts you, I can too."

"My mom and sister are her guests," Simon told him. "I'm not involved in it."

Bach smiled secretively, like a poker player about to show his unwitting opponents a full house. "You're involved," he said. "You're gonna end up chest deep in this thing. I can feel it."

Simon scoffed and gave a dismissive wave of his hand. "That's some Miss Cleo tarot card shit."

"No." Bach scratched his head, ruffling his blond hair and inadvertently showing a scabby wound on the underside of his arm. "See, when I look at a person, any person, I feel information about them flowing into my head. I don't immediately know what it is and a lot of it flows back out in an instant if I don't focus. Just walking down a crowded street can give me an information overload unless I let that crap pass right through me without stopping. But here's the thing: when I focus on a person, sometimes I can see their whole life—past, present, and future—in crazy detail. But I only get that kind of detail when it's some random person I have no connection to. The more tied up with my life that person is, the less information I get. I get a fair amount about acquaintances; much less, though still some, about friends. But about myself . . . nothing. Not one goddamn thing for my whole life. Ra—I get a little information about her but not a lot, which tells me that she and I are going to see a lot of each other in the near future. I get roughly the same level of information from Leda and from you."

Simon's cheeks flushed with irritation. "Man, that's some bullshit. You don't really think I'm gonna buy that crap, do you?"

The corners of Bach's lips twitched and his eyes danced like lightning on a cloudless sky.

"You wanna be wowed, is that it? You want me to tell you something about your life that no one could possibly know?"

"Fuckin' con artist trick," Simon said. "That's just cold reading; anybody can learn how to do it. You don't know shit unless I drop a hint about it."

"Okay then." Bach stared off into the distance, his gaze seemingly fixed on the blurry horizon. "In college you had an affair with the wife of a teacher's aide. You didn't even like the woman; you just hated her husband and liked the idea that you were getting the better of him. When he found out about you two, he left her. She dumped you the next day, but you didn't care. I think you had already started up with some other girl by then. What else . . . There's a stray cat that hangs out around your apartment building. Last year she had four kittens and they all died because she couldn't find enough food. She almost starved to death. You felt bad about it, so you started leaving food out for her. She just had another batch of kittens; look for them in the neighboring building's garden shed. Let's see . . . last month you noticed some growths—hard little bumps—on the soles of your feet. They aren't painful but they make walking uncomfortable. You're going to the doctor next week to get them looked at. Don't worry, though. I get the feeling it's not serious."

His eyes blazing above his amused smile, Bach raised an eyebrow. "Convinced? Or did you drop hints about that stuff?"

Without realizing it, Simon had moved to the edge of the step he was sitting on while Bach was speaking. Now he was overcome with dual urges: one to punch Bach, and the other to take off running.

Bach chuckled, and the sound knocked Simon to his senses. He quickly leaned back on the steps in what he hoped was a relaxed pose.

"Somebody's been talkin' about me, that's all," he said.

"Who the hell do you think's been talking about your feet? The only person you told was your doctor's receptionist, when you made the appointment."

"So?"

"So?" Bach's eyes narrowed at Simon in a mixture of concentration and annoyance. "When you were nine, you stole from the collection plate at church."

The surge of that long-suppressed memory surfacing jolted through Simon's veins. He could not have been more horrified if Bach and plunged his hand down his throat and turned his stomach inside out. Confronted with a piece of himself so long sequestered in the darkest corridor of his mind, he felt an overwhelming urge to scream. He jumped to his feet before he could control himself. Out of breath from the adrenaline filling his veins, he stood, panting and staring down at Bach, too shocked to be angry.

"Your father had just died," Bach continued, meeting Simon's stare without blinking. "You spent every day trying to be strong for your mom, who was a wreck, but you spent every night crying into your pillow. Without your dad, it was like a hole had been drilled into your heart that leaked constantly; no matter how much love you got from your mom, your sister, and the rest of your family and community, your heart just couldn't stay full. Seeing that you were struggling, the priest pulled you aside one day and told you that your father had gone to a better place. Those words grabbed your chest in a vise and squeezed all the love inside your heart out of that hole. You were tired of adults talking down to you and patting you on the head like you didn't understand what had happened. And here came this guy telling you that your father was better off in the grave than with his wife, who never smiled anymore, and his children, who deserved to have their dad's hand to hold."

Bach's voice was flat, emotionless. Simon felt paralyzed.

"You didn't want to go to church that Sunday, but your mother dragged you along. You spent the whole service glaring at the priest while he talked, just getting madder and madder, until they passed the collection plate and you saw a chance to get even. While passing the plate, you palmed a twenty-dollar bill. No one saw you. You went home feeling pretty damn proud of yourself but for some reason you couldn't spend that twenty. You kept it under your mattress for almost a month, just thinking about it. You didn't feel guilty, not exactly, but you didn't feel free to use it either. In the end, you snuck it into your mother's purse." Bach's stare intensified as he leaned a little closer. "You never told anyone about it, did you?"

"No," Simon mumbled. "Nobody."

"Are you wowed yet?"

"That's not funny."

"No," Bach agreed, "it's not. But it's in my head just the same."

"Man," Simon said, slowly taking his seat, "you can't tell anyone about that."

Bach smiled and laughed a hollow laugh. "I've been living under a bridge for six months," he said. "Some shit happened, my sight-beyond got twisted into a knot, and my mind just snapped. I ran off, raving like a lunatic, and apparently no one tried to stop me or came looking for me. If I hadn't met Ra, I'd probably still be sleeping on the river rocks and screaming at strangers. At this point, I've broken ties with my family; my so-called friends won't take my calls; my ex threw away most of my shit; and whatever was left, my landlord sold when I didn't pay my rent. Who the hell am I gonna talk to about it?"

Simon watched as Bach shook his head and chuckled hu-morlessly to himself. Fear twittered in his stomach, but his mind was eaten up by curiosity.

"So," he said, "what else do you know?"

CHANGE OF HEART

Inside the house, Leda and her mother were preparing to leave. Leda had promised to meet Rachel later that afternoon near the Greek restaurant that hid the entrance to the local office, and Mrs. Morley had promised to dig through her family records and contact a few relatives to gather more information.

"I'll try to answer any questions you come up with," Rachel said. "If I don't know the answer, I'll find someone who does. Thanks for meeting with me today, Mrs. Morley."

"Call me Vivian, please," she said.

"Vivian. Let me walk you out."

"Oh, yes." Mrs. Morley shuddered. "I don't care to walk through that tunnel alone."

"I don't know what you're complaining about, Mama," Leda said as she struggled to balance herself on her crutches. "At least you can *walk* through it."

"How on earth do you pass through that frightful thing every day, Rachel?"

Rachel noted but did not comment on her guest's pronunciation of her name: RAY-chel, instead of Rah-KEL. It happened constantly, and it was probably easier just to accept the mispronunciation as part of working with Notans rather than correcting everyone. Regardless, it made her homesick.

"I'm used to it," she said. "Tunnels like that one are placed all over the Arcana. It's our primary mode of travel."

"I can't imagine getting used to *that*," Mrs. Morley said.

"There's no quicker way to get where you're going," Rachel said, "especially across dimensional borders."

The three women stepped out onto the porch to find Bach and Simon on the steps, talking. Bach's dog was curled up at his feet, its head resting against his ankle. Bach stroked the puppy's oversize ears with one hand while he spoke.

Seeing their approach, Simon climbed to his feet, carefully avoiding his mother's stern gaze.

"It's time we were on our way," announced the matriarch. With a sharp look at her son, she added, "It was kind of Rachel to give up her day for our benefit."

"Yeah," Simon mumbled.

Vivian glared at her son, her dark eyes all fire and ice. Simon sniffed and turned his head aside, the stunted reaction of someone well-accustomed to such a gaze, then offered Bach a quick nod.

"See you tomorrow, man."

Bach smiled. "Thanks again."

Simon descended the front steps and waited, silent, for his mother and sister. Mrs. Morley carried her purse as well as her daughter's while Leda slowly maneuvered herself, crutches and all, down the steps. Then, with Rachel in the lead, the family headed for the passage at the end of the short walkway.

Just before they reached the shadowed threshold, Rachel heard Leda whisper to her brother—"What was that about, Sy?"

"What?" he hissed back.

"You talking to Bach. You'll see him tomorrow?"

"Yeah," he said quietly. "I'm gonna give him a ride."

"Where?"

"I dunno. He says he needs to get around town, take care of few things, but he doesn't have a car anymore and he can't get a hold of anybody else to give him a lift. Says he'd take the bus but he's broke and he's got no ID. I've got a few days off coming up, so I said I'd help."

"Really?"

"Yeah."

Rachel heard Leda make an odd sound—half huff and half chortle. To her, it suggested that Leda was surprised by her brother's act of charity. Simon did seem changed from their earlier interaction, more subdued and collected, as if his resentment and irritation had been forgotten in mere minutes. *Seems like Bach made quite an impact on him*, she thought.

Well, that's an oracle for you.

OCEAN / ISLAND

His most recent encounter with the boy
sent him reeling
to a landless stretch of ocean;
a state of affairs he found especially irritating.

Finding his way back to his abductor's home was
challenging under any circumstances,
but reorienting himself took twice as long
when he had to do it from the air.

If he flew too high,
he became disoriented,
losing all sense of which direction
would take him to the boy,
so, he stayed low,
suffering the water for the sake of his vengeance.

Every splash of the waves
that sizzled against his flaming skin
dimmed him,
slowed him.

The long flight gave him ample time
to curse every hair
on the human boy's head.

This island had been his home for centuries.
In all that time, he had seen no one.

Aside from the fish that kept him from starvation,
he was the only living creature within this
speck of existence.

The ocean that encased the island,
as blue as his own skin,
appeared endless
when standing on the beach,
but he knew this was not the case.

There was nothing beyond those waters.

This place was as
encapsuled
and
contained
as oil in a lamp.

He,
the lone, burning wick,
could not escape.

When deposited over land,
he could

move between
layers of reality—
slip easily through the
borderlines of existence
to find his way back to his target.

But without solid ground beneath his feet,
he couldn't make the transition to that plane.

Flying was painfully slow by comparison.

Nevertheless, he would find his way back
to the boy
and his mother.

The door to the island dimension remained sealed.

The door—
an invisible but solid slab,
cool and abrasive to the touch,
exactly his height,
exactly his width—
had not opened since the day he arrived.

When his jailer
first thrust him into this place,
he had spent every waking moment
assaulting it,
pounding
and
clawing,

desperate to return to the world he had left,
wanting only to seize that bastard by the throat.

The door never opened—
and slowly,
unhappily,
he adapted to his situation.

The other side of the door—
a small, portable container—
he knew it sometimes moved
from place to place,
though he never felt the movement himself.

No one could hear him shout,
but he'd learned he could listen
to the faint drone of voices
on the other side of the door
in the real world.

All were distant, muffled,
but they were frequently discernible,
and every voice was human—
not his own kind.

Time marched on.
The container that held the doorway
changed hands
again and again.

He listened as empires rose and fell.

BLUE FLAME

The languages he heard evolved;
he learned the new grammars and vocabularies.

Time burned away like paper,
his years nothing but wispy embers.

Forgotten,
he waited.

THE ASSIGNMENT
OFFICE

Weekly assignment was not what Leda had expected.

Accessing the local office via the back door of the Greek restaurant was a little unsettling to her—she wondered how many buildings she passed each day with similar, unnoticed doors—but it turned out to be the least surprising aspect of the meeting.

After leading her down an empty-yet-noisy office hallway, Rachel left Leda in a large room with mismatched tiles on the floor, promising she'd be back momentarily.

Frosted windows lined one wall of the room, clear enough to show vague, shadowy forms moving about on the far side, but too opaque to allow for identification. While various cracks and dents in the walls had been spackled, no attempt had been made to paint the spackled areas to match the rest of the room. All the obvious repairs made the hallway look like it was one sledge-hammer away from crumbling apart.

Leda tried to tamp down her disappointment. Everything here belonged to another dimension, and yet it just seemed so . . . dingy. She had expected a more professional setting, something akin to the staff meetings at the museum where she worked—something at least semi-formal. Instead, she saw a large, cracked screen that covered about two-thirds of one wall and many folding chairs assembled loosely into rows. The room housed a night court–like smell of dusty leather speckled with old book glue, all with an underlying whiff of body odor. The only door into the room bore strange words on it that Leda's language-loving brain scrambled to translate.

Before she could make an educated guess, Rachel reentered the room, a gray-haired man in her wake.

"Leda," she said, "this is Mr. Creed. He runs the Skiptrace department of this office."

As he shook Leda's hand, Mr. Creed gave the slightest of nods, accompanied by a long blink of his eyes. This was a gesture Leda had seen Rachel make when meeting her mother for the first time. Maybe it was some sort of ritual in their culture. Always eager to learn, her mind stowed away this knowledge for future reference.

"I am very pleased to meet you, Ms. Morley." Despite Mr. Creed's excellent English, Leda detected the hint of a mystery accent, and her intellect reflexively strove, without success, to identify it. "I am Creed Serge len Norov. This is quite an occasion for me. I have never met a gatekeeper face-to-face before, and I have not had occasion to speak directly to a Notan in ten years. Furthermore, your presence seems to have achieved the impossible: Ms. Wilde is actually the first to arrive to assignment."

Leda smiled politely as Rachel rolled her eyes. "The pleasure is mine, Mr. Creed. Is there anything I'm expected to do while I'm here?"

"No, nothing," he replied. "You are here to observe and that is all you need to do. I'll instruct the collectors to speak English while they're here."

"I don't want to cause any inconvenience."

"It's no inconvenience," he said. "I have them speak English at assignment periodically to make sure everyone is keeping up with their training. As you have no doubt noticed"—he pointed to his lips—"I am out of practice myself, but I don't work in the field anymore so my having an accent is of no concern. The collectors are another matter. They have to pass for American, and that means no Arcanan accents. If I have them speak English around me once in a while, I can hear for myself if anyone is slipping. Besides," he added with a gleam in his eyes, "it keeps them on the toes."

Leda smiled uncertainly. "Well, shouldn't I introduce myself at least?"

"Oh, that won't be necessary," Creed said with a chuckle. "After everything that's happened with you and Ms. Wilde, they all know who you are. You just watch the meeting. I only hope it won't be too boring for you."

Rachel took a seat next to Leda and pulled out her phone while Creed turned on the wall screen. A very long list appeared on the right half, each item of the list seemingly written in the same language as that on the door. On the left half of the screen, only one item was listed.

Though many of the letters strayed from the Latin alphabet, Leda quickly deduced the meaning. She pointed to the left column. "That's your name?"

"Yes," Rachel responded, her eyes still on her phone. "My name popped up because I opened a program on my phone."

Leda glanced over Rachel's shoulder and saw that the phone had a list on it identical to the right-side column. Rachel touched one of the items and a lengthy paragraph appeared.

"So those are the jobs for this week?"

"Right," Rachel said. "I'm gonna take a peek to see which ones might work for me."

"How long until the meeting starts?"

"About ten minutes."

"Ten minutes?" Leda said in surprise. "We're the only ones here. Where is everybody?"

"They'll show up."

Within minutes, a steady flow of people entered through the open door. A handful of others came through one of the frosted windows. Their clothes ran the gamut from sport jackets to T-shirts and, in one case, pajamas. They chatted among themselves in several languages as they found seats and fired up their phones.

Leda watched with interest to see the name of each new arrival appear in the left-hand column, though she could not accurately read the names until Rachel engaged a translator on her phone to Romanize the words. Many were simple enough to read and categorize—Baker, Vogel, Kuramitsu, Malik, Rivera—but, looking around the room, Leda found it nearly impossible to guess which name matched which person. The names never seemed to match her visual expectations of their ethnicities. One blonde collector, an ivory pale woman whom Leda guessed to be the owner of a distinctly Nordic name, turned out to be Cavi Monika len Mehmet—not Nordic in the least.

The collectors gathered themselves into groups of four and chatted loudly as they waited for the meeting to begin.

"Why four?" Leda mumbled.

"What?"

"Why are they all in groups of four?"

"Everyone tends to sit with their square," Rachel told her.

"Square?"

"Collectors are trained in groups of four," she said. "Traditionally, each member of a square comes from a different continent of the Arcana—North, South, East, and West."

"Why's that?"

"Officially, it's to build bonds between communities and encourage us to learn about other Arcanan cultures. Honestly, though, I think it's just because it's always been done like that and no one's ever bothered to do it differently."

Leda nodded. The Central Office, like most bureaucracies, was not fond of change. Some things transcended dimensions.

The seats nearest to Leda and Rachel were soon occupied by Suarez, Wu, and another man who introduced himself as Reuben Omri len Bnai Arba Achayot—"but you can call me Benny." Rachel conversed with these three in her native language for only a moment before reverting to English.

"Thought you'd be out another week, Wilde," Wu said, stretching his lanky form as far as the chair would allow. "You're not still concussed?"

"The doctor says my head is fine."

"What about your ribs?" Suarez asked.

"Still healing, but the Central Office says I'm fit for light work."

"Since when does this job involve 'light work'?" Benny said with a snort. "I had to climb five stories of scaffolding in the middle of the night last week to catch a mark."

"Yeah," Suarez said, "this isn't a 'light work' kind of job. They must be really worried about the conspirator situation to put you back on the job so soon."

Conspirator situation. The invasive touch of memory prodded Leda. That man—the one who abducted her, who locked her and Rachel in his basement. All this talk of conspiracy started with him. His face burst into her thoughts before she could block it out. Those hard, soulless eyes glared into her, stripping away every defense in their path, leaving her painfully naked. Leda's heart galloped in her chest as if trying to flee from her body.

"There's no evidence of a conspiracy," Wu said, waking Leda out of her daylit nightmare. "Don't feed the rumor mill."

"If there's no evidence," Suarez said, "why has the Central Office doubled security measures?"

"And why," added Benny, "are the auditors reexamining departments that have already been cleared by the year-long systems check? What are they looking for?"

"And what about this?" Suarez showed his phone's screen to the group.

Leda's racing heart twisted about inside her like a squealing animal, so much so that it hurt. The screen showed a photograph of *that man* under the heading "The Breach Killer." The sight of him turned her breath to ice. She wanted to scream. She wanted to run. She wanted to curl into a ball and cry until her tears washed the world away.

"The fuck's that?" Wu asked, his voice exploding into Leda's manic thoughts.

"The Central Office is posting updates about the search for the murderer," Suarez said.

Wu shrugged. "Nothing weird about that."

"It also says they're searching for anyone who's helping him," Suarez told them. "Why say that if they aren't concerned about a conspiracy?"

Leda forced the memory of her captor back into the dark, prickly parts of her mind and focused on the conversation at hand. "Is anything posted?" she asked, willing her heartbeat to slow. "About that guy?"

Suarez shook his head. "Nothing new."

"That page isn't proof." Wu wagged a finger at the phone. "Just because the wording is out of the ordinary doesn't mean it's evidence of a crime. Right, Wilde?"

"Yeah, Wilde," Suarez said. "You were there when the murderer talked about working with Arcanans. There *is* a conspiracy, right?"

Rachel caught Leda's eye and made an exaggerated expression of frustration. Leda gave a little nod. *This isn't the first time she's heard this argument*, she realized, *and she's tired of it.* That was a feeling Leda understood intimately. When she first showed up to work on crutches, her coworkers had bombarded her with repetitive questions—what happened, what happened, what happened? She'd invented a story about a mugging, but after telling it for the thirtieth time she'd started evading the question altogether. Her refusal to talk had led to the circulation of bizarre rumors. She was so fed-the-fuck-up with it all that she kept her office door closed at all times now to avoid wandering eyes drifting in her direction from the hallway.

"I don't know any more than you do at this point," Rachel said. "Until I hear otherwise, I'm just going to keep doing my job, injuries and all. I'll just"—she rubbed her ribs—"take a smaller workload for a while."

The men shot each other a few glances—doubtful, challenging, curious—before leaning back in their seats and looking at their phones.

"I don't know . . ." Wu scanned the list of assignments. "Everything here looks pretty intense. You may end up sitting it out this week by default."

"No, no, no," Rachel protested. "Look here: I see at least three fact-finding jobs. Those tend to be pretty light."

The three men laughed and took turns pulling up their sleeves and pants legs to show off scars they'd received on fact-finding jobs. Even Rachel, at their prodding, showed Leda a triangular scar on her shoulder.

In the process of showing off that scar, Rachel inadvertently flashed several others. Leda eyed the marks and imagined the bloody wounds that had birthed them.

"This isn't a job for the squeamish, is it?" she asked.

"You don't know the half of it," Wu said.

"Are injuries really that common?"

"What we do is tough." Rachel gave a little shrug. "I don't know anyone in this job who goes a full year without at least one new scar."

"I don't know too many who haven't broken a bone or ruptured an organ," added Benny.

"And," Wu said somberly, "we've all known someone or known of someone who's died on the job."

"Died?" Leda gasped. Until that moment, she had not grasped how extremely different Rachel's daily routine was from her own. Her own work, while often tedious, was cerebral and took place almost entirely in an office. Rachel's work apparently necessitated some pretty extreme physical activity. Daemon collecting was not the fascinating, intellectually challenging endeavor she had imagined; it was more akin to animal control. "Are you for real?"

"It happens," Rachel said, "but not often. Most collectors only stay on the job for the required time, then they move on to other work."

Leda felt her growing list of questions leak into her expression. Suarez seemed to recognize it, because he leaned toward her and explained, "This job is an eight-year stretch. Upon reaching age twenty, each Arcanan has a choice of three services to join. Working as a collector is the longest stretch—eight years —but it's the least dangerous. It also allows for the most time off, except in the case of a year-long systems check like the one going on now. Some collectors stay on after the eight years are up, but it's rare for a collector to stay at the job for more than twelve."

"So, what'll happen to you when you retire?" Leda asked. "Do you get a pension or something?"

The foursome shared an amused smile that irked Leda. It reminded her of her coworkers snickering at her from across the room or down the hall as she maneuvered her crutches around the museum.

"No." Rachel shook her head. "When we leave this job, we'll move on to other work. A lot of collectors take jobs in other, less physically demanding areas of daemonic monitoring. Creed used to be a collector; now he works with Skiptrace. Most of the guys in the repairs department used to be collectors."

"I want to work in the daemonic research office eventually," Benny told Leda. "The job's not strenuous and it's a fascinating field."

"For you, maybe," Wu said. "When my eight years are up, I'm going home and working in the vineyard with my cousins."

"And I'm going to work on my family's farm," Rachel said with a wistful sigh. "I'm gonna sow the fields, shear the sheep, milk the goats, and never look at a daemon again."

"What about you, Mr. Suarez?" asked Leda. "Do you have plans for 'retirement'?"

"I have hopes, not plans," he replied. "I hope Lola's clan will admit me, so she and I can be together."

The warmth on his face when he spoke the name Lola instantly told Leda everything she needed to know about their relationship.

"No word from Lola on that yet, huh?" Benny asked.

"No." Suarez sighed. Raising his eyes to Leda, he said, "The Prushell clan matriarch isn't too keen on me."

"Prejudiced old hawk," Wu muttered.

"Prejudiced?" Leda raised an eyebrow. The blip of surprise brought on by the word faded almost immediately. Naturally the people of Rachel's dimension had prejudices. Prejudice, sadly, was as human as language. "What prejudice?"

"Some people cling to this old idea that Hallans are barbarians," Rachel said.

"Hallans?" Leda's mind was off and whirring. "That's your clan, Mr. Suarez?"

"Halla is a city," Suarez told her, "but it has clan status in the Arcana. Anyone born there is given the clan's name 'Halla.' And yes, Hallans have a reputation for being barbarians. It's not a fair reputation, but it has a historical basis."

"Are you for real?" Benny snorted. "Anyone who thinks Hallans are killers is a moron."

"That all Hallans are barbarians is prejudiced dogshit," Suarez said. "That Hallans acted like barbarians in the past isn't dogshit; that's true. I was born and raised there, Benny, I've read the Hallan history books. They're written in blood, sometimes literally. Hallans used to be vicious. We still live a very . . . military lifestyle, but nothing like the old days."

"The point is," Rachel interrupted, "Lola's clan matriarch thinks modern Hallans are still the same bloodthirsty savages of the past. Because of that, she won't let Suarez join their clan, and that means he can't be with Lola."

"'Savages', huh Wilde?" Suarez said with a tilt of his head.

"Oh, sorry," she said with a wince. "I didn't mean that! I was channeling my mom for a second."

"It's okay." Suarez gave her a friendly bump on the arm. "The good news is the matriarch is about ready to step down. The heir-presumptive for the Prushell clan is Lola's aunt, and she likes me. Once she's the new head of the clan, we'll probably get her blessing. So, Ms. Morley, my hope for retirement is to join Lola's clan, have kids, and find work somewhere local."

Leda's analytical mind put all the proffered knowledge into order and immediately wanted more information to fill in the blanks. Every bit of information she collected spawned a dozen more questions.

Before she could probe the subject further, Creed strode into the room, stepped in front of the wall screen, and waved his hand. A loud tone issued from the screen, something reminiscent of an old church bell. The sound brought all conversation to a stop.

Leda sat up straight and leaned forward in her seat, eager, hungry, and prepared to absorb it all.

A LIGHT LOAD

C reed made one brief statement in an Arcanan language—to Leda's ears, the same one she had heard Rachel use several times—and then proceeded to speak in English.

"There's quite a long list this week," he said. "I hope those of you who are running behind with last week's work will hurry up and finish, because you'll get no sympathy from me."

"What's with the pileup?" shouted a young man in the back of the room. "The list's almost twice as long as it was four months ago."

Creed nodded, waved his hand dismissively, and said, "Address all questions about the rate of daemonic breakdown—"

"To the Central Office," droned half of the collectors.

"Just so," Creed said. "I have no answers for you."

"Can't we at least get some backup from collectors in other districts?" asked another man. "Rate of daemonic breakdown may be the Central Office's business, but making sure there are enough collectors to do the work is your job, right Mr. Creed?"

He sighed. "Yes—and I've looked into it, Mr. O'Neill. Unfortunately, the pileup is happening worldwide."

"Does that have anything to do with Wilde's psycho?" a woman asked.

The abductor's face—bushy eyebrows, graying dark hair,

and vicious eyes—exploded into Leda's mind once again and her gaze darted around the room. Every face she saw was painted with worry, disbelief, or a blend of the two. Nothing she saw came close to matching the raging panic inside her.

"Yeah," another collector chimed in. "Is it related to the terrorist conspiracy?"

The room suddenly rumbled with whispers and chattering. Leda's chest tightened, squeezing the air from her lungs, and her bandaged injuries prickled with pain. She looked at Rachel and saw that her jaw was clenched, as were her fists.

Creed clapped his hands, yanking Leda's focus out of herself and back into her surroundings. "Officially," he said, "there is no conspiracy and there are no terrorists. The investigation is ongoing, but as of right now there is no concrete evidence of a terrorist organization in the Arcana."

Leda noticed Wu poking Suarez in the side, an I-told-you-so grin on his face. Suarez smacked his hand away.

"We have no idea why there's a worldwide increase in daemonic activity," Creed continued, "but since there is, we have to deal with it. There are no collectors to spare. At least, not until the year-long evaluation is complete." He smiled wearily. "I'm sure we're all looking forward to the interdimensional passages reopening, yes?"

To Leda's astonishment, the room erupted with hoots, hollers, and clapping. From all corners of the room, Leda heard exclamations of "I want to see my family!" and "I miss my girlfriend!" and "Notan food is gross!"

Good Lord, she thought, her eyes sweeping over the boisterous crowd. *I can't imagine a staff meeting at the museum going like this.*

Creed hooked his pinky fingers into his mouth and whistled

until the noise in the room subsided to a light chatter and then stopped.

"Let's get started!" he said. "We'll begin with the worst of the worst this week. He waved his hand and one file from the right column jumped to the foreground of the screen. Though the paragraph was split by the jagged crack in the glass, Leda saw the words clearly enough on the phone screens of everyone near her. "Two ragers in the same location. Any volunteers?"

"Screw that!" called a man's voice.

"Yeah," agreed someone else. "You can't expect one person to take on two ragers at once!"

"It's not impossible," a woman said. "I've seen it done."

"Then you do it, Vogel."

"Kiss my ass!" she shot back. "I brought in those chatters last week and I've got the bruises to prove it. *You* passed on that one, Tambe!"

"And I'm passing on this one, too."

"So am I."

"Who gets it?" Creed asked.

A cacophony of negative responses filled the air. Creed scanned the room, his eyes boring into each person as if searching for a hidden nod among the crowd of shaking heads. His eyes fell upon one collector. Leda looked at the young man, his arms loosely crossed over his stomach, one hand just barely clutching his phone. His legs were stretched out in front of him and his head was bowed so low that his chin almost touched his chest. Amid the chorus of grumbling, he was conspicuously silent.

Creed glowered at him. He walked through the rows of chairs and stood over the quiet man with his fists jammed into his hips. The other collectors, who obviously knew what was about to happen, fell silent behind snickering smiles.

"Ms. Wilde," Creed said, "tell the room what happens to collectors who sleep through assignment."

"Well, if they're me," Rachel said, "they get sent after a serial killer who smacks them around until they hurt every time they breathe."

"Exactly." He turned on his heel and marched away from the sleeper. With a wave of his hand, he sent the chosen file on the screen flying to a name on the left side. "Somebody wake up Mr. Owens and tell him he's been nominated for this week's least desirable job. Now then"—he brought up a new file from the right column—"any takers on a missing riot?"

"Here!" shouted a man just behind Leda. "I got that!"

"And it goes to Mr. Ironsi. Next, a defective muse daemon."

"Mine!" said a woman in the front row.

"Ms. Rattanakosin, it's all yours. Next, a defective depressive."

"Right here!" yelled a woman near the door.

"Ms. Varga. Next . . . ."

The meeting continued in a routine fashion from there, with only a few jobs on the list generating more than a cursory discussion. Suarez, Wu, and Benny all chimed in to accept various jobs or to briefly discuss details with fellow collectors. Rachel spoke up a few times but her colleagues kept taking the jobs off her hands. She argued with them each time, but they wouldn't hear of her pushing herself while she was healing, even though it meant more work for them. Leda felt a swell of admiration for their camaraderie; while she had gotten some assistance from her colleagues in carrying boxes and documents from room to room, no one had offered to lighten her workload while she was recovering.

As Creed approached the end of the work list, Rachel had

acquired only two fact-finding jobs, both of which were considered "simple," yet both of which she'd had to fight to receive.

"Defective hoarder," Creed read from the list. "Let's see, who's gotten off light this week? Mr. Saar, I'm looking at you."

"I've got fifteen jobs," Saar complained, "and two left over from last week. How is that getting off light?"

"Keeping up with your work is your responsibility. And by my count most everyone else has been assigned eighteen jobs this week."

"Okay, fine, I'll take it."

"Good. That's just leaves one last fact-finder. Who wants it?"

"Give it to me," said Rachel.

"Wilde, put your hand down," someone called out.

"No, let me have it!"

"No need to feel left out," said someone else. "We'll be sure to make you suffer for this time off once you're better."

Many collectors chuckled while others nodded their agreement. Rachel vigorously shook her head.

"I should take this one!" she insisted. "I go by that market all the time. The owner, Mr. El Sayed, knows me by sight. I can check out the situation without looking suspicious. Injured or not, I'm the best one for the job."

Other collectors started to argue with her but Creed quickly shouted them down.

"Quiet! Quiet! Ms. Wilde," he said, "you really feel you can poke around this place without arousing suspicion?"

"Absolutely."

He peered into her face, still and intent. Leda watched him watch her, wondering what he was looking for. A sign that she was lying? A crack in her resolve? Whatever it was, Rachel didn't flinch. Finally, Creed nodded and waved his hand at the screen. The last item from the right column soared to the left and disappeared behind Rachel's name.

"It's all yours," he said. He waved both hands and the two columns on the large screen vanished.

"We're finished here," he said. "Anyone who requires additional equipment for this week's assignments, see me at the main desk in five minutes. Ms. Ruiz and Mr. Niemi, you're both overdue for your six-month physical. Get it taken care of before the next meeting. Ms. Lakatos, the housing department wants a word and they can't seem to get a hold of you. They're talking my ear off about it. Call them already. Now, everyone get to work. Contact me with any problems. Be safe out there."

With the meeting concluded, Leda was startled to find herself suddenly surrounded by collectors who had been ignoring her only moments before. One after another, they introduced themselves—a barrage of names that Leda had no hope of remembering—and eagerly shook her hand. She waited for them to ask questions about herself, her family, and her ordeal, but no one asked her anything. All they seemed to want was to meet her before going on their way.

When the last one shook her hand and walked off, Leda glanced at Rachel, bewildered.

"What was that about?"

"It's not every day that collectors like us get to meet a gatekeeper," Rachel said. "And besides, after what we went through, you're a bit of a celebrity." She gestured toward the door, then started walking in that direction.

"But no one asked me anything," Leda said, hobbling after her. "No one asked me a question or tried to make conversation. All they did was tell me their names."

"What should they ask you? They read my report about the incident, so they know what happened. You're new to being a gatekeeper, so they probably know more about that than you do, and odds are they'll never see you again anyway. What did you want them to say?"

"Well . . . never mind." Leda sighed, but her ever-racing mind was already cataloging everything she had learned. She found what little information she'd culled so far sorely lacking; her thirsty brain demanded more. As she took in every corner of the office building before they exited onto the street, she felt sure that no matter how many sips she got, her thirst would never be quenched.

7
PINK-SAND DESERTS / EMERALD MOUNTAINS

Wing-weary,
he was forced to rest
more and more often.

During those times,
he thought of his family,
his home.

He felt their absence
as an unhealed wound
in his chest.

Memories of vast pink-sand deserts
under burnt ocher skies
made him ache with longing.

Each time he thought of
his world,
he wept scarlet sparks.

He wanted to go home.

Damn that boy for keeping him here.
Damn him.

The container that held the doorway
somehow passed into the hands
of his own people.

They could not hear him,
but he learned from their talk,
listening at the invisible door,
that they knew he was there.

Briefly,
he felt the teasing breath of
freedom
on his face.

Home was within reach!

The sulfur lakes,
the emerald mountains—
he would see them again.

Surely,
his people
would free him.

They tried.

They failed.

Wounded by hope,
he sat by the door
with his head in his hands.

He waited.

RECKONING

B ach was waiting on the curb when Simon pulled up in his Ford Taurus. In spite of the fact that it was the agreed-upon time and place, Bach looked a little surprised to see him.

"Thanks," he said as he climbed into the passenger seat. "Wasn't sure you'd show."

Simon frowned. "Told you I'd be here. Didn't you believe me?"

"I thought you might wig out a little when everything I said had time to sink in. I've seen it happen before."

Simon signaled and pulled away from the curb. "Well, it did get to me a little," he admitted. "Couldn't think about anything else all night. But then I went to look in that garden shed for the cat, and she was in there with her three babies. She walked right up me like she'd known me forever, rubbed against my leg. Maybe she knew my smell from the food I'd left her, I don't know."

"She's lost weight since you saw her last," Bach said with a little tilt of his head. "And one of her kittens looks suspiciously like your neighbor's mangy orange tomcat, the one that jumped to your balcony last year, snuck into your apartment, and ate the turkey out of your sandwich while you were in the bathroom."

"That kitten ain't ugly enough to have come from him," Simon muttered. "We going the right way, by the way?"

Bach nodded. "Just keep going straight for now."

"Gotcha," Simon said. "Anyway, I took 'em all home and put 'em in my kitchen, but she moved 'em to my closet. They're sleeping on my old Steelers sweatshirt."

"They'll be fine there."

"Yeah . . ." He stared ahead at the road. *I shouldn't be believing this shit so easily*, he thought, despite knowing that he did believe it. His tongue prodded his teeth as if trying to loosen something stuck in his gums. "So," he finally asked, "where are we going?"

"A lot of places." Bach puffed a breath through thin lips and eyed Simon nervously. "You sure you don't mind driving me? This is gonna take a while."

"If I minded, I'd say so. Where are we going?"

"Turn left at the light," Bach said. "I talked to my bank and someone's been withdrawing money out of my account since I lost my mind. I've got a pretty good idea who it was." Bach hissed through his teeth. "I want my life back, and I'm gonna start by getting my wallet."

TEN MINUTES LATER, they pulled over in front of a three-story apartment building, a giant brick box with dirty windows and postage stamp balconies spaced regularly at each level. It was one of many similar buildings that lined the street. The whole neighborhood had an institutional feel; the structures looked dull and impersonal, like they had been built from matching kits by a contractor who had run out of fucks to give about his job. It was the sort of street you could drive down a dozen times and never notice a damn thing.

The front door, made of thick glass framed by black metal, was guarded by what looked like a punch code intercom. Bach jumped from the car before Simon even brought it to a full stop.

"Whoa!" he shouted. "You need any help?"

"No, just wait here, okay?" Bach called back over his shoulder. "I got this."

He charged up the walkway leading to the front door with both fists clenched. Simon put the car in park and leaned over the passenger seat to watch. Bach rattled the locked door, and then punched a number into the intercom system. Simon couldn't quite make out what he was shouting.

Bach fought with the locked door handle for several long seconds and then, after one last slap to the glass, ran halfway up the front walk and whipped around to face the building. His head turned back and forth, his eyes scanning the ground. He bent down, grabbed a rock from the lawn, and flung it at a second-story window, missing it by inches.

Simon grinned and leaned over just a bit more. "This is getting good," he whispered.

"SHANNON!" bellowed Bach. He grabbed another rock and threw it, this time chipping the windowsill. "SHANNON! GET THE FUCK OUT HERE! NOW!"

Two figures appeared behind the glass: a man with shaggy hair and a woman in red lipstick, both clearly screaming at Bach though neither voice breached the window. Bach grabbed another rock and flung it. It hit the glass, fracturing it and making the woman shriek.

The man pushed her aside and opened the broken window. "What the fuck's your problem?!" he shouted.

"I WANT MY WALLET!"

"Fuck you!"

"I'm calling the police!" screamed the woman over the man's shoulder.

"DO IT!" Bach's voice was verging on hysteria. "CALL THE COPS! I TALKED TO THE BANK, SHANNON! MY WALLET'S IN THAT APARTMENT, AND SO'S THE MONEY YOU'VE BEEN STEALING FROM ME! CALL THE COPS! CALL 'EM!"

The man at the window exchanged a troubled glance with the woman. They spoke to each other softly for a moment, and then the phone dropped from the woman's hand.

The couple disappeared from sight. Neither returned to the window. Moments ticked by. Bach grabbed another rock and hurled it. It flew through the open window and crashed inside. The man reappeared and screamed what sounded like a string of obscenities as the woman tossed something over his shoulder—through the open window and down to the lawn.

Bach ran forward and scooped up the fallen object. With a shout of triumph, he walked toward the car and held out the item, his wallet, for Simon to see. Simon responded with a wave and a nod.

As Bach thumbed through the contents, his expression darkened, and he spun and ran back toward the building.

"Where's the money!?" he shouted up at the still-open window. "Where's my goddamn money!?"

The man flipped him off and slammed the window shut.

Bach clenched his jaw. "Oh, hell no!"

Just then, a resident exited the building. She watched Bach carefully out of the corner of her eye but seemed determined to avoid at all costs whatever insanity was happening on the front lawn. As she slipped quietly away, Bach rushed the closing door and caught it just in time. He flung it open and charged inside with the force of an invading army.

Simon chuckled. "Better and better."

Less than a minute later, he spotted Bach behind the cracked window. The shaggy-haired man was right in his face, jabbing him in the chest with his finger, while the woman fought in vain to get between them. Suddenly, Bach stepped around the couple and vanished from sight.

Simon wondered briefly if he should try to get up to that apartment, just in case Bach didn't have as good a handle on the situation as he hoped, but then Bach reappeared. He pitched open the window, shattering the fractured windowpane in the process, and started throwing things onto the lawn below.

"What the hell?" Simon said.

"Sy!" Bach shouted as he tossed out a pair of sneakers. "Grab that shit for me!"

After hesitating only a moment, Simon jumped out of his car to obey. Fueled by adrenaline, he snatched up the falling items—shirts, pants, shoes, and a leather jacket—and stuffed them all into his trunk. As he did, more items rained down on the lawn: books, blankets, a frying pan, and more. Simon loaded them into the car as quickly as he could while anxiously glancing around for the police car he was sure would arrive any second.

More things flew from the window, as did a steady stream of obscenities. Simon was toting another armful of clothes to the car when the woman blocked the window with her body and shrieked at Bach to stop. The man shouted something too, but all Simon heard was Bach screaming, "Fuck you both!"—and then the slam of a door.

For a long moment, all was quiet; then Bach stormed out through the front door, a laptop in his arms and a backpack slung over his shoulder.

"We're done here," he announced. He swung himself into the passenger seat and tossed the bag and computer to his feet. "We can go."

"Hold up." Simon slammed the trunk lid and rushed to the driver's seat. "Okay. Let's get the hell outta here before the cops show up."

"There won't be any cops," Bach said. "The stuff I took won't impress the police as much as them committing identity theft or fraud or whatever the hell crime it is to use someone else's bank card. They know it. I know it. Nobody's calling the cops."

Simon pulled the car away from the building but found he couldn't keep his eyes on the road. His heart was roaring like a diesel engine. "Is all this shit yours?"

"Not exactly," Bach admitted. "When I saw that my wallet didn't have any cash in it, I just wanted to get back what I'm owed. When I got upstairs, I demanded the money, but they said they didn't have any. Then I saw my laptop."

"YOUR laptop?"

"Yeah. I guess Shannon decided to take more than just my cash. The laptop's mine, some of the clothes are mine, the shoes are mine—"

"The leather jacket?"

"Not so much."

"What's in the bag?"

"A bunch of stuff." He unzipped the backpack and peered inside. "An iPhone—mine. An iPad—not mine. Watch—not mine. Sunglasses—not mine." He held up the Ray-Ban sunglasses with a proud grin. "Took those right off his head. I'm pretty happy about that."

"Yeah, I saw that guy." With half a smile and a shrug, he added, "Bitch replaced you while you were gone, huh?"

"Whatever," Bach mumbled, eyes on the open bag. "Hmm. I thought that was my Xbox when I grabbed it, but now I'm not sure. Oh well. It's mine now. But the most important thing is this." Bach held up his open wallet, the driver's license inside smiling for all the world to see. "I got my ID back! I am me, and I can prove it!"

He looked so absurdly pleased with himself that Simon couldn't help but chuckle. "That's awesome, man. Glad I could help."

"Me too. Sorry for making you an accomplice."

"It's fine," Simon said, heaving a deep breath to calm himself. "I've been involved in worse."

"Yeah, I know. Like that time you let your friend sell weed out of your apartment because the cops were watching his place. Good thing you only did that once. He got busted not long after that."

The distant memory stepped forward in his mind, far more vivid than he expected. He guessed that was due to Bach's influence. Maybe his "sight-beyond" was like those chemicals people used on old paintings to clear away the grime and bring out the colors. "Man," he whispered, "you gotta stop that. It's just weird."

Out of the corner of his eye, Simon saw a pained expression cross his passenger's face.

"Sorry," Bach said. "A six-month hiatus from sanity kinda put a dent in my ability to self-censor. I gotta remember to think twice before I open my mouth."

Simon shook his head and flexed his fingers on the steering wheel. As he drove on, the discomfort of Bach's intrusion into his history passed, replaced by a growing curiosity about where this day would lead. The first stop had been a riot. Hopefully the next would be just as exciting.

"Where to next?"

Bach settled back into the passenger seat. He held tight to his wallet, tapping it against his leg. "To the university," he said. "I want my degree."

A BUMPY RIDE

Seated next to Rachel on a city bus slouching its way downtown, surrounded by throngs of morning rush-hour commuters, Leda scanned the notepad in her hand, rereading every scribble she'd made in the last hour. She had millions of questions jumbled up in her mind—questions about the Arcana, questions about Arcanans, so many questions about Arcanan languages—but she had chosen to begin her study of this new world with Rachel personally. *Always start with what's in front of you, that's the best way*, she reminded herself. *Start with that and you'll inadvertently learn about any number of adjacent matters.* So far, she had learned about Rachel's family and clan, and everything she'd gleaned from that was slowly helping her to form a larger picture of this new culture.

"Okay," she said, glancing up from her notes, "so your clan is led by your grandfather, Brom."

"Right," Rachel answered without looking up from her phone screen.

"You said that's unusual. Why?"

"When my grandparents founded Clan Wilde, the town assumed my grandmother would be the head, but she insisted that my grandfather should lead. There's a lot of old-fashioned people in our town who still think a woman should always have the final word, and my grandparents wanted to show everyone that they were forward-thinkers."

Intrigued, Leda wrote, *Matriarchy?* in her notepad.

The bus stopped suddenly at a red light and simultaneously hit the curb. The entire right side of the bus heaved upward like an unexpected tidal swell. Leda grabbed her crutches before they could slide into the aisle as Rachel groaned and held her ribs.

"*Fuck*," Rachel moaned.

"Damn it," Leda said. "You okay?"

"Peachy." Rachel rubbed her torso and grit her teeth. "You?"

During the stop, Rachel went back to looking at her phone. Leda snuck a glance at the screen and saw, to her horror, a photo of *him*. Rachel was looking at the page about The Breach Killer that Suarez had shown them at the meeting. Leda's eyes fled from the sight, darting away as if the photo could burn her retinas. Briefly, she wondered if she should ask if there had been any updates in the case, but a rush of panic whipped the curiosity out of her brain. Scrambling, her mind refocused onto a safer topic.

"So," she said, picking up her pen again, "your grandparents. They're not married?"

"No."

"Your parents—Filip and Elafina—are they married?"

"No."

"And your brother Wilham and his baby mama?"

"Her name's Rettie. No, they're not married."

"Is anyone in your family married?"

"I don't know anybody who's married," Rachel replied, shooting Leda a puzzled glance. "The whole idea sounds weird to me."

No marriage, Leda thought. *How bizarre.*

"So, Rettie didn't marry your brother, but she did join your family, right?"

"Yes, of course." Rachel gave Leda another odd look. "That's how it works."

"And Rettie—shit!"

The bus lurched forward, and just as the front wheel bounced down to the street, the back wheel struck the same curb it had just left. The back half of the bus kicked up, knocking several passengers into each other and momentarily sliding others out of their seats. Leda's crutches toppled into the aisle. She and Rachel strained through their injuries to collect them.

"Rettie," Rachel continued, "was interested in collection fabric, which happens to be our town's primary product."

"Collection fabric?"

"The fabric used to make collectors' gloves. It's what allows me to touch daemons."

"And Rettie wanted a job working with that fabric?"

"Right, so she signed up for a matching tour. In the past, only men signed up for those; it's become more common for women in recent years, but of the thirty-some people who took part in that tour, she was still one of only three women."

"What's a matching tour?"

"On a matching tour, people get the chance to live in different areas that specialize in their field of interest. Rettie lived one month in four different towns that specialize in collection fabric. When she visited Kritt, she went around to the different clans to meet the men of the town, and that's when she met my brother. They liked each other and our clan had room to grow, so my grandfather invited her to join us."

"And . . . that was it?"

"'It?'" Rachel repeated, brow furrowed. "*What* was 'it'?"

"They only knew each other for a month," Leda said, trying not to sound too incredulous, "and then she moved in so they could start a family?" She cocked one eyebrow. "That's awful damn quick, don't you think?"

"Why would it need to take longer?" Rachel said with a shrug. "They got along, they wanted the same things out of life, and our clan had room to expand. Why drag it out?"

Leda made a mental note to add to her scribbles once she got a chance to set down her crutches: *abbreviated courtship, semi-arranged marriage.*

"That's certainly efficient," Leda said, "but not very romantic."

"Romance is for fun, not commitment," Rachel confidently replied, sounding like she was reciting a lesson learned long ago. "Passion is a poor foundation for a future."

"So . . . no passion at all?" Leda said. "That doesn't sound fun."

"There's no rule against fun," Rachel said. "Passion is great; everybody should have it and enjoy it. It's just not a good reason to commit to someone. It's important not to confuse a purely physical attraction for something meaningful."

There was some logic to that— Leda reluctantly conceded— some boring, grandmotherly logic. Still, she couldn't imagine building a life around someone without some mad passion to make it worthwhile.

Rachel stretched her neck to read the passing street signs. "I think our stop is next," she said, pocketing her phone.

Leda put a hand on Rachel's shoulder and pushed herself to her feet. Rachel put out an arm to steady her while she hefted the crutches under her arms.

"Damn these things," Leda muttered.

The bus jerked to a stop at the corner of a downtown inter-section. The sudden jolt sent one crutch sliding out from under her but, with Rachel's arm for support, she kept her feet. Rachel retrieved the lost crutch, scooped up Leda's handbag, and led the way down the steps. Leda glared at the driver on her way out, telepathically scolding him for his shitty driving, but the man smacked his chewing gum and ignored her.

The doors slammed behind them and the bus careened away to continue its route.

DEJA VU

"**W**here are we headed?" Leda asked.

"First job: Memorial Park."

"Mr. Creed said it had something to do with a déjà vu daemon, right?" Leda said, recalling what he'd said at the meeting. "Why is déjà vu a problem?"

"Déjà vu is almost always the sign of daemonic interaction," Rachel said. "It most often happens when a daemon's whispers, for whatever reason, penetrate the wrong part of the human brain."

"Is that a malfunction? Something that needs correction?"

"Not always." Rachel readjusted Leda's bag on her shoulder. "The whispers of a daemon can affect two different people in two very different ways. Some people just don't receive the whispers of particular daemons and that can result in a déjà vu feeling. There's no malfunction, just a genetic fluke, so there's nothing to fix."

"So, what's the problem in Memorial Park?"

"Too many déjà vus happening in one location. Something could be wrong."

"But you don't have to catch the daemon?"

"No one does, if it's not broken. It might just be a coincidence. My job today is to check it out and report what I see. Someone else will make the call based on what I tell them."

Leda crutched along at a good pace, but even so, she noticed Rachel had to slow her step several times to match her stride. Side by side, they took up more than half the width of the sidewalk, forcing others to edge around them when passing. Rachel kept glancing from side to side, giving anyone who eyed them a thorough-but-subtle scan. Leda made a mental note of this and guessed that Rachel was uncomfortable with how extremely conspicuous they were to passersby. Invisibility in Notan society was crucial to Arcanan operations—a lesson that, from what she'd learned, had been drilled into Rachel and her colleagues from the very start of their work. Not that Rachel needed to worry. With her crutches, Leda was by far the more eye-catching of the two of them. Next to her, Rachel was hardly worth a glance.

"So," she panted, "Rettie. Unusual name."

"It's short for Alazerette," Rachel said. "Her full name is Yatran Alazerette len Wilde."

"Alazerette . . . I've never heard that name before. It's pretty. Does it mean something?"

"It means 'color of lapis lazuli.'"

Leda thought of the ancient Egyptian displays at the museum—the brilliant blue hues of the art and jewelry. Lapis lazuli. She'd always loved that color. There was something special about it, something brilliant and royal. "I like that," she said. "It must have a special significance to her family or her culture, right?"

Rachel snorted. "I doubt it. Color names were a huge fad around the time I was born. Growing up, I knew a lot of girls named 'Virti'—that's 'green'—and several boys named 'Karmarem'— 'crimson.' My cousin is Indigo. Those names are out of fashion now, but I still meet a lot of people my age who are named after colors."

"Oh." Leda felt a flush of disappointment. A naming fad. What a letdown. Nevertheless, she plowed ahead with her questions, determined to make the most of this outing. "Your brother and Rettie have a son?"

"Right. Wilde Hart len Wilde."

"Len Wilde means 'of Clan Wilde'?"

"Everyone has to belong to a clan to retain citizenship privileges—that's the law."

All this walking on crutches was exhausting. Breathing hard, Leda tried to focus her mind through the physical strain to line up all the facts she was gathering.

"You said that women typically stay with their birth clans; does that mean children almost always take their family names from their mothers?"

"That's true."

Leda mentally underlined the word *Matriarchy* in her notes.

"What if the father's in a different clan? The kids don't take his name?"

Rachel chuckled and shook her head. "Until I started studying to be a collector, it never occurred to me that someone would find that strange. Where I'm from, fathers are only a part of their children's lives if the mothers agree to it. Well," she corrected herself, "that's not exactly true anymore. There's this thing called a 'hinge option.' When a baby's born into her mother's clan, the father's clan can attach a hinge option to her birth certificate that gives the kid an open invitation to join her father's clan when she comes of age, twenty years old. It also gives the father limited rights to her while she grows up."

"Limited?" Leda's mind jumped back to the assignment meeting, to Rachel and the other members of her square talking about Arcanan prejudices. "That sounds a little discriminatory."

"Hinge options are less than three hundred years old," Rachel said. "It used to be that a father had no rights to any kid born outside his clan—or even inside his clan, if he pissed off the mother. A hinge option sounds like progress to me."

Leda thought of her father. It was no secret in her family that even though her parents were deeply in love, they had married because her mother got pregnant. She tried to imagine her life had she been born in Rachel's society. Her parents would not have married and, had her mother so chosen, her father might never have been a part of her life; she would have been raised in a family unit compromised solely of her mother's family. She thought of her uncles—one of whom traveled for a living and was seldom home, the other of whom took great delight in teasing her. They would have been the primary male influences in her life. For a moment, the empty place in her heart left by her father's death felt much bigger. The idea of a childhood without her daddy was too heartbreaking to bear. She filed away the things Rachel had told her, silently said a prayer of thanks to her father in heaven, and kept her face expressionless.

Rachel peered around the corner. "This is it."

In a rising wave of color, the concrete and metal of the city gave way to grass and trees. Tall, bushy oaks shaded the stretches of trim grass, their branches intertwining across winding sidewalks. A light dusting of multicolored leaves rustled over the ground, the herald of an incoming autumn. The sound of rushing water announced the presence of a circular fountain in the heart of the lush vegetation. A spout of water continuously erupted from a concrete tower in the center; from there, the water flowed over an enlarging series of bowls before emptying into the final bowl, a round, ten-foot-wide structure standing in the middle of a cross section of sidewalks. A handful of chirping finches bathed in one of the smaller bowls under the watchful eye of a stray cat lurking in a nearby shrub. The last few morning joggers raced out of the park, passing the incoming herd of mothers with strollers. Amid the rolling sounds of the city rush-hour, singing birds and chattering squirrels filled the park with a peaceful air—a small bite of the natural in an artificial world.

As soon as they stepped inside the bounds of the park, Leda plopped herself down on a bench and let her hated crutches drop to the ground. She heaved as big a breath as her lungs could hold and let her screaming muscles go limp.

After picking up the crutches and leaning them neatly against the back of the bench, Rachel pulled out her glasses and began to case the park. As she wandered, Leda took out her notebook and jotted down some of the things she had gleaned from their conversation. It was strange to hear Rachel talk so casually about her society when so many aspects of it ran contrary to what felt natural to Leda. She tried to look at her own life from Rachel's perspective and suddenly thought that being immersed in a male-dominated society must be very disorienting. The idea of marriage, of being legally tied to one person for a lifetime, might seem upsetting to someone of her background. Leda's brain teemed with questions. There was still so much to learn.

Rachel returned to the bench and, glancing at Leda through tinted lenses, shook her head.

"Nothing unusual."

Leda couldn't help but laugh at this. She had looked through those glasses enough times at this point to know that they made *everything* look unusual. Through those lenses, she had seen swirls of light with no source, splatters of shadow attached to nothing, and transparent colors drifting about in fractal forms. On a few occasions, distressingly, she'd seen daemons—weird, out-of-focus little monsters whispering their temptation songs to passersby. Once she saw a ripple, a dimpling in reality that left wrinkles in the air and ground, which Rachel said was a sure sign that a daemon had passed from this plane of existence to another within the last few minutes. According to Rachel, all of these bizarre, inhuman, nightmarish things were perfectly ordinary.

"Nothing unusual," Leda whispered to herself. "Lordy."

After a few more minutes of searching, Rachel turned around in a huff and marched back toward Leda, her hand on the glasses, clearly about to swipe them from her face—until something over Leda's shoulder caught her attention. Suddenly focused, Rachel walked past the bench where Leda rested, knelt down with a grunt of discomfort, and stared at something in the grass.

"What is it?" asked Leda, shifting awkwardly in her seat.

"Hmmm," Rachel mumbled. "If it's what I think it is . . . here"—she pulled the glasses from her face and shoved them toward Leda—"take a look."

Leda slipped on the glasses and gazed at the spot Rachel indicated. Just a yard or two behind the bench, there was a strange fluttering of color, small but intense; the strobe-like flashing, which seemed to be cycling through every imaginable color, was almost painful to the eye. In the center of it all there was a stagnant point, a colorless smudge around which the flashes orbited. One especially violent flash threw off a handful of red sparks. Rather than drift into the ether at large, the sparks were quickly sucked into the black center and swallowed up.

Leda stood and, not bothering with her crutches, hopped

closer and plopped down on the grass with her braced knee awkwardly extended. "What the hell is that?" she whispered.

"Weird, huh?" Rachel waved at the spot and Leda saw her hand pass harmlessly through the thing. "I learned about this phenomenon years ago, but I've never seen it happen in person."

"Is it a daemon?"

"Yeah. But it's dying."

Leda started at the word. "Dying?"

"Well, 'suffering a catastrophic failure' might be a better description. It's broken and it's breaking more and more as we watch."

"Is this what caused the déjà vu?"

"Without a doubt. This thing whispers like any daemon, but the moment its malfunction went critical, those whispers hit the wrong frequency. It probably triggered déjà vu in everyone it tried to tempt."

Leda leaned in closer, holding her breath, waiting. Finally, she shook her head. "I don't feel any déjà vu."

"At this point, it's probably too broken to whisper at all. See that blackness in the center? That's the daemon's core consuming its substance. It's—crap, what's the word?—imploding. Its substance is breaking up and being sucked through its core into the wastes. Once there, it'll break down into its basest elements within the daemonic primordial ooze."

It was a strange thought—those crawly, freakish things dissipating into nothingness as if they were castles reduced to sand by the ocean's waves. *Strangest things in all of God's creation*, she marveled.

"Will you take it in to the Central Office?" Leda asked, still staring at the lights.

"No reason to," Rachel said. "It's dying a natural death and it's too far gone to repair. At this point, it couldn't hurt anyone if it tried. I can't even tell what kind of daemon it was. In another day or two, it'll be completely gone." She pulled out her phone. "I'll send in a report, but I guarantee you the higher-ups will just let this one go."

Leda stared at the decaying creature for a few minutes, her mind tingling. It was fascinating yet overwhelming, captivating yet repulsive. She couldn't decide if she should edge away from it like it was a rattlesnake or creep closer and try to touch the dying, but still mesmerizing, embers. The dual urges struggled within her briefly before canceling each other out, leaving her content just to look.

Rachel sat back on the ground next to Leda and began typing a message, presumably a report to her superiors. The two women sat in silence, side by side, as the morning grew bright and warm. A young couple wandered past them, arm in arm and whispering through secretive smiles. Leda tried not to stare at them, despite the kaleidoscopic whirl of colors and patterns that followed their motion. Memories of bygone romance flitted into her thoughts, leaving her pensive, resentful, and longing for human connection. As the pair wandered out of earshot, Leda removed the glasses and turned to Rachel—who, she noticed, was also casting furtive gazes at the couple.

Leda gave her a gentle nudge. "The way your brother and his baby mama hooked up; is that what you'll do?"

"Could be," Rachel said, tucking her phone into her coat. "I'm not planning to leave my clan, so I guess I might meet some guy on a matching tour." She sighed and crossed her arms over her chest. "It wasn't supposed to be that way."

"Wasn't supposed to?" Leda tilted her head. "What's that mean?"

For the first time, Rachel looked reluctant to answer a question. Typically, she rattled off responses in a matter-of-fact way, regardless of the topic. To see her with a tightly clamped mouth and cheeks drained of color made Leda both curious and uncomfortable.

Rachel drew a hissing breath through her teeth and stared down at the ground. On the exhale, she replied, "There's a clan in my hometown that works some land just a few miles from ours. Clan Kash. I've been involved with Kash Dhruv since the two of us were about thirteen. We were all swept up in each other, probably way more than we should've been. The thing is, both of our families were happy about it so they encouraged us. Two kids from the same town, neighboring clans, childhood friends . . . I guess we looked like a perfect couple. By the time we were sixteen, everyone just assumed we'd always be together, so I think we started to assume it, too. We broke up a bunch of times, but everyone said we would get back together, and we always did."

"Are you still together now?" Leda asked, already suspecting the answer.

Rachel shook her head.

"What happened?"

"Do you remember when Suarez told you that every Arcanan has a choice of three service options when she turns twenty? I chose collections. I thought Dhruv would do the same, but he picked military service." She gingerly rubbed her sides and puffed a breath through her nose. "I had no idea he was even considering it. He shipped out and we just . . . stopped talking and went about our separate lives. I think I still assumed we'd end up together once we were both back on our family farms. Maybe he thought that, too, but not long ago he told me that he's decided to stay in the military after his five years are up."

"He's not going back to your town," Leda said.

"Exactly." Rachel wrinkled her nose and glared at the grass. "He only called to make our breakup official. I heard he's involved with someone else now." She turned her head and stared at the retreating young couple, who were happily oblivious to everything around them. "I never really thought about having to find someone else."

Leda experienced a flash of déjà vu that she was sure had nothing to do with the imploding daemon. She had lived this exact scenario before. After breaking up with her last boyfriend, a man she had dated for almost two years, she had sat side by side with a friend complaining that she had never thought she'd have to find someone new.

She remembered the last time she saw her ex: right after their graduation ceremony, when he passed by her on his way to hug his mother. There was a new girl on his arm. Leda didn't know her but an image of her was forever burned into her memory: skinny, pale, horse-toothed, flat-chested, and bony-kneed. She was also wearing a designer dress, her hair was elegantly styled, her nails were perfectly manicured, and she wore real diamonds in both ears and on two fingers. Money. The bastard had dumped her for an ugly girl with money.

She tried to tell herself she was better off without him, but the sting of rejection lingered even now. The knowledge that, in his eyes, she had been measured and found lacking was a hurdle she simply could not clear. That the relationship hadn't been very good to begin with and was probably doomed in the long run hadn't make the breakup easier. It hurt to know that she was expendable. Leda felt her heart expand to empathically encompass Rachel. They were very different women on multiple levels but this, at least, they had in common. Cultures differed, languages differed, upbringings differed, but heartache was universal.

"You know what we need?" Leda said. "A night out."

Rachel glanced at Leda, eyes pinched. "Out?"

"Hell yeah. Once I'm off these damn crutches and you can breathe again, let's you and me go clubbing some night. We should go someplace so loud that we can't hear ourselves think about our exes. We'll dance and drink until the losers who hit on us are interesting. There's plenty of men out there we can use for a night and never think about again. Right?"

Rachel smirked; her expression showed surprise, but also amusement. Leda supposed she understood. After all, until now she had treated Rachel solely as a source of information. She certainly had never suggested that they spend recreational time together.

But after she got over the initial shock, Rachel smiled. "I could do that. I can't remember how long it's been since I had a night out."

"Same here. I'd say we're due."

Rachel grinned and nodded. The two smiled at each other in commiseration as only discarded women can. Then Rachel chuckled softly and climbed to her feet.

"If you've got to get back to the museum tomorrow," she said, "then we'd better go ahead and look into the other two jobs on my docket while we're out today."

"Yeah, okay," Leda said, sighing resolutely. With Rachel's help, she managed to pull herself upright and tuck her crutches into place. "Work now, men later, and never the two shall meet, right?"

"Right."

Side by side, they started back the way they had come, leaving the daemon to complete its catastrophic failure unobserved.

DISGRACE / DISMAY

11

Out of breath,
he glided down and landed on a rocky beach,
whereupon he immediately collapsed.

The weight of his wings seemed to triple
as he lay face-down on the shore,
gravity pulling his wing-arms to the ground
until the membranes were nothing
but limp folds.

Exhausted and damp,
his flames dimmed
his body reduced to a dull burgundy.

His fire-born muscles were so drained of energy
that he couldn't raise his head.

When he finally mustered the strength
to lift his chin and open his eyes,
he sensed that he was several continents away
from the boy.

All four eyes pinching shut,
he groaned and lowered his head
to the wet rocks beneath him.

He would sleep,
he would wake up thoroughly sore,
and then he would travel
half a world
to resume his vengeance.

The rocks below him stank of salt and bird shit
and the continuing spray from the crashing tide
kept his flames dim.

The thought of another journey across this
human-infested planet
made him feel worn out and unclean.

And then the worst realization of all:
this would likely not be the last time it happened.

Was this really better than returning home in disgrace?

He sat in the shade of a tree—
a tropical thing that was always green
and produced fragrant fruit
that he could not digest.

A pile of fish at his side
marked his latest meal.
He often did not eat for days,

his mind lost
to the passing of time.

The sun
that was not the true sun
rose and set at random
as if obeying a madman's whim.

The moon appeared rarely,
seldom accompanied by stars.

It was all as the cascade of a waterfall,
ever-changing water
but an unchanging sight.

Voices of his people wandered—
muffled, hushed—
through the closed door.

He wasn't sure how long it had been
since they had taken possession
of the sealed door
but their words,
his own language,
sounded foreign to him.

The poisonous speech of humanity
lingered in his ears
like ghosts
haunting an old ruin.

When had the ways of men become his normal?

THE FLYER

Simon loitered outside the English department building, his eyes sweeping up and down the university's city-bound campus. Though he had graduated just one year earlier, everything looked a little different. He had never really noticed before how small these little oases of green were, or how odd they looked surrounded by towers of steel and concrete. Then again, he hadn't been to this building since completing his freshman year English requirements, so maybe he'd just forgotten.

While Leda excelled in English—and every other language— Simon's brain more readily embraced science-related topics. Though initially unsure of where his interests would lead him, he'd done well in biology, chemistry, and physics before eventually taking an interest in therapy. While he had no use for shrinks and others who sat around listening to whiners bitch about their lives, he found he had a limitless reservoir of patience for people struggling with physical issues.

When tackling a problem—a *real* problem, something he could see and touch—Simon intuitively understood the value of working slowly and steadily to reach the goal. That was the beauty of physical therapy: when done correctly, it yielded solid progress, even if only a little at a time. The mind and its intangible dance confused and repulsed Simon, but the body could be dealt with in a scientific manner. It was just the sort of work he was made for.

Loitering by the English's department's front door, still waiting on Bach, he stepped over to a large bulletin board papered with various flyers and announcements. Most of them were about test prep classes, apartments for rent, and people in need of a roommate. Some advertised items for sale, everything from furniture to guitars. One ad in particular tickled him. *For sale: small fold-out sofa, hideous blue pinstripe pattern, mystery stains on one cushion, ugly mattress inside has rip underneath. Looks like shit but comfy as hell.* Several tabs with the owner's phone number had been torn off.

Simon grinned. Apparently, he wasn't the only person who respected honesty.

Beneath the sofa ad, an old flyer poked through. With nothing else to engage his time, Simon flipped up the ad and tore away the hidden paper. Much to his surprise, it was not college related; it was a missing person notice. There was a grainy photo in the center of the paper, a gentleman with deep smile lines and crinkly eyes. Underneath was his name—Javier Alvarez—and a description of him, first in English and then in Spanish. The flyer ended with a painful plea: *Someone knows where my father is. Please call me. I miss him so much.*

The pain of a lost father gripped Simon's chest and his heart went out to the missing man's child. "Damn," he murmured. "Hope they found him." Then he checked his watch. Bach had said picking up his degree from his adviser would take no more than ten minutes. That was twenty-two minutes ago. What was the hold up?

Just as Simon's impatience grew to a boil, Bach appeared in the doorway.

"Sorry about that. One of my professors was withholding my last three credits. He said I was absent too many days."

Simon heaved a deep breath, consciously calming himself. "Were you?"

"I dunno," Bach said. "Maybe. But never once while I was in that class did he actually take attendance, so I don't think he could prove it. Anyway, I had to go talk to him to get those credits back."

"So, you got 'em?"

Bach grinned and held up an elegantly decorated paper, complete with signature and symbol.

"I'm a college graduate," he said proudly.

"Congratulations. How'd you get that guy to change his mind so fast?"

"Are you kidding?" Bach laughed. "Now that I'm back in control of my sight-beyond, there's not a person in this building I couldn't blackmail."

"Really?" Curiosity engaged; Simon leaned closer. "What'd you have on him?"

"You don't wanna know. It's nasty. And not a fun, kinky nasty. Sick nasty. Illegal nasty. You should've seen his face when he realized how much I knew."

Simon smiled and chuckled quietly. He could well imagine that expression. Seized with a sudden impulse, he said, "Hey, you got any dirt on my landlord? I've been trying to get that ass-hole to replace the fridge in my place for months. Damn thing doesn't stay cold and it smells like an old gym sock. Be great if I had something on him that would get his ass in gear."

"I'll let you know if I come up with anything." Bach rolled up the paper and then tapped it in the palm of his hand to neaten up the ends. "And speaking of landlords, I need to visit mine. Ready to go?"

"Yeah, okay."

Simon glanced at the missing person flyer still in his hand and stepped up to the bulletin board. He plucked out a tack and affixed it to the board in a prominent spot, covering several ads. Satisfied, he headed down the walk in the direction of the nearest street, toward his parked car.

He was halfway there when he realized no one was behind him. He looked back and saw Bach frozen in front of the bulletin board.

"You coming?" he called.

When Bach didn't respond, Simon approached him. As he drew close, he saw that Bach was staring at Javier Alvarez's flyer—his electric blue eyes pulsing with energy, his muscles shuddering as if trying to shimmy out of his skin. His fingers dug into the newly acquired degree still clutched in his hands.

"What is it?" Simon asked. He looked at the flyer again. "You know that guy?"

"Never met him," Bach whispered.

"Then what's the problem?"

"I don't know," he said, eyes wide and unblinking. "I have this feeling. It's like I'm seeing something I wasn't supposed to see. It's weird. Terrifying. Wrong." He started to turn his head, but his eyes stayed glued to the smiling man in the photo. "I wasn't supposed to see this. Not yet."

"Huh?" Simon's brow furrowed. Bach's labored breathing sent a prickle down the nape of his neck. "What the hell's up with you?"

"I don't know," Bach said, his voice strained. "I think . . . I think I was supposed to see this later. Maybe. Or not. God!" Bach wrenched his eyes away from the paper and covered his face with his hands. "When I look at that thing, I feel like there's something I have to do, something vital. But I also feel like it's too soon to do it. It's like . . ." He thrust his fingers deep into his hair. "It's like getting slapped awake in the middle of the night by your own brain reminding you that you forgot to pick up a prescription. You know you've gotta do it so you'll have your meds, but it's midnight and the pharmacy is closed. You're worried about not having them, but you can't get them until tomorrow, but you need them, but the pharmacy is closed, and your thoughts just keep going in a damn circle!" Bach pinched his eyes shut. "It's like that," he said, speaking much slower, "but more."

Simon looked over Bach's bowed head at the bulletin board. Javier Alvarez smiled at them from some long-gone moment in time. He looked back at Bach and saw his hands grasping and ungrasping fistfuls of his hair. The hard-won degree had fallen to the ground, dirty and forgotten. Bach looked up at him—the edges of his eyes twitching, his lips curled back from his teeth. The image of a rabid dog flashed across Simon's mind and he took half a step back.

"You okay?" he asked, unsure of what was happening.

"There's a gun to my head," Bach gasped. "My mind is too clear. There's no sight-beyond coming in like there should be. It's all been blown out. It's just wind in an empty tunnel. I don't understand. What am I supposed to do?"

Simon stared at Bach as if he was a naked lunatic screaming in the street. In the short time he had known this man, he had come to expect their conversations to be odd, but this time his words were alarming. Bach's weird gift might not be scientifically logical, but at least he usually made some kind of sense. Seeing his once well-ordered behavior crumble filled Simon's gut with coiling snakes.

"You're supposed to go see your landlord, remember?" Simon said. "We were heading back to the car, right? We should go now."

Bach stared at the ground without responding, trembling hands still pulling at his hair. Simon's eyes darted all around to make sure no one else was witnessing this spectacle—or his own association with it. Then, wanting to put an end to this insanity before anyone saw, he edged a little closer to Bach's shaking form and put a hand on his shoulder.

"You gotta stop this, man," he said firmly. "You don't wanna end up under that bridge again."

The word bridge jolted Bach. He drew himself upright, looked at Simon—his too-blue eyes full of dread and determination—shook his head, and exhaled through his nose. "I'll never sleep under a bridge again," he said. "I can't control the information that comes into my head, but I won't let it control me. Never again."

With that, the blaze of madness that had engulfed Bach died away. A few deep breaths, and he once again looked firmly in control of his body and mind.

Realizing that he wasn't going to have to deal with an outburst of crazy, relief washed over Simon. "That's right," he said. "Let's get outta here."

"Yeah." Bach's eyes drifted toward the flyer again but he stopped himself and resolutely turned his back to it. He leaned down, scooped up his fallen degree from the ground, and brushed away the dirt. "Thanks."

"It's nothing."

Bach flashed a weary, unamused smirk and met Simon's gaze. "If you had ever been homeless because you couldn't keep yourself in your own head, you'd know it wasn't nothing. Now let's go. I never wanna come back to this place again."

They walked away from the university and toward Simon's car, leaving Javier Alvarez's smiling photo in the center of the bulletin board, afloat in a sea of lesser causes.

METAL AND GLASS

L eda was sore from the crutches, making it hard for her to hobble down the bus steps as she and Rachel disembarked at a street corner. Both of her hands were developing blisters where she held the grips and her arm muscles wailed with each movement. Following her usual routine was enough to make her body ache, but this morning had involved considerably more walking than she was used to. As fascinating as all of it had been, she wished she had put off joining Rachel at her job until her knee was healed. *But*, she told herself, *since I'm already here, I should see it through.* Gritting her teeth, she soldiered on.

Just a few steps from the bus stop was a walkway lined with a well-manicured row of hedges. The glass and steel monstrosity the walkway led to stretched high above the street, carving out a place in the city skyline. Throngs of people, most of them in suits, moved in and out of the building, each one absorbed in his own business and paying no mind to any other person in his path.

Standing in the plaza out front, Rachel checked the file on her phone and squinted up at the tower's dozens of floors above her.

"This is the address," she said. "What is this place?"

"This is the Konyha building," Leda told her. "They're a kitchenware manufacturer. This is the company's regional head-quarters."

Leda noticed an odd look on her companion's face—suspicious and a little uncomfortable. "Are you bad with heights?" she asked.

"Heights? No," Rachel replied. "It's just . . . we don't have buildings like this where I'm from. The tallest building I ever saw back home was maybe ten stories tall and that was in Bhaleti."

"What's Bhaleti?"

"The Arcana's largest city."

"How big is it?"

"Oh, it's not like here," Rachel said with a dismissive wave of her hand. "I mean, I read somewhere that New York City is the biggest city in the United States and that has, what, eight million people? Bhaleti only has about 250,000, last I heard."

Leda's eyes widened. "Just 250,000? That's it?"

"Yes. And the city of Halla has, I think, about 200,000."

"So small," Leda mumbled in wonder. "How big is your hometown?"

"Oh!" Rachel said, grinning. "Kritt has less than 2,000 people. You can't compare Kritt to Halla or Bhaleti. It's metal and glass."

"It's what?"

"Metal and glass—you know, two completely different things."

Apples and oranges, metal and glass, thought Leda. *Interesting figure of speech.*

"Come on," Rachel said. "I've got work to do. Let's have a look inside."

They entered the building and stood together inside. The

lobby was gigantic—four stories high, with tall, tinted windows that bathed the room in filtered sunshine. Five separate escalator pairs trafficked long lines of people to and from the first few floors. The longest of these upward-bound lines led to a colossal desk manned by eight people, half of whom greeted the people coming up the escalator while the other half answered telephones, their eyes fastened to computer screens.

Rachel scanned the entry desk and glanced at the other escalators. Leda followed her gaze. At the bottom of each escalator, there was a turnstile requiring a key card swipe to allow passage.

Rachel frowned. "Let's step outside."

She turned around and held the door open for Leda, then led her to a bench just outside the entrance. As Leda made herself comfortable, Rachel took out her phone and swiftly composed a message.

"Who are you texting?" Leda asked.

"Creed," Rachel said. "I'm explaining the situation. He'll take care of it."

"How?"

Rachel shrugged as she sent the message and pocketed her phone.

"You're not curious how he'll do it?"

"I don't care how," Rachel said. "I only need to know how to do my job, not his."

To Leda, Rachel's tone sounded flippant and a little annoyed. It wasn't the first time she'd heard someone take that tone when discussing their job, but in this case, it made her wonder. "I get the feeling," she said, "that you don't like your job much."

"I have three years left of my eight-year stint before I can work on the farm full time. It doesn't matter whether or not I like the work. I have to do it."

"I guess I'm wondering why you picked this job if you don't like it and you had two other choices."

"Well . . ." Rachel squinted at the light reflecting off the skyscraper's windows. "I thought long and hard about military service since it's five years instead of eight, but I wanted to be able to go home during harvest times, when my clan needs every available hand to bring in the crops. Collections offers the most flexible schedule. It's also not as dangerous as military service."

"Dangerous," Leda repeated, her interest piqued. "You-all at war with somebody?"

"Not as such," Rachel hesitantly replied. "'War' isn't really what our army's for."

Leda was puzzled. "Then what is it for?"

"Hmm . . ." Rachel ran her tongue over her teeth. "You see, the Arcana is unified. While we do have lots of different regions, we don't have different countries with different leaders anymore, so we don't need to war with each other. Our army exists to protect all of the Arcana against outside threats."

"Outside the Arcana? So, threats from other dimensions?"

"Essentially."

Leda pondered this information for a moment and then attempted to sum it up. "The Arcana is at war with people from another dimension?"

"No, no, no." Rachel groaned, one hand on her forehead. "You're still limiting your thinking to Notan experience."

Her exasperated tone, which seemed unjustified to Leda, stung. She was working hard to understand something that Rachel wasn't explaining well. If anyone should be frustrated by this conversation, it should be *her.*

"Your country's army exists to fight other armies," Rachel said. "That's what it trains for, that's its purpose. Ours doesn't train to engage other soldiers." Rachel turned a grim expression to her companion. "There are scarier things out there than human beings."

A chill ran down Leda's spine as she absorbed this knowledge. It raised dozens of horrifying questions, the answers to which she feared. A huge, monstrous thought, its silhouette akin to the freakish riot daemon she had seen in the basement, rose from her imagination and loomed tall just over her shoulder, its mouth agape and ready to swallow her whole. She shuddered. In recent days, she had broadened her worldview to integrate daemons, the Arcana and all its people, interdimensional passages, and so many other foreign concepts. A threat like the one Rachel hinted at . . . it was too alien. She pushed this colossal thing into her memory files and grabbed on to a neighboring thread of the conversation, a human thread.

"What's the third option?" asked Leda.

"What?"

"The third option," she repeated. "There are three options for every citizen, right? Daemon collection, military service . . . what's the third?"

"Oh," Rachel said, her voice lighter. "Dredging."

"What's dredging?"

"It mostly involves scavenging technology and artifacts from the Apsa, another layer of the human dimensional spectrum. There are no Apsans anymore, haven't been for ages, but they left behind a lot of tech and knowledge that we gather for our own use. The technology isn't always safe, though; lots of people have died. That's why we also keep our prison colony there: since they've chosen to not be productive members of society, dredgers put them to work scavenging tech that, while potentially dangerous, might be useful to us."

Leda shifted her weight, trying to push off the sense of un-ease that came upon her as Rachel talked. What she described struck her as a rather severe punishment for the average criminal. The Arcana was not the only society to use prisoners for unsavory work. Still, it made her uncomfortable.

"How long is the dredging term of service?"

"Three years. A lot of the people who pick that option plan to continue their education and don't want to wait five or eight years when they already have a lot of school and training ahead of them. My brother, Wilham, chose dredging because he's studying to be a veterinarian. I hardly saw him for three years, and when he finally came home for good, he was fifteen pounds lighter and had some freaky-looking scars that he doesn't like to talk about."

Leda remembered the scars she had seen on Rachel and her friends the previous day and how nonchalant they had been about their old injuries. It was hard to imagine what sort of wound Rachel would consider "freaky-looking."

"How big is your prison?"

"Small," Rachel told her. "Nothing like the prisons here. Very few offenses in the Arcana are worthy of prison. We only incarcerate the worst of the worst."

Leda's treacherous mind immediately conjured an image of the psycho from the basement, his horrible face smirking down at her. Pain shot through her bandaged knee as she instinctively cringed, as if she could bodily hide from the memory.

"Worst of the worst?" she said quietly, fixing Rachel with her wide-eyed gaze. "Like that man?"

The mention of their shared experience visibly affected Rachel. Her eyes darted around restlessly, and she clutched her cracked ribs. "Yes," she said. "Yes, definitely that guy."

"So, if they catch him—"

"*When* they catch him," Rachel said, "his ass will go directly to the Apsa." She smiled darkly at Leda. "Imagine how much better you'll sleep at night knowing that not only is he locked up, but he's in an entirely different dimension."

Though overwhelmed by the immensity of everything she had just learned, Leda did feel a touch of premature relief come over her. The idea of not having to walk the same earth or breathe the same air or even see the same stars as that man was deeply appealing; she longed for such a future.

"Is there a conspiracy?" she asked in a hushed voice. "Do you think it's true? Are your people involved with him?"

Jaw clenched and fists balled against her thighs, Rachel stared intently at the concrete sidewalk beneath their feet. Briefly, Leda wondered if she was angry, but then Rachel exhaled sharply, licked her lips, and shook her head.

"I don't know," she finally said. "I know the guy who grabbed us spouted off some Arcanan terminology, but . . . I don't know if I believe that he really was working with Arcanans." She picked at a scab on her thumb until a liquid red dot appeared. "Maybe I just don't want it to be true. If a daemon like Apep gets loose, it'll cause mass destruction, both to the planet and everything living on it. That someone from my world would want that to happen . . . it just . . .." Her mouth remained open, as if to allow the unspoken words to fall from her lips. Then she straightened up. "I don't know," she said again. "Fuck it all, I just don't know."

A sharp ding cut the air, startling both women. Rachel fished out her phone, read the newly arrived message, and nodded.

"All set," she announced. "Let's go in."

DILIGENCE

They reentered the building and joined the line of people ascending to the main desk.

When their turn came, a woman with a well-trained smile gave them a once-over. "How can I help you?"

"My name's Rachel Wilde, and this is Leda Morley," Rachel told her politely. "We're supposed to visit the trademark department."

With her smile still pasted on, the woman turned her attention to a nearby computer screen. "Who in the trademark department are you scheduled to see?"

"I don't know their name," Rachel said. "My boss made the arrangements."

Leda watched how easily this casual deception came to Rachel. While she had not told the woman an actual lie, she certainly wasn't telling her the whole truth, and yet she seemed quite comfortable with that.

The lies didn't sit quite so well with Leda, but her curiosity kept her discomfort at bay.

"I need to see some ID, ladies," the smiley woman told them, holding out one manicured hand.

Rachel fished Leda's driver's license out of the purse she was still carrying for her and then pulled another card from her own pocket. From over her shoulder, Leda caught a glimpse. It bore a photo of Rachel, along with some writing that appeared to be English, but it didn't have any of the state symbols that Leda's license displayed. Then she recognized the color and design. The card was a student ID. *Why . . .* she began to wonder, but then the answer occurred to her: if Rachel was stopped by Notan authorities, they could check on the authenticity of a state–issued ID pretty easily, whereas university records weren't so easily accessible. *I'm starting to think like an Arcanan,* she thought, pleased with herself.

The woman behind the desk scanned the cards, pausing only to glance up and compare the photos to the two women, and then returned them to Rachel.

"You can go on up, ladies," she said, eternally pleasant. "Trademark is on the forty–seventh floor. Elevators are just down this hall. Be sure to take the elevators on the right. The ones on the left only service floors fifty and above."

Rachel nodded. "Thank you."

The two of them boarded the elevator alone. Despite the smooth ascent, Leda repeatedly shifted her weight on her crutches; her blisters were screaming. She glanced at Rachel several times, noting the slightly tense and uncertain expression on her face. Her companion's eyes were glued to the illuminated numbers marking their ascension.

"I guess it's a little weird for you going up this high," she ventured.

"It's unnatural," Rachel said. "A building this tall just isn't right."

"There are skyscrapers all over the world, you know. This world, anyway."

"People aren't supposed to be this high off the ground."

"I would argue that people aren't supposed to cross between dimensions."

"I guess we disagree then," Rachel muttered, still staring at the rising numbers.

The doors slid open to reveal a wall covered by an orange and gray smear of a painting. After blocking the elevator door long enough for Leda to exit, Rachel stepped into the hallway and allowed the elevator doors to close behind her. Leda scanned the list of offices on the directory plaque in front of them.

"Trademark's this way," she declared as she pivoted her crutches to the left.

Rachel slipped her glasses onto her face as they walked. They turned a sharp corner, and large glass doors marking the entrance to a bustling office came into view.

The etched words "Trademark Department" guarded a palace of cubicles containing a pulse of activity unlike anything Leda had seen before. Every person she could see appeared to be in constant motion; whether carrying a file from one cubicle to another or furiously typing at a desk, each and every employee was working at peak efficiency.

"Hell of a work ethic they got here," said Leda with a nod of appreciation. "Wonder if they're hiring."

Rachel scrunched up her nose. "This place is weird."

"I know, right?" Leda said. "Nobody at the museum puts this much energy into their work, that's for damn sure."

"No"—Rachel removed her glasses and held them out to Leda—"I mean this."

Balancing awkwardly on her crutches, Leda took the glasses and popped them on. Much to her surprise, the visual assault she had come to expect from Rachel's lenses did not occur. The typical swirls, fractals, and color bursts from the ether were conspicuously absent from the office, replaced with only a few dim dribbles of varying color and the occasional blotch floating through space.

"It's pretty still," Leda said. "Not much to look at."

"Because there are no daemons," Rachel told her. "Look again. I didn't see even one."

As instructed, Leda looked again. Through the doorway glass, she watched the mad bustle of the office. Amid the human activity, the lenses showed her only a few thin streaks and scattered dots of spectral color. Sure enough, there was not one daemon in sight. The only movement in the trademark department came from the humans.

"The ether is almost clear," Rachel said with a shake of her head. "No daemon tracks at all. With this group of people in the same space for eight or so hours each day, there should be daemons. One or two at the very least."

Leda removed the glasses and handed them back to Rachel. "These people look really productive. Maybe that's from the lack of daemons. Isn't that a good thing?"

"Hmm . . ." Rachel donned her glasses again and scanned the office with great intensity, as if ready to pounce on the slightest clue. "Not one daemon. Definitely not normal."

Moments passed and Leda shuffled on her crutches. "So, what should we do abo—"

Leda's question was cut short as Rachel strode forward and pushed her way through the double glass doors. The girl at the trademark reception desk briefly tried flagging her down while simultaneously typing and continuing her telephone conversation, but Rachel breezed past her with little more than a wave.

Flustered, Leda was wondering what to do when Rachel, just

a step away from being out of sight, suddenly stopped and stared at something at the far side of the office—and then, seeing that Leda was not on her heels, gestured impatiently for her to follow.

Nostrils flaring, Leda drew a long, slow breath and flexed her blistered fingers around her crutch grips. Using her good leg, she pivoted around and backed into the door, pushing it open with her backside and pulling her crutches in after her. As the heavy doors swung shut behind her, Rachel continued to stare through the glasses across the sea of cubicles.

"Thanks for the help," Leda said, seething, when she finally caught up with her.

"You won't believe what I'm looking at," Rachel said, oblivious to Leda's anger. "Take a look over there"—she motioned with her chin—"and tell me what you see."

Still quietly fuming, Leda peered over the tops of the cubicles toward the far wall. Inside the first office, she saw a plump man with a receding hair line wearing a suit and tie. He was standing quite still, his hands poised over his desk like a piano player's just moments before the start of a concert.

"That man's just standing at his desk," she said.

"That doesn't look weird to you?"

Leda wrinkled her nose. "A guy with his name on the door not working as hard as his subordinates? Looks normal to me."

Rachel removed the glasses from her face and handed them to Leda. "Look again," she pressed.

Leda put on the glasses and looked at the balding man again. This time, she saw a strange aura around him—a skittery, skeletal thing that vibrated out from his stout body and then refracted back into him, shaking and jittering through the bounds of his skin. Similar movement nearby drew her eye and she looked around the rest of the office. The other employees had their own quaking auras, though none were half as clear or active as that of their supervisor. Leda turned her head and saw something pulsing around the receptionist's ever-moving form as she talked on the phone, filed papers under her desk, refilled the paper tray of her printer, and typed seventy words per minute at her computer. The woman's strange aura seemed to jab at her, poking her, driving her on.

"Okay," Leda said, tipping the glasses back onto her crown, "that's weird. What is it?"

"A daemon has set up shop here," Rachel said. "It's compelling them to work this hard."

"So why isn't the suit working?"

"He's trying to," Rachel said. "Look at how his hands are twitching."

His hands were, in fact, twitching, so much so that Leda marveled that she had not noticed the first time she looked. If only looking at his hands, she might think he was having a seizure. She glanced around the office, searching for another person with the same symptoms, but saw none.

"So, what does it—"

Again, Rachel marched away before Leda could finish asking her question.

Curiosity overshadowing her annoyance, Leda followed and eagerly kept pace.

Initially she carefully copied Rachel, keeping her head high and her eyes forward, adopting the stride and stance of a person on a mission, a person whose right to be there need not be questioned. She soon wondered if such an act was necessary, however, since the frenzied employees went about their work without a glance at either her or Rachel. The only ones who noticed them were the ones who knocked into them during a mad dash across the office, and even they could not be bothered to stop and figure out why two unfamiliar women were in their office; every person who bumped into Leda ducked and weaved to regain his or her path without so much as a "sorry." Whatever was affecting the department had put blinders on every person under its control.

The two women peered through the glass window into the office of the supervisor. Now less than six feet away, Leda could clearly see that his hands were not the only part of him twitching. The muscles in his unshaven face jumped, tensing and convulsing, as different expressions fought for control. He jerked back and forth, rocking back on his heels and forward onto his toes as if he had conflicting urges about where to go. His mouth opened and closed like a caught fish gasping for life. Though the two women stared at him through the window, he took no notice, caught up in his own contradictory impulses. Leda tilted her head forward and the glasses slid down her brow and onto her nose. Immediately, her eyes were assailed by the ethereal, needle-like protrusions exploding from within him. Like an electric porcupine with osculating quills, the colorful spikes vibrated about his person so violently that Leda could hardly see his body. Leda took the glasses from her face and shoved them toward Rachel, who slipped them on and squinted at the man. After only a moment, she lowered the lenses and rubbed her eyes.

"What're we seeing?" asked Leda. She looked at the twitching man and felt a swell of pity amid her curiosity. "What the hell is happening to him?"

"Best guess, this man and the defective daemon are occupying the same space. The daemon isn't as fully out of phase with the world as it should be; it's poking into our level of reality in the same spot where he's standing. That explains why these people are falling over themselves to get their work done: its whispers have gotten too loud now that it's a little too far into this world. That's also why this man isn't acting like all the others: he's paralyzed by the daemon's presence. It's like the daemon is a hook that caught him, and now the two can't separate or move on." She glanced around at the bustling employees. "It's probably a diligence daemon. It's compelling these people to work at peak efficiency."

"Diligence." The word struck a strange chord in Leda's ears. "Diligence is one of the seven heavenly virtues."

"I don't know what that means."

"Seven heavenly virtues," Leda repeated, louder. "Practicing them is supposed to protect us from the temptation of the seven deadly sins."

Rachel stared at her blankly. Leda pressed on.

"Diligence is supposed to drive out temptation and pave the way to happiness. It's the good that drives away the evil of sloth. That's what I was taught as a child. Why would people need to be tempted to act virtuously?"

Rachel's expression remained impassive. "Good and evil don't enter into a daemon's function. Morality is in the mind of the tempted."

"But then . . . this thing you're calling a daemon . . ." The weight of Leda's upbringing pulled her analytical mind off course as the echoes of childhood church lessons grew louder in her mind. All the peculiar things she had learned since meeting Rachel began to slip out of the well-labeled cubbies where she'd stored them. The word "daemon" shimmied out of the label of "natural phenomena" and poked its head into the Sunday categories, shedding the "a" from its name as it did so. But this thing

Rachel described did not fit the brimstone variety. The conclusion slipped through her thoughts and to her lips, neither embraced nor rejected: "That thing is an angel."

"It's a daemon," Rachel said. "It's a malfunctioning diligence daemon."

But the word had already taken root in Leda's brain. *Angel.* Childlike longing overrode her logical adult brain and her heart suddenly ached. Those tender years of her youth when she was mourning for her father, those years when her only comfort was in knowing her daddy was in heaven, crept up on her. A primal need, rising up from the daddy-shaped hole in her heart, overflowed. She snatched the glasses from Rachel's hand and put them on. Her dark eyes strained through the kaleidoscope of stabbing colors to find form behind the trapped man.

"From the state of his clothes and hair," Rachel said, "he's been stuck here for a day or two. He and the daemon can't separate from each other." She shrugged. "I can't handle this myself. I'll have to kick this assignment to a cleaver."

Leda's eyes stayed glued to the supervisor even as the ingrained researcher within registered Rachel's words. "Cleaver?"

"Someone who can untangle a daemon from a human," Rachel said. "Nasty job. Not many people would sign up for it."

"You mean an exorcist?"

"Huh?"

"A priest who uses God's light to expel a demon from the human it possesses."

"No." Rachel snickered. "That's bullshit."

Leda's jaw tightened but she couldn't bring herself to look away from the ethereal display. Though it still hurt her eyes, she now saw an alien beauty in the spectacle. The motion was jagged and unearthly, but it radiated with a pulse that held her eyes captive. Still flooded with childhood yearning, her heart thundered in her chest. With every skittering dart, she hoped to see something meaningful. With every flash of color, she strained to find significance.

Out of the corner of her eye, she saw Rachel lean against the window, phone in her hand.

"Let's see," Rachel said, scrolling, "who's the cleaver on duty? Keene."

"What's keen?"

"Keene Dante," Rachel said. "I've heard good things. Well, about his work, anyway. I've heard the man himself is intimidating. I'll just send this assignment to him and message Creed so he can update the file. And . . . done!" She pocketed her phone and turned to Leda with a smile. "I'm finished here. We can go."

"Go?" Leda tore her eyes from the imprisoned supervisor. "You're gonna leave these manic people to burn themselves out?"

"No, I'm going to leave these manic people in the more capable hands of a professional trained to deal with situations like these."

"But shouldn't we keep an eye on things until he gets here?"

"What for? There's nothing we can do, and the longer we stay the more likely it becomes that someone will notice that we don't belong. Let's go."

"But . . ." Leda felt rooted to the spot. "What does it look like?" She trained her eyes on the man once again.

"Huh?"

"The ang . . . the daemon. What does it look like?"

"I don't know," Rachel said, her tone growing impatient. "It's inside that man. I can't see it."

"But you must know."

Rachel huffed out a sigh. "Diligence daemons usually have long spikes and huge eyes, okay? Let's go."

But Leda continued to stare, trembling on her crutches. More than twenty years of church lessons replayed in her mind, accompanied by storybook images of human-like creatures made holy by their great wings and gold halos. Through Rachel's glasses, she could see the spikes but no wings. What she could see, and what Rachel described, did not fit her childhood expectation. And besides, angels were supposed to do the work of the Lord, not pollute an office with misplaced temptations.

Rachel snatched the glasses off her face, making her yelp and drop one crutch.

"What the hell?" she yelled.

"Let's go," Rachel said as she bent down and swept up the crutch. "I've got other work to do."

"I don't see how you can leave these people—"

"Because there's nothing I can do for them!" Rachel exploded. "These people are so far gone to this daemon that they don't even care that I'm standing in the middle of this office screaming at you!"

It was true. Throughout their visit, not one person in the trademark department had paid them the slightest mind. But this man—his utter helplessness, his obvious torment, was so difficult to walk away from. And if she stayed to see the man separated from the thing inside him, then maybe she would finally get see it clearly.

"But that man—"

"What about him!?" Rachel turned and marched across the office, headed toward the front door. A clerk with his arms full of papers bumped into her and she shoved him out of her path. He hurried on his way without a word. "Keene will be here soon," she called over her shoulder, "probably within the hour, and he'll separate the man from the daemon. If you want to stay, be my guest. But he'll probably chase you out as soon as he gets here and even if he lets you stay . . ."

Rachel stopped, spun around, and clamped her mouth shut, and for a full thirty seconds the two women glared at each other in a silent battle of dogma and willpower.

Finally, Rachel drew a slow breath, balled her fists, closed her eyes, and exhaled slowly.

"Even if he lets you stay," she repeated, softer now, "it's just a defective daemon. He will separate it from the man, and he'll take it in for correction. That's all."

Liquid heat flushed through Leda's skin. Insult felt as tangible as the crutches under her arms, and yet she couldn't give it a name. Her eyes burned and her lips tightened into a thin, tight line.

Rachel watched this happen with no sign of sympathy. "This is my job," she said plainly. "I know it's new to you, but for me there's nothing mysterious or . . . sacred about it."

"What business of yours is it if I see something differently?" Leda said.

"I don't care how you see it or what you believe, so long as it doesn't interfere with my work. Stay if you want, but I'm going."

Leda looked at the supervisor again, but without the glasses he just looked like a man in the throes of a full-body muscle spasm. Her childhood yearning began to feel heavy in her chest, changed from a feathery hope to a lead burden.

"It's just," she said, "I always believed "

"I don't care," Rachel cut her off. "Whatever's happening in your head, it's got nothing to do with me. The only thing I care about right now is the fact that I've got one more job on my docket and if I get it done today, I can spend a few days resting up so I can be at my best for assignment next week."

Offense reared its head again and Leda bit her tongue to quiet it. *The attitude on this bitch!* cried her heart. *She's told me so much about her society and the way she lives; shouldn't she be willing to hear a different point of view? But,* the analytical part of her brain chimed in, *I asked her to tell me about those things. She didn't ask for my thoughts.* That fact in and of itself struck Leda as rude, but she conceded that she was not entitled to change Rachel's mind. *And,* she thought as she glanced around the hectic office, *this is hardly the time or place to get into an argument about it.*

Rachel turned and walked away, stopping only when she reached the door, which she held open, waiting in silence. Leda sighed, gathered her strength into her weary arms, and began to move.

As she hobbled her way through the crazy sea of overstimulated employees, she tried not to resent Rachel. While her words might have been insensitive, it wasn't on her to deal with Leda's internal conflict. Whatever reconciliation she made between facts and beliefs, it would have to be done without the help of her guide.

YOUNG / ONCE

He was young,
healthy.

No matter how many times
the boy sent him
spinning off to distant waters,
he was strong enough
to find his way back.

As long as that was true,
he must persevere.

His people
would not excuse failure.

Either a human died
for the insult dealt to him,
or he must die
in his quest for vengeance.

The only other option
was to continue

his pursuit
until the boy
grew old and died.

The options were
unappetizing.

Still,
they tasted better
than the unpalatable choice
of returning home
unavenged.

One human lifetime
deprived of his own kind
and the comforts of home
could not compare
to his own lifetime
spent with a tarnished reputation.

That boy
grown into an old man
would still find him
young
and capable
of rising to prominence.

Avenged, he could be a court adviser,
a general,
a spiritual leader.

BLUE FLAME

He could lift his family
to the heights of society
and move them into the palace
while he served royalty.

His parents
would hold their heads
a little higher
every time his name was spoken.

Their enemies
would cower before him
and beg for mercy.

Unless
he was dishonored.

Summoning hidden reserves of strength,
he plunged ahead,
racing toward
his target.

He was young
once,
on the other side of the door.

On the island,
he had aged.

He no longer felt
the wild impulses

that had ruled him
in bygone years.

Anger
was still with him,
but not rage;
he no longer felt
the urge to destroy.

Annoyance
he still felt,
but far less
impatience;
he had grown accustomed
to waiting.

Hatred lingered
in various forms;
he resented
his imprisonment,
he loathed
his jailer,
and
he reviled
humankind.

Some days,
hate
was the only thing he felt.

KNOWING

Bach's former apartment building was a twelve-story work of art on a fashionable city block. The front doors, brass-and-glass beauties, were crowned with a royal blue awning trimmed in gold fringe. Upon seeing the face of the building, Simon refused to be left in the car and insisted on accompanying him inside.

As they approached the front doors, a uniformed doorman unabashedly looked them up and down. He took particular interest in Bach's hole-filled sneakers and ill-fitting clothes, although he gave Simon's locs a disdainful glance as well.

"Can I help you?" he said in a nasally sneer.

"I used to live here," Bach told him.

The doorman raised an eyebrow and looked pointedly at Bach's shoes again. "Really?" he scoffed.

"Yeah," Bach said firmly, "really. I've been away for a while and I need to talk to someone about the stuff I left behind. I'm just gonna be inside for a minute."

The doorman chuckled and shook his head. "You're not going inside. I'm going to have to ask you to leave."

"No," Bach replied.

"If you don't leave, I'll have to—"

"You're not gonna do anything," Bach cut him off. "You're

afraid if you call the police, the cop who shows up might recognize you and then your boss will find out that you lied about not having a criminal record. Call the cops on us, and I'll call your boss on you."

Shock burst over the doorman's face, his jaw falling slack under his pudgy cheeks. Bach brushed past him while Simon flashed a huge smile and boomed, "Whaddup, my man?" The doorman grimaced and backed away as Simon, grinning, crossed the threshold.

The lobby looked like a photo from a magazine. The plush rugs accented the marble floors, the lighting was crisp and white, and the walls were immaculately painted and adorned with modern artwork. The air smelled strongly of air-freshener, a scent a bit too chemical to achieve the vanilla it wanted to be. At the far end of the lobby, two golden-doored elevators stood side by side.

Simon let out a low whistle. "This place is swanky," he said with an appreciative nod. "On my salary, I might be able to afford a broom closet in this building. Might."

"My parents paid the rent," Bach said. "My dad knows the owner. They went to college together."

Simon chortled. "My dad served with a guy who owns an auto repair place. When I take my car to him, he gives me a two percent discount. And then he charges me for the coffee in the waiting room."

"My dad wrote up the template for the lease agreement the landlord uses," Bach said. "Dad also represents him when a tenant sues. And they *do* sue. No one from this building, I think, but other buildings, definitely. And for good reason." Bach took a deep breath and ran his eyes over the lobby. "I really hate the landlord. Always have. He's a total douche nozzle." He froze and stared into space for a long moment. "And he's not even here."

"What?"

"He's not here," Bach repeated, throwing out his arms in exasperation. "Why did I feel like I needed to come here if he's getting tan on a beach somewhere? Shit."

"Ah, man . . ." Simon sighed. "You sure?"

"The sight-beyond doesn't lie."

"Well," Simon said, stuffing his hands in his pockets, "what'd you want the guy for?"

"He sold all my furniture when I disappeared. I was hoping he might have held on to something of mine that I could get back."

"You think that's likely?"

"No."

"If he and your dad are tight, wouldn't he have given it all back to your folks?"

"They wouldn't want it."

There was something in Bach's voice, something sticky and unsightly. Having known the man for just two days, Simon could only guess that what he was hearing was pain. Although Bach wore that pain without complaint, Simon felt embarrassed to see it. He looked away and cast his eyes around the lobby, avoiding Bach's emotions as if they were a virus he could catch.

"Is there someone else we can talk to?" he asked. "Hate to think we drove out here for nothing."

"Hmm," Bach murmured, deep in thought. "Actually, yeah, there is someone. Maybe he was the reason I was drawn here in the first place."

To Simon's surprise, Bach turned away from the elevators and headed for a door tucked back in the corner, his ragged sneakers squeaking on the marble floor. Simon followed him. The door opened onto a set of stairs that they trotted down into a sub-level floor, their footsteps echoing in the concrete stairwell. The picture-perfect lobby gave way to a hallway lined by cinderblock walls and gurgling exposed pipes on the ceiling.

Bach led Simon to the far end of the hall toward a door marked "Supply Closet." He rapped on it.

"Mr. Petrillo?" he called. "You in there, sir?"

A burst of coughing exploded from behind the door. Bach stepped back and motioned for Simon to do the same just before the door swung open, releasing a monster cloud of smoke. The stink of burnt dog hair hit them and both young men reeled backward, covering their noses and swiping at their eyes. Simon felt like he'd just been pepper-sprayed.

"Mr. Petrillo?" Bach said through a cough.

"Bach?" rasped a deep voice from the far side of the smoke. "Where you been?"

"I, uh, kinda checked out," Bach said. "Good God, sir! What the hell are you smoking?"

"Ohhh," the man said affectionately. "My son-in-law sent me this. 'Pure Gold,' it's called. Excellent stuff! You boys want a puff?"

Bach and Simon waved their hands in refusal, both still coughing. Simon opened his eyes through the burn of tears to see the owner of the voice fully emerge from the noxious vapor. He was an older man, white-haired and skin streaked with wrinkles, but his back was straight and his shoulders square. His grandfatherly face beamed at them with bloodshot-but-sparkling eyes and a warm smile.

Mr. Petrillo strode forward, arms wide. "Where you been, my boy?" he said as he drew Bach in for a hug and clapped him heartily on the back. "You didn't come home that night!"

"I know," Bach said, his eyes still squinty and watering. "I'm really sorry."

"When you didn't show," Mr. Petrillo said, still holding him in a kindly one-arm embrace, "I called the boss. When he didn't do nothing, I called your parents. When they didn't do nothing, I called the police. When they didn't do nothing, I drove all over the city every night for weeks. Nobody wanted to look for you, damn it! What the hell is wrong with your family?" He gestured emphatically with his free hand. "Why did your parents tell the police you weren't missing when you damn well were?"

"We didn't exactly . . . our last conversation wasn't a happy one."

"It don't matter," Mr. Petrillo said, shaking his head. "Family takes care of family. That's how it works."

"Not always," Bach said with that same sticky something in his voice. He coughed, shook his head a little, and then grinned. "How has nobody busted you for stinking up this supply closet yet, Mr. Petrillo?"

"Eh, nobody goes in there except me. Bobby, that damn doorman, tattles on me all the damn time, but"—the old man's tone turned conspiratorial—"I'm not worried about the boss. I've been around so long I know where all the bodies are buried. Don't matter what Bobby says, I can smoke when and where I want."

"You gotta find something less pungent," Bach said. "'Pure Gold,' my ass. It oughtta be called 'Pure Sewage.'"

"I only smoke once a week these days," Mr. Petrillo said dismissively. "I'm way, way down from before. Eating better, too. I'll outlive everybody in this building!"

Bach looked like he wanted to say something in response, but Simon saw him think better of it and shift gears. "Sir, I want you to meet my friend Simon. Sy, this is Mr. Petrillo, the super."

The old man grinned and thrust out his hand, which Simon took.

"Nice to meet you, sir," Simon said, voice raspy from smoke inhalation.

"You too, young man," he replied. "What brings you boys here today?"

"Simon's driving me around to help me get my life back on track," Bach said.

"Ah, good man." Mr. Petrillo nodded. "Good to see someone's helping this kid after everybody turned their backs on him."

"I didn't know about all that," Simon said. "That's pretty messed up."

"It's inexcusable! You know"—Mr. Petrillo put his arm around Simon's shoulders and pointed at Bach with his thumb—"this boy saved my life."

The stink of cigar smoke surrounded the man like a fog. Simon's eyes watered as the air in his mouth took on the taste of leather, but he smiled and waited for the coming story.

"One day," the super began, "outta the blue, this kid knocked on my door and told me I needed to go the doctor. I didn't know what the hell he was on about, but he said I had to go right away and he wouldn't shut up about it. He followed me around half the day, just getting underfoot. I couldn't get any damn work done! So, I called the doctor, just to shut him up. Do you know—it turns out the arteries in my heart were clogged. Doc says it was a miracle I hadn't dropped dead of a heart attack. So, they cut me open, unclog me, and look at me here today, huh?" The old man laughed and slapped his palm to his chest. "I don't know how he did it, but I'm alive today because of Bach. This boy's got the touch of God in him."

Simon shot Bach a look but Bach, his cheeks bright red, shuffled his feet and refused to raise his eyes.

"Listen, Mr. Petrillo," he said, eyes still cast downward, "I came by to ask about my stuff."

"Oh yeah." The old man grimaced. "Sorry, son. The boss sold all your furniture. Your car, too."

At that, Bach lifted his head and his eyes blazed. "Damn it!" he said through clenched teeth. "I knew about the furniture, but I wanted the car back!"

"Claimed he was recouping lost rent and repairing damage you left in your apartment."

"I didn't damage shit."

"Hey, I know that, kid." Mr. Petrillo patted him on the shoulder. "I tried to say something but . . . well, you know."

"I know," Bach mumbled. "I'm not surprised."

"The rest of your stuff," Mr. Petrillo said, "it wasn't worth much, so he told me to throw it in the dumpster."

Bach groaned and his shoulders slumped. Simon opened his mouth to offer his condolences, but Mr. Petrillo caught his eye and winked. "Lucky thing I don't listen so good," he said.

Bach stared at him for a moment and then, with a twitch of his head, asked, "Sir?"

"Yeah, I packed all your stuff up into one of the storage lockers," he said with a grin. "How about you boys help me bring it up?"

BACH, SIMON, AND Mr. Petrillo carried seven cardboard boxes of clothes, photographs, linens, and various other items out the front door. Simon's car was parked directly in front of the building, much to the fury of Bobby the doorman, who kept threatening to have it towed. The old super responded only with a "Bah!" and a wave of his hand.

Bobby huffed and steamed and, finally, pulled out a cellphone. Bach stared at the man intently as he began to dial, and then suddenly shouted, "Pearl necklace!"

Bobby jolted so powerfully that he dropped his phone. It fell to the pavement, but instead of retrieving it, the doorman stared at Bach with his mouth hanging open and his eyes wide. Bach nodded, gaze locked on him, and tapped one finger to his temple.

Trembling slightly, Bobby slowly bent down to pick up his phone and then backed away and through the front door, far away from Bach.

Mr. Petrillo laughed aloud, wagging a finger at the spot where the man had once stood.

"Hey," Simon asked, shoving a final box into his overflowing car, "the guy stole a pearl necklace?"

"That's half the story," Bach said in a whisper. "Have you ever heard of 'Seven Knots to Heaven?'"

"No." Simon squinted at him. "Sounds like a sex thing."

"It is. And it's the second half of that story." A spark flitted through Bach's electric blue eyes as he cringed and shuddered. "I really wish my sight-beyond wouldn't broadcast strangers' sexual kinks in my head."

Bach stepped around the car with his arms wide, and Mr. Petrillo happily embraced him again.

"You gotta come back to see me, my boy," the super said, his eyes squeezed shut. "Don't leave me here alone with these jackasses."

"I'll come by if I can," Bach said. "Thank you for everything you did for me. Because of you, I got a piece of myself back today."

Tears appeared in the corners of the old man's eyes. "You're a good kid," he whispered. Then he released Bach, smiled through his tears, and held the young man at arm's length. "So, any last-minute warnings for me? Or any advice?"

Simon smiled at the sight. A man old enough to be his grand-father was asking a twenty-something guy for advice. In any other circumstances, this scene would make no sense, and yet everyone present understood the logic of Mr. Petrillo's request.

Bach closed his eyes. A moment later he opened them again, revealing blue irises dancing with electric sparks.

"Your daughter's going to call this evening," Bach told the old man. "Keep your phone on you and be sure to answer when it rings. You'll wanna take that call."

"Yeah?" Mr. Petrillo shot him a sly but kindly look. "What's she gonna tell me?"

"My lips are sealed," Bach said, smiling. "You'll have to hear it from her."

"A surprise, huh? Will I like it?"

"You'll love it."

"Better get my phone out of the supply closet, then. And since it sounds like I'm getting good news today . . . maybe I'll smoke another Pure Gold while I'm in there."

"I thought you were cutting back," Bach said.

"Just once a week," he said as he turned toward the doors.

"You've already had one!"

"One *day* a week."

Mr. Petrillo gave Simon a smile and a wave before barging back into the building. Through the glass doors, Simon saw the super fish a new cigar out of his pocket and hold it to his nose, inhaling lovingly. Bobby the doorman reappeared and, pointing at the cigar, started to yell something. Mr. Petrillo pointed back at him and shouted, "Pearl necklace!"—and Bobby yipped and promptly vanished.

The old man grinned, waved once more at Bach and Simon, and ducked out of sight.

"Man," Simon said, chuckling, "that guy's a trip."

"I'm gonna miss him," Bach said. "He was the only person in that building I liked."

BACK IN THE car, Simon smacked his chest, and shook his shirt, nose wrinkled. "Fucking Pure Gold's gonna follow me all day."

"Same here." Bach gave his shirt a sniff. "Damn, that's rank!"

"That shit's gonna kill him."

"It will, actually," Bach said. "Lung cancer. He's been smoking since he was fifteen. It'll catch up to him before too long."

A twinge of grief caught Simon in the chest, surprising him with its intensity. That sweet old man was dying of cancer? He hardly knew the guy but . . . *Goddamn.* He gave Bach a sidelong look, perplexed. "Why didn't you tell him that? You saved him from a heart attack, but you won't warn him about lung cancer?"

"He knows the risks and he still smokes," Bach said. "I've told him again and again that he should quit but he loves those cigars too much. It's out of my hands."

"Then why go nuts to save him from a heart attack? Why'd you badger the guy into going to the doctor then but not now?"

"Because the heart attack was going to take him any day." Bach cast a look at the building in the sideview mirror. "The cancer won't get him for another ten years—twelve if he gives up smoking completely. I badgered him about the heart condition, so he could have the next ten years to spend with his family. And believe me, he'll be grateful for those years tonight when he finds out his daughter's pregnant." Bach smiled. "He's gonna adore that little girl. And he'll be around long enough that she'll have a lot of sweet memories of him to look back on."

"And that's all she'll have, because he'll be dead before she's in middle school," Simon said, accenting his words with palm slaps to the steering wheel. "Why not drag his ass back to a doctor to get him treatment before the cancer gets to him?"

Bach crossed his arms over his chest.

"How many times should I do that, Sy?" he demanded, his voice climbing in volume. "How many times am I obligated to drag him to a doctor? How closely do I have to watch him? Do I have to stay with him every moment for the rest of his life, just in case he needs to be reminded to look both ways before crossing the street? And what about all the other people whose futures I know? That doorman? In about five years, he's gonna accidentally asphyxiate in his bedroom. Do you think it's my responsibility to tell him so, or is it his responsibility to not choke himself while he jerks off? Or, hey, what about my landlord? I've known since I was a kid that he's gonna OD on cocaine. He's only got about eight months left. Whose fault will that be, mine or his?"

Simon squirmed with discomfort, but Bach wasn't done yet.

"Or what about her?" He pointed to a woman on the sidewalk as they passed her. "Gonna die in a car accident in four years. Her nine-year-old son will die with her. Her husband will live, but he'll feel so guilty that he was driving the car that killed them, that he'll shoot himself in the head two weeks later. And that guy?" Bach pointed to the driver of a car headed in the opposite direction. "A stroke when he's ninety-three. I can go on if you want! Hey, look at that office building! There are hundreds of people in there, and if I concentrate hard enough, I can see how most of them are gonna die! How many of them would you like me to help? How many of them would you like me to terrify by telling them about their last day on earth?"

Simon stared at the road ahead, knuckles white on the steering wheel. He had been wrong, that was clear. It stung a little to be called out like this, but more than that, he was stunned. The inside of Bach's head sounded like some horrid mixture of Big Brother and the ninth circle of hell. At the very edge of his vision, he could see him staring at him, those creepy blue eyes seeing things that no one had a right to see. Simon set his jaw and tried not to think about what scenes from his life Bach was watching.

"If it would really make a difference," Bach said, his voice leveling out, "I would try to save every person I met. But despite everything I know, the future is not written in stone. I knew, *knew,* that Mr. Petrillo was going to die of a heart attack, so I helped—and the moment he went in for heart surgery, I knew he was going to die of lung cancer. If I somehow saved him from the cancer, he'd still die from something else. It would never end."

"Forget it," Simon said quickly. "I shouldn't have said anything."

"I would have helped him," Bach said, his voice now strangely distant, as if coming from someplace far away.

Simon's gut twisted and his face hardened. The old wound in his heart suddenly felt inflamed. "Don't."

"Your father," Bach said. "I would've told him not to go to work that day."

"I said don't!"

"I would've told him there'd be a robbery at the pharmacy—"

"Stop!"

Simon slammed on the brakes. With a piercing squeal, the

car skidded several feet and then thumped to a stop in the middle of the road. Bach dug his fingers into the seat beneath him and stomped his foot to the floor, right where the brake would have been had he been driving. The car behind them swerved wildly to avoid a crash and then drove off, blasting its horn all the way to the next intersection.

"Do not talk to me about my father!" Simon roared. "I don't give a fuck how much you 'know' about me, you do not know what it's like to be nine years old and have to bury your father because of some asshole with a gun!"

Honking cars squealed around them, coming within inches of the sideview mirrors, the drivers shouting or making obscene gestures. Bach gripped the seat with one hand and slammed the palm of the other to the dashboard, bracing himself against the near collisions.

"You're right," Bach said, his eyes pinched shut. "You're right, and I'm sorry. I don't know what that's like."

"Damn right," Simon said, his lips drawn tight.

"When I was nine, I went to give my mom a hug and I suddenly knew that she had only gotten pregnant with me so my dad would have to marry her." Bach paused a moment, panting, then said, "She didn't love him and she didn't want me. She just wanted his money. Every time she looked at me, all she saw was a dollar sign. I never tried to hug her again. She didn't notice."

Simon reluctantly turned toward him. The two men stared at each other as a line of cars piloted by angry drivers swerved around them.

Eventually, Bach gave a little nod. "Okay?"

Simon drew a long, slow breath and nodded once. "Yeah," he said, "okay."

He pressed on the gas and rejoined the flow of traffic.

Thoughts of his father gradually retreated to the private spaces of his brain, where they were accustomed to living.

The remaining simmer of his anger passed after a few blocks. At a red light, Simon glanced at Bach. "Do you know how I'm going to die?" he asked.

"No," Bach said as he settled back into his seat and rubbed his eyes, "and I hope I never do."

The light turned green and the car rolled on.

17

ORANGE LIGHTNING

Rachel watched as Leda's eyes inhaled the pattern on the awning above the market door, an elaborate work of cherry red, sky blue, and brilliant gold. Giving it a closer look, Rachel could see that the interlaced lines, angles, and loops were very pretty, but she couldn't imagine what Leda found so engaging. She looked like she was trying to absorb every inch of the awning, to know it intimately.

"Geometric shapes," Leda whispered. "Non-representational. Regular tessellation. Symmetrical." Her dark eyes sparkled, the colorful pattern reflected in them like twin copies. "Islamic. Handmade, from the look of it. It's spectacular."

"Yeah, it's nice," Rachel said, yawning.

"Who made it?"

"Why don't you ask Mr. El Sayed about it when we go in? It'll distract him while I look around."

"And what will you be looking for?"

"The file says the Central Office has detected recurring interdimensional breaches at this address."

A visible, shivery jolt went through Leda as her face whipped toward Rachel in alarm. "Another psycho trying to break down barriers? Like . . . like *him*?"

Him. Rachel didn't have to ask who she meant. The psychopath's hateful face popped into her mind and she reflexively rubbed her achy ribs. Annoyed at the mental intrusion, she replayed part of their encounter—specifically, the part where she beat him over the head with his own padlock.

Satisfied, her brain allowed the memory to retreat and she met Leda's eyes. "No," she assured her, "nothing like that."

Leda let go of the breath she had been holding.

"These breaches," Rachel told her, "have been split-second, just flashes. Normally, no one would be concerned. Split-second breaches happen pretty frequently. They're a naturally occurring phenomenon. They're like lightning strikes—startling, sometimes damaging, but totally natural. The only reason these breaches turned up on our radar is because there have been so many. I'm supposed to figure out what's causing them."

"Is it a daemon?"

"Maybe. Usually daemons move between dimensions freely, without causing breaches, but malfunctioning daemons do all kinds of crap they shouldn't." She gestured to the market door. "Let's go see what's what."

There was graffiti on the front door—a collection of misspelled, foul words in drippy black and red paint. Unfortunately, Rachel recognized the style; she had seen similar work, with the same misspellings, on other nearby buildings. *The Bell brothers*, she thought in disgust. The neighborhood trio of juvenile delinquents had struck again.

The door jingled as Rachel stepped inside and held the door open for Leda. The autumn chill gave way to the cozy embrace of the market's warmth and the chorus of traffic was swept away by the faint hum of the refrigerators.

Mr. El Sayed—a thin, dark-haired, pleasant-looking, middle-aged man—sat behind the counter reading something on his smartphone. He lifted his eyes as they entered.

"Hello, crazy girl," he said politely to Rachel, his strong accent woven through his speech.

"Hello, Mr. El Sayed," Rachel replied. She nodded back at the door. "Those brats again, huh?"

He glared at his front door. "They smashed the camera as well," he said darkly. "Those boys are a disgrace to their family."

"Truth." Rachel glanced around the store and found it empty. "Where's your wife today? Not still sick, I hope."

"Not still," he told her. "Again. For a while, she was fine. Yesterday, she woke up sick again. She has been in bed ever since."

"I hope she feels better soon."

As Mr. El Sayed nodded, he cast a curious eye on Leda, whose gaze had been snared by the colorful painting behind the counter. "Is this your friend from the bridge, crazy girl?"

"No sir," she said. "This particular lady wouldn't be caught dead under a bridge."

He nodded his approval and returned his attention to Leda. "I see you have an eye for artwork, yes?" he said, gesturing to the painting she was examining.

"Yes sir," Leda said, nodding. "I work for the Rigaceen Museum, so it's part of my livelihood."

"Ah, the Rigaceen!" He smiled fondly. "I take my son there often. It has a wonderful collection of Egyptian artifacts."

"Are you Egyptian, sir?"

"Yes, my wife and I."

"I thought you might be. The painting there and the design on the awning are suggestive of the Egyptian style. Did you bring them with you when you came to the US?"

"No. My wife painted them."

"Really?" Leda's eyes widened. "I'm impressed. Has she ever displayed her work outside this store?"

"No, no!" Mr. El Sayed laughed. "My wife is very private about her work."

"That's a shame. If I had talent like hers, I'd show the world."

"I have told her this."

Leda tapped a finger on the counter. "You know, there's an art gallery downtown that offers a free showcase of local artists once a month. I know someone who works there, and she'd love to display a piece like this . . ."

Rachel took this opportunity to pop on her glasses and wander up and down the aisles undisturbed. Several daemons scurried about the area, their oddly proportioned bodies disappearing into or poking out of fractal swirls and color smears. A rotund daemon with iridescent skin sat in the back corner. It regarded Rachel with one dime-size eyeball then heaved its bulbous body forward and rolled through the wall into the street.

Another daemon—this one long and flat, with cactus-like spikes running down its body—slithered along the length of the ceiling. The tips of its spikes emitted occasional puffs of pink vapor that sparkled, then dissipated into the ether. A small flock of tiny, fork-shaped daemons swam through the air in a triangular pattern, passing through shelves and walls alike as they darted and soared as one.

Rachel sighed and marched to the far side of the store, where she retrieved a cherry cola from a refrigerator. She twisted the top off the bottle, leaned against the wall, and took a long gulp as she continued to scan the market for anything unusual.

A jagged line of orange suddenly shot through her vision, like a silent lightning bolt bursting across the sky. In the instant that it appeared, the daemons in the market jumped and scattered like cockroaches. The flock of fork-shaped daemons broke apart, each tiny creature zipping off in a different direction; the flat, spiky daemon fell from the ceiling and, writhing, passed straight through the floor in a puff of pink smoke. Rachel choked on her cola, leading her to cough so violently that she almost didn't hear the crash that occurred a split-second later.

At the front of the store, Mr. El Sayed made a loud exclamation in Arabic and pounded his fist on the counter. "Naji!" he shouted.

A muffled voice yelled back.

Rachel slid into the aisle next to her to get a clear view of the action.

"Excuse me please, Miss Morley," Mr. El Sayed said, politely but in a harried tone. He glanced at Rachel, then dashed through a door behind the counter, into the storage room. "Crazy girl!" he barked as he disappeared from view. "You must pay for that drink!"

"Yes sir," Rachel said through her coughs.

She heard him race up the flight of stairs. A moment later, the sounds of a muffled argument taking place above her head drifted down to her.

Leda caught her eye. "Who's Naji?"

"His son," Rachel answered.

The father's heavy footsteps thumped overhead. The two women followed the sound with their eyes, tracing a line across the ceiling and toward the stairwell in the storage room. Shortly thereafter, the owner returned to the counter with his tousle-headed son in tow. The little boy's arms were crossed over his chest, his eyes darting between his father and the ceiling.

"Sit," Mr. El Sayed ordered.

Naji took a seat behind the counter but immediately began to squirm. "Gotta stay upstairs," he mumbled.

"You are disturbing your mother," his father said. "She needs her rest."

"She needs *me*!" he cried, then jumped up and lunged toward the back room.

He took only two steps before Mr. El Sayed caught him by the collar and yanked him back to his seat.

"She needs you crashing around the apartment?" his father said. "She needs you waking her up? Sit down!"

"She needs me!" the boy repeated, stamping his foot and trying to pry his father's fingers off his shirt.

"Enough! Stay here if you cannot keep quiet. Sit!"

The boy plopped down; his arms pulled even tighter across his chest. Rachel watched him staring up at the ceiling, anxiety whirling through his eyes.

"It is a teacher workday or something?" Leda asked.

"No," Mr. El Sayed said, fuming. "He was sent home because he tries to leave the school grounds to come home in the middle of class. Now I ask you, how does it punish this boy to send him home when that is where he wants to be? It doesn't! It punishes me!" He looked down at his sulking child. "Tomorrow you return to school," he said, "and you will stay there!"

"No!" the boy barked back.

The father clenched his jaw and stared heavenward, shaking his head, as if imploring the universe for an explanation. Leda smiled sympathetically.

Rachel cleared her throat and swiped at her eyes, then pushed her glasses back into place and glanced around.

The flock of fork-shaped daemons had reformed and resumed its sweeping movements. The fat daemon in the corner had rolled part of its great girth back into the store, though its eye remained outside of the building. The ether, with all its colors and swirls, was as it should be. There was no sign of the lightning.

She turned back toward Leda—and gasped. Beyond her, Naji El Sayed sat where his father had commanded . . . but was now entirely engulfed in orange light.

A soft orange glow illuminated his eyes. Tiny orange sparks played about his fingertips like atomic faeries. Brief flashes of orange light emanated from his skin with each move of a muscle. The boy shifted his weight and the orange flashes lit up the market. The intensity of the colorful flares was startling.

Rachel watched as the swarm of fork-shaped daemons swung wide of the boy but maintained their triangular pattern. Another daemon, an undulating lump of a thing, floated through the market, paused within arm's reach of the boy, then floated on. The flat, spiky daemon rose through the floor like a sea serpent, rippled its way through the store, and passed through the wall. Its pink smoke bounced off Naji's glow without touching the boy himself. Rachel observed this bizarre daemonic behavior with fearful fascination as she wondered how on earth the boy was causing it.

The kid grumbled and shot a seething glare at his father. The market's owner was continuing his pleasant chat with Leda, his back turned to his unruly son. Keeping one eye on the conversing pair, Naji quietly slipped out of his shoes and pushed them away with his feet until they were just beyond the reach of his toes. He stared at the shoes, and the light in his eyes grew brighter, as did the sparks around his hands. He flexed his fingers, digging his nails into his arms, and the flashes around him flickered like a dozen strobe lights. Tiny clouds of orange puffed from his nostrils as his breath came quicker and quicker.

Rachel's hands tightened around the cold bottle of cola as she waited, eyes wide, breath held.

In one swift motion, Naji nodded, blinked, and flung his fingers outward. Silent orange lightning split the air again, scattering the daemons, making Rachel's heart jump into her throat, and momentarily bleaching the lenses of her glasses.

A full fifteen seconds later, when she could finally see through layers of reality once again, Rachel saw Naji smiling spitefully, his eyes still fixed in the same place—except that, she realized with a jolt, his shoes were gone.

"Shit!" she exclaimed.

Leda stopped talking in mid-sentence and stared, her expression shocked and disgusted. Remembering herself, Rachel slapped a hand over her mouth and snapped her gaze to Mr. El Sayed, who gazed at her in surprise.

"Sorry!" she said from behind her fingers. "I just . . . I thought . . . I, uh . . . I forgot to buy milk. I need milk and I forgot to buy it and I need it."

Leda winced at Rachel's babbling lie.

Mr. El Sayed shook his head. "I have milk, crazy girl," he told her calmly. "Buy all the milk you need. There is no need for profanity in front of my son."

"Very sorry," she said. "It won't happen again." She looked at the boy, who was looking at her with surprise eerily identical to his father's. "Sorry about that, Naji."

The boy tilted his head at her a bit and narrowed his eyes, not out of anger but rather puzzlement. Rachel smiled, but let Naji see her gaze move to where his shoes had been. The boy tensed, eyes wide, until Rachel smiled at him again and offered him a tiny nod, one finger tapping her glasses. With that, the boy relaxed and a smile grew over his face until he finally resembled that happy kid she had come to know from prior visits.

"It's okay!" he said. "Miss Crazy Girl? Can I see your glasses?"

"Naji," his father cut in, "sit quietly."

"I don't mind," Rachel said. "It's the least I can do since I was so rude."

Mr. El Sayed opened his mouth, but before he could refuse, Leda, reading the room, jumped in to resume their conversation. Thankfully more interested in a discussion of art than in dealing with his disobedient son, the store owner willingly let himself be distracted.

Rachel slowly knelt next to Naji, the glasses in her outstretched hand.

"Don't be scared," she told him softly. "Nothing you see through these can hurt you."

Naji slipped the glasses onto his face; when they proved too large, he used both hands to hold them in place, his eyes darting every which way. From the opposite side of the lenses, Rachel could still see the orange glow in his eyes.

"Whoa," the boy said, his eyes tracking something that was crossing the market from one corner to another. "What are they?"

"Part of my job," she said.

Naji smiled as he swung his head left and right, up and down, to devour all he could. Then his smile faded.

"They don't look like the other one," he said.

"What other one?"

"The one from upstairs. The one that keeps coming back."

Rachel frowned. She held out her hand and the boy obediently placed the glasses in them.

"This other one," she said, "you can see it just by looking? I mean, you can see it just like you're seeing me?"

"Yeah," he said, casting a nervous glance at his distracted father. "I'm the only one who sees him." His lower lip trembled. "Nobody believes me."

"What does it look like?"

"Big and scary," the boy said. "He's all . . . raaagh!" he growled, waving his arms. "And, and he's got these wing things, too big for inside. He's yellow and red, and where his hair should be it goes *whoosh*." He wiggled his fingers over his head. "He's got these big, clawy feet and pointy hands. And he—"

"Stop," Rachel jumped in. "Where did you see this . . . whatever it is?"

"Upstairs," Naji said. "It keeps coming into my house. I saw him there earlier, looking at Mama. So"—he leaned in close, a gleam in his eyes—"I poofed him!"

"Poofed?"

"Like my shoes. I made him disappear. I like to poof things. I send things to my 'away' place. But not him. I always send him farther, as far as I can."

"But he comes back?"

"Yeah." Naji's eyes grew watery and his lip trembled again. "I send him really, really far—a *lot* farther than other things I poof— but he always comes back. Every time I find him, he's always trying to hurt Mama. When he gets close to her, she feels sick. She prays, but it doesn't help. I don't want him to eat her." He sniffed and swiped at his eyes. "It's my fault," he croaked. "I was poofing things around, just for fun, and I think I poofed him here by accident. I didn't mean to. I won't do it anymore. Can you help me?"

Rachel's heart ached a little as she watched Naji cry. The boy looked so worn down. Whatever was happening was too much of a burden for a young child to bear—yet he had been resolved to fight this battle alone. Until Rachel and her magic glasses appeared. Now he looked at her with such hopeful desperation, like she was his last chance to defeat the enemy.

Gently, she brushed a tear off his cheek. "I'll take a look."

Mr. El Sayed glanced down at his son and noticed the boy sniffling. With fatherly concern flooding his expression, he put a hand on the boy's shoulder.

"Naji?" he said.

"Oh, not to worry, sir," Rachel said with a smile. "I guess my prescription is a bit too strong for him. I think he went a little cross-eyed for a minute." She tapped Naji on the tip of his nose. "Right, kid?"

Naji, summoning strength from his dwindling inner reserve, managed a laugh. "Those glasses make everything look funny."

Mr. El Sayed smiled at his son and affectionately ruffled the boy's already messy hair. "All right then."

The door jingled and a pair of young men entered, both of them laughing over some joke. They gave Mr. El Sayed a friendly nod as they moved deeper into the store.

Leda shifted her weight on her crutches. "I don't want to distract you from your customers, sir, but please do tell your wife about that gallery I mentioned. Next month, I want to see her work on the south wall."

"I will tell her," the store owner said, chuckling. "But do not get your hopes up, Miss Morley."

"I'll try." Leda grinned. "And next time you come to the museum, you have the front desk give me a call. I can give you and Naji a private tour and show you the artifacts that don't make it to the display cases."

"I look forward to that very much."

"Rachel," Leda said, shooting her companion a sharp look, "time to go, isn't it? You best buy your milk!"

"Milk?" Rachel repeated, staring blankly—then the lie came roaring back to her and she nodded rapidly. "Right! The milk!"

"And you will pay for your soda, too, crazy girl!" Mr. El Sayed called after her as she dashed back to the refrigerated section.

AS SOON AS Rachel and Leda left Mr. El Sayed's store, Rachel set the half-empty soda and carton of milk she was carrying on the curb and, without a word to Leda, ran around the side of the building. In the back alley, she paused and took a deep breath to steel herself against the pain she knew she was about to subject herself to.

As ready as she would ever be, she climbed onto a dumpster and reached for the fire escape ladder. Slowly, quietly, ribs burning, she scaled the ladder and pulled herself onto the second-floor landing.

On the fire escape balcony, her elbow brushed a row of potted herbs, stirring up an aroma of basil and rosemary that briefly overshadowed the stink of the alley. She inhaled appreciatively as she peered into the window and scanned the apartment.

There was a hallway with a row of doors and an open space at the far end where she could just make out one arm of a sofa and the edge of a kitchen countertop. Framed photographs lined the hallway walls, their glass surfaces reflecting the sunlight in rectangular shine. The walls were painted a soft gold, accented with rich reds and cozy browns. An ornate painting, presumably one of Mrs. El Sayed's, adorned the far wall, adding a splash of royal blue to the color palette.

She looked carefully for any sign of movement both inside the apartment and in the alley behind her, but saw only Leda swinging her way into the back alley on her crutches wearing an expression that was both curious and reproachful—equal parts "What's going on?" and "What the fuck is wrong with you?"

Rachel held up her hand in a "wait here" gesture—to which Leda rolled her eyes—then hooked her fingers into the grooves of the windowpane and tried to lift it. Locked. She nibbled her lip and looked around.

Just beyond the rail of the fire escape there was a second window. She climbed over the rail, held the fire escape railing with one hand, and leaned over as far as she could. Pain shot through her ribs, but she held on.

Through the window, she saw a large bed with a brightly painted headboard. Sitting on the bed, with her back to Rachel, was a woman wrapped in a blanket. Mrs. El Sayed's hunched form slowly rocked back and forth, one visible curl of her long black hair gently swaying with the motion. She turned her head slightly, and Rachel saw her pale lips moving, forming words that she could not hear. Her vacant gaze rose from the floor and stopped near the ceiling. One quivering hand reached out and batted weakly at the air, as if swatting away a fly. Then she closed her eyes, one hand wrapped around a gold locket hanging from her neck, her lips still moving.

Rachel pulled herself back to the fire escape and softly drummed her fingers on the railing. What was Naji seeing that she wasn't? She fished out her glasses and popped them into place before leaning over to look through the window again.

Mrs. El Sayed swatted at the air again, and this time Rachel saw something—a strange flicker of orange light, like a candle flame in the wind, erupting at the spot where her hand swiped.

Then a series of similar flickers lit up the air around Mrs. El Sayed and she pressed her hand to her brow. Rachel strained her eyes, trying not to feel the pain in her ribs or the increasing numbness in her arm, and gradually the tiny flames morphed into long, jointed lines that bent around the woman's head. An area near the ceiling began to show a faint, luminescent outline, betraying a form. The longer Rachel stared, the more of that form she saw.

After several long minutes, during which she lost most of the feeling in her arm, Rachel saw an outline of the thing take shape. It was a man-like figure, arms and legs and a head, but it had two extra appendages that extended from its shoulders and beyond the boundaries of the room. No features were visible on its face, if indeed it had one. Its elongated arms reached halfway around the room, and its fingers, spindly and multi-jointed, flexed greedily around their victim.

Mrs. El Sayed swayed and fell back on the bed. The creature moved forward and leaned over her, its color changing from gold to ginger to scarlet. It placed both hands over Mrs. El Sayed's face as if to smother her.

A chilling spasm hit Rachel and her heart sank. She recognized the being.

The bedroom door banged open, making Mrs. El Sayed jump and the creature rear back. Naji stood in the doorway, his arms crossed and his eyes fixed on the thing standing over his mother. The woman sighed heavily and rolled over, waving at Naji to leave, but he stood rooted to the spot, his schoolboy face twisted with a grown man's rage.

Impossibly, Naji was seeing this thing with his naked eyes— and he was brazenly staring it down.

The boy strode forward, his eyes fixed on the creature.

Much to Rachel's amazement, the creature backed away. The boy balled his hands, sparks leaping from his skin—and with a blinding orange flash, the creature vanished.

Naji looked around the room to check his work; seemingly satisfied that the creature was gone, he then went to his mother's bedside and threw his arms around her. The woman lifted her head a bit and tried to wave him off. When he continued to hug her, she smiled wearily and reached to stroke his messy hair. Then she settled down into the bed, her eyes closing and her lips finally becoming still.

Naji rested his chin on his mother's shoulder and sighed, tears rolling down his cheeks.

Rachel pulled her body clear of the window and swung her legs one at a time over the railing. As soon as she was able to shake sensation back into her arm, she climbed down the ladder to the alley.

Leda was waiting.

"What in the hell are you doing?" she demanded through clenched teeth.

"Something I shouldn't," Rachel replied. "Come on. I gotta get back to the house. I've got some un-fun calls to make. I'll fill you in while we walk."

As the two women headed back around the building, they heard Mr. El Sayed's voice from within. Most of his words were lost, muffled by the brick walls, but at the very last Rachel heard him bellow, "Where are your shoes!?"

RAIN / BURN

He had only just begun
to inflict suffering
on the mother
when the damned boy burst in
and blasted him away.

Roars of exasperation
shook his fire-born body
as the tear sealed behind him—
erased by a coat of liquid sky—
trapping him
in a cold rainstorm
over choppy waters
without a hint of land in sight.

His frustration was spent
with the first beat of his wings.

For the first time,
he felt encouraged.

The woman was weakened.

Every time he saw her of late,
she was in bed.

His presence was,
as he had been taught could happen,
sapping her energy.

He looked forward to discussing this phenomenon
with his elders when he returned home
after killing her.

Out of phase,
out of sight,
he landed on a huge cargo ship
stacked with truck-size containers,
perching like a scarlet vulture
on the top of the mast.

While the ship traveled for him—
its pace absurdly slow—
he hunkered down,
his wings folded around him
like a cocoon,
shielding his body
from the hideous rain.

Allowing his natural heat
to warm him,
he rested
and schemed.

The burn mark on his palm was itchy.

That was the only thing
that distinguished
today
from
yesterday.

He scratched at the burn,
listening to the muffled sizzle
of his claws on his skin.

From listening at the
invisible sealed door,
he knew that the container
that held the passageway to this island
had spent the last few decades
in a storage room,
stacked on a shelf
with other such containers.

He wondered
if he
and the other prisoners
shared the same jailer.

If so,
they all bore this burn.

Were their burns itchy today?

Was it day or night where they were?

He would likely never know.

He would likely grow old
and die
on this island
without ever speaking
to any of them.

Or anyone at all.

Hatred
once again
rose in his gullet
only to slide down
into his stomach
like sludge.

Fuming at ghosts
took more energy
than he had today.

The old numbness washed over him,
silencing the itch
and lulling his brain into a stupor.

Drawn
by the siren call
of sleep,
he reclined against the tree,

lifted his chin
toward the cloudless sky,
and let his four arms
go limp at his sides.

All four palms,
including the scarred one,
faced up
as if to collect pools of sunlight
in their webbed fingers.

Is this how the rest of my life will pass?
he thought vaguely.

Will I fade in and out of myself
until I fade away completely?

Perhaps I should sleep
until the end comes.

Or perhaps,
he thought
as he passed into the
dream-like state
he had come to know so well,
when I wake this time,
the door will be open.

Perhaps.

THE BULL UNDER THE BRIDGE

Traffic roared overhead, accentuated by the occasional honk or screeching tire. The stink of car exhaust mingled with the stench of the polluted river to create a sort of underworld cologne that invaded the nostrils. Simon's pained expression told Bach that he was probably remembering Mr. Petrillo's cigar smoke fondly at this point. Bach found the odor just as repulsive, and yet it also triggered a kind of nauseous nostalgia, flooding his mind with hazy memories that he wished to forget.

Simon turned his head left and right, his eyes squinting in the sunlight, his breath choppy. Bach couldn't really blame him for feeling nervous. He felt the same way, though for an entirely different reason. For Simon, their current surroundings were a wasteland, a hefty step outside his social understanding of the world. He had no knowledge of how this alien world functioned nor how he should navigate it. Bach, on the other hand, was nervous because he had lived in this world for half a year and seeing it now, after having once again firmly stepped into mainstream society, he felt too at ease. He knew this world; he knew its rules and its necessities. And he didn't want to know so much. He wanted to believe that the real world was where he belonged but now that he was here, just a few yards from the spot where he had once slept, he knew with unsettling certainty that he could pick up his homeless life without missing a beat. Actually, it would be quite a bit easier than resuming a "normal" life, as he was trying to do. And that terrified him.

A few people were asleep in the shadow of the bridge, though it was barely noon. Bach had counted on this. The nights grew cold, so it was safer to sleep during the day, when it was warmer and then keep active after dark. Bull was probably here.

Bach scanned the array of bundles and blanketed forms huddled in the dark places.

"There," he said, pointing with his chin. "That's him."

He clutched the large roll under his arm a little tighter and climbed the hill; Simon followed close behind. They passed from the sunlight into the bridge's shadow and Simon quick-stepped to shorten the already minimal distance between them. Bach could hear his breath just behind his ear.

The heap Bach approached was larger than most under the bridge, and conspicuously isolated from the other bundled forms. It twitched irregularly and uttered strange, sometimes alarming noises.

Bach stopped about two yards from the quaking figure. "Bull? Sir? Hey, Bull!"

The form jerked. One arm flapped up and smacked the ground as it fell. The noises continued.

Bach shook his head and tried again: "Sir!"

"Why don't you just, you know, poke him or something?" Simon asked.

"I would never touch this guy to wake him up," Bach said quietly.

"Why not?"

"The last guy I saw try it lost four teeth."

Simon's eyes widened a bit and he looked at the ragged heap of a man with new respect.

Bach stamped his foot a few times. "Bull!"

The man finally became silent and still. Then, suddenly, he jolted upright, arms swinging in every direction, a feral roar bursting from his lips. A moment later, he was sitting cross-legged, fists pressed into the ground, panting like he had just run a mile.

Bach gave him a good look. Very little had changed. The middle-aged Bull was still a mountain of a man with broad shoulders, a square jaw, and enormous hands. There were a few fresh cuts and bruises on his face and a couple of his knuckles were newly split, but that was to be expected. This was a hard life, and he was a hard man.

Bach cleared his throat and Bull's eyes zeroed in on him. He heard Simon take a step back, probably startled by the intensity of his stare. Addled though his mind had been for those six months, Bach vividly remembered the first time he saw this man's red-veined eyes.

"Sir?" Bach said again. "Sorry to wake you."

"Then why did ya?" he snapped. "What the hell do you two fuckwads want?"

"I'm just here to repay a kindness."

"A what, now?"

"You were good to me, sir," Bach said. "I mean, not always—I'm not sure, but I think you're the reason my pinky finger doesn't bend so good anymore—but you did more for me during my six months here than any other person on this planet. So, I came to say thank you and to give you this."

Bach set down the roll and stepped back, motioning for Simon to do the same.

Narrowing his eyes at them, Bull reached out slowly, closed

his fingers around the bundle, and carefully drew it close, his suspicious gaze shifting between it and the two young men. He partially unrolled it and his eyebrows twitched. "A coat?"

"Winter's coming, sir," Bach said. "It's an old coat and you're bigger than me, so I don't know if you'll be able to use it, but I don't have much else to my name right now. And I remember you told me that's it's better to have any kind of coat in bad weather than no coat at all. I think you said that after you beat the snot out of Old Quinn and took his coat."

"Quinn?" Sparks of memory danced across Bull's face and he leaned forward, turning his head from side to side as if trying to see through a disguise. "'S that you, Blue?"

The forgotten nickname came back to Bach in a flash of foggy memories. There was a time, months ago, when Bull had stood over him as Bach crawled along the river's edge, mumbling idiotically, and asked for his name. Bach had stuttered something, a "B-B-B-B" sound, but never formed a word. Bull had grabbed him by the shirt and yanked him to his feet. Then he'd seen Bach's blue eyes, dancing with electric insanity, and blanched. From that moment on, he'd called him "Blue."

"Yes sir," Bach said, a bit sheepish. "It's me."

Bull leaped to his feet and closed the space between them with just two long strides. He spat a bark of laughter and shook his head. "Shit on a stick! I thought you might turn up here again sometime, but I didn't expect you t'be all cleaned up!"

"I didn't expect it myself," Bach said.

"How'd it happen?"

"My head cleared and a friend took me in. I'm getting my life back on track."

"Fuck and shit!" the man bellowed. "Of everybody here, you're the last one I'd expect to claw your way out!" He laughed, a great boom of a sound. "I kinda figured you'd choke on your own puke some night."

"I probably came close once or twice." Bach felt his cheeks grow red. "Bull, I just wanted to thank you."

"For what?"

"You looked after me some. When you had enough to share, you gave it to me. When I didn't know how to get by, you tried to teach me. I got beaten up plenty, but you kept the worst of the worst away from me. I don't remember too much of my time here, but I do remember you. So, thank you."

"Ah, fuck it, Blue," Bull mumbled, turning away from him. "I wudn't doing you no favors. You were a good pet to have. You scared the shit outta people with all your ranting and those crazy eyes. I didn't hafta fight near as much if I kept you nearby."

"I kinda figured," Bach said with a nod. "That's okay. It's actually nice to know I was useful."

Bull held up the coat and looked it over. "Thanks for this. It's in better shape than the one I've got."

"Yeah . . ." Bach trailed off. He took a deep breath and, despite trying not to, looked at his shoes. He had spent a long time last night preparing for this moment and still the words stuck in his throat. He squeezed his eyes shut and gathered his nerve. "There's something else, sir."

"Hmm?"

"I . . . made a call the other day. I got in touch with Crystal."

As Bach knew it would, the name instantly drew Bull's attention. The older man straightened his back and drew himself up, which made Bach's heart jump. He had seen Bull square himself up like this more than once—just before throwing a punch.

"Whatchu want with her?" Bull asked. "She divorced me when I got back, kicked me out."

"Yeah, I know," Bach hurriedly replied, "but I needed another number and she was only one I could think of who could give it to me."

"What number?"

"Jenny's."

This name provoked a very different response. The tension slipped from Bull's face and he blinked rapidly, his brow furrowed. He shook his head and leaned forward slightly, as if he hadn't heard correctly.

"Jenny?"

"Yeah, Jenny, your little cousin. You told me about her. How she lived with you and Crystal for years after her mom got sick. I thought—"

"What the hell'd you want with her?" Bull's tone was jagged, sharp. The burn in his eyes grew hotter. Behind him, Bach heard Simon catch his breath and take a step back, loose pebbles crunching under his feet. Bach fought the urge to do the same.

"I told her I'd seen you," said Bach. "She'd been looking for you, you know." When Bull didn't reply, he pressed on. "She asked me to tell you that she has her own place now and she's making a good living. She wants you to come stay with her. I got her address and phone number. It's in the pocket of that coat I gave you. She's looking into what services the local Veterans Center offers—"

"I don't need 'services,'" Bull said, his eyes scorching Bach's soul. "I'll take the coat. You can go now, Blue."

Exhaling slowly, Bach allowed his stomach to unknot. "Bull—"

"Get out, kid," said Bull, turning his back and plodding away. "You don't belong here no more."

The ex-soldier walked away, returning to the depths of the

shadows. Vague memories of his broad shoulders and swinging arms teased Bach's brain but they were all cloudy and incomplete, dirtied by his sight-beyond insanity. There were a few things about Bull he remembered with some clarity—beating up Quinn; sharing a few bites of something with Bach; pinning him down while Bach screamed like a loony about an old man time-traveling into his brain—but most of those six months were like smoke in a glass jar. Now Bach was watching his only concrete tie to this place walk away from him for the last time. And it was the last time. His sight-beyond was hideously clear about that.

"Goodbye, Bull . . . sir."

If Bull heard him, he gave no sign. He slung the coat around his shoulders and sat down in the darkness with his back to the two young men.

Bach cast his eyes down at the loose stones and patches of browning grass in front of him. He had slept on these stones and knew the feel of them intimately. Since leaving the bridge, he sometimes woke up in the morning and, for just a moment, could feel the cool, rough surfaces of these stones on his skin like the lingering touch of a lover. He suddenly wanted to go back to Rachel's house, to lie down in the bed that wasn't his and cover his face with the pillow until the smells of this place disappeared from his memory as they had disappeared from his skin and clothes. And yet, he had lost so much of himself during those six months that any memory, no matter how disturbing or hurtful, was a gift.

He knelt, plucked one stone from the riverbank, and held it to his nose. The putrid stink of the river floor filled his senses and, to his relief, lit up his brain. Bits of memory surfaced—scattered and incomplete, like crumbs left under a table when the meal is long over, but *real*. The memories were in there and could be recovered, at least in part, with the right trigger. He slipped the stone into his pocket, rubbing the smooth surface like a lucky charm.

"Bach," Simon said, his voice strained. "Come on, we gotta get outta here."

Bach glanced up to see Simon already turning and hurrying away from the shadow of the bridge. He stood and followed after him at a jog, the cold stone in his pocket jangling against his thigh.

His thoughts returned to Bull. He examined his sight-beyond, searching for hope.

Before he could find some nugget of Bull's future, he heard a voice on the wind. The speaker was above him, probably on the bike path that swung by the bridge at the top of the riverbank. Though he couldn't see the person it belonged to, the voice echoed through the corridors of his mind. His pace slowed and he listened carefully. There were no words, only a soft vocal melody that clawed at him relentlessly.

"Javier Alvarez," he whispered.

The voice was that of a girl looking for her father. In his mind's eye he saw her perfectly: a young woman who wore a smile above all else and refused to cut her long hair because she remembered how her mother used to brush it. She had a round face and small nose, long fingers with many calluses, and a confident step. Around one ankle, she wore a gift from her father: a thin anklet with tiny bells on it that jingled softly when she walked. Though he couldn't hear those tinkling bells with his ears, Bach's brain was deafened by the sound. All activity in his mind stopped, including his sight-beyond. As Javier Alvarez's daughter waltzed through his brain, he began to feel that same sense of urgency that he had experienced when looking at the flyer. The timing was still wrong. It was too soon. There was something he was supposed to do, something connected to this girl, but it wasn't meant to happen until later. It would happen eventually, though—it *had* to happen. This girl, this anonymous no one, was vital. He had never met her, yet she consumed him.

Bach deliberately inhaled the stench of the river and thrust his hand into his pocket to feel the stone. He imagined losing his mind again and having to return to this place. He imagined spending another six months covered in dirt and shit while digging through trash cans for rotten food. He imagined never repaying his debt to Rachel and leaving behind his puppy to starve. The Alvarez girl faded into the closeted areas of his mind. The inflow of knowledge from his sight-beyond returned.

With a sigh of relief, he hurried after Simon.

With the resumption of his sight-beyond, he suddenly knew two things: Bull was going to down a six-pack before he took a long, hard look at Jenny's information. Whether or not he would contact the girl who called him Dad, Bach didn't know. But he did know, with sudden clarity, that Miss Alvarez's quest to find her father was doomed.

Javier Alvarez had been dead for months.

20

SHOES

"So," Leda said, "Naji accidentally brought something from another dimension into his home, and that thing is trying to hurt his mother?"

"Yes."

"But you won't help him?"

She and Rachel were walking through the interdimensional passageway that led to Rachel's house. Upon crossing the threshold, the first thing Leda saw was the riot daemon wrapped in its coat and wandering around the yard. Its long sleeves dragged behind it like two limp tails as it shuffled through the dry grass.

Bach's puppy laid on the top step, watching the daemon closely as it moved from one side of the yard to the other. The dog's absurd ears stood tall as he tilted his head this way and that, listening to the daemon's invisible, shuffling feet.

"I don't think I *can* help," Rachel said. "That thing in their bedroom—he's not a daemon."

"What is he?"

"A Djinni."

"A Djinni?" Leda hobbled up the walkway after Rachel. "You mean like a genie in a bottle?"

"Bottle?" said Rachel, brow furrowed. "I don't understand. It's a Djinni. There's no bottle involved."

Images of Disney's *Aladdin* and *I Dream of Jeannie* sprang to Leda's mind, but neither of those genies seemed to fit the description Rachel had just given her. She dug a little deeper in her memory and found a few mythological tales, *1001 Arabian Nights*, and a lecture she had once attended about pre-Islamic culture.

"A race of sentient beings," she recalled, "made by God from smokeless fire just as man was made from clay. Like humans, the Djinn had the option of being God-fearing and good or of being blasphemous." Rachel's forehead smoothed as her confused expression melted away, and she nodded.

"Daemons have no free will. They're cogs in the cosmic machinery." She reached out to hold Leda's elbow and helped her up the stairs. "The Djinn are a free-willed species with their own culture and laws, just like humans. So, it's not like I can catch this Djinni and bring him in for correction." She held the front door open for Leda. "I can't even address him directly," she continued, seemingly talking more to herself. "I don't know the Djinn language, and there's no guarantee he knows any language other than his own. If I go straight to him and we don't understand each other, I could make things worse. If I try to drag him out of the El Sayeds' home, I might hurt someone and I could cause an interdimensional incident." She clucked her tongue and tugged on her hair, staring out the door at the shuffling daemon in the yard. "My best option is to get in touch with the Solani clan and see what they suggest."

"Solani?" Leda asked. She propped her crutches against the staircase railing and sat on the steps, relieved to be done hobbling for the moment. "Who are they?"

"A clan. They represent Arcanan interests to the Djinn."

"Like an embassy?"

"Of sorts. We don't actively maintain contact with Djinn society. The Solani clan just reaches out to them when necessary. It's more of a courtesy than anything else since the Nota isn't our world and the Djinn have no connection to the Arcana."

"No connection to the Arcana," Leda repeated, "but they do have a connection to the Nota?"

"Yes."

Leda added this tidbit to her mental databank, but in doing so, found an insurmountable gap in her knowledge. "I don't understand."

Rachel nodded, acknowledging the statement, but she didn't respond. Instead, she ducked out the front door, trotted down the steps, and crouched in front of the porch.

Unwilling to pick up the hated crutches again so soon, Leda pulled herself to her feet, hopped on her good leg to the doorway, and grabbed the doorframe to support herself. She watched Rachel seize one of the crosshatch pieces and yank it, causing it to snap and fly off, then get onto her hands and knees and crawl through the small opening until she disappeared from view.

Unable to crouch or crawl with her knee in a brace but too curious to simply wait where she was, Leda carefully lowered her body until she was face down on the porch. Through a crack between the slats of wood, she could just make out Rachel's wriggling form.

"What are you doing?" she called out.

"Just wondering if . . . yep!"

Rachel scooted back out through the hole and got to her feet with her find held in one hand, smirking.

Leda blinked and shook her head a little. "Shoes?"

"Naji's," Rachel told her, grinning in triumph. "Bach said no one was coming through the passage to dump all that crap under the house. I didn't know how that was possible, until today. Naji 'poofed' it there."

21
CHESTERFIELD MANOR

B ach stared at the phone in his hand with a strange look on his face. Simon watched him, wondering if that look indicated disgust or fear. Neither made any sense to him. He leaned forward, draping his arms over the steering wheel and resting his chin on the top of it. A greasy spot near his nose still smelled like the burrito he'd eaten driving home from work last week. His stomach growled.

"If you're not gonna call," he said, "get off your ass and go ring the doorbell."

Bach just uttered a closed-lipped grunt, shook his head, and continued staring.

Simon rolled his eyes and lifted his chin to see over his companion's head. They were parked next to a manicured lawn, complete with decorative lampposts lining a circular driveway and a bubbling fountain within a ring of rose bushes. The four-story house towered over its beautiful surroundings. Simon remembered passing this house every Sunday when his father would drive them to church. As a child, Simon had gotten the impression of a grumpy old man in a three-piece suit glowering at everything in the street. He'd asked his parents who lived there one day, and his father's only reply had been, "Some white lawyer." Today, when Bach asked him to pull over in front of the house, he hadn't immediately realized that it was a planned stop —that this was, in fact, his passenger's family home. But that was ten minutes ago, and they'd been sitting in the car ever since. He looked at Bach again and saw that he had not moved.

"Call the damn number!" Simon commanded.

Bach snapped to attention—and pocketed his phone.

"This was a bad idea," he said. "Let's just go."

"Wha—oh, hell no!" Simon grabbed Bach by the coat and wrestled the phone out of his pocket. "How d'you get face-to-face with that guy Bull like it was nothing, but you're afraid to call your mom!?"

"Let go of me, damn it!" Bach said. He tried taking back the phone, but Simon smacked his hands away. "I'm not ready! I'll call later!"

"You're here right now," Simon said, already scrolling through Bach's contacts. He found the number labeled "Home," pressed the button, and held up the cell as it began to ring. "How the hell hard can it be to talk to your folks?"

"I don't want to do this," Bach said, his eyes darting about, looking for an escape route. "This won't go well. It won't."

The phone rang again and again. Bach stared at it—expectant, suspicious, as if waiting for the device to transform into a viper.

After the sixth ring, a recorded message played.

"You have reached the Chesterfield home," said a man's voice. "We are unable to speak to you at this time. Leave a message and we'll know you called."

Bach lunged, snatched the phone out of Simon's hand, and ended the call. Simon stared at him, slack-jawed, as he stuffed the thing back in his pocket.

"Man," he said, mystified, "what is your problem?"

"I don't have a problem."

Whether because of the audacity of the lie, or the way Bach refused to meet his eyes, Simon felt anger bolt through him. "If you don't have a problem," he yelled, grabbing the edge of Bach's coat and shaking him, "then leave a fucking message for your parents, so they know you're alive!"

"Fine!" Bach yelled back. He held out his hand. "Give me your phone!"

Simon squinted at him and shook his head. "What the hell are you—"

"I can't use mine! Give me your fucking phone!"

Confused, Simon pulled out his phone and handed it over.

With a resolute sigh, he dialed and—copying Simon—held it up as it rang, so both of them could hear.

"How the hell's it different to leave a message with my phone instead of yours?" Simon asked.

"There won't be a message."

Two rings into the call, someone picked up. Simon blinked in surprise, but Bach only closed his eyes and leaned back in his seat, his jaw set.

"Hello?" said a woman's voice.

"Mom."

Simon heard the woman on the other end catch her breath. He stayed silent, waiting for her to speak to her son, but she didn't say a word. His mind flooded the silence with everything he had expected to hear—the mad rush of relief and tears that would have come from his own mother—but no sound entered the car. Bach kept his eyes closed but nodded just slightly, his lips pulled into a humorless smile.

"Mom," he said, "I'm out front. Can I come in?"

Silence.

Bach opened his eyes and looked out the car window, his gaze sweeping over the lawn and up to house. Wondering if Mrs. Chesterfield might run out the front door to find her son, Simon leaned forward, so he could see out the passenger window. No one came out of the house. Simon saw just a bit of Bach's expression reflected in the window. The man's usually electric blue eyes seemed dull.

"I just wanted you to know that I'm okay. I wasn't okay for, like, six months but I'm fine now. I'm staying with a friend while I get my life together." He paused and licked his lips. The hand with the phone in it slowly fell and came to rest on his knee. "It's kinda weird that you didn't report me missing or anything, but whatever."

The cell's screen cast a glow over Bach's jeans, indicating a call in-progress, but Mrs. Chesterfield wasn't making a sound. Bach continued to stare at the house, his eyes leaping from one window to another. A knot formed in Simon's gut—a growing regret for having pushed Bach into this confrontation. It had not occurred to him that Bach's parents could be so different from his own. He dug his fingernails into the steering wheel.

"Mom?" Bach said, his voice raspy. When he got no response, he closed his eyes and leaned his head against the window. "Fine," he said. "I'll come back later and maybe you can think about talking to me then, okay?"

He paused and then added, "I don't want anything, I just . . . thought we could talk." He opened his eyes again and looked down at the glowing, silent phone screen. "Mom," he nearly pleaded, "you haven't heard from me in six months. Can't you say something?"

Simon held his breath, listening, but he heard only his heart thumping in his ears. Bach stared at the phone through squinting eyes. Then the woman on the other end inhaled sharply, startling them both.

She hesitated only a moment before saying, "I'm happier without you."

The phone clicked, and the screen went black.

Bach's fingers went limp and the phone slipped down his leg to the floor mat.

"Bitch!" Simon blurted at the phone.

A knot twisted viciously in his stomach. How could a decent guy like Bach have such a shitty mother? What the hell kind of woman let her son go missing for six months without looking for him and then refused to acknowledge him when he came home?

Bach clucked his tongue. "You know," he said softly, "I think that's the first completely honest thing she's ever said to me."

"I'm sorry," Simon said. "I didn't think it would be like this."

"I did. But it's okay."

"Man, I'm so sorry. I—"

"It's okay," Bach repeated. "If you hadn't made me call, I would've kept stressing about it. It's over now. I actually feel relieved. Oh!" he exclaimed, reaching down to his feet. "I dropped your phone. Sorry about that."

Simon stared at him a moment and then sputtered with laughter. The sound made Bach blink and pull back, but Simon just grinned and shook his head.

"*You're* apologizing to *me*?" Still chuckling, he took the phone and tucked it away. "Man, you are something else."

Bach let out a huge breath and smiled. "You know what's weird? I'm getting so much sight-beyond info on my mom now. I never get this much information from people close to me. Before, I would get maybe one or two things a year on my mom, and less than that on my dad. But since I got right in my head, I'm learning so damn much about them both." A weird expression was spreading across Bach's face, something tired but intrigued. "I lived twenty-two years with those people and I'm just now realizing how little I knew about them. I never knew my dad wanted to be a teacher before my grandfather told him he had to go to law school. I never knew my mom had an abortion in college. I suspected, but didn't know for sure until now that my mom's had a lot of affairs while she's been married to my dad. And my dad knows about most of them. Dad almost ran away with another woman eight years ago. He only stayed because she called it off." He leaned back in his seat, his eyes shimmering blue. "It really drives home how drastically my life has changed."

The whole, naked truth of Bach's ability assaulted Simon with the force of a boxer's punch. It was useful, even amusing, when Bach used his gift to blackmail an asshole. It was gruesome and depressing that he could see the deaths of strangers. It was unthinkable that he could suddenly know so many hateful things about his family and still apologize for dropping a phone.

"How the hell did it take you twenty-two years to lose your shit?" Simon asked.

Bach shrugged. "If I'd known how much of a relief it is to be insane, I would have done it a long time ago."

Simon looked at the house and grounds. Classically beautiful. It must take a lot of time and money to maintain that perfection. From deep in his chest, he felt a swell of anger toward the people who lived there. "Okay," he said, smacking the steering wheel with his palms, "what do you wanna do now?"

"Let's leave."

"You sure?" he asked, even as he turned the key in the ignition. "Did you do everything you needed to?"

"No," Bach whispered, rubbing his eyes, "but I'm done. Can you take me to Ra's and help me carry my stuff inside?"

"No problem." Simon put the car in gear and pulled away from the curb. At the last second, he gave the steering wheel a quick jerk and struck the mailbox with his bumper. Bach grunted in surprise as the wood pole snapped, the box flipped into the grass, and the momentum rolled it across the lawn. Simon drove on, trying not to smirk and keeping one eye on Bach, who watched the reeling mailbox in the sideview mirror with a glazed expression.

"You okay?" Simon asked.

Bach slumped down in his seat, arms crossed over his chest, and stared at his feet. "Yeah," he said. "It went about as well as I thought it would."

"Yeah." Simon glanced at the house in the rearview before turning down a side street. The Chesterfield home vanished in a blur of sidewalks, houses, and trees. "Hey," he said. "To hell with 'em."

"Yeah," Bach said softly. He lifted his head and took a deep breath. "Yeah," he repeated. "To hell with 'em." His gaze drifted toward the sideview mirror but then he shook his head and focused on the road ahead. "I hope I never see that house again. But I will," he added in an undertone, "soon."

"Really?" Simon cocked an eyebrow. "Hard to believe your mom's gonna come around. Think your dad'll call?"

"No," Bach said firmly, "he won't. In his mind, I'm not worth the fight with Mom that phone call would cause. I don't know why I'll be back, but I know I will. And I don't think it'll be a happy occasion."

Simon nodded. Given everything he'd heard today, that made sense. What could possibly have happened six months ago to make a mother, even an ice bitch like Mrs. Chesterfield, turn away from her son? Simon truly could not imagine the horrors he would have to commit to lose his place in his mother's heart.

"So," he said, "'Chesterfield,' huh?"

"Yeah," Bach mumbled, a blush climbing his neck, creeping over his cheeks, and kissing his ears.

"Is Bach your first name? Sounds a little strange. Bach Chesterfield."

"No, Bach's a nickname I came up with. 'Chesterfield' is where the 'ch' in 'Bach' comes from."

"So, what's the 'ba' from?"

"Uh . . . that's from my first and middle name."

"Which are?" Simon pressed.

Bach's cheeks deepened to crimson as he stared doggedly at his feet. "My full name is Bertrand Archibald Chesterfield V."

Simon snorted a chuckle. Bach scowled and looked away, and the chuckle turned into outright laughter.

"Damn," Simon said, "that is bad. I see why you went for the nickname. The fifth? For real?"

"Yes," he said, almost growling, "and I'm the last one, believe me. I mean, after five generations we've run out of things to call ourselves. My great-great-grandfather was Bert, my great-grandfather was Baldo, my grandfather was Arch, my dad's Rand, and I'm Bach. We've totally mined this bastard dry for nicknames. No son of mine will ever be the sixth to inherit this shit. Especially now." He ground his teeth. "It stops with me."

Simon nodded. That sounded like the healthiest possible outcome of this crapfest.

BRIDGING THE GAP

Rachel helped Leda settle into a kitchen chair and then took a seat across from her. Leda glanced down at her watch; was it really possible that it was only a little past noon? She felt she'd lived a lifetime in the last five hours. She couldn't believe she still had half a workday ahead of her at the museum.

She glanced over at Rachel, and noticed that her eyes were focused on something in the small yard behind the house.

When Leda looked out there, the thing that stood out to her most was how the grass became smeared and out of focus at the edges of the pocket dimension, as if the reality of this place lost its cohesiveness the farther you got from the house. But that wasn't where Rachel was looking. Her gaze seemed to be locked onto the sapling tree rising tall above the overgrown grass. It was an odd tree in that it was nothing but a skinny trunk with no branches, but to Leda it was utterly dull compared to how insubstantial this tiny world became just a short jog from where they sat. It was strange to think that Rachel was so used to the pocket dimension that the spindly tree was more interesting to her.

"Okay," said Rachel, tearing her eyes from the backyard. "So, you wanted to know about the human dimensional spectrum."

"Yes!" Leda opened the pocket notebook on the table in front of her and clicked her pen. The promise of more knowledge put her brain in a state of readiness and she leaned forward to receive whatever Rachel could offer. "Go on."

Rachel took a deep breath and placed her forearms on the tables, her fingers knitted together. "I'm gonna explain this to you the same way it was explained to me in school. It's a simplified explanation of a complicated phenomenon."

Leda straightened her back and set pen to paper.

"Picture the colors of the rainbow," Rachel said, "all lined up the way you would expect to see them: red, orange, yellow, green, blue, indigo, violet. The way you see these colors is the way the human dimensional spectrum is laid out. Each color is a level in this spectrum."

"But that's seven levels," said Leda. "You said only four levels have humans in them."

"That's true—my dimension, yours, and two others are human dimensions. But the daemons that tempt all the humans in those four dimensions travel through seven levels, which is why we call it the 'human dimensional spectrum.' As far as we know, the daemons are contained by these seven levels and do not travel beyond them."

"But there is something beyond them?" Leda asked.

"Yes, but honestly, I don't know too much about it. I can tell you about this spectrum, but others . . . not so much."

"Then let's start with this spectrum," Leda said, writing furiously and wishing she had thought to record this conversation. "Tell me what you know."

Rachel licked her lips, stretched her fingers, and gave a nod.

"Remember the colors of the rainbow," she said. "The 'red' level is what we call the Tinoha. The Tinoha is a void, just empty space—no earth, no stars, no nothing. The 'orange' level is the Asuta. It's an inferno of primordial elements, just a swirling hot soup of horrible. There is an earth there, but nothing lives on it. The 'yellow' level is the Lata. There are a few human settlements there, all of them Arcanan colonies. We started colonizing it once we confirmed that there were no humans already living there. It's a wide-open space full of life, it just hadn't been touched by humans until we got there. The 'green' level of the spectrum is the Nota, your world, and the 'blue' level is the Arcana. The 'indigo' level is the Apsa, which I told you about earlier. The 'violet' level is the wastes, the Jarus, where daemons go to die." She paused as Leda continued to scribble. "Okay?"

"I've . . . just about . . . got it." Leda's pen came to a halt. "Now, what about the other spectrums? Where do they come in?"

"Well," Rachel said with a sigh, "see, the Nota—again, that's the 'green' level in the human dimensional spectrum—is also the 'green' level in other spectrums. Think of those other spectrums as other rainbows that exists at a slight angle to this one, intersecting our rainbow at various levels. They're not part of the human spectrum . . . but that doesn't mean that nothing lives in them."

The missing bits of knowledge in Leda's thought process began to appear and line up in her mind. "The Djinn are from another spectrum," she said, "a non-human spectrum, that intersects at the green level—my world's level. It's a separate spectrum that includes my world, the Nota, but not the Arcana."

"Yes," Rachel said. "Their world is called 'Kaf' but aside from that, I don't know much about it. I do know that they have ways of traveling between dimensional layers, and they've been visiting this world since . . . forever. My people met them during our work here, and we established a limited relationship. They try not to interfere in our work, and we try not to interfere with whatever they might be doing." She shook her head. "I'd actually never seen one before today."

"What about Naji? Is he . . . possessed or something?"

"No." Rachel's brows lifted in surprise. "Why would you think so?"

"How else could he do what he does?" Leda asked, bewildered. "I mean, people don't . . . what'd you call it? 'Poof' things?"

"Oh. He can do that because he's an *ukiba*."

"*Ukiba*," Leda repeated. She quietly sounded out the word as she wrote it in her notepad. "What's that?"

"*Ukiba*," Rachel said, "literally means 'rupture.' It's someone who can open a breach in dimensional boundaries. It's very rare. It's actually a highly-valued ability, because opening a passageway between worlds using technology takes time, and maintaining that passageway takes energy and skill. A person who can open a passage naturally saves us a lot of time and resources." Rachel groaned and rubbed her face. "I really don't wanna have to call the Central Office about that kid."

"Why not?"

"Like I said, *ukiba* are rare and we need them. The Central Office will want to use Naji and his gift. That means they'll need someone to discuss it all with the El Sayed family—and what with our manpower being limited right now, they'll probably want me to do it. And I don't want to." She inhaled and exhaled slowly. "I've got enough beyond-my-job-description crap going on right now."

Leda shot Rachel a look, her lips tight. *'Crap,' huh?* It wasn't like she'd signed up for this "gatekeeper" business, yet she was soldiering through this unfamiliar territory, making the best of it in every way she could and being courteous all the while. Did

Rachel think she was too good to do the same? *Of all the lazy, stuck-up attitudes . . .*

But before she could unleash her anger, Rachel pulled out her phone. "Do your job," she murmured as she tapped her phone's screen, not seeming to notice the look on Leda's face. "It's your job. Do your job." Shoulders slumped, she put the phone on the table, tapped the speakerphone button, and waited.

Hardly a moment had passed when a female voice spoke through the phone and Rachel began to talk. Leda's ire quickly faded as a steady stream of Arcanan words and phrases filled the air, including some words she had heard before, like "*ukiba.*"

Suddenly, the other woman interrupted Rachel mid-sentence and began to speak louder and faster than before. Rachel tried to resume her end of the conversation several times before finally surrendering to the onslaught. After a minute of listening to the speaker and occasionally adding a word or two here and there, she grunted and shoved the phone across the table. The woman continued talking rapidly.

"What's she saying?" Leda asked, eyes glued to the phone.

"She's excited to hear about Naji's gift," Rachel said. She leaned back in her chair and gently hugged her ribs. "She's already making plans for it."

The woman on the other end of the line talked on and on, but Rachel showed no sign of interest. Leaving the phone where she'd dropped it, she slowly rose from her chair and walked to the kitchen sink.

"Shouldn't you listen?" asked Leda.

"She's not talking to me," Rachel said. "She's talking to herself. Besides, the less I say, the less likely she is to include me in her plans."

Rachel filled two glasses with water, returned to the table, and set one glass near Leda before sitting down, holding the other to her chest as she did.

Minutes ticked by and still the woman on the phone prattled on, heedless of how one-sided the conversation had become. Leda sat quietly, listening intently, while Rachel sat back in her chair with her eyes half closed.

"What's so interesting about Ms. Dokgo's voice?" Rachel asked.

"Your language has so many fascinating elements to it," Leda said. "If I ever decided to map it out—"

"There's no reason for you to do that."

Leda shot Rachel a harsh look and jutted out her chin. *First, I'm a "crap" job; now she's dictating what I do with my own time.* "I realize you didn't ask to be my 'liaison,'" she snapped, "but that doesn't give you the right to—"

"I mean," Rachel interrupted, "that there's no reason for you to map out the language when it's already been mapped out."

Leda blinked and pulled back a bit. "What?"

"It's been mapped out," Rachel said. "We have digital dictionaries, translators, and programs for learning any Arcanan language you want."

"Any . . . ? Wait," Leda said, reeling, "how many languages do you have?"

"How many do you have in the Nota?"

"But . . . you said everyone from the Arcana knows one language."

"Everyone is required to learn the common speech, yes," Rachel said, "but we have as many different languages as you do. I grew up speaking Common Arcanan, but I learned K'Maz from my mother. I also learned some N'Ocav and Mibu during my abroad years in school."

The voice on the phone chattered on, eager but forgotten, as Leda absorbed this knowledge.

Rachel's weary gaze slowly transformed into a thousand-yard stare. "N'Ocav is hard to learn," she said pensively. "The grammar is intricate, and one word can mean ten different things depending on the context. The N'Ocaving people take their language seriously, too. They consider it a matter of pride for their culture that everyone who speaks the language does so perfectly. Every time I slipped up, they gave me an earful. Mibu is much easier by comparison, but I still can't speak it perfectly. I learned enough to get by but for a native Bayan, Mibu words are difficult to pronounce. It has a very . . . nasal sound to it. It's Wu's native language. Ask him to speak it for you sometime. You'd swear he's talking out of his nostrils."

Leda felt her cheeks burn with embarrassment as she suddenly realized her amateurish mistake. This was not one culture or one society that she was studying, it was many. The breadth of the world she was trying to grasp was as great as her own. Focusing only on Rachel's culture was like trying to study all European cultures based on interactions with a single Italian. More importantly, while it was all unknown to her, it was not a new discovery. Not only was she making incorrect assumptions about the number of cultures that overlapped her line of inquiry, she was trying to investigate something that had already been thoroughly studied. Far from being an adventurer discovering a new world, she was a tourist journeying through a foreign land. She felt like a pompous fraud.

Pushing aside her mortification and donning a cool, professional expression, she put down her pen and closed her notebook. "Could I get access to a digital English-to-Arcanan language program?"

"Easily," Rachel said. "I'll talk to Creed about it."

The voice on the phone began to shout, "Wilde! Wilde!"

Rachel groaned but reached for the phone and moved it to her side of the table.

For the next two minutes, she was allowed to speak briefly in response to each of Ms. Dokgo's questions, though she mostly continued to listen to the other woman talk. But as Leda looked on, her heavy eyes suddenly opened wide, and she launched into a lengthy speech that she forcefully pushed through every attempted verbal hijacking Ms. Dokgo made.

When Rachel was finished, Leda was surprised to hear a long pause. When Ms. Dokgo spoke again, it was only briefly and in a subdued tone—then there was a loud click.

Rachel slumped down in her chair with a sigh of relief.

"So?" asked Leda. "How'd it go?"

"Oh, she's full of ideas for Naji, just like I knew she'd be." Rachel took a long gulp of her water. "She wanted me to talk to the El Sayed family."

"Just like you thought."

"Yeah, but I told her that I'm already a liaison to a gate-keeper family, a job I'm not qualified for. I told her I've been dragging a gatekeeper all over the city to observe me at work, and that I'm doing so while dealing with cracked ribs and a light work load, which means the gatekeeper's probably getting a very skewed view of Arcanan life. I made also it clear that I know even less about *ukiba* than I do about gatekeepers, so I can't even imagine how badly I would screw *that* up. I then pointed out that Naji's father calls me 'crazy girl,' so he might not be too receptive to hearing about his son's 'magic power' from me. That shut her up." She took another drink of water and stared at the silent phone; her eyes pinched. "It's weird to hear my language spoken so much at once after hearing English for so long."

Leda smiled a little, swallowing what remained of her anger. Rachel's expression suggested that her mind was well outside her body—that her eyes were seeing a world far beyond that phone on the table.

"Arcanan and English don't sound much alike," Leda said. "I'm betting the grammatical structures are completely different."

"Oh man," Rachel said with a snort, "English is so imprecise. You need three times as many words to say something that could be said very simply in Arcanan. No matter what I say in English, I don't feel like I'm getting my point across."

Everything Rachel had said before suddenly made perfect sense to Leda. Silently, she scolded herself for thinking badly of her without possessing all the facts.

"Is that why you think you're not doing a good job explaining things to me?"

The focus returned to Rachel's eyes and she looked at Leda. "It's very frustrating," she said, clutching her water glass in both hands. "It's difficult to teach anything when I can't use my own language to do it. Add to that the fact that I know very little about gatekeepers and understand your society only well enough to blend into the background . . ." She closed her eyes and held her breath, her lips brushing against the edge of the glass. "I'm feeling a little . . ."

"Homesick?"

"Yes," Rachel said. "Yes, I am. I want to be back on the farm with my family, my language, my people, and everything that's familiar." She huffed a sigh. "I'm sick of this job."

Being sick of a job was something Leda understood very well, thanks to her jackass boss. She also understood what it felt like to be homesick. She remembered crying into her pillow at the start of every summer camp—and, during her first week at college, calling home in tears every night, desperate for her mother's comfort. Rachel was much farther from her home than Leda had ever been, and with the interdimensional passages closed for a year, she didn't even have access to family comfort. *How sad she must be!* Leda thought. *And how lonely.* The thought of being an entire world away from her mother stung Leda's heart—and made it warm to her Arcanan guide.

"Well," Leda told her, "from where I stand, you're doing your job very well."

"Thank you," Rachel said. "I still don't think I'm the best person for it."

Leda chuckled softly. "I've probably been making it worse with all my questions."

They locked eyes a moment and then Rachel returned her smile.

"Your questions are strange to me. Everything you want to know is so ordinary. They aren't things I think about much. Imagine if you had to explain something from your daily life that you take for granted. Could you explain to someone from another world why you have your father's last name instead of your mother's? Could you explain the cultural significance of marriage? Or retirement? Or what about high-heeled shoes?"

"Or," Leda said, "a prayer before bedtime." She thought of the crazed trademark department and the obscured diligence daemon. "All my talk about angels and heavenly virtues probably sounded like an entirely different language to you, didn't it?"

"It's not something I'm used to," Rachel said. "I mean, just coming out and talking about faith . . ." She shook her head and looked into her drink. "Nobody does that. It's . . . it's just—"

"Where you come from, it's inappropriate," Leda concluded.

So, it wasn't her beliefs that Rachel had reacted negatively to, it was that fact that she was expressing *any* faith-based belief out loud. Unknowingly, she had violated a cultural taboo. "This is weird for both of us, huh?"

"Yeah, I guess it is."

They regarded each other, smiling a little but saying nothing, and Leda felt a sense of mutual understanding settle over the room. She and Rachel had been through a lot in the short time they had known each other: they had fought off an attacker, returned knowledge of gatekeepership to her family, and traveled all over the city looking for daemons. Still, this was the first time she felt that they'd really seen each other. The veil of mystery between them had been dropped and, Leda felt, it had put them on more equal footing. Rachel's smile and even gaze suggested that she felt it too.

Rachel picked up her phone again, reluctantly. "I still have to call the Solani clan," she told Leda. "You can listen in if you like."

"That's okay." Leda slipped her notebook and pen into her purse. "I'll wait for that program I asked for. Is this it for you today?"

"Most likely. It'll take the Solanis a little while to get back to me. Until I hear from them, all I can do is wait."

"God," Leda said quietly, "that poor kid." The memory of Naji's little face tugged at Leda's heart. "I hope he and his mom will be okay."

"I'll make sure the Solanis understand it's urgent. But I'm kinda at the mercy of their schedule."

"Well then, I'll go into the museum for the afternoon. I'm sure my jackass boss is filling up my inbox. I can catch up on some work until I hear from you."

"You still want to be involved with this assignment?" Rachel looked surprised.

Leda stopped, her fingers still pinching the half-closed zipper of her purse. "Sure. Why wouldn't I?"

"Well," Rachel said, "the idea was that you would follow me around for a day to learn a little about what my people do. You did that. You don't have to do any more." She gave a little shrug, sending a ripple through the water in her glass. "Unless you want."

"I'd like to see it through," Leda told her. "I don't like leaving things half-done. Unless," she added, "you'd rather I not."

"I don't mind." Rachel frowned at her phone screen. "I'll reach out when I hear something."

"Okay then. I'll keep my phone on." Leda slung her bag over her shoulder and scooped up her crutches. "Give me a call when you know something. Or," she added as she hobbled out of the kitchen, "if you wanna get dinner. Whatever."

Rachel nodded without looking up and gave a little wave with the fingers holding her water glass. "I'll be in touch."

Leda headed up the hallway into the foyer and swung open the door. The daemon shuffled over the threshold and into the house, dragging its coat in its wake. Leda stepped back into the foyer to get out of its path as it shuffled around the corner and then sidled her crutches through the doorway. As she did, she saw her brother and Bach emerge from the shadow passage, their arms laden with what looked like clothes, shoes, and a bookbag. Simon caught sight of her and nodded an acknowledgment. Leda nodded back. This was fortuitous. Simon could give her a ride to work. With pain radiating through her hands and arms, she was relieved she wouldn't have to ride another bus.

As she reached to close the door, she paused and then stuck

her head back inside. Across the hallway, through the doorframe into the kitchen, she and Rachel briefly locked eyes and exchanged gentle smiles.

"Later, girl," Leda said.

"Later."

STRATEGY / MOTION

The cold rain had drained his energy,
lulled him into unconsciousness.

Hunched over like a gargoyle
atop the ship's mast,
his wings drawn tight
around his body,
he slept.

When he awoke,
he parted his wings and gazed up
at the clear night sky,
at the glamorous moon
and her twinkling attendants.

It was still cool
but free of the rain,
his fiery skin glowed
a healthy gold.

The waters around him were
still

and
vacant.

Everything he saw—
ocean, ship, and sky—
seemed a shade of bluish-gray,
save for a long silver streak
of reflected moonlight on the water
bisecting the darkness.

The boat glided along,
quiet but for the
gentle splash
of the waves against the hull.

He could have taken flight
and soared quickly back to land,
but he had a mind not to.

The boy
would be expecting him.

That was the pattern he had set:
the boy blasted him away,
he rushed to return.

This time,
he would wait,
travel at a leisurely pace,
save his strength.

The boy would grow
anxious
and
jittery
with anticipation.

He would jump at shadows,
bolt at the slightest sound,
so sure
that his enemy had returned.

He smirked.

Before long,
the mother would get well;
distractions would creep in,
as they were wont to do;
and the child
would grow less attentive.

Eventually,
he would leave the woman
unguarded.

That is
when he would strike.

That is
when the mother would die.

That is
when he
would go home.

The icy stupor
that encased
him gradually melted,
bringing him back to awareness.

He stretched all four arms,
reacquainting himself,
not for the first time,
with the feel of living
in his own rippling skin.

Then he heard noise—
much more than usual.

A mishmash of languages,
shouting,
cursing.

Intrigued,
he pressed his fin-like ear
against the sealed doorway
like an eavesdropping child.

He could hear only
a smattering of words:
"disrespect,"

"humans,"
"inexcusable."

All of these were
in the language
of his own people.

But there were also
Arcanan words.

His rusted knowledge of Common Arcanan
made comprehension a challenge,
but he understood enough to know
that nothing the speaker said
made the slightest bit of sense.

He seemed to be responding
to the shouts and condemnations
with pleasantries and compliments.

It was as if
he was overhearing conversations
taking place in two different rooms.

It was baffling.

And that was fascinating.

The volume of the various voices
changed multiple times,
suggesting that,

despite the lack of motion around him,
the container that held him and his island
was being moved.

Soon enough,
his people's languages
spiraled away,
leaving only a sole human voice
that hummed brightly
like a strange, voiceless bird.

Mystery, he thought,
smiling.

So much after so much nothing.

A tasty mystery.

RUNES

S imon was ten minutes late picking up Leda in the morning. When he finally arrived at her apartment, he offered no apology or explanation. Leda threw every dirty look she knew at her brother, with no visible effect. Eventually, she gave up and slouched in the passenger seat, casting her anger out the window instead of at the man who had incurred it. This slight was just another drop in her pool of ire.

Due to her injuries, Leda had taken to bringing paperwork home from work to keep up her usual pace. She'd arrived to her office the previous day only to overhear her boss complaining about her. According to him, she had stacks of untouched paperwork that were growing by the day, and what little work had been finished was far below acceptable standards.

Wounded and furious, Leda had burst into his office to defend herself, startling the two other employees within. She'd presented him with all the completed paperwork she had taken home the night before and had begun to rattle off everything she'd done in her long list of her projects—only to have him cut her off, insisting that her reduced hours were cutting into the quality of her work. She typically did much more, he told her, and her work was usually much more thorough.

It took a moment before Leda realized he was referring to

his *own* work—the work Leda often did for him but didn't have the energy for right now. Anger pricked her lungs as she drew a hot breath, met his squinty stare, and—as calmly as she could—informed him that she was performing every task for which she had been hired and was performing those tasks exceptionally well. Any other task that wasn't being fulfilled was certainly the responsibility of some other employee—one who was not pulling his weight.

The flash of indignation in his eyes had momentarily elated her—then filled her stomach with lead. Though the confrontation had ended there, she sensed that it was going to resume, probably quite soon, and it wouldn't be pleasant.

She glanced into the backseat of Simon's car where her crutches lay, felt the ache of them under her arms, and scowled.

The alleyway that hid the entrance to the pocket dimension was blocked by a long line of parked cars. Simon swore under his breath and shook his head as he stopped in the middle of the street and put the car in park. "I'll let you out here and drive around the block. It'll be easier for you with those things," he said, jerking a thumb toward the backseat. "If it takes me a while to park, tell Bach not to go anywhere. I gotta talk to him."

He jumped out, yanked her crutches out of the backseat, and held them in position while she hauled herself to her feet. As she hobbled down the partially-obstructed alley, swinging her crutches awkwardly to avoid the cars, he drove off.

Tottering through the pitch-black passageway, Leda felt the world around her vanish, consumed by the endless abyss. She heaved a breath of relief as she exited into the pocket dimension and once again felt the comforting embrace of reality. *I'll never get used to that*, she thought with a shudder.

Rachel's house was draped in shadow from an overcast sky

and a crazed wind whipped the yard's unkempt grass about. Leda worked her way up the front walk, shaking her head several times to dislodge her hair out of her eyes. When she arrived at the front door, she reached out to knock—only to find that the door was cracked open.

She heard Rachel speaking sharply and another voice, a man's, reply with calm.

Curious, she pushed open the door and let herself in.

Rachel was clutching three or four oversize leaves of burnt-yellow paper in her shaking hand and staring at the person before her.

Leda gave the boy a quick scan. Though seemingly an adult, he was definitely young—no more than twenty. He was short and lean, with shoulder-length brown hair that covered his ears and most of his neck. Baggy clothes and a slouched posture accentuated his sinewy look. A necklace made from multicolored woven twine peeked out from between his hair and the collar of his loose shirt. The boy stood before Rachel with his hands in his coat pockets and his face supremely relaxed. Leda had a sneaking suspicion that if she got too close to him, she would smell some recreational herb.

Seeing Leda enter the room, Rachel shifted from Arcanan to English. "Tell me again what happened," she said, her jaw tight.

The boy shrugged, smiling. "I wrote it all up."

"I read your report," Rachel said. "What I don't understand is how you managed to single-handedly ruin generations of your clan's hard work in just one meeting."

"It was an accident," he said, still smiling. "Totally unavoidable."

"An accident?" Rachel shrieked. "How is mooning the entire delegation an accident!?"

"Ah," he said, chuckling, "you had to be there. But no worries! You got a response to your inquiry, right?"

"Oh yes," she said, waving the papers under the kid's nose, "I got a response. And if the translation is accurate, it's absolutely the most eloquent way I've ever been told to go fuck myself."

"Aw, don't worry about that," he said through his eternal grin. "That's just how they do things. It's pretty positive that they wrote it all out for you."

Rachel sputtered, opening and closing her mouth again and again, a snarl forming and melting on her lip each time. To Leda, it looked like she was struggling to find a word that would uncork her boiling rage, but in the face of this unflappable young man, she couldn't do it.

After a few more failed attempts, Rachel took a deep breath, drew herself up to her full height—bringing her eye to eye with the slumping boy—and glared at him.

"You are a disgrace to your mother and your clan," she said.

"Yeah," he said, chuckling. "I've heard that before."

"You are also," she continued through clenched teeth, "a thundering moron."

"Wow!" He laughed, nodding, eyes wide. "'Thundering!' That may be a new one! I like that. 'Thundering.'"

Rachel stared at him as if he had birds flying out of his ears. Then she scoffed and swatted at the air before him. "Get out!" she said. "*Tulira!*"

"Okay," he pleasantly replied. "But hey, before I cut out, I gotta give you this."

From a sagging coat pocket, he produced a small box. Leda craned her neck to get a good look at it. The item was wooden but had a strange metallic glint to it, giving the otherwise brown box a peculiar could-be-blue shine. Carved into its surface were a number of symbols and runes, some of which Leda immediately recognized, some of which were new to her. When Rachel crossed her arms over her chest, eyes burning twin holes into the boy's face, the visitor calmly turned and offered the box to Leda instead.

"What is this?" she asked.

"Dunno," he said with a shrug, "but it came with the letter. Something about how humans shouldn't plead poverty if they can afford to throw away their conquests."

"What does that mean?"

"Hard to say. They hurled the box at me while they were talking, so I might have heard them wrong." He pushed the box into Leda's fingers, stuffed his hands into his pockets, and winked at her. "Wilde's pissed off so I gotta run. Otherwise, I'd stay right here and get lost in those eyes. Later, beautiful."

Humming brightly, he sidestepped around Leda and strolled up the hallway toward the front door. Leda, bewildered, stared after him, trying to decide whether she was offended. As the boy sauntered past the crumpled coat on the floor he grinned and exclaimed, "A daemon wearing clothes! I love it!" He slumped way down and gave the daemon a chummy slap on the back without breaking his stride.

The coat shuddered, quickly shuffled away, and wiggled its way into a crack between the wall and the sofa.

Leda stared after the kid until she heard the front door open and close. Then she turned back to Rachel, who was still silently fuming.

"Who the hell was that?" Leda asked.

"Solani Zek len Solani," she said.

"Solani? Isn't that the embassy clan you told me about?"

"Yes. Zek is the ambassador's son. Apparently, he was the

only one available to make my request. Ugh," she said, nose scrunched. "His poor mother."

"Was he flirting with me?" asked Leda, her mind still grappling with their interaction.

"Probably. He had the nerve to flirt with me when he first got here. And this elegantly written refusal I'm holding reports that he also flirted with half the Djinn delegation at the meeting. He even flirted with the Djinn ambassador's wife, and when the ambassador took exception to that, he turned around and flirted with the ambassador himself. *Tulira!*"

"So, he completely fucked up your chances of getting help."

"He fucked up more than that. His clan will have to spend the next fifty years rebuilding the bridges he's burned."

"The hell," Leda mumbled. "Is he stupid or just crazy?"

"Oh, who knows?" Rachel said. "But whether or not it was deliberate, it might be a blessing in disguise for his clan. Now his mother will have no choice but to keep him out of sight. Maybe she'll ship him off on a matching tour, so he can become some other clan's problem. If any other clan will take him, that is." She groaned and rubbed her eyes. "*Tulira.*"

Leda plopped down on the sofa and let her crutches slide to the floor. Behind her, she heard a scrape as the coated daemon shifted positions.

"What does that mean? *Tulira.* I've heard you say it before, usually when you're pissed."

"Oh." Rachel opened her mouth to respond, but then stopped and scrunched up her face in thought. "It doesn't translate well. How to explain? It refers to someone or something that could or should be serving a useful purpose but isn't, usually by choice. It means 'useless' and 'failure' and 'wasted potential' all rolled together." She suddenly smiled for the first time since

Leda's arrival. "My mother uses *tulira* about twenty times a day. I remember her leaning out of an upstairs window to scream it at my brothers when they accidentally left the goats out of their pen and they decided that the garden looked tasty." In spite of her recent fury, Rachel chuckled. "I can still her voice echoing in my brain. '*Tuuuuuullliiiiiiirrraaaa!!*'"

Leda set the strange box on the coffee table, fished her notebook out of her pocket, and wrote "*tulira*," along with a quick definition. She would have to look it up when she received the language software Rachel had promised.

"Is Bach still in bed?" she asked.

"No, he left early, before that idiot Zek got here. Why?"

"Simon's looking for him."

The front door opened and slammed, making both women jump. Simon stormed into the living room, eyes wide, one finger wagging behind him. "Who the hell was that?!" he demanded.

"A thundering moron," Rachel said.

"You okay, Sy?" Leda asked.

"Hell no! That guy smacked my ass! He disappeared into the passage before I could punch him!"

Leda put a hand over her mouth to hide her grin, while Rachel rolled her eyes and pressed her palms to her forehead.

"*Tulira, tulira, tulira,*" she chanted.

"Forget him," Leda told her brother, failing to hide her smile.

"It's not funny!"

"Yes, it is," she said. "But forget it. Oh, and Bach's not here."

"That's right," Rachel said, hands still to her head. "He left early. He had his arms full of stuff and he took that dog with him."

Simon threw up his arms in frustration. "So, what do I do now?"

"He's got his phone on him," Rachel said. "Just call."

"Fine." Simon shoved his hand in his pocket and fished for his phone as he marched toward the door. "But," he added, low and dangerous, "if I see that guy on my way out, I'm kicking his ass."

Leda's grin slipped away and she clicked her tongue. "Sy—"

"Kick it good!" Rachel called out.

The door slammed.

Leda huffed and glared at Rachel. "Do not," she said, "encourage my brother to throw a punch. If he gets arrested, he could lose his job."

"I doubt he'll even see him," Rachel said, "unfortunately. If ever somebody needed an ass-kicking . . . but never mind." She dropped her hands and exhaled through her teeth, her eyes closing as the breath left her. "The Solani clan can deal with Zek. I've got more important things to worry about."

Rachel handed the peculiar papers to Leda, who examined them with immense interest. The paper was so crisp and crinkly that it made tiny crunching sounds with each touch of her fingers. Its yellowish color was unusual, but so too was the purplish tint of the ink. Together, they made a strange yet appealing contrast, like amethyst in a sea of sunlight. The words were inscribed in vertical columns on the letter, trails of curves and swivels accented by dots and dashes. At the bottom of each vertical line of writing, an ornate, box-like character was stamped onto the page. Leda was put in mind of a row of votive candles with long waves of smoke twirling up into the atmosphere.

"It's a little bit Arabic here and there," she said as she took in the forms. "Other than that, it bears no resemblance to anything I've ever seen before."

"Or ever will again," Rachel told her. "It's the Djinn language. There's nothing like it anywhere."

"It's lovely. So's the paper."

"I thought you might like that. Keep it if you want."

"Are you sure?" Leda asked. The paper crinkled as she clutched it a little tighter. "You won't need it later?"

"There's no 'later' with Djinn stationery," Rachel said. "It kind of . . . dissolves in a few hours. Whatever it's made of, it doesn't transcend dimensions very well."

Leda gently rubbed the paper with her thumb and felt the wafer-like consistency of it as it crackled under her touch. The color danced in her eyes. She drew it close to her face and inhaled, discovering a scent of floral ash. Her heart ached. Only a few hours? That was tragic.

Settling into an armchair, Rachel picked up the box from the coffee table and examined it closely, turning it over and over in her hands.

"Weird little thing," she said. She held it closer to her face and squinted. "I don't see a latch or a hinge. It just looks like a block of wood." She tapped it with her index finger. "Sounds hollow, though."

Leda reluctantly tore her eyes from the letter and took a closer look at the box. "I recognize some of those markings," she told Rachel. "That's a *nazar*. That's a *khamsa*. That one's the Seal of Solomon. These others . . ." She traced one of the symbols with her finger. "I'm not sure."

"Well, I know this one," Rachel said, pointing to a shape that reminded Leda of an inverted bell curve. "It's *The Hermit's Tongue*. Oh! I know this one, too." She pointed to a horizontal line with a fan-like shape above it. "It's *The Empress Brush*."

"What do they mean?"

"*The Empress Brush* was the emblem of the Arcana's old monarchy. *The Hermit's Tongue* is almost as old, but we still use it today. It's a symbol of the people who overthrew the monarchy—a symbol of the united Arcana."

"So, they're both power symbols," Leda said. "The *nazar* is a symbol to ward off evil and the *khamsa* signifies blessing. The Seal of Solomon is supposedly a symbol that gave King Solomon power over demons."

The daemon squeezed out from behind the sofa and shuffled between the two women. It stopped and the coat that surrounded it fluttered. The neck hole shifted, tilting toward the box. Leda looked at the coat, but only saw the same empty space inside that she had seen before. She glanced back at Rachel and caught her breath. Rachel was staring down at the coat in absorbed silence.

"Is it talking?" Leda asked.

"Yeah."

"What's it saying?"

"It says there's something written on the box that we aren't seeing," Rachel said. "Apparently the symbols we see are just a superficial layer of writing on this thing. There's more underneath." Rachel pulled out her glasses and, much to Leda's surprise, offered them to her. "What?" she said in response to Leda's expression. "You're the linguist. You've got a better chance than I do of reading whatever's on this thing."

Filled with pride, Leda nodded appreciatively as she accepted the glasses.

The first thing she saw after sliding them into place was the daemon's bulging eye gazing up from within the coat, colorless and unblinking. Bits of wrinkled green skin framed the orb and one long, pointed ear (also green, rimmed with pink) jutted out over the coat's collar. The hint of a vein surfaced in the white of the eye, colorless but distinct. Suddenly the vein shimmered, dashed in a whip-like motion across the eye's membranes, and dove into the pupil like a snake into its hole.

Leda shuddered, then turned her attention to the box. The symbols she had seen before were gone, except for Solomon's seal. In their place was a continuous coil of words that wrapped around the box seven times. She turned the box over to find the beginning and then slowly spun it in her hands, taking in the message.

"Can you read it?" Rachel asked.

"Mostly," Leda replied. "It's a mish-mash of languages but . . . I think I'm getting the gist of it." She turned the box one last time to reach the end. "It says something like . . . *'This is the captive, cloaked in blinding rune. Place it in the hands of the master.'* After that, it just repeats."

"'Blinding rune'?"

"I'm thinking all those symbols we saw were just a distraction. The only one I still see is the Seal of Solomon."

Rachel clucked her tongue and shook her head. "I should've guessed," she said. "The symbols I saw are polar opposites. They wouldn't normally be placed together. During the Empire War, whenever the dissident army beat the Imperial forces, they would paint *The Tongue* over *The Brush* on government buildings to signal their victory."

"'The master.'" Leda took off the glasses and stared at the symbols with new eyes. "If the only true symbol on this box is the seal, then maybe Solomon's the master?"

"So, we're supposed to put it in his hands? Okay, where is he?"

"Solomon?" Leda said. "He's long dead."

Rachel blinked. "Really?"

"Yeah," she said, surprised. "He's a legendary king of Israel from three thousand years ago."

Rachel wrinkled her nose and huffed. "This means more phone calls. Crap."

Though she tried not to marvel at Rachel's ignorance, Leda was astonished by the woman's disgust at being inconvenienced by a three-thousand-year-old death. Leda set the box down next to the letter and saw, with dismay, that the edges of yellow paper were curling and fading to gray. It was like watching a butterfly with a broken wing try to fly as it sank through the air.

"Who can you call about this?" she asked.

"I think I'll probably have to call Wentrivel at historical records. Ugh."

"What? Is the guy a jerk or something?"

Rachel picked at the arm of her chair. "He's got a little crush on me. I don't like to encourage it."

Leda smirked. "Is he good looking?"

Rachel rolled her eyes. "I don't know. He's just really persistent. It's annoying."

"Persistent, huh?" Leda leaned forward, grinning. "How long has he been after you?"

"I'm not sure," Rachel said stiffly. "A couple of years."

"That long?"

"I guess." Rachel squinted her eyes and cocked her head slightly. "Is that right? The first time he got flirty with me was at the last license renewal, so . . . yeah, about two years. I was still with Dhruv at the time but now that we've broken up, he's been a lot more forward."

"Has he asked you out?"

"No," Rachel said with a jolt. "That would be rude."

"Rude?"

"If we were going to do something together," Rachel told her, "I would really need to be the one to suggest it. For him to come right out and ask me . . . no, that wouldn't be appropriate."

The shock on Rachel's face reminded Leda of a man she had been interested in a year earlier—a man who had been stunned when she'd taken the initiative and invited him to dinner. Though he had accepted her invitation, he'd canceled at the last minute and never contacted her again. Leda had always believed that he'd ghosted her because he'd been intimidated by her forward manner. She found the mental note she had made about Arcanan society having matriarchal roots and underlined it again.

"But if he didn't ask you out," she pressed, "then how is he being forward with you?"

"It's the way he addresses me."

"How's that?"

"It has to do with our language," Rachel said. "You really don't have anything like it in English. See, there are different ways to address the people you know. There's one way for addressing family, another for addressing friends, another for colleagues, another for acquaintances, and another for strangers. There are others, too, but those are the primary ones. I address Wentrivel as a colleague, but he addresses me as a friend. It implies that we have a closer relationship than we do and it's unsettling."

Leda's brain eagerly cataloged this information but she stopped herself from diving into comparisons to other languages, so she could concentrate on Rachel's personal issue.

"Okay, so he's using these 'honorifics,' I guess, to press his intentions on you."

Rachel thought for a moment and then nodded. "That's more or less right."

"So, he's getting too familiar. I can see how that would make you uncomfortable." Leda's eyes drifted to the decaying beauty on the table. The tip of one corner broke off and floated to the tabletop, crumbling into nothing as it fell, like a kiss of ash. "But," she continued, "since you and your man broke things off, maybe now's the time to give it a chance."

Rachel glanced at Leda as if she had offered her a plate of moldy cheese. "Um . . . no."

"Why not?" Leda chuckled.

Rachel licked her lips. "It's just . . . I'm not at all drawn to him."

"You don't find him attractive," Leda said.

"Or interesting," Rachel said. "He doesn't seem to have much of a personality. I just don't feel any heat between us."

"Oh?" Leda raised an eyebrow and smirked. "I thought passion was a poor foundation for a future."

Rachel drew back. Leda saw something leap into her eyes, like a spark on flint. With a strange sort of squint, Rachel stood up and pulled out her phone. "You're right," she said calmly, eyes on the screen. "I'm gonna call."

Her acceptance of Leda's playful admonishment left Leda surprised and gratified. She had expected an argument—a light-hearted debate, at the very least—yet Rachel hadn't put up a fight at all. Leda wasn't used to that. She was used to people defending their position long after she had poked it full of holes. For Rachel to shift her point of view so willingly was weirdly refreshing.

While Rachel put the phone to her ear, Leda turned her gaze to the crumbling letter and watched the yellow slowly get devoured by the gray. She reached out and brushed the edge of the paper. A third of it instantly dissolved into a dusty pile. *Too beautiful to last*, she thought. That was the way of things.

"Extension 184, please . . . Paavo, hi."

HELPING HANDS

A text to Bach brought a reply with an address several miles away. Still fuming from his hand-to-ass encounter, Simon returned to his car, brought it roaring to life, and raced away from the curb.

Less than three minutes later, he pulled to a stop and double-checked the address Bach had sent him. This was the place. Simon wasn't sure what he had been expecting to find, but it certainly wasn't this.

The building was small, dwarfed by the apartment towers that framed it, but the scrawny steeple and crosses in the windows unmistakably marked its identity. Simon locked his car and stood by the damaged fountain out front, listening to the trickling water rolling over cracked concrete, as he stared up at the building. It was a church.

At the sight of it, the childhood wound on his soul reopened a bit and bled anger and resentment into him. In a flash, he reexperienced his father's death, the priest saying he was in a better place, and the stab to his aching heart that followed. He had to drag himself all the way to the front door before he could shake off his disgust and enter with his shoulders back.

As he stepped inside, he found himself staring up the center aisle of the nave, rows of pews lining it on each side. The morning sun peeked through the windows at odd angles, creating a shadowed patchwork on the far walls. A faint floral scent dusted every surface; it stirred as Simon moved. The muffled sound of his shoes on the wood floor traveled farther than it should have in the stillness and the puff of air through his lips threatened to echo from the rafters.

Holding his breath, he glanced around and quickly spotted Bach in the very back row. He slid down the pew, sat next to him, and reclined in silence.

Bach sat with one hand on a stack of clothes—many of the same clothes Simon had helped him retrieve from his ex—and the other on the head of his dog, whose chin rested on his knee.

"Why're you here?" Simon whispered.

"Waiting for someone," he replied.

"Who? There's nobody here."

"It won't be long." Bach took a deep breath and leaned back in the pew. His eyes seemed to glow in the marbled shadows.

"There was someone I wanted to visit yesterday," he told Simon, "but I didn't know how to find him. Then, this morning, I knew. I knew who he was and where he would be. I just had to get there—here—first. He'll be here soon." Bach scratched the puppy's ears, triggering a tail wag. "I was surprised to get your text," he said, turning his eyes to Simon at last. "I had a hunch I'd hear from you soon, but I wasn't expecting that text. It's fun for me, you know."

"What is?"

"Being surprised. Really surprised, I mean, the type of surprise that bowls you over. Doesn't happen all that often."

Simon nodded, mulling over the thought. Life without surprises. Sounded less fun . . . but also easier. Interesting trade-off.

He looked around the church but no one else had appeared.

He shifted his weight. "You said you had a hunch," said Simon. "About me texting you. What was your hunch?"

"Ah." Bach looked down at the dog leaning against his leg. The puppy gazed up at him and pressed a little closer, his huge ears flopping to the side and his tongue dangling from his smiling jaws. "You drove by my parents' house this morning on your way to pick up Leda. It has something to do with that."

"Yeah." Simon tried to swallow but found his mouth was dry. He exhaled through his teeth. "There's a whole lotta shit piled up on the curb out front. I stopped to take a look and . . . I think it's your shit."

"Mine?"

"Yeah. There's clothes and photos . . . lots of stuff. I was gonna cram it all in my car but I was already late to get my sister."

Bach stared down at the floor, at the happy dog and at the ruined sneakers just barely covering his feet. After a few long breaths, he slowly nodded. "That makes two surprises today," he said. "Well," he added in a whisper, "sort of."

The bang of a swinging door burst like a gunshot through the nave and startled the two young men. A voice weaved its way among the pews, echoing faintly as it sang an upbeat tune. Bach sat up straight and tried to find the singer while his puppy stretched his ears to their full height and cocked his head back and forth in time with the song.

Swiveling in his seat, Simon caught sight of a man at the far end of the church, standing just beyond the crooked sunlight in the shadows.

"That's him," Bach said.

He scooped up the pile of clothes and slid his way to the end of the pew with Simon just behind him and the dog half a step ahead. No sooner had the puppy cleared the pew than it spotted the man and let loose a sharp bark. The sound bounced violently from the walls, alerting the man and terrifying the dog. The animal jumped behind Bach's legs and cowered from the echo, not daring to bark again even as the man walked toward them.

"It's rather early, gentlemen," said a chipper voice. "Can I help you with something?"

"Father Nathaniel?" asked Bach.

"Yes."

The man was no taller than Simon but thinner and older by three decades. The clothes he wore seemed appropriate for his height but not his weight. They all hung from him in loose folds as they would from a scarecrow. He had a long face and a short crop of thinning hair and wore wire-rimmed glasses on a hawk-like nose. To Simon, he looked like a stretched-out owl in a white collar. Bach smiled at the priest and nodded at the clothes in his arms.

"My name's Bach. I, uh, came to give you these," he explained. "I know there's a donation bin for this sort of stuff, but I wanted to thank you personally."

"For what, son?"

"For the clothes and food you gave me when I was living under the midtown bridge."

The priest opened his mouth to speak but then slammed it shut as he blinked and stared. He leaned forward, adjusting his glasses, and turned his head from side to side as if hoping to catch a familiar glance of Bach from an atypical angle. Suddenly, a smile crept over his face.

"I wouldn't have known if I'd passed you on the street, but I see it now. Those eyes! You're the young man the bridge folks called Blue."

"Yes Father," Bach answered with a weak smile. "Bull started calling me that when he couldn't get a name out of me. I didn't realize the others picked it up."

"Bull, Bull . . . oh yes, yes! The soldier."

"Back then, I wasn't really . . . I don't remember a whole heckuva lot. I was a little . . . touched in the head."

"I remember," Father Nathaniel said. "I brought you something to eat one day and you looked right at me—very nearly gave me a heart attack with those eyes—and you said, 'Car'll crash.' The next day someone rear-ended me at a stop light." The priest smiled behind his hand, his fingers offering Simon only a glimpse of his crooked teeth. "The next time I saw you, you kept saying 'Fire, fire, fire.' I came back to the church that day and found the wastebasket in my office all in flames. I think someone had dropped a lit cigarette in there. Not much damage, thank God, but that was the start of a pattern. Every time I saw you, you said something prophetic. I tried to discuss it with you, but every time I brought it up, you ran off."

"Yeah, well . . ." Bach passed a hand over his face. "I wasn't in a good place."

The priest shook his head. "You don't sound surprised to hear about your predictions."

"It's a thing I do."

"Is that right? Does it happen often?"

"It happens."

"And are your predictions always true?"

"So far." Bach shrugged. "Here, I brought some clothes and blankets for you. I don't have the ones you gave me anymore, but I thought these might be okay as a replacement."

"Sure, sure." The priest accepted Bach's outstretched offering. "Every little bit helps. Thank you, son."

"Thank you, sir, for looking out for me when I needed it."

"Oh, don't mention it, don't mention it," the priest said. "I'm so glad you came by. People come and go and I so seldom get to see where their lives take them." He hugged the clothes to his chest and looked Bach up and down. "You look like you've come a long way since last we met."

"I'm, uh . . . I'm getting there."

"That's good, that's good. Is there anything else you need? Can I get you some coffee?" He turned to Simon for the first time. "Or you, son?"

"I'm fine," Simon quickly answered. "I'm just here to give Bach a lift."

"My friend's been driving me around while I gather up my life," Bach said, gesturing to Simon.

"Ah!" The priest clapped him warmly on the shoulder. "God bless you, son."

Simon repressed a flinch and tried to smile as he nodded. The fatherless wound pained him, filling him with bitterness, but the emotion had no outlet in the face of this well-meaning priest. He felt as out of place in this building and this conversation as a dancer on a football field.

The dog at Bach's feet whined and nosed his master, his large brown eyes darting nervously from one corner of the church to another.

Bach rubbed his ears. "I think the echoing in here has him upset. I better take him outside before he makes a mess on your floor."

"Fine, fine," said the priest. "Thank you for coming by to-day . . . Bach, was it? Bach. And you if need anything or if you'd ever like to talk to someone about your . . . unusual, God-given talent, please feel free. I'm intrigued."

"I prefer not to discuss it. And you may be the first to call my 'talent' God-given, Father."

"Oh? Isn't that what it is?"

"I don't know." Bach sighed. "Never gave it much thought."

"Really? It seems like the sort of thing that would occupy a man's thoughts."

"I guess that . . ." Bach shrugged. "It doesn't really matter to me where it came from. It's here, it's mine, and I've got to cope."

"So its origin has never troubled you?"

"No. I don't remember a time in my life without it. Whether it came from God, the devil, Mother Nature, or Uncle Sam, it wouldn't change how I live with it."

"Interesting, interesting," the priest murmured, his eyes wide behind his glasses. "It must be quite an adventure, living in your head."

Adventure's not the word I'd pick, thought Simon. He exchanged a knowing glance with Bach.

"You can't imagine," Bach said. "Thanks again, Father. Take care."

"Don't mention it, son." The priest reached out to shake his hand. "Come back any time. The door's always open." He then held out his hand to Simon, who, after casting a brief look of doubt his way, accepted it. "Take care, son. God be with you."

"Yeah," Simon said. "Sure."

The puppy led the way to the front door and onto the street, glancing back at Bach every few steps. Simon felt his chest untwist as he stepped into the open; his lungs expelled the floral dust and filled with fresh air. The morning sun, though still climbing the autumn sky, warmed his skin and whisked away the shadows of the church.

He clapped his hands together. "So, do you wanna go get your shit off the curb or—"

He stopped when he saw the frozen expression on Bach's face. He was staring in the direction of the street, those luminous eyes of his burning a hole in something with creepy intensity.

Following his gaze, Simon turned and saw a piece of paper stapled to a telephone pole. With a jolt, he recognized the same missing person flyer they had seen the day before. He stepped in front of Bach, marched to the pole, and ripped away the paper.

Bach caught his breath and buried his face in his hands, his fingernails digging into his forehead. "Alvarez," he croaked. "Alvarez."

"Get it together," Simon warned him. "Don't lose it."

"I'm okay."

Keeping one eye on his friend, Simon crumpled the flyer and, not seeing a trashcan, shoved it into his coat pocket. Simon glanced back at Bach and saw, to his horror, that tiny trickles of blood had appeared under his friend's fingernails.

"Shit!" He grabbed Bach's hands and yanked them away from his face. "What the fuck! Don't hurt yourself!"

"Tatiana," Bach whispered.

"What?"

"Javier's daughter, the one who made those flyers . . . Tatiana."

"Okay . . ." Simon said. "So what?"

"Why can't I get anything else on her?" Bach said, his voice coming out as a squeak. "Why don't I know more? Who the hell is she and why is she doing this to me? *How* is she doing this to me? What am I supposed to do about it?"

The puppy lay down on the sidewalk and stared up at Bach,

whining. Deaf to the worried animal, Bach stared at his bloody fingertips as if he didn't understand what he saw.

Simon grabbed him by the arm, dragged him to the dilapidated fountain, and thrust his hands into the water. The contact seemed to bring Bach out of his trance; he started washing away the blood of his own accord. The dog rose and approached the two men with his tail tucked between his legs.

"I don't understand why this is happening," Bach said as he splashed water onto his face. "Why does this Tatiana girl clear out my mind?"

"Maybe she's too close to you?" Simon suggested. "You told me that the closer a person is to you, the less you know about them."

"But I don't know her," Bach said. "I've never even seen her."

"Okay. Well . . ." Simon's mind raced to find some answer that would keep Bach from overreacting again. "Maybe you will."

"Huh?"

"Maybe she's a major part of your life in the future," he ran with the thought, "and that's why you don't know anything about her."

Bach gripped the edge of the cracked fountain and stared into the bloodied water, eyes squinting. His blue irises rippled in the surface.

"I hadn't thought of that," he said. "That might make sense. It's still weird how . . . urgent it feels. Whoever Tatiana is, I feel like she's . . . she's possibly the most important thing ever. Or she's supposed to be, anyway."

"Hey, that could be cool," Simon said him, thumping him on the arm. "The most important thing in your life. Maybe she's 'the one,' y'know?"

"No," Bach shook his head. "That's not what this is about."

"You not into Latinas?"

"Not into girls."

Simon's line of thought abruptly broke off as this revelation exploded to every corner of his brain.

"Whaddya mean?" he said. "Not at all?"

"Not at all."

"But that Shannon chick—"

"Chick?" Bach chuckled, his tone cold. "Nope. Guess again."

A memory of the woman in red lipstick flashed through Simon's mind. He saw her standing at the apartment window, staring down at the lawn as Bach screamed at her to open the door. But no; he now realized she wasn't the one he'd been screaming at. In his mind, he looked past the woman and saw her shaggy-haired companion.

"Ah, shit." He exhaled. "Shannon was the guy."

"Yeah."

An assumption Simon had made about Bach was stripped away, leaving a peculiar emptiness in its place—one he did not know how to fill—and blurring the previously well-defined boundaries he had sensed between them. His mind raced to reestablish those limits.

"I'm straight, you know," he blurted out.

"Fuck you, man," Bach snapped. "I know you're straight. I'm gay, not stupid."

There was a tense pause as they stared at each other. Then Simon burst out laughing.

Bach blinked and pulled back.

"It's not funny," Simon said between laughs. "I know it's not funny. It's just . . . Ha!"

In a moment of crisis, Simon did the same thing he had always done ever since he was a child: he reached into the father-shaped hole in his heart for guidance. Often enough, there was nothing there to hold and he had to redirect his search, but this time he found what he sought. Somewhere, whether in the corridors of his memory or in the shadows of the beyond, Simon heard his father laughing at him. When he opened his mouth, he heard that voice all the louder.

"Sorry." He tamed his laughter to a light chuckle. "Forget everything I said."

"Yeah," Bach said, raising an eyebrow, "sure."

"Okay, so," Simon said, collecting himself, "she's not gonna be the love of your life. That doesn't mean she's not gonna be important. I mean, plenty of people come and go in our lives and have a major impact. And that's not always a good thing, you get me? Sometimes they light you up, and sometimes they burn you out."

"Yeah." Bach scratched his puppy's head thoughtfully. "You mean she might end up causing me a lot of trouble."

"Women have a way of doing that."

"But I still feel like I'm supposed to help her."

"Can't help ya there, man. Just throwing out some ideas."

"Yeah, I know." He smiled. "I appreciate it."

Simon heard his father's laugh again and couldn't help but smile back. "It's cool."

The dog nosed his master's leg and continued doing so until he dropped one hand to the pup's head again and rubbed his ears. Bach looked down at his feet and tapped his toe, causing his rag of a sneaker to flap.

"I guess we should go pick up that crap on my parents' curb before trash day rolls around," he said. "Plus side: maybe they threw out some of my shoes. It'd be nice to wear something that doesn't look like I dug it out of a dumpster."

"Now you're talkin' sense," Simon said. "Let's go. I bet if we put that dog on the floor at your feet, we'll just manage to cram it all in."

"If it doesn't all fit, I'm sure I can just leave some of it behind." Bach closed his eyes. "You'd be surprised how little a person actually *needs*. After living under the bridge, I know exactly what I need versus what I'd like."

"True that. But I bet we can fit in plenty of the shit you like."

"Yeah. Hey"—he opened his eyes and held Simon's gaze— "thanks for all your help."

"No problem."

"Maybe so. But for me, it's huge. I'm rejoining civilization and you've been a big part of that process." He smiled and tapped Simon on the shoulder. "I won't forget it, man. Thanks."

Caught off guard, Simon stared at Bach in silence. Since his first visit to Rachel's house, he had often thought about all the things he wasn't: he wasn't an interdimensional traveler, he wasn't an oracle, he wasn't gifted with language, and, most of all, he wasn't a gatekeeper. From his perspective, he had observed the events of the last few days from the sidelines. He hadn't once thought that in someone else's eyes, he might be a significant part of the action. That special place deep in his core lit up and he heard his father laugh again.

Simon smiled a bright, genuine smile and nodded. "It's okay. But someday, sometime . . . you're gonna owe me for a tank of gas."

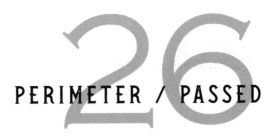

PERIMETER / PASSED

When he returned this time,
he approached
the boy's home
slowly,
inching his way
ever closer.

The moment he saw the child
react to his presence,
he marked the spot
and retreated.

He did this repeatedly
from multiple directions
until he had marked
a perimeter
around their building.

From outside this circle,
from neighboring rooftops,
he watched
and waited.

As he'd hoped,
when the boy sensed
but didn't see him
again and again,
he grew jumpy.

For a time,
the child stood guard
at his mother's door,
crouched at the threshold,
rocking back and forth on his heels.

He taunted the boy several times,
stepping inside the circle,
alerting his abductor,
only to immediately retreat.

These little teases
wreaked havoc
on the boy's confidence.

Every time he sensed
his adversary
but could not locate him,
he looked more
confused,
concerned.

The plan was proceeding perfectly.

New voices;
human voices.

He thought he heard
Common Arcanan again
only to lose the thread of it
rather quickly
and then,
English.

The realization drained him.

His people
had given him over
to humans.

Two women spoke
to one another,
an insipid conversation
about symbols
and men.

He felt his interested piqued
when he heard his jailer's name.

The moment passed.
The insipidness continued.

He heard
his jailer's name again,
spoken in Arcanan this time.

ALISON LEVY

Oddly,
the speaker,
one of the women,
seemed to be talking
to herself.

*Into whose hands
has my fate been passed?*

Leaning on the sealed door,
he held his breath,
and, as usual,
waited.

27

INTERRUPTIONS

Rachel's conversation with Paavo captivated Leda. The sounds of the Arcanan language were gradually beginning to lose their alien air. Many words sounded familiar and a few she even recognized.

Of equal interest was the casual tone Rachel adopted with her erstwhile suitor. While her facial expressions suggested she wasn't entirely happy with the conversation, she maintained a pleasant voice and never stiffened; she remained at ease and even laughed once. Paavo's voice through the phone was muffled, but even from several feet away, Leda could hear how animated he sounded. Whatever Rachel was saying, he was obviously into it.

By the time Rachel ended the call and sank into the sofa, the Djinn stationery had long since dissolved into a light dusting of ash. Leda watched the gray dust gradually dissipate into the air with a twinge of sorrow. *Too beautiful for this world*, she thought.

"Okay," Rachel said. "Wentrivel did some digging and found references to this box."

"Did you ask him out?"

"No!" Rachel said, scowling at Leda's grin. "Focus!"

"Fine." Leda gave a theatrical wave. "So, what's with the box?"

"He's not sure. The records aren't clear. But"—she pointed at the box with both index fingers—"the inscription's reference to

'The Master' doesn't necessarily refer to this Solomon person."

"But the seal—"

"Oh, you were right about the seal," Rachel said. "Solomon is the master the box alludes to, but we don't necessarily need to put the box in *his* hands. We just need the hands of someone from his bloodline—probably a male descendant."

"A direct male descendant?"

"Probably any male descendant—but, again, the records aren't clear. Seems to make the most sense to try the first descendant we uncover and see if the box reacts."

"Well," Leda mused, "Solomon supposedly had hundreds of wives, so he's likely to have a few descendants still running around. Of course, the Bible only mentions three of his children."

"Well," Rachel said, "apparently Solomon's name isn't listed in the Arcana family records, but since he was a Notan king, that's not a surprise. Wentrivel thinks the records of the clan Bnai Arba Achayot—that's Benny's clan—are the best place to start. He's going to take a look, says he'll send along any information he finds."

Bnai Arba Achayot—*Children of the four sisters*, Leda translated in her head. She didn't know the term, but the words were Hebrew, suggesting a connection to Solomon. Leda wondered whether Benny's Arcanan clan predated Israel's United Monarchy. *Regardless, the variations in language and culture must be intriguing*, she mused. Yet another subject to read up on someday. She turned the box over in her hands, trying to look past the counterfeit inscriptions with her naked eyes. "So, what do we do now?"

Rachel set her phone on the arm of the sofa and leaned back, hands in her armpits and head bowed. "We wait."

LEDA AND RACHEL'S quiet conversation was interrupted minutes later, not by the phone but by the front door. They rose from the sofa and peered around the corner to see Bach and Simon carrying boxes and garbage bags up the stairs.

Rachel put a hand on her hip. "Are you bringing trash into this house?"

"Just 'cause one person throws it away doesn't mean it's trash," Bach said.

"It does if it *is* trash," Rachel said. "What's in the bags?"

"Mostly my clothes and shoes."

Leda rounded the corner and was assaulted by the puppy as it charged into the house and knocked one crutch out from under her arm. Oblivious to her curses as she sought to regain balance, the dog jumped and yipped and darted every which way—until he laid eyes on Rachel, at which point he skidded to a stop, took a slow step in her direction, and whined.

Rachel waved a hand and barked a command in Arcanan. The puppy seemed to take this for approval, because he raised his head and beamed a floppy-tongued canine smile at her.

Rachel rolled her eyes. "*Tulira.*"

"Where'd you get all this stuff?" Leda called up the stairs.

"My parents threw it out," Bach answered from out of sight. He reappeared and trotted down the stairs, and Simon handed him another armful of trash bags. "Sy saw it all sitting on the curb in front of their house, so we went to pick it up."

He marched back up the stairs without acknowledging Leda's mournful expression or Rachel's wrinkled nose.

Mumbling something under her breath, Rachel stepped forward, snatched a boxout of Simon's arms, and followed Bach up the stairs.

SOMETHING BLUE

Upstairs—at the end of the hallway, through the last door on the right—Bach tried cramming the final trash bag into his tiny, and now overstuffed, closet. Several other bags littered the floor of the small bedroom, and boxes were stacked on either side of the bed. As Rachel set down her box, she brushed a curtain, stirring up a moldy smell.

"Gross," she murmured. She looked at Bach. "I never realized how empty this room is. The bed's okay but the rest of this furniture . . ." She gestured at the crumbling dresser and another wooden heap in the corner, possibly the ruins of a desk or end table. "There are other pieces in this house you could pilfer."

"I don't need much," he said, closing the closet door. "Besides, I don't wanna get too comfortable." He looked at her and smiled. "This isn't my home."

"I know." She worked her way back toward the door. "Doesn't mean you can't be comfortable while you're here."

"Thanks, Ra. But I'm happy just to have a roof over my head. The bed is a bonus. Anything else feels like excess."

She watched him look around the room at his bagged and boxed possessions and caught a glint of panic in his eye—the look of a poor man suddenly confronted with the responsibility of ownership. "Right now, I've got all I can handle. The last thing I want is to have more things."

"Well, if you change your mind," she said, "go ahead and help yourself."

"Sure." Bach took a deep breath and opened his mouth to say more but seemed to think better of it. Blinking rapidly, he looked away from his belongings, as if the sight of them was too much to take in. "Sure," he repeated softly. Then he brushed past Rachel and headed into the hall.

The puppy wagged his tail and yipped as Bach descended the stairs, Rachel behind them. Once Bach entered the living room, he took a seat on the floor and playfully rolled the dog onto his back, inciting a chorus of barking. Swinging wide of Bach to avoid stepping on the animal, Rachel moved to the far side of the living room, phone in hand.

Without thinking about it, she pulled up the Central Office's page relating to the ongoing conspiracy investigation. She had been checking this site a lot more than she meant to ever since Suarez showed it to her. There was no reason to. There hadn't been a break in the case, updates were minimal, and if ever someone did find the escaped killer, she would certainly get an alert about it, either from the Central Office or from Suarez. All she got from checking was an uneasy feeling about the future and a reminder of what the murderer looked like. *As if I'd ever forget,* she thought bitterly, glaring at the photo.

"Rachel," Leda said, startling her out of her thoughts, "how long should we sit here waiting on Paavo?"

"I don't know," she said. Redirecting her thoughts, she swiped away the Central Office's page and checked for messages from home. "I'm sure he's hard at work on it."

"Who's Paavo?" Simon asked.

"A guy Rachel knows," Leda said. "He's gonna help with this box."

"Oh."

"And," Leda added with a raised eyebrow, "he's seriously into her."

Rachel rolled her eyes and looked away from Simon's smirk. "I don't understand why you're latched on to this," she said to Leda. "It's not half as interesting as you're trying to make it."

"It would be if you'd just go with it," Leda said with a laugh. "What's holding you back?"

"I'll 'go with it' when I'm good and ready," Rachel said.

"Better get ready soon. You don't wanna wait too long or he'll lose interest."

Lose interest? The very notion of it being her job to maintain a man's interest in her made Rachel feel dirty. Considering how lightheartedly Leda was talking about the subject, she thought it unlikely that her Notan friend was trying to insult her, but even if this was a cultural difference, she couldn't fully tamp down her anger. "I've been ignoring him for two years and he hasn't lost interest yet," she said, her jaw tight. "Today was the first time I was a little more friendly and he ate it up. He's not going anywhere."

"Oh, you don't know," Leda said, a teasing edge to her words. "Could be some other girl waiting to stake her claim."

Rachel bristled. "Let her!" The vitriol in her voice seemed to surprise Leda, who drew back, the smile dropping from her face.

For a tense moment, they stared at each other, eyes locked, expressions firm. Rachel looked away first.

"Look," she said in a steady voice, "I don't know how Notans do things, but I wouldn't lower myself to competing with someone over a man."

"Lower?" Leda's face and voice were as blank as snow.

Bracing herself for an argument, Rachel mentally formulated an apology for her harsh tone, though not her actual words.

"So, you would just step aside if some other woman wanted a guy you wanted?" asked Leda.

Rachel blinked. Far from angry, Leda sounded intrigued. *Oh crap*, she realized, her energy spiraling down the drain, *I just triggered another cultural exchange.*

Already, Leda was digging through her bag, presumably looking for that notepad she carried everywhere. Rachel opened her mouth to protest but never got the chance to speak.

"Ah!" Bach exclaimed. "Man, that reeks!"

All eyes turned toward him. Bach was still seated cross-legged on the floor, the puppy draped over his lap. In his hand was the ornate box—with its lid wide open.

Bach took another hesitant sniff and then dropped the box to the table. "Ugh! Smells like dead fish! Sick!" Before anyone could say a word, he reached out and flipped the lid shut.

Rachel, her mouth hanging open, stepped forward, eyes locked on the box. "How did you open that?"

"What do you mean?" Bach shook his head slightly. "I opened the lid."

"But how?"

"With my hands," he said slowly, as if speaking to a child.

Rachel reached out and seized the box. She hooked it with her fingernails and pulled, without success. She gave it an annoyed look and then handed it to Leda, who made a few of her own attempts to pry off the lid before shaking her head.

"Here." Leda pushed the box toward Bach. "Do it again."

"Um . . . okay." With a flick of his thumb, he snapped the lid open. "There."

Leda took the box from his outstretched hand. Carefully holding the lid open, she turned it around and gazed inside. When she brought it closer to her face, she winced and turned her head aside.

"Ew," she said, her face scrunched up. "That really does stink."

Simon sniffed over her shoulder. His face convulsed and he leaned away, one hand covering his nose. Leda held her breath and brought the box in close for another look.

"I don't see anything in there," she said, "but it looks way too damn deep."

Rachel craned her neck to get a look. "Deep?"

"Yes," she said, gazing into the opening. "It's like there's no bottom."

Rachel held out a hand for the box. She drew a deep breath and held it before bringing the item to her face and peering in through the open top. Just as Leda had said, it appeared bottomless. She stuck her fingers into the opening and wiggled her hand through until she was up to her wrist, several inches deeper than the box should have been. "It's a portal," she said, pulling her hand free. "That's the only explanation."

"Like the one that gets us into this house?" asked Simon.

"Much smaller, but yes."

"Huh," Simon said pensively. "Where's it go to?"

"Very good question." Rachel glared at the box as if challenging it to explain itself. It was dark in there, but she thought she could see sand. "Why would anyone make a portal with such a tiny door?"

"To restrict the stink?" Bach shrugged. "What's the story with that thing, anyway? Why's it here?"

"A moron gave it to me," Rachel said, eyes devouring the inside of the box for a clue.

Bach looked at Leda, who nodded confirmation. "*Right*," he said. "So why could I open it when you couldn't?"

"Says on the box only a descendant of King Solomon can open it," Leda told him.

"Oh." For a moment, Bach looked distrustful, like the box was an illusion that might disappear if he waited long enough. Then, with a glimmer in his blue eyes, his expression mellowed. "Me, huh? 'Kay."

"You didn't know?" asked Simon.

"How the hell would I know something like that?"

"Well," Leda said, "where'd your family come from?"

"Philadelphia."

"Before that, smartass," Leda said as Simon snickered. "Before they came to America."

"I dunno. We've got some English, French, German, Russian . . . Swedish . . . some Irish, I think. I'm just your basic Euro-mutt."

"Didn't hear about a Hebrew branch of the family?" Simon asked.

"News to me."

Rachel continued to stare into the box as they talked. The darkness inside it was odd. It seemed to shift, changing color and intensity, like shadows moving with a changing light source, as if there was something . . .

Her entire body tensed. "There's something moving in there."

She felt all eyes turn in her direction—and as they did, the box began emitting a soft whistle. The puppy jumped up from Bach's lap and circled Rachel, his ears fully erect and his eyes trained on the object in her hands. He growled.

"What's doing that?" Simon asked as he scooted to the very edge of the sofa. "What do you see in there?"

"There's a . . . a distortion," she said. "There's a ripple in the air, or—"

The box rattled and shook. Startled, Rachel dropped it, letting it clatter to the floor with its lid wide open. The whistling grew louder, filling the room until it became deafening. The dog howled as everyone covered their ears and scrambled away. Simon climbed over the coffee table and moved toward the kitchen doorway, stopping short to grab Leda under her arms as she staggered, crutch-less, across the floor. Rachel backed into the far wall, fumbling to retrieve the phone in her pocket. Bach crawled on his knees and elbows, hands over his ears, to the edge of the fireplace. The box rumbled and jumped while the dog danced around it, his howls barely audible above the wail.

Then the shriek died and the box became still. The Morleys stood up, Simon still supporting Leda, as Rachel lowered her phone and took a few hesitant steps forward. The dog flattened his ears and backed away from the wooden cube, his teeth bared. Bach uncurled and sat up. He scooted toward the dog, one hand reaching toward the upright fur on the animal's back.

"What's up, boy?" he crooned. "It's all right."

The dog barked again, lunging toward the box—then yelped. He tried to back away but stumbled, his front leg jerking awkwardly, as if caught by a puppeteer's string. He cried and tried to scamper away, but his leg remained stuck in the air. A fold of skin on his ruff bunched and yanked. The puppy squealed, his claws scratching deep lines into the wood floor and a stream of urine puddling under his feet, as something unseen dragged him inch by inch across the floor.

Rachel, Leda, and Simon just stood and stared, mouths agape, but the crying animal electrified Bach. Snarling, the young man leaped from the floor and swung his fists at the air.

"Let go of my dog, damn it!" he bellowed. "STOP!"

With a yip, the puppy fell backward. Free, he bolted to the far corner of the room, hid behind an armchair, and whimpered. Bach followed him, whispering and cooing. Rachel put on her glasses and scanned the room while Simon held tight to Leda, who was wide-eyed and trembling.

"What do you see?" Leda asked, gripping a fistful of her brother's T-shirt.

"Something . . . blue?" Rachel said. Blue was the only definite description she could formulate. It looked like a luminous blue . . . something. "I see blue light floating . . ."

The blue glow began to expand and take on the rough semblance of a form. It took only seconds for her to identify what she saw. "Oh shit."

"What?" When Rachel didn't immediately respond, Leda shook her hands up and down. "What, what, what?!"

"It's a Djinni," Rachel said decisively. "I can see it a little." She pointed to the center of the room next to the coffee table, which had been displaced in the scuffle to escape the noise. "It's standing there."

"A Djinni? In here?" Leda's fear clearly forgotten, she eagerly scanned the room. "It's like the other one you saw?"

"Basically, but the one in the El Sayeds' apartment was yellow and red," Rachel said. "This one's blue. It must've come through the portal when Bach opened it."

Leda pushed away from Simon and, swinging her arms to maintain her balance, hopped toward the spot Rachel was examining. Three hops into her journey, Simon grabbed her, muttering, "Nuh-uh, nuh-uh," and pulled her back.

"What's it doing?" Leda asked.

"Just standing, I think." Rachel stepped forward, squinting

through her lenses. "Good morning," she said with a sharp nod. "Would you mind having a word with us, please?"

Through the glasses, Rachel saw a fluid dance of blue flame. The peculiar sparks grew, swelling in size but not in brightness. Her heart skipped a beat when she realized that the Djinni was moving toward her. She took a step back, bumping into the wall, as the flames of the Djinni came within inches of her nose. Though the features of its face remained obscure, two distorted blue sparks surrounded by rippling air hovered above her head, blaring at her like twin welder's flames.

Nerving herself, Rachel took a breath and stood tall. "I am Wilde Rachel len Wilde," she said. "The box containing your portal was given to us by your people. They implied that you would be able to help us with a Djinni who's injuring a woman not far from here."

The blue flames crept closer to her and tilted back and forth, as if regarding her from every angle. Rachel balled her fists and maintained her gaze while trying to swallow the feel of cotton coating her mouth.

From the far end of the room, the puppy poked its head around the side of the chair and whined. The Djinni swung toward the noise and swooped, its talon-like fingers reaching for the animal. Rachel gasped, her eyes following the Djinni's movement. The dog yelped and ducked behind the chair again. The creature lunged for it, jostling the armchair in its attempt to seize the whimpering creature. Unable to reach, it shoved the chair aside, startling the wide-eyed Morleys. The dog yelped and darted for cover and the Djinni once again lunged after it—only to rear back when Bach stood squarely in its path, blocking its way.

"I don't know what the hell is going on here today," Bach

said, rigid with anger, "but I don't care if you're a Djinni, a human, or a fucking unicorn—don't you dare touch my dog again!"

The room stilled. Without shifting from his position, Bach cast a glance at Rachel. "Where is it?" he asked.

"Right in front of you," Rachel replied. "You know," she added as the thought popped into her head, "that's the second time it's obeyed an order from you."

"So," Bach said slowly, "that maybe means it has to do what I say?"

"I don't know."

"I know what it does mean," Leda chimed in, disentangling herself from Simon's grasp. "It means the Djinni understands English."

"That's true," Rachel said. "Give it another order."

"Like what?"

"Anything," she pressed, gesturing at the collection of blue light. "Do it."

"Okay." Bach opened his mouth, but no command came out. Looking slightly perplexed, he shook his head and tried again. "Um . . . make yourself visible . . . if you can . . . please?"

An eerie hiss erupted, like air escaping a punctured tire. Then the air folded and puckered as a form, emerging from nothingness, crept into view.

The torso appeared first—a thick, rounded chest that tapered sharply to the waist. Six limbs sprouted from the torso as four hands and two feet simultaneously materialized independently, the limbs gradually growing to connect with them. The creature's bluish flesh rippled continuously, a steady flow of rolling flame with ill-defined boundaries. The head appeared last, close to the ceiling, large and domed. The ears resembled fins and gently flapped against the head. Each nostril of the broad nose was split several times up the side, like gills on a fish. The eyes were perfectly round and a shocking shade of green.

When the creature was fully formed, he cast a glance at every person in the room. When he saw that all eyes were on him, he pinched his eyes shut and snorted; a faint string of words sizzled from his throat.

"What was that?" Rachel asked, leaning forward.

"He called us filth," Leda said as she took up her crutches. "Filth, trash, or something like that. The language he's speaking is quite archaic, but—"

"The language you speak," the Djinni hissed, "is inferior. I detest the feel of these words in my mouth. I would prefer to gargle sewage."

Disdain oozed from his every word and thickened the air long after the room went silent. After exchanging glances with the Morleys—Leda looked fascinated, Simon bewildered—and Bach, Rachel stepped forward.

"Nice to meet you too," she said. "You're welcome, by the way."

The Djinni snarled at her, his indigo lip curling halfway up his cheek. "Are you fishing for gratitude, Arcanan?"

"We did let you out of that box."

"*You* did not." He swung his head completely around until his chin was perched above his spine and he was staring at the unsettled Morley siblings. "Nor did you," he said to Leda. "Certainly not you," he snapped at Simon, whose mouth was hanging wide open. The Djinni continued to turn his head, completing a full circle atop his body, then glared down at Bach. "It was you," he spat.

"It *was* me," Bach said. He stared up at the creature, his eyes dancing with electric sparks. "You've been in that box a long time, huh? Last time you were out, you were part of a cadre of Djinn that Solomon brought into his service."

"Enslaved," the Djinni said, the word rumbling deep in his chest.

"Most of the others were freed when he died," Bach continued, "but Solomon didn't feel comfortable breaking the seal that held you. He felt you were a danger to humans. There's a lot of blood on your hands."

The Djinni roared, his cavernous throat loosing a voice that boomed through the house, shaking walls and cracking glass. Bach held his ground, but the other three humans stumbled backward. Rachel smacked into the wall behind her and Leda and Simon thudded into each other. The puppy yelped and huddled behind his master, shivering.

The Djinni exhaled the stink of rotting fish through his pointed yellow teeth—an odor Rachel could smell across the room—as he thrust his face into Bach's. "Another," he said. "Another beast with eyes in the unseen."

"Another?" Bach asked.

"The king," the Djinni bitterly clarified. "Your cursed forefather. He was a seer as well."

Bach's eyes glittered. "Cool."

"Okay, you're clearly unhappy to be here," Rachel said. She stepped to Bach's side and looked up at the tall being, locking eyes with him. "But we need you. We're having a problem with one of your people and we were told, indirectly, that you would be able to help."

"Your problems do not interest me, sow." The Djinni waved his third hand at Rachel, his webbed fingers fanning her with the salty odor of his skin. "I have no obligation to assist you. You are but a seed caught in my teeth."

Though the Djinni's words were overtly rude, Rachel found that she wasn't offended. She also quickly recognized that his bluster didn't match his actions. "Then why are you still here?" she asked. Filled with a competitive need to hold her own, she glared at the glowering Djinni and crossed her arms over her chest. "Why not just bolt when the lid of your box was opened?"

The blue creature tilted his head. A wrinkle climbed his nose.

"Because," he said, "I am bound to the king."

"The king is dead," Leda said. "He's been dead for thousands of years."

"I am aware of that. However, in his absence," he said, rolling his eyes, "I am reduced to obeying him." He pointed a long, webbed finger at Bach, who took half a step back and blinked rapidly at the claw thrust in his face. Fin-ears flapping and a purplish flush flowing through his skin, the Djinni offered the slightest of bows in Bach's direction. "How," he snarled, "may I serve you, sir?"

PART

GAINING / LOSING

R epeatedly,
he swept into
the woman's bedroom.

Once inside,
he pressed
the air from
her ailing body,
weakening her further
but prolonging her illness.

Then,
just as swiftly,
he fled,
exiting before
the boy
 could find him.

During his most recent attack,
the boy reacted to his presence
but, after a moment

of visible doubt,
chose not
to rush to his mother's side.

He grinned.

Soon, the child would second-guess
everything he sensed.

Soon, the boy would not react.

Soon, the woman would die.

Soon, he could go home.

With a creak and a hiss,
the invisible door unsealed
and swung open,
a tall rectangle
punched out of the scenery,
giving him his first view
of the real world
in thousands of years.

Jubilation filled him
and his flames blazed wildly
as the new air of a distant place
blasted through the passageway.

Feather-light with elation,
he plunged through the doorway

and left the island
for the first time
in thousands of years.

His joy vanished almost at once.

He was beholden
to another human,
a new jailer,
descendant of the former.

He felt it
in his brand,
in his core.

Iron weight filled him up.

He was not free.

Is this *the king's scion?*

A piteous, skeletal man—
barely a man—
with not a hint
of his forefather
on his sallow face.

How could this scarecrow
possibly have descended
from a king who commanded
a legion of Djinn?

Invisible to the gawking humans,
he should have fled
and never looked back,
burn mark be damned.

But
the Arcanan woman
saw him
and knew him.

And then he—
impulsively,
regrettably—
lunged for the yapping animal.

The pale man barked an order.

By his brand,
he knew for sure.

The pain returned.

Freedom
remained
a dream.

30
PERSPECTIVE

"Y ou have to serve me?"

"Yes," the Djinni growled.

"Me?"

"Yes."

"For how long?"

"For as long as you command."

Still scrubbing the dog urine from the floor, Bach glanced up at the blue Djinni, who towered over him. The idea that this massive being was going to obey him seemed laughable. Bach felt it would be more appropriate to beg him not to hurt him. "Is this, like, a three wishes kinda deal?"

"No, simpleton," the Djinni replied. "There are no limitations on my enslavement. I am bound to your orders."

"Okay." Bach pitched the scrub brush into a bucket of soapy water and climbed to his feet. "Well," he said, still skeptical, "I'm ordering you not to hurt my dog—ever."

"Yes . . . sir," the Djinni said through his bared teeth. Under his breath, he added, "Muck-mouthed swine."

"And please stop insulting us," Bach added. "It's totally un-called for."

The Djinni turned up his nose as if he smelled something disgusting. "Very well."

Bach carried the bucket into the kitchen, passing by Rachel and the Morleys, who were all seated at the table. The three of them watched the Djinni's every move, their eyes glued to his undulating blue flesh. It was mesmerizing. When looking at it, Bach was reminded of a lava lamp.

He tipped the bucket over the sink, pouring out the dirty water. "Why *did* you attack my dog?" he asked over his shoulder. The water sloshed as he jostled the bucket, splashing onto the counter. "He wasn't hurting you."

"I . . ." The Djinni closed his eyes, all four fists balled. "I am hungry."

"You were gonna eat him?" Bach spun around. "He's not food! He's my pet!"

"It is an inferior beast with no purpose."

"*Tulira*," Rachel said quietly.

"That doesn't mean you can eat him." Bach tossed the empty bucket and brush under the sink and then charged toward the front door, whistling sharply. The puppy scurried to Bach's side —tail tucked, ears flat, one eye on the Djinni. Speaking softly to soothe his friend, Bach opened the door. With one last glance at the glowering Djinni, the dog bolted into the yard and slipped under the porch.

"I left half a bucket of chicken in the fridge," Bach said as he closed the door. "You can eat that."

"You serve chickens in buckets?" the Djinni asked, his eyes narrowed to green slits. "Do you also eat from troughs?"

"It's not a *bucket* bucket," Bach said. "It's a *chicken* bucket."

"Repulsive," the Djinni said with a shudder.

"It's chicken. Do you want it or not?"

The Djinni grumbled under his breath, turned away, and slouched into the kitchen. Bach approached the kitchen table and reached for a chair while watching the Djinni turn his head in a full circle. *Too many arms, moving blue skin, webbed fingers and ears,* he thought, *and his head spins around like "The Exorcist" kid. He should creep me out more than he does.*

"What and where is a 'fridge'?" asked the creature.

"That thing there," Rachel said, pointing.

The Djinni approached the refrigerator, tilting his head back and forth. Leaning close, he wrapped the webbed fingers of one hand around the handle and pulled cautiously. The door creaked open, exhaled a frosty puff, and cast its light over the kitchen. The Djinni's jaw fell open. He crouched low to closer examine the interior.

"Remarkable," he said, tapping the light bulb with one finger. "It is quite cool."

"That's the point of a refrigerator," Rachel said. "To keep food from spoiling."

"Obviously. I'm amazed that humans could invent something so useful."

Bach saw Simon raise an eyebrow as he glanced at his sister, and Leda shake her head. Irrationally, Bach felt embarrassed, as if by being the one to open the box he was responsible for this poor behavior.

"Yeah," Rachel said sarcastically, rolling her eyes. "We never invent anything useful. Like a refrigerator. Or a portal box."

The Djinni's shoulders tensed. Shooting daggers at Rachel, he said, "Tart-mouthed whore."

"What the hell?" Leda said. "I just heard Bach order you to stop insulting us!" Whirling on Bach, she pinned him with her eyes. "Right?"

"Uh, yeah," he said. Feeling awkward, he looked back at the Djinni. "I did ask you to stop that. Okay?"

The Djinni's round eyes swept over the meager contents of the refrigerator and quickly locked on to the only bucket-shaped object. He seized the red and white cylinder and plunged two hands inside. "It is of no consequence. Tartness of speech is a virtue among Arcanan women, and there is no word for 'whore' in their language."

"But you . . . really?" Leda stared at the Djinni a moment and then her eyes, aglow with the sparks of her hungry mind, scanned the tabletop. "No word for the world's oldest profession?" she whispered rapidly. "I need to write that down. Where's my notebook?"

"That really doesn't insult you?" Simon asked Rachel.

"No," she said. "I don't really understand the word 'whore.' I mean, I understand that it's someone who has sex in exchange for money, but I don't see why that's an insult. A person can do what she wants with her own body. And money . . ." She uttered a disgusted grunt. "When I decided to work as a collector, I had to take a class to learn about currency. I had so much trouble with the concept that I had to take it twice." She shook her head. "As an insult, 'whore' seems pretty tame."

"I gotta tell ya," Simon said, "from my perspective, it doesn't sound that tame."

It didn't sound tame from Bach's point of view either. The creature was obviously trying to push the limits of his instructions—and Bach didn't like it. Yet he couldn't bring himself to speak up. Descendant of a legendary king or not, he wasn't comfortable giving orders.

"Perspective is everything," said the Djinni as he popped a chunk from the bucket into his mouth. There was a loud crunch as he bit down. His eyes closed and he exhaled through his nose, the many nostrils flexing and expanding. "I imagine from your perspective an Arcanan insult would sound quite tame. Perhaps if I called you an isolated, idling hoarder?"

Shrugging, Simon looked at Bach, who shook his head.

"What the hell does that even mean?" Simon asked the creature.

"Ask the tart-mouthed whore."

"Hey!" Rachel yelled at the Djinni. At the sound of her ire, Bach shifted his weight away from her. "Take your condescending attitude and shove it up your ass, or wherever your people shove things."

The creature ignored her and continued to eat, his teeth crunching behind his smiling lips.

"Isolated . . . idling . . . hoarder," Leda murmured as she scribbled in her notebook.

Deciding he couldn't let this continue, Bach stood up and put himself between the kitchen table and the Djinni. "Looks like you're a fan of the chicken," he said.

"It is edible," the Djinni said through a stuffed mouth, "but insufficient in quantity."

"So . . . more chicken?"

"Indeed."

The Djinni thrust the bucket at Bach's chest, returned to the refrigerator, and opened the door slowly, his wide eyes fixated on the glowing bulb inside. Bach turned to toss the bucket into the trash but stopped when he looked inside.

Brow furrowed, he brought it to the table. "This thing's full," he whispered.

Rachel squinted at him. "What?"

"Look." He turned the bucket to show them the contents: a

pile of meat and fried skin. "That's all the chicken. What the hell did he eat?"

"Probably the bones," Leda said.

"The bones?"

"Sure. I've read legends about Djinn that say they eat bones and dung."

"Dung?" Simon gawked. "Jesus."

"Would he like the dog's shit?" Rachel asked, shooting the Djinni an irritated glance. "I'd be happy to make that happen."

"No way," Bach said, shaking his head. "I'm not giving any-body shit to eat."

"If that's what he wants—"

"Ra," he said, louder and firmer, "I'm not giving him dog shit." He straightened up and put the bucket on the table. "There's a chicken place just up the street. I'll run out and get some more. He's a guest here, I'm gonna treat him like one."

"A guest?" Rachel scoffed. "No. You are a guest, in that you were invited and you stay here with my permission. He's neither of those things."

"Well, where is he supposed to stay if not here?"

"His box."

"What?" Bach looked stunned. "Why?"

"He's hostile!" Rachel said, leaning forward on the table. "He hates humans, and you said he was locked up all these cen-turies because he's dangerous. I don't want him wandering around this house while I sleep. It's bad enough I have to hear that daemon thumping around in the dark. At least the daemon's small and gets out of my way when I tell it to. That Djinni's huge and he keeps lobbing insults that border on threatening. I want him back in his box when you're not here to—"

A creak split the air, cutting her off. Seconds later, there was a splintering snap. All eyes turned toward the living room threshold. The Djinni stepped into view, crossed a pair of arms over his chest, and, with his other hands, tossed two pieces of wood onto the table.

The larger of the two pieces clattered to a stop in front of Leda. She picked it up, examined it, and then held it out for the others to see. "The box," she said.

"And the lid," added Simon, holding up the smaller block of wood.

Rachel cursed and snatched the two pieces from the Morleys. She shoved the lid back into place and tried to straighten the twisted hinges, to no avail. No matter what she tried, the lid popped off and clattered to the tabletop. Cursing again, she slammed both fists onto the table and then pushed away from the table, rose, and stalked away.

After watching her mutter darkly under her breath and pace the room for a while, Bach glanced back at the Djinni to find him also watching her, a smirk on his blue face.

"Well, that's settled," Bach said with a sigh. "I'm gonna get more chicken."

Simon perked up. "Hey B, get me some biscuits?"

"Okay. Ra, Leda, anything?"

"What?" Leda was holding the box up to her face and tilting it back and forth, inspecting the interior. "Oh . . . nothing for me, thanks."

"Take him with you," Rachel said.

"What?"

"Take him with you," she repeated, pointing at the smug Djinni. "You're the only one he has to listen to. If you're leaving, he goes with you."

Bach looked the Djinni up and down, from his towering head

to his webbed feet. "Kinda think someone's gonna notice him."

"Figure it out," Rachel said. She scowled at the Djinni, who continued to smirk down at her as if she were a small child throwing a tantrum. "I need to call some people and find out just how much I'm allowed to interfere in the El Sayeds' lives."

"I thought your Central Office had big plans for Naji," Leda said.

"True, but that doesn't give me license to jump into the middle of their problems. I need to know what I'm allowed to do and how I'm allowed to go about doing it." Rachel sighed and rubbed her face. "I really wish I'd never volunteered for this job."

"Probably good that you did," Leda said.

"Why's that?"

"Probably not everyone in your position would've tried to help that kid. And he needs help." Leda turned to the Djinni. "He does, right?"

"If," the Djinni mumbled through a yawn, "the Djinni the Arcanan describes is, as she claims, assaulting a human woman, then the family in question is certainly in danger of harm."

"And you could help, right?"

"It is unlikely that human intervention will be sufficient."

"So," Leda pressed, "*you* could help, right?"

The Djinni rolled his eyes. "If so ordered, I am capable of providing assistance."

"You'd need to be ordered to help a child?" Leda asked sharply.

"It is none of my affair."

Leda shot the Djinni some intense side-eye. "And here you were talkin' shit about humans. Doesn't sound like you have a moral high ground to stand on."

The Djinni stared at her, lip curled his lip, but she met his gaze with equal resolve.

Between their standoff and Rachel still cursing under her breath, Bach felt the air getting thick and sticky with emotion. He desperately wanted to get out of the house.

"Let's just go," Bach said to the Djinni. "Just come with me, okay?"

"Very well." The Djinni tossed a last look at Leda. "Clan-less doll."

Confusion washed over Leda's features and she stared at the Djinni, lips parted in a silent question. Rachel, meanwhile, spat a string of angry Arcanan words at the Djinni, who responded with a barely audible chuckle.

Bach looked back and forth between all the beings in the room, then settled his gaze on the Djinni. "No idea what that was about, but I'm pretty sure it's your fault. Let's just go."

The Djinni turned his back and strolled out of the room toward the front door, Bach a ways behind him.

As Bach turned to leave, he heard Leda, over the sounds of scribbling, murmur, "Clan-less . . . doll."

AZRAQ

"**Y**ou're gonna need to make yourself invisible again, but I want you stay near me at all times," Bach said.

The Djinni offered Bach a mock bow. "As you wish."

As they crossed through the black passage, Bach experienced the same brief but overpowering sensation he felt every time he traveled it: his head was completely drained of sightbeyond. The utter lack of ebb and flow in the tide of data that occupied his every waking moment was replaced by a vacuum. The silence screamed at him like an unhinged hermit—but just before it became unbearable, he reemerged into the world. In an instant, his mind was awash with fresh information, and he relaxed.

A rustle announced the Djinni's exit from the passage just behind him. Bach glanced over his shoulder and saw only a slight distortion in the air—a strange wrinkle akin to light and shade dancing on the surface of water.

"So," he said, thrusting his hands into his coat pockets as he walked, "what's your name?"

The shimmer kept pace with him, silent.

"I need to call you something," Bach said. "I don't wanna keep calling you 'Djinni.' I mean, that seems kinda rude."

The shimmer floated along without responding. Bach shook his head.

"Look," he said, "I'm not gonna order you to tell me your real name. If you'd rather keep it to yourself, I'm cool with that. I hate my name too. That's why I go by 'Bach.' Just give me something to call you. Anything you want."

The wrinkle in the air fluttered, then the distortion quietly grunted and a disembodied voice said, "Azraq."

"Azraq," Bach repeated. "Is that your real name?"

"No."

"Hmm. Okay. I'll call you that."

At the end of the block, Bach and his companion entered a restaurant with floor-to-ceiling windows and a crooked sign. Waves of hot air rushed into the street as Bach opened the door, releasing the aroma of cooking oil and meat. He was ordering a regular bucket when something poked him twice in the back, striking like a viper's fangs between his ribs. Flinching, he canceled his initial order and asked for two extra-large drumstick buckets instead, plus Simon's biscuits.

No sooner had he stepped into the street than one bucket was seized by invisible hands. It disappeared into thin air, and muffled crunching ensued.

"Give me back the meat when you're done," Bach said. "I can't afford to throw away food." He looked down at the plastic bag hanging from his arm. "Guess I'm eating chicken for the next few days."

The wrinkled air grumbled a string of foreign words. The mildly threatening tone left Bach exhausted. He was just getting his life back on track after six months out of his mind. He didn't have the energy or mental fortitude to deal with this.

"What is it now?" Bach asked through a sigh.

"I am awaiting your forthcoming command," the Djinni said.

"Oh yeah? What command is that?"

Azraq spat. A wad of chicken skin struck the sidewalk near Bach's feet.

"Money," the Djinni snarled. "Gold, silver, diamonds . . . Humans always make the same demand. It was the first thing commanded by that damned king."

"Oh." Bach fished a biscuit out of the bag and took a bite. "No thanks."

"No thanks?" The distortion circled behind Bach and approached him from the opposite side. "What deception is this?"

"Deception? No. I just don't wanna take somebody else's stuff."

The wrinkle thrust itself close to Bach's face. "Explain yourself."

Bach drew back and turned his face aside to avoid the Djinni's breath, a putrid cocktail of old fish and new chicken. "Um . . . 'kay. You'd have to get that stuff from somewhere, right? It can't just appear out of thin air. I'm not gonna order you to steal. I don't want anything I didn't earn."

The distortion inched closer, nearly connecting with Bach's nose. His skin crawling from the assault on his personal space, Bach ducked, sidestepped the Djinni, and continued on his way, but he could feel his companion's eyes boring into his head.

He tried not to let it bother him. The Djinni wasn't human, after all. Maybe the rules of social interaction were different for his people. Besides, he had been imprisoned for thousands of years. Confinement like that would mess with anyone's mind. Maybe that was why Azraq was so arrogant and challenging; maybe it was just an act that allowed him to cope with the difficulties of his life. *Or,* Bach reluctantly thought as he listened to the crunching of chicken bones, *maybe Azraq's just an asshole.* He took another bite of biscuit and kept his gaze on the path ahead.

"You refuse that which you did not acquire by your own hand?" the disembodied voice asked, its tone threaded with disbelief and suspicion. "Are you not living under a roof not your own, by the charity of that Arcanan woman?"

"Yes," Bach said, "and I'm gonna repay her for everything. Don't know how yet, but I will."

The Djinni did not respond and Bach saw no reason to press the issue. He had a hard enough time convincing himself that he would be able to return Rachel's kindness without having to convince someone else. He knew what was in his heart, but he could guess that an outside observer would find his determination comical and pointless; after all, he was unemployed and nearly broke. But if the Djinni thought he was nothing but a moocher, he didn't mention it.

Bach turned off the main street and down the alley toward the passageway. Before he could step over the shaded threshold, the wrinkled air blocked his path.

"Then," asked the Djinni, "what is expected of me while I am in your service?"

"I told you," Bach said, "we need your help to stop that other Djinni."

"And then?"

"What do you mean, 'and then?'"

The shimmer fluttered, shrinking and growing in the shaded light of the alley.

"When the offender is removed," Azraq said, "what is to be my function? How am I to serve you?"

Bach's shoulders slumped and he sighed. "Dude, I really

don't need or want anyone to serve me. Kinda makes me squeamish just thinking about it. When we're done with that other Djinni, I'd rather you just took off."

"You won't return me to the box?"

"No. Even if you hadn't broken it, I wouldn't put you back in there. I mean, I get the feeling you've done some bad shit, but that was what—three thousand years ago? That's a long damn prison sentence."

"You will . . . release me?"

There was a strange tone to the voice that Bach had not heard before: inquisitive, submissive, and oddly genuine.

"Release?" he repeated. "You mean, free you?"

"Yes."

"I will if I can," Bach said. "Can I?"

"I do not know." One of Azraq's hands materialized before Bach's face. He held open his fingers, revealing a dark scar nestled in the palm. "This is the mark of my enslavement," he said. "It is the king's mark. Thousands of years ago, I was captured and rendered unconscious. When I awoke, this mark had been branded into my skin. I have no memory of how it was placed there. As long as it remains, so does my bondage. While it mars my body, I am compelled to obey the sons of the king. It is by this mark that I knew you. It is this that binds me to you. If I am to be free, this must be erased."

The hand disappeared back into the shimmer, but the sight of it was burned into Bach's mind. In a flash of sight-beyond, he experienced Azraq's memory of the scar's birth. For one immeasurable moment, he felt the pain of the brand and smelled the scorch rising from his skin, both unpleasant and unfamiliar. The Djinni, who had only rarely known the phenomenon of smoke, had been horrified by the odor. In that moment, there had been anger and fury, followed by defeat, hopelessness, and resignation. It had been the first moment of a lifetime of slavery.

The moment fled but it left a coat of bile in Bach's mouth.

"I'm sorry," he said at last. "That's horrible. And I'm sorry that I don't know how to undo it. Still, I'm not about to rope you into serving me. I just wanna help that kid and his family. They don't deserve whatever that Djinni is doing to them. And, besides, I owe Rachel a big debt—I wanna help her with this. When it's taken care of, as far as I'm concerned, you can go."

Azraq was still; the blend of light and shadow that was his hidden body rippled gently. Bach waited, casting expectant glances behind the Djinni at the passage to Rachel's house.

The half-consumed bucket reappeared, thrust out of the shimmer. Bach grunted as it struck him in the gut.

"Warn me next time, okay?" he said as he tucked it under one arm.

No response. Bach glanced around but saw no sign of the wrinkled space. For a moment he wondered if the Djinni had entered the passage, but then he spotted the distortion behind him, on its way back to the street.

"Where is this market?" Azraq called out.

"What? Where are you going?"

"Where is this offending Djinni that I am to remove?" he asked. "If this task is to be the only obstacle between me and my freedom, then I would tackle it now and be done." The shimmer oscillated at the intersection of the street and the alley, its peculiar puckering effect intensifying. Suddenly, it bolted across the street.

"It is there—I sense its presence," he called out. "The matter will be settled momentarily."

"Wait!" Heart thundering, Bach chased after him, struggling

to keep a grip on the food. "I'm gonna text Ra! Don't do anything until she says it's okay! Azraq, do you hear me!?"

The wrinkle raced ahead of him and darted out of view.

Bach fought with the bag and bucket to free up one hand for his phone as his mind scanned through a long list of undesirable outcomes to this development.

"This is not gonna get me outta Ra's debt," he said. He typed furiously, drumsticks bouncing from the open bucket onto the sidewalk, as he speed walked after Azraq.

AGREE TO DISAGREE

The defective daemon huddled in a corner near the front door, its ripped and dirty coat hanging limply from its invisible form. The neck hole sagged to the side, offering Rachel an unobstructed view of the seemingly vacant space within the coat. She wondered if the daemon was looking at her. More and more often, while wearing her glasses, she had caught the unwelcome creature with its eye fixed on her, tracking her every move. Then again, she also saw it staring at other things: the wall, the floor, a table, or the empty air. She didn't know if there was intent in the direction of its gaze, and she didn't care enough to ask. All she knew for sure was that the longer it shared the house with her, the creepier it acted.

Faced with the possibility that it was watching her now, she turned her back on it, leaned one shoulder into the wall, and hunched over her phone, trying to convince her brain that the creature was nothing more than an old coat left on the floor. Still, the thought of it lingered.

I bet all this conspiracy crap means no one is prioritizing the repair of this riot daemon. I'm gonna be stuck with it until I move out. Ugh. I can't wait to go home.

On the other end of her phone call, two voices argued. Ms.

Dokgo was arguing in favor of recruiting Naji for the Arcana, especially in the face of the possible terrorist threat. The opposing voice (belonging, Rachel believed, to Ms. Ladera) maintained that there was no terrorist threat and this whole situation was, at best, a Notan–Djinn dispute, which meant Arcanan intervention of any kind was inappropriate. Every time Ms. Ladera adhered to rules and facts, Ms. Dokgo increased her volume until she was very nearly screaming. Ms. Ladera's voice stayed calm, but Rachel thought she could detect a slight strain—a small but undeniable note of defeat that was destined to overrun her resolve. Rachel held the phone a few inches from her ear and waited for the two women to finish their battle. In the meantime, she listened to the other argument taking place within her earshot— one between the Morley siblings.

"I'm not saying it's not weird," Simon said, "I'm just saying I don't get why you give a shit."

"How can you not understand?" Leda asked. "Don't you get the cultural significance of a society that has no word for 'whore' but considers 'isolated' and 'clanless' to be fighting words?"

Simon looked bored. "Not really."

"It's *huge*! Not having a family is a bigger insult than selling your body! That's shocking by our standards! It has so many implications!"

"Like what?"

Leda sputtered, staring at Simon as if he had just jammed a finger up his nose. "'Like what?'" she echoed. "Really? For one thing, it means Arcanan culture places greater importance on being connected to family and society at large than on being chaste. In fact, from the way Rachel describes it, her society couldn't care less how much or how little sex a person is having."

"I don't care how much sex anyone's having."

"Oh, bullshit," she said, scoffing. "Do you know how many times I've heard you call a girl a 'slut'?"

"That's not about her having sex," Simon said. "It's more about how she acts. Or maybe how she looks."

"Then think of it this way: The very fact that English has multiple words to shame a woman for how much sex she tells you something significant about *our* culture. The fact that Rachel's culture doesn't have a single word for that . . . the implication is that her people don't feel the need to shame women for sexual things."

"Who's shaming women?" Simon asked, spreading his arms wide. "Where the hell are you getting this?"

"Oh my God, I can't even." Leda pressed her forehead into her palms. "I can't walk from the parking lot to my office without some asshat shouting, 'Show me your tits!' or 'Love that chocolate ass!'"

"They think you're hot. How's that shaming you?"

"Holy shit!" Leda exploded. "You're an idiot! How the hell did the same woman give birth to us?"

Rachel did not understand their conversation. If any Arcanan man spoke to a woman the way Leda described, his clan would get an earful about it. If his disgraceful behavior continued, the community would most likely demand that his clan disown him. If they refused, the whole clan might be cut off from communal support and possibly even lose citizenship. That Leda and Simon could argue about such a thing struck her as otherworldly. Surely there weren't two sides to this issue.

"Can't you respect my opinion?" Simon said.

"Your opinion disrespects me!" Leda snapped back.

On the distant end of the phone, Rachel could no longer

hear Ms. Ladera over Ms. Dokgo's repetitive shrieks. It seemed logic had finally bowed to volume.

Before the victor could fully commandeer the line to give her instructions, Rachel felt her phone vibrate, indicating an incoming text. She allowed Ms. Dokgo to continue crowing while she read the message—just two short sentences from Bach, both of which tested her mastery of English: *Geni gn 2 mrkt. Wht shd I do?*

Rachel muttered one of her mother's most commonly used oaths, a string of words that loosely translated to "Go sweat blood from your ass crack." The daemon stirred behind her, momentarily drawing her eye, but then it settled into statue stillness again.

Her jaw tight, Rachel brought the phone to her ear and emitted a quick cough. "Pardon me," she said in formal Arcanan, "but I'm going to have to ask the two of you to wrap this up. The, uh, situation has become urgent."

OTHER

A day
like each before.

Until,
perched on a roof,
he sensed the other—
and then saw him,
an isolated,
sentient
heat distortion
soaring up the street.

The power
of the other
radiated in waves,
so potent
that he could
feel it
from the rooftops.

He smiled.

Another Djinni!
He had not seen
one of his kind
since coming to
this world.

Then he frowned.
With all the world
to choose from,
why would
another Djinni
come here, now?

Fear seized him.

Had this other come
to interfere?

If he was robbed
of his vengeance,
he would lose
his chance
to restore
his honor.

If that happened,
he could not
go home.

He dove from
the roof

across the street
and into
the woman's window.

The other leaped
up from the street
and met him
in the bedroom.

There,
face-to-face,
he saw
past the distortion.

Blue and green,
four arms,
and webbing.

A Marid.

He now understood
why this other
had approached
without hesitation.

The Marid
were not known
for being
respectful.

"You cannot have her!"
he screamed.
"Nor the boy!
I am here
to repay an insult
the boy
has dealt me!"

"The insults
of children
do not interest me,"
the Marid replied.
"You will
forgo your vengeance
and leave.
If you refuse,
I will remove you."

Yellow and red, wings,
and four eyes.

An Ifrit.

That explained
the bluster.

The Ifrit
were not known
for cool-headedness.

He'd sensed
the Ifrit's influence long before
reaching the building.

The youngster
had spent
a great deal of time
around this building;
his residue was
everywhere.

This was quite
an obsession
to result from
a mere insult.

He frowned.
He did not want
his first interaction
with another Djinni
in millennia
to be hostile.

Then he smiled.
On the other side
of this hostile interaction
was his freedom.

Staring down
the Ifrit's scowl,
he filled with resolve.

Just an hour ago,
he had been
trapped
on his pocket island.

Now,
true freedom
was in sight.

This was a day
like none
before.

INDECISION

Bach arrived at the El Sayeds' store with his phone still in one hand and the quickly emptying bucket of chicken bouncing in the other. Even with Rachel shouting at him through the phone, demanding information, he could hear yelling from inside the market. The rough blend of voices made it difficult for him to pick out words from the cacophony, particularly as both Rachel and Mr. El Sayed were losing their grasp of English as they got louder.

He struggled to communicate what little he knew with Rachel, but he couldn't focus through all the noise. After a few more incomprehensible shouts, she hung up on him. Flustered, he pocketed his phone and charged into the market.

Mr. El Sayed's shouts boomed through the building, drawing some concerned stares from the smattering of customers perusing the aisles. Bach scanned the market. Though his voice was everywhere, the shop's owner was nowhere to be seen.

Following the sound, Bach ducked into the back room and peered up the staircase that led to the apartment above. A second voice, smaller but also shouting, finally reached his ears as a boy with a mess of dark hair appeared at the top of the stairs. He was pointing at something and shrieking, "Two! Four hands! There! There! With the other!"

"Is he blue?" Bach shouted. "Hey kid! The second one! Is he blue?"

Naji looked down at Bach and, without a hint of concern at this stranger's presence, nodded vigorously and pointed again, poking the air with one small finger.

"Yes!" he shouted back. "He's blue! He's with the other one! There!"

Bach dropped the chicken and raced up the stairs. Almost immediately upon reaching the top, he collided with Naji's father.

The older man jumped back, momentarily stunned beyond speech; then his expression of surprise hardened to suspicion and he demanded, "What the hell are you doing here?"

"I'm sorry to barge in, sir," Bach said as he brushed past the man. "I have to keep an eye on my—well, he's not exactly my friend, but it's my fault he's here, and I have to watch him. Sorry!"

Naji darted around his father, grabbed Bach's hand, and dragged him down the hall. They entered a bedroom littered with toys and books. Bach quickly located Azraq's shimmer floating near the window, its alien essence puckering the air like a shadow woven into light. He scanned the area but saw nothing else.

"Where's the other one?" he asked Naji. "Where's the one that's been haunting you?"

Naji pointed to a spot near Azraq, but Bach couldn't see anything there. If the other Djinni was there, he was better hidden than his blue counterpart.

Mr. El Sayed burst into the room, his dark eyes blazing and his fists balled. "I will call the police on you!" he said, shaking a fist a Bach. "Step away from my son this instant!"

"I know you won't believe me," Bach said, holding up his

hands, "but I'm here to help." His eyes flashed as a stampede of sight-beyond information charged through his mind. "Please believe me, Amr," he pleaded. "I'm not some punk like those little bastards who trashed your store, and I'm not like that drunk asshole who threw a brick through your window in the middle of the night. I'm not the one who's been making those threatening, racist phone calls, and I'm not the one who made that false police report about you being affiliated with terrorists. I'm no danger to your family, but there's someone here who is. Please let me help."

Mr. El Sayed tensed and froze. It was a reaction with which Bach was well-acquainted. This wasn't the first time someone had been so startled by his inexplicable knowledge that they couldn't react.

The expression on Mr. El Sayed's face shifted as his outrage quickly pushed him through his surprise. "You are the only intruder here!" He grabbed Bach's arm and yanked him away from Naji. "How dare you come into my home!"

The shimmer darted across the room, inserted itself between the two men, and shoved them each in the chest, driving them apart. The push sent a bolt of pain through Bach, promising to be a colorful bruise in the near future. Mr. El Sayed stumbled backward and struck the door frame with a gasp of half pain, half confusion. Rubbing his shoulder, his befuddled gaze swept the room as he mumbled something in Arabic. A deep voice erupted from the air where no person stood, responding to his words in Arabic as fluent as his own.

Mr. El Sayed's eyes darted to Bach, and widened when he saw that the younger man's lips were not moving.

"Don't push him, Azraq," Bach said. "We did barge into his house, you know."

"You are the key to my freedom," said the voice. "While that holds true, I will not allow you to come to harm."

"What about the other Djinni? What's he say?"

"Djinni," Mr. El Sayed said, eyes now saucer-wide. "How . . ."

Naji ran to his father, threw one arm around the man's leg, and held out the other toward the unseen menace, as if preparing to hold it at bay. Looking dazed, Mr. El Sayed laid one hand on his son's head as he stared at the empty spot that contained the rumbling voice.

"He is an Ifrit," Azraq said.

"Ifrit?" Bach repeated. "I thought he was a Djinni, like you."

"He is Djinn," Azraq said, his voice lowered to a growl, "but not like me. I am Marid, he is Ifrit. He is as unlike me as a gorilla is unlike you. And this particular Ifrit is a young, contemptible brat. He speaks to me, his social better and his elder of many centuries, without respect."

"Why is he here?"

"The boy brought him."

"It was an accident!" Naji wailed, tightening his grip on his father. "I didn't know!"

"Why's he attacking the kid's mother?" Bach asked.

"Safiya?" Mr. El Sayed took a step forward.

"I told you, Baba," Naji said, still holding out a protective hand. "She's not sick. A monster's hurting her."

"An Ifrit," Azraq said. "Call him what he is, boy."

"Ifrit," Naji said, testing out the sound of the word.

"He makes claims of avenging his integrity," Azraq told Bach. "He believes his social standing and that of his family will be ruined if he returns home without making the child suffer for drawing him into this world against his will."

"Is he still here?" Bach asked. "I can't see him."

"Yes," Azraq said. "He is standing there."

"Where?"

"There."

"You're invisible, dude. Can't see where you're pointing."

The voice grumbled and the shimmer started to expand. Rippling blue arms emerged from the air. Mr. El Sayed clutched at his child, his knees shaking, but Naji slipped out of his grasp and stood in front of his father with his arms crossed over his chest. The boy's big eyes watched with interest, not fear, as the Djinni materialized.

Mr. El Sayed was not so stoic; he made a strangled noise through clenched teeth and swayed back and forth. Alarmed, Bach grabbed him by the shoulders to steady him as he lowered himself to the floor then stared up at the huge blue creature, his mouth agape and his eyes wide.

Naji smiled at his father and patted his knee. "He's okay, Baba," Naji said. "He pulled the bad one away from Mama." He cast a gaze of admiration up at the four-armed being towering over him. "He's good."

Azraq peered down at the smiling child. He tilted his head slightly, squinting, and then turned to Bach. "There." He pointed to the far side of the room. "The Ifrit stands there."

Though he saw nothing, Bach advanced on the indicated area.

"Excuse me," he said, offering a nod in greeting. "Hi. You've been causing this family a lot of trouble. I'm gonna have to ask that you leave these people alone. If you could just go back where you came from . . ."

Azraq snorted through his many nostrils. "Do not be idiotic," he said. "That plebian filth is not going to obey you. If you want him to desist, I will have to remove him."

Anxiety nipped at Bach. He was unaccustomed to being put in a position of authority and was wholly uncomfortable with being expected to take control in this way. Furthermore, though he wanted to help, he did not want to accept responsibility for the well-being of this family. Nothing about the situation was making him eager to act.

"I . . . no. Can't do that. Ra hasn't given me instructions."

"There is no other possible solution to this problem," Azraq said, his nostrils flaring. "He is not going to vacate this building by choice and these humans are helpless before him. The Arcanan woman will agree. Let me remove him."

Bach's every urge to act ground to a halt. Not so long ago, he had been a raving lunatic under a bridge. Surely, he wasn't qualified to make a decision like this. "No," he insisted, his breath coming quicker now. "It's bad enough that we're here without Ra's permission. We need to wait. Don't touch him."

Suddenly, both Azraq and Naji snapped their attention to the far corner—the corner Azraq said the Ifrit occupied. A great whoosh of air roared through the room, sending toys, books, and clothes whipping up from the floor and slamming into the walls. Azraq bellowed with anger, and Naji dove into his father's chest.

Bach ducked and shielded his face; the force of the wind stung his eyes and made it difficult to see Azraq, but he could hear him shouting, his voice rising well above all other sound.

Without warning, Mr. El Sayed, with Naji in his arms, was knocked onto his side by an unseen force. The door swung shut with a bang, followed by a flash of light from the hallway outside.

Naji squealed, burst from his father's embrace, and rushed the door. After fighting the knob without success, he threw his meager weight against the door, but it didn't budge. Bach rushed to the boy's side and added his shoulder to the effort. The door was as immobile as a concrete wall.

"What the hell just happened?" Mr. El Sayed asked, climbing to his feet.

"I don't know," Bach replied, bewildered.

"He ran out!" Naji cried. He pounded his fists on the door and kicked as hard as he could. "The bad monster—the Ifrit! He ran out!"

"Assaulting the door is futile," Azraq said with a sigh. "Look."

He pointed with two of his hands and all three set of human eyes followed his gesture.

Bach felt the blood drain out of his head. The door's hinges had liquefied and re-hardened into brass lumps.

Feeling lightheaded, Bach put one hand on the nearest wall while grabbing his hair with the other. "What happened?"

"Your indecision happened," Azraq replied, jabbing one finger in his direction. "Hearing you refuse to order his removal, the Ifrit determined that he was free to act as he pleases until the Arcanan arrives. He then insulted me," the Djinni hissed through his teeth, "calling me a dog on a leash and a branded piece of livestock." He spat a flicker of white sparks. "Filth! He is most likely in the process of smothering the woman as we speak."

Naji shrieked and slammed his body against the immobile door so hard that he bounced off the wood and fell to the floor. "MAMA!" Naji screamed, jumping up and pounding his fists on the door. He ran to the window and tried to open the rusted latch. "MAMA!"

"Not h-happening," Mr. El Sayed stammered, his gaze never leaving the carpet. "*Hadha la ymkn 'an yahduth*. This cannot be happening."

"What will you do now, seer?" Azraq asked. He stepped closer to Bach and glared down at him through glowing eyes. "Do you have such faith in the Arcanan woman that you believe she will arrive in time to seize control of the situation? And what, in point of fact, do you expect her to do? What action could she take against an Ifrit, a being many times stronger than she? She is a daemon catcher," he said, his voice low and flat. "Far from the procurer of miracles you envision, she is a laborer— no better than a wrangler of stray dogs. She is as low and ordinary a human as ever you will see."

He leaned closer, his meaty breath bathing Bach's face. "But you . . . *You* are descended from kings. Your mind is a way station for the crossing paths of time. Most pertinent of all, you are the descendant and inheritor of the king who branded me."

Azraq glanced away and Bach followed his gaze. Naji, sobbing, was throwing toys at the window in a feeble attempt to break the glass. Mr. El Sayed was huddled on the floor, his entire body quaking.

"Look inward, if you must," the Djinni said, "and see within your excess of knowledge that I am right. I am a weapon waiting to be employed, but I am useless without the hand that wields me." He flared his many nostrils and flashed his pointed teeth. "What is your command?"

Azraq stood with both pairs of arms crossed over his chest, glaring at Bach. Heart thundering in his ears, Bach felt his resistance crumble under the weight of his unwanted leadership. A cold, hollow sensation occupied his chest.

He hardly heard his own voice slip through his lips.

"Go."

SAFIYA

Safiya El Sayed was half-gone into sleep, slipping into a hazy dreamscape, when distant noises tugged at her. Though her mind and body were heavy with exhaustion, she recognized the agitated cry of her son. And there was another voice, one she didn't know. She felt a tinge of alarm—but before she could drag herself into full consciousness, she heard her husband's voice rising above the others. She relaxed. Amr was there. Naji was with his father.

Sleep crept over her and she sank into its pillowy depths. No further sound broke the slumber seal and she eased into her dream. . . . Then, a world away, her child's terror-laden voice stabbed at her, stirring her mother-blood and puncturing the dream, which dissolved like sand.

Her eyes fluttered.

"Naji," she murmured over chapped lips.

The sickness that had left her bedridden for weeks returned all at once, slowly squeezing the air from her body. As with every time she experienced an attack of this nature, she closed her eyes, focused on her breathing, and whispered a prayer. The words drifted from her mouth like dandelion seeds in the breeze even as the weight on her chest grew heavier. The locket strung around her neck pressed down into her skin as if someone was pushing it toward her heart. The pressure blossomed into pain and then spread like fire until every nerve in her body was ablaze. She gasped and tried to scream but there was no breath left in her to do it.

Grabbing fistfuls of the sheets, she struggled to get out of bed, but a great weight pinned her to the mattress. Fear exploded into panic and the last of her energy burst throughout her body. She kicked, flailed her arms, and fought against the unseen thing holding her down. One arm knocked over a lamp, sending it crashing to the floor, and one foot smashed against the bed's footboard.

Unable to draw breath, her strength soon failed and she grew still. As her spark of life flickered, the barrier between worlds faded. She saw a huge being made of twitching yellow fire towering over her, its two clawed hands on her chest. Two red, flaming wings sprouted from its back, their span so wide that they, ghost-like, passed through the walls on opposite sides of the room. On the creature's face, she saw an expression of hateful determination.

Safiya's lips began to move again as she unconsciously resumed her prayer. The being's face rippled; it curled its lip, revealing a mouthful of pointed teeth and a forked red tongue. It pressed down on her even harder. Her eyelids fluttered and began to close.

There was a loud crash, and then an enormous blaze of blue cut through her vision. The weight on her chest suddenly vanished. She heaved a breath and filled her lungs, which instantly revived her. Rolling onto her side, she panted wildly. As she gasped for air, she cast her eyes about the room, searching for some sign of the creature she had seen in her breathless moments, but she saw nothing. *Of course there was nothing*, she reasoned, *it was just a hallucination brought on by my illness.* The vision seemed more distant and less real with each passing second.

Naji burst through the door and flew into her arms, nearly knocking the air from her lungs again. "Mama!" he shrieked, digging his fingers into her skin. His entire body was trembling. "Mama!"

"Naji," she rasped, smoothing his hair. "Why are you shaking? Are you cold? Have you been playing in the freezers again?"

"Safiya!" Amr lunged into the room, out of breath, his eyes wide and red-rimmed. He threw his arms around them both and held them to his chest. "Are you hurt?"

"No, no," she said, "but I think this illness is taking its toll on me."

A strange man entered the room. "Where are they, kid?"

"I think they went through the wall," Naji said. "Over there."

Cheeks trapped between her child's head and her husband's shoulder, Safiya watched the unknown blond man. His clothes were too big for his gaunt form and there were sunken hollows in his pallid face that gave him a sickly appearance, but his peculiar blue eyes sparkled with a young, healthy, ethereal energy. As he rushed by her, she caught a whiff of fried chicken. To her surprise, she discovered that she was hungry for the first time in days.

Her revived appetite overshadowed her exhaustion and gave her a gust of unexpected strength. She extricated herself from her husband's arms, straightened, and whispered, "Amr, who is this man?"

"I don't know," he said. "I think he means well."

"Azraq!" the man shouted at the wall. "Azraq! Can you hear me?"

Azraq? she thought, baffled. *"Blue?"* She tapped Amr on the arm. "He is shouting 'blue' at our wall. Why?"

Amr exhaled a blend of a chuckle and a groan and shook his slumping head. He pressed his face to her hair and hugged her tight. Squirming, she watched the blond man as he paced back and forth by the wall, pausing now and then to shout "blue" again.

"I don't understand," she said to her husband.

"I don't understand much of anything today," he said in reply. "I am just so thankful to find you unharmed."

"I only have a cold," she said.

"You're not sick, Mama," Naji said. "I told you! It's the monster!"

"Oh, Naji." She sighed. "Not again."

"It's the monster!" he said insistently. "But he's not really a monster. He's an Ifrit. The other Djinni said so."

"Ifrit? Djinni? Amr, what on earth is he talking about?"

"The Djinni," Naji repeated. "One is blue, and he's good. That man"—he pointed at the stranger—"brought him here."

Heedless of their conversation, the blond man moved to the window and scanned the world outside with such intensity that Safiya saw his shoulders quiver.

"Azraq," he said, "where did you go?"

Safiya's brow furrowed. Her son was babbling nonsense, her husband was an emotional wreck, and there was a stranger standing in her bedroom saying "blue" repeatedly—in her language—for no discernible reason. How on earth had her house gotten so out of control in her absence? This could not continue.

She sat up straight, adjusted her clothes, and smoothed her hair. "Amr, I have obviously been in bed too long. All of this silliness must stop. First"—she nodded in the stranger's direction—"this very odd man has no business here. Please ask him to leave. And then I should like to know why Naji is not in school, and why you are not at the register!"

Amr exhaled, and as the tension left his body, he seemed to deflate to half his size. He put his hand on his son's shoulder and squeezed. Resting his head against his father's side, Naji just grinned at his mother.

Safiya continued to stare at them, arms crossed over her chest, fingers impatiently drumming her arms.

At the far end of the bedroom, she noticed, the blond stranger was still staring out the window.

THE CHASE

The chase rocketed through
the between spaces of existence,
a patchwork forest of
corners, cracks, and edges.

Along protracted stretches of borderlines
dividing light from shade,
separating one minute from the next,
isolating one molecule from another,
Azraq pursued the Ifrit.

Muscles long restricted by the bounds
of a pocket dimension
felt their power return.

Like a dwindled fire suddenly tossed
a fresh supply of dry wood,
the light inside him roared and blazed.

Centuries of half-death and waking sleep
were cast aside
and he felt himself fully alive.

BLUE FLAME

He grinned at his fleeing prey
and threw every ounce of himself into the pursuit.

The pair flew through
walls and structures.
Streets turned to meadows
and into streets again.
Cities and nations fell into their wake
with not a footprint to keep.

The sun remained high,
a lone fixture in the fluid landscape,
but it quickly grew warmer
as the Ifrit fled south.

Cropland and greenery
shifted into swamps
and then vast expanses
of desert sand.

Oceans flitted into Azraq's peripheral vision,
filling his nose with misty salt,
but at each appearance of beach or cliff
the Ifrit bolted for land.

Clouds exploded overhead,
drenched the world,
and blinked out of existence.

Jungles grew into mountains and plateaus
as the air dried and cooled.

The scent of the sea grew stronger.

Water repeatedly appeared in their path
and the Ifrit leaped,
his immense speed propelling him
over the blue
and landing him on soil
again and again.

The earthen islands vanished,
and they passed over rocks and glaciers.

The unbroken sea loomed large
on the near horizon.

The Ifrit spread his enormous wings.

Azraq smirked.
The moment had come.

With his wings extended,
his prey could not
maintain the same pace.

As he struck his last footfall
and jumped,
Azraq closed the short distance
between them and pounced.

For a moment,
the Ifrit's wings held them aloft;

but before he could catch the wind,
Azraq grabbed the end of one wing
and yanked with all his might.

They spun in a corkscrew twirl,
cold air whistling through their ears.

The Ifrit's wings flamed,
a sunburst of red and yellow
that leaked into the standing world.

A colony of seals on the rocks beneath them
barked furiously
and plunged into the water.

Seabirds squawked and darted out of the way.

As the water rushed up to meet them,
the Ifrit shrieked in fear,
but Azraq clung to him,
dragging him down.

The ocean swallowed them.

The shock of cold flooded Azraq's body
but his blue Marid flesh
maintained its flaming integrity.

The Ifrit's flames, on the other hand,
were lost in the splash.

With a great sizzle,
his ignited body deadened
and his skin grew dull.

Azraq dragged his extinguished foe
from the waves
and onto the seals' rocks.

The Ifrit trembled,
his ashen skin
limp and clammy.

The wing in Azraq's hand was tattered,
ripped nearly in half,
its pieces swaying in the polar wind.
Flittering drops leaped
from scrapes and abrasions
like embers from a fire.

The Ifrit groaned
and hacked up a lungful
of seawater.

He lifted his thin face,
narrowed his eyes,
and bared his teeth.

"I must," he said.

Azraq looked at his quarry.
The excitement of the chase had subsided

and he sighed to see that his catch
seemed smaller when still.

"You must torture humans
for a foolish mistake?" he asked,
his great green eyes alight with disdain.

"You must exact revenge on a mere child
because he innocently drew you to his home
against your will?
Is your pride so fragile?"

"I cannot go home until I do!" the Ifrit said.
"You know this!"

In his raspy voice, Azraq heard anger
but also a painful longing.

Homesickness.

It was a feeling Azraq had felt
for so much of his life
that he had accepted it
as his default state of being.

"Are you so young that you cannot differentiate
between a deliberate act of malice
and a childish blunder?
Are they equal offenses
in your pitiful eyes?"

"Offense sees no age," said the Ifrit
with a weary huff.
"The boy insulted me.
If I let the insult stand
and return home unavenged,
everyone close to me
will shoulder the affront.
Shall I cause them all to suffer
for my failure?
The death of one human
keeps my family
in good standing
and my future intact.
What is the boy, or his mother,
compared to our collective success?
One life—
one paltry human life—
for the sake of many."

Trying to flex his torn wing,
the Ifrit winced and clenched his teeth,
his long claws digging into
the rock beneath them.

All four of his eyes locked on to
Azraq's marked hand.

"Did you not seek revenge, old man?
Did you quietly accept
the dishonor of that mark?"

Azraq looked at the burn mark in his palm,
the millennia-old sign of his enslavement.

For a moment, he felt himself
in the Ifrit's place.

Caught and branded by the king,
he had lusted for revenge
as madly and desperately
as this pup.

All the years of his youth were spent
howling for satisfaction.
To return home
without inflicting a wound . . .
unthinkable!

Then the moment passed,
age reasserted itself,
and his eyes cleared.

The king was dead.
Time had removed vengeance
from his hands
as age had removed it
from his heart.

"The scale you put forth
does not balance," he said.

"An insult is an insult!

Mine is no less than yours!"

"That you would equate our situations
speaks volumes about you," Azraq muttered.

The Ifrit snarled and lunged at his captor
but Azraq—
bigger, stronger—
caught his wrists
and wrenched his arms.

The Ifrit wailed, strained,
and then crumpled,
his wings drooping
in Azraq's grip.

"I have wasted enough time already!"
the Ifrit pleaded.
"Let me go!
Once I kill the woman,
I will go home and never bother
with this human realm again!
Is that not what you want as well?
To leave this detestable maggot world
and go home?
Is there anything you would not do
to be among your own kind again?"
A low moan escaped the Ifrit.
"In all this time among humans,
I have seen only you.
I have never been so alone."

The Ifrit exhaled heavily,
flimsy in Azraq's grip.
"I just want to go home,"
he whispered into the stone.
"I just want to go home."

He has seen only me?

The Djinn had been visiting this world
since long before Azraq's time.

They had always been here.

Then again . . .

Azraq's mind turned to the chase
that had just ended.

Not once in all those places they passed
had he seen or sensed another of their kind.
Not one.

He hurled his senses into the between
and searched—
he was an elder of his breed,
stronger than most;
his sharp senses were capable of
a wide reach—
but there were no Djinn.

Iron fingers gripped his heart.

In his day, the Djinn were everywhere.

Had they surrendered their holdings
in the human realm
and slunk back to their own world?

The Djinn he knew
were a conquering people,
never retreating
when they could expand.

Were they grown weak? Lazy? Stupid?

Azraq's chest constricted
and he closed his eyes
to contain
his disgust and despair.

This world had changed.

What was once a smattering of kingdoms
between vast frontier and wilderness
was now a continuous construction of
glass and metal.

If the humans could affect such change,
how wildly transformed
his people's world must be.

"All these centuries
I have longed to return to my home,"

he said quietly,
more to himself than to his prisoner,
"but now I wonder
if I would recognize it as mine."
He stared at the Ifrit,
limp and bleeding in his hands.
In his heart,
Azraq felt the pain of his
long-fortified hope crumbling.
"It would perhaps be better for me
to remember what once was
than to learn what is."

Lifting the compliant Ifrit,
Azraq held his wrists with one pair of hands
and his wings with the other pair.
The captive did not make a sound.

Azraq turned to face north.
"Would that the king's fool of a descendant
had never opened that box.
Nothing appeals to me so much now
as to dwell solely
in my memories."

Carrying the weight
of his melancholy,
he held his captive aloft
and ran.

PROBLEM SOLVED

S afiya El Sayed stood in her kitchen, a mug of hot tea in one hand and her other hand on her hip. Naji sat at the table, his loving gaze on his mother and his sneakered feet swinging over the tiled floor. Amr sat across from their son with his face in his hand, taking in slow, deep breaths.

Raising the cup to her lips and taking a sip, Safiya's eyes darted from her husband to her son and back again. The drink slipped down her throat, warming her from the inside, and she slowly exhaled through her nose, flexed her fingers around the mug, and brought it to her lips again. The fragrant steam of the tea bathed her face, the invigorating scent of mint steadying her nerves.

The blond stranger waited just over the kitchen threshold in the hallway. His electric blue eyes alternated between watching the master bedroom door and stealing glances at Safiya, whose cool stare never strayed from him.

One more sip and she set the mug on the counter, the ceramic cup clinking against the tile.

"So," she stated. "Djinn?"

"Yes ma'am," the blond man replied.

"Two of them," Naji said. "The bad one that hurt you and the good one that stopped him."

"Quiet, Naji," she said.

"But Mama—"

"Enough!" she shouted. "This is absurd!"

"Safiya," Amr said, lifting his head from his palms, "I saw it with my own eyes. It appeared out of nowhere in Naji's room and it spoke to me."

Safiya's lips drew to a thin line as she closed her eyes. "I blame my father," she said. "He is always filling Naji's head with his stories. But you, Amr—how could *you* be swept away by this?"

"It was real." He jabbed a finger into the tabletop. "Four arms, as tall as the ceiling, and blue skin that moved!"

"Ridiculous! You imagined it! And how could you let this strange man into our home?"

"He let himself in!"

"That's true, ma'am," the stranger interjected.

She shot him a scathing glare, and he cringed.

"Sorry about that," he said weakly.

"What about the door, Safiya?" Amr asked. "Did I imagine that as well?"

A flicker of doubt crossed Safiya's mind. Naji's bedroom door was cracked in half, each side crushed and splintered as if it had been struck by a battering ram. The El Sayeds had been married for nearly ten years; Safiya felt unshakably confident that her husband could not have caused such damage. She was equally sure that this underfed blond stranger was not strong enough to do it. Even the two of them together could not possibly have shattered a solid wood door.

And then there was the matter of the melted hinges. A blow torch, perhaps? But that would have taken a considerable amount of time, and Amr would never sit quietly while their son was being sealed into his room.

The door was a mystery. But it did not confirm the existence of Djinn.

"I do not know what happened to the door," she said. "I do know it was not caused by a Djinni."

"Two of them," Naji said. "The bad one locked us in, the good one busted us out."

"Quiet!" Safiya said. "Why are you even here, Naji? Why are you not in school?"

"I stayed home to protect you, Mama!" Naji said. "I had to be here to poof away the Ifrit!"

"'Poof?'" Safiya shook her head. "What on earth is poof?"

"Naji has a special gift, ma'am."

The blond man flinched and shrank into himself as Safiya narrowed her eyes at him. Though he couldn't meet her stare, he pressed on.

"Naji can move things, or people, over long distances," he said. "I have a friend from . . . a different place and her people know something about what Naji can do. I'm waiting for her to call me back right now."

"And who are you?" Safiya said, quickly losing patience with this intruder. "What was your name? 'Beak'?"

"Bach, ma'am."

"And this Djinni you claim to have brought to our home, what was his name?"

"He wouldn't tell me his real name, but he said I could call him Azraq."

"Azraq," she repeated. "That is Arabic for 'blue.' Your Djinni calls himself 'Blue'?"

Bach blinked and tilted his head. "I didn't know that," he said. "Makes sense. He is blue."

"It's an absurd name!"

"Hey now," he said, pulling himself up tall. "My name was 'Blue' for a while."

"What?"

"Yeah. For the six months I spent under a bridge. I was too crazy to tell anyone my name, so a guy who looked out for me named me 'Blue.'"

"Ah!" Amr smiled at Bach. "You are the crazy girl's friend! The one she spoke of!"

"Yes sir," Bach said, smiling back.

Feeling bombarded with information, Safiya held up her hands and shook her head. Six months under a bridge? Too crazy to say his name? The crazy girl's friend? Everything this odd man said seemed to beg a thousand questions, and she didn't have a damn to spare for any of them.

"I believe I passed out when I could not breathe earlier," she said decisively. "Melted hinges, Djinn, and poofing—the world cannot be this mad. I must be hallucinating."

"Safiya." Amr stood and put his hands on his wife's shoulders. "You are safe. Naji is safe. We have a broken door but nothing important was lost. Let us be grateful."

"But this man!" she said, pointing at Bach. "I do not understand! Why—"

A sudden gust of wind whipped through the kitchen, turning her half-asked question into a gasp. Safiya was sure the windows were closed, and yet now there was a wild breeze swirling around the apartment—hot and foul, like a devil's breath. Naji squeaked and jumped from his chair. He stood between his parents and the twisting wind, his arms thrown out in a protective gesture.

"Azraq!" Bach shouted as he held an arm in front of his face and backed into the wall.

There was a crackle of dim light in the kitchen corner. Before Safiya's eyes, the very air ripped open in a long, thin, jagged line. The tear puckered and tugged against itself like skin blistering under heat. Slowly, something blue began to emerge from inside it, undulating as it pushed its way out of the tear.

For a moment Safiya stared, her breath shallow. Then she snapped out of her trance, lunged forward, and threw her arms around her son, pulling him back.

Over the top of Naji's head, she stared at the rip. The strange blue thing grew larger as more of it passed through the tear, but Safiya could not give its form a name. Only when it suddenly straightened up and turned did she realized, with a soundless gasp, that what she saw was a huge, man-like being with no hair, four arms, and skin that flowed like liquid smoke. When it locked gazes with her, she saw the depths of an alien sea in its eyes.

"Clear this area," the creature commanded. "I require space."

Bach jumped forward and dragged two chairs and a trashcan out of its path. Safiya tried to pull Naji tighter against her chest but the boy somehow slipped her grasp. He took a step forward, then looked over his shoulder and smiled at her. In his eyes, she saw trust, respect, and not a hint of concern for their safety. She and Amr were clinging to each other in terror, but their child stood with the confidence of a veteran soldier.

The blue being stepped fully into the room and dragged something through the tear after him. Safiya leaned forward, trying to make out what it held in its four hands.

With one last yank, it brought its burden into view. It was another creature, but how very different it was. It had only two arms, each held immobile at the wrist by its captor, and long, thin hands with spidery fingers. Two great wings sprouted from its shoulders—both of them firmly pinned by the blue one's hands—and its skin looked like living flame, a shifting palate of red, orange, and yellow. While the blue creature's skin flowed like water, the captive creature's skin prickled and twitched like points of candle flame. Its four eyes, all of them blazing red, glared at its captor as it hissed through pointed teeth.

The blue one, with one swift yank, forced its captive to kneel on the kitchen tile.

"This inbred whelp," it said in a deep, rolling voice, "is the source of your troubles."

"Oh, thank God." Bach dropped into one of the chairs he had moved. His shoulders sank as if a weight had slipped away from them. "You got him."

"My success was never in doubt."

Safiya looked back and forth between the two creatures, her mind awash with disbelief. She felt Amr's arms around her but though she gripped his forearm with both hands, she never glanced in his direction; her eyes stayed fixed on their inhuman visitors.

Before she could stop him, Naji approached the creatures and examined the captive's angular face. "He looks different now," he said.

"Naturally," the blue one said. "I have brought him fully into this reality, where he cannot hide."

"Oh." Naji cocked his head and smiled. "He's not so scary now."

The defeated being spat at the boy, showering him with a spray of sparks. Yelping, Safiya burst out of Amr's embrace and yanked her child away; simultaneously, the blue creature tightened all four of its hands, squeezing the red creature's wrists and wings until they sizzled. It cried out and fell still.

"How long can you hold him?" Bach asked.

"As long as you require. It would be easier, however, to simply break both of his legs so he cannot flee."

"Um . . . no," Bach said. "Let's not do that."

A muffled ringtone burst into the room, jolting Safiya's already frazzled nerves.

Bach quickly dug his cellphone from his pocket. "That's Ra," he said with audible relief. "Good. I have no idea what to do with a Djinn criminal. Are there jails for that? Do your people have prisons, Azraq?"

Azraq rolled his large eyes. "A futile solution."

"So what would you suggest?"

"I would not."

Bach shook his head. "Not helpful, dude. Just hold on to him, okay?"

"As you wish."

With the phone to his ear, he stepped into the hallway.

Though she could hear a few words of his conversation, Safiya did not attempt to eavesdrop. Instead, she continued to watch the inhuman pair in her kitchen, one hand still restraining her curious son.

"Your name's Azraq?" Naji asked.

"No," the blue creature said, "but that is what I choose to be called."

"What's gonna happen to him?" Naji pointed at the captive.

"That is for the king's scion to decide."

"Who's that?"

"Him." Azraq nodded toward Bach.

"What do you think he'll do?"

"Drawing upon the limited knowledge I have gathered of him from our short time together, I would guess his decision will be something as ineffective as it is absurd."

Naji stared, blinked, and said, "Oh."

Azraq turned his head and peered closely at the child, making Safiya nervous. Despite hearing repeatedly that this was "the good one," her eyes were drawn to the creature's sharp claws and pointed teeth. Safiya's father had told her many stories of the Djinn, many of which had ended badly for the humans involved.

"You are a bold one," Azraq said to Naji. "There are few grown men who could look me in the eye as you do, boy."

"Why?"

Azraq's forehead creased. "Am I not a fearsome thing in your eyes?"

"What's that mean?"

"Look at your parents." The creature whipped his gaze to the El Sayeds. Safiya gasped and shrank back against Amr. "They fear me. Why don't you?"

Naji shrugged. "You're not scary."

"Is he?" Azraq gave his captive a shake, drawing a growl.

"Not anymore."

"Why not?"

"Because you've got him," Naji said. "He doesn't look like he can hurt me anymore."

"Indeed."

Naji smiled at Azraq, then spun around to face his parents. "Don't be afraid. Everything's okay now." He suddenly grew morose and bowed his head. "I'm sorry I brought the bad Djinni here. I didn't mean to poof him inside. I'm very, very sorry."

"Y-you brought   " Safiya stammered. She squirmed out of Amr's grasp and knelt down by her child. "How did you ever bring such a monster into this house?"

"I didn't know!" Naji pressed his small face into her chest. "I was just poofing things," he said in a muffled voice, "and then he was here!"

"About that," Bach said as he stepped back into the kitchen. "Like I said, your son has a rare gift that my friend's people value very highly, and they'd like to discuss it with you. She's on her way here. But first . . ." He glanced over his shoulder and gestured toward the stairwell that led down to the market. "Um, seems like one of your customers heard all the yelling and called the cops. A patrol car just pulled up out front."

Amr cursed under his breath. Safiya watched her husband straighten his clothes, take a deep breath, and turn his eyes firmly away from the two Djinn. With his back to the inhuman visitors, he quickly grew tall and calm.

"I will deal with this," he said. "Naji, stay with your mother."

"Amr," Safiya began, "I should go with—"

"No." He leaned over to kiss her forehead. "I will handle the problem downstairs," he assured her. "You stay and keep an eye on . . . all this." He looked at Bach. "You and these Djinn will not be in my home by this evening."

"Of course, sir."

Amr swept through the doorway and down the hall.

Feeling more confident now, Safiya scanned the Djinn carefully. In all her adult years, she'd never given any thought to her father's old stories. Now there were two Djinn standing in her presence. Her father would have a wealth of things to say in this situation, but she could think of nothing except that, despite everything that had happened, her family was safe.

Naji reached for her and squeezed her hand, a smile on his sweet little face, and her heart warmed, his confidence easing her worry. She pulled him close and kissed the crown of his head.

The blue Djinni glanced at Bach.

"You spoke to the Arcanan at last?"

"Yeah," replied Bach, sighing. "I told her everything that happened and . . . well, first there was this really long pause. Like, really long. And I was just waiting for her to hand me my ass. Then she said something like, 'It's a Notan issue, a Notan solved it, so it's not my problem anymore!' She actually sounded kinda happy."

Azraq snorted and shook his head. "Arcanans," he muttered.

GUILTIER PARTY

Rachel and the Morleys arrived at the El Sayeds' market to the sight of flashing red and blue lights illuminating the ornate awning. After a quick phone conversation with Bach, Rachel hung up, pocketed her cell, and took in the scene. A handful of people, customers and passersby, loitered near the entrance, many of them holding up phones to snap photos. Just inside, Rachel saw two officers—one checking out the aisles, the other digging around behind the counter.

Mr. El Sayed appeared from the back room and greeted them, and immediately both officers approached him, turning their backs to the crowd outside.

"I need these policemen to leave," Rachel said.

"I don't think they're gonna ask your opinion," Leda said.

"Even so." Rachel dug two chunks of wood out of her coat pockets and handed them to Simon. "Here," she said. "The Djinni's box and its lid. Would you mind taking these upstairs?"

Simon raised an eyebrow. "Yeah," he said with a humorless chuckle, "I'll just walk right on by those cops and head up the stairs. They won't mind, huh?"

"I meant go around back and use the fire escape. Bach's up there, he'll let you in."

He took the box and lid from her and jammed them into his own pockets. "Sure, a Black man climbing the fire escape; those cops won't have a problem with that."

"They won't see you."

"Yeah," Simon said darkly, "they better not." Without another word, he weaved his way through the small crowd and disappeared around the corner.

The two women watched as the officers continued to press Mr. El Sayed with their questions. When he hesitated before answering one question, the shorter officer puffed out his chest and leaned in until he was within inches of his face. Mr. El Sayed leaned back but kept his feet rooted to the spot, his expression tight. His discomfort was so tangible that Rachel could feel her own skin crawling.

"That's not a 'here to help' sort of stance they're taking," she said.

"Somebody called the cops on a Middle Eastern man," Leda replied. "They're gonna presume he's guilty until proven innocent. Maybe even after that."

Rachel exhaled through flared nostrils. This struck her as a spectacularly unproductive attitude, particularly for armed authorities. "How do we make the police leave?"

Leda nibbled her lip in thought. "Point them toward a guiltier party?"

"Hmm . . ." Rachel said, turning this over in her mind. "I think I can do that."

"Yeah? How?"

"I know a guiltier party, and I'll bet the police know them too."

"Okay," Leda said. "Dangle it in front of them and maybe they'll take the bait." She gestured with her chin toward the three men in the market. "It would probably help to defuse the tension in there first, though."

"How?"

Leda's dark eyes scanned the officers intently, a sharp, calculating light shimmering in their depths. "Guys like this . . . a 'damsel in distress' type of act should do the trick."

Her words skimmed across Rachel's brain without finding a place to take hold. Rachel stared at her without the slightest comprehension.

"Damsel in distress act? Is . . . is that a thing? How do you do it and how does it work?"

To Rachel's surprise, Leda looked at her askance, as if wondering if she was serious. Then her expression relaxed and she nodded. "Matriarchy," she said wistfully. "Must be nice. No problem—I got this. Let's go."

Rachel swung the door open, and they moved inside.

" . . . lotta shouting," the taller officer was saying. He took a step back and swept his eyes around the store, one hand hooked into his belt, the other casually scratching his jaw. "Caller said you took off up the stairs, left a bunch of people unattended in the store."

"Yes." Mr. El Sayed sighed. "Yes, there was a situation with my son. I certainly did not mean to alarm anyone."

"The caller said there was a lot of noise upstairs," said the second officer, a man with graying red hair. His expression was stony and tight-lipped. "A lot of crashing around or something. That have to do with your son too?"

Rachel saw the color drain from Mr. El Sayed's face as he leaned back another inch, clearly wanting to increase the distance between himself and the officer but not daring to take an actual step back.

"W-well," Mr. El Sayed stammered, "I am not sure what your caller heard, exactly—"

"You a citizen?" the redheaded cop asked.

"No, sir. I have a green card."

"Do you now," the officer said coldly.

"Mr. El Sayed," Leda interrupted, hobbling her way up to the men. "I came to see if your wife had changed her mind about those paintings."

The cops snapped their attention to her.

"Miss," said the tall officer, "I'm gonna need you to stay back until we're finished here."

With the grace of a seasoned actress, Leda gently shrank before the two men, her posture slumping a bit and her expression softening like that of a chastised child.

"Oh my God," Leda said breathily, her eyes as wide as Rachel had ever seen them. "Is everything all right? Are Mrs. El Sayed and Naji okay?"

Rachel watched, impressed, as Leda's performance sliced through the tension and drained some of the officers' stress. Leda was right. This "damsel in distress" thing was defusing the situation. She took a mental snapshot of the act and resolved to review it later so she could figure out how it worked.

The redheaded man rolled his eyes and then returned his attention to Mr. El Sayed, leaving the tall officer to deal with Leda. "Right now," he told her, "it's just a noise complaint."

"So no one's been hurt?"

"No."

"Oh, thank you Jesus." Leda heaved a sigh, placing one hand over her chest. "Oh, it would just crush me if something happened to these good people."

The officer sighed and, after a glance at his sneering partner, said, "No one's been hurt that we know of. We're just respond-ing to a call about a disturbance."

"It was those boys again, huh?"

All eyes turned to Rachel as she casually strolled to the back of the store, snagged a cherry cola from behind a refrigerator door, and twisted off the top.

"What boys?" asked the tall officer.

"Those Bell brats," Rachel replied in between gulps. "You know, the three brothers. They've caused you trouble before, right Mr. El Sayed?" She flashed him a glance. It was too brief to offer more than a hint of rescue, but it was enough.

"Yes!" the owner said, pointing a finger at Rachel. "Yes, that is just so! Those boys! They were here before! They smashed all of my tomatoes and painted profanity on my door!"

"And they were here again today?" asked the redheaded of-ficer.

"Yes!" the owner said. "They were . . . throwing something at the upstairs windows!"

"You saw them?"

"No, no, I never see them! No one sees them! I hear boys laughing, I hear something hitting my windows, and then I see three kids running away!"

The two officers exchanged a new glance—one of weary familiarity.

"The Bell brothers," the redhead muttered as he rubbed his forehead. "Goddamned little pricks."

"Pains in our ass," his partner said. "We get at least three calls a week about those punks and still nobody's actually *seen* anything." He shook his head. "I thought we'd get 'em when they let all the animals loose in that pet store, but no such luck. Little bastards know exactly where the cameras are."

From across the store, Leda shot Rachel a look and gave the slightest nod. Rachel smiled behind her drink. A guiltier party: delivered.

"I'm sick of those three shits," the redhead snarled as he whipped out a notepad and a pen. He faced Mr. El Sayed again, this time with a professional expression. "You wanna file a report, sir?"

"I filed a report the last time they came here," Mr. El Sayed said with a wave of his hands. "Would it do any good to file another?"

The cop's pen hovered over the notepad a moment; then, with a grunt, he snapped it shut and pocketed both items. "Nope," he said. "We've got a file two inches thick on those little fucks and nothin' to show for it. I'll make a note of this incident but there's no reason to waste your time with a formal report." He looked at his partner. "Let's go."

"Yeah." The tall officer nodded smartly at the owner. "Sir."

Mr. El Sayed nodded politely in return and, visibly relieved, ushered them to the door. The small crowd outside parted to let them through, their eyes darting from the officers to the market and back again.

From inside the store, Mr. El Sayed watched the patrol car drive off, Rachel and Leda standing at his elbows. When the car disappeared from view, he leaned forward against the window and rested his forehead on the glass. Eyes closed, he drew several deep breaths, exhaling slowly after each one. Gradually, his arms and hands stopped shaking until, calm, he stood up. Then his eyes drifted upward and a very different fear flooded his face.

"Does the problem upstairs have something to do with you, crazy girl?" Mr. El Sayed whispered.

"Nope," she said, smiling. "I started to get involved but it all worked out without me."

"But you know the young man who came here with the . . ."

"With the Djinni," Leda finished for him.

"Yes, I do." Rachel took a sip of her soda. "He's the friend I told you about."

If Mr. El Sayed was surprised by this news, his expression did not betray it. He flipped the sign on the front door from "Open" to "Closed," turned the deadbolt, and rubbed the back of his neck. "What is to be done?"

"Don't worry." Rachel scanned the dwindling group of people just outside the door. With the police car gone, the bystanders seemed to have concluded that the entertainment was over—and the few that remained were rapidly losing interest. *Notans*, she thought, rolling her eyes. "An expert will be here any minute."

"An expert," Mr. El Sayed said wearily. "Could there be such a person?"

"Yeah. The Central Office—that's my, uh, employer—said his name is Odero Lemath len Odero. He's an expert *ukiba*, so he can help with Naji. Not sure if he can help with the Djinn issue—speaking of which, is that under control?"

"There are two Djinn in my home," Mr. El Sayed said. "Absolutely nothing is under control."

Leda pointed her crutches toward the back room. "I'll check in on that. Probably shouldn't leave the boys unsupervised too long."

"Can you make it up those stairs with your crutches?" Rachel asked.

Leda grimaced. "I'll manage." With heavy, uneven footfalls, she heaved her way from one step to the next, and soon disappeared from view.

Walking slowly around the store, his hands brushing against the metal shelves, Mr. El Sayed inclined his head toward Rachel. "'*Ukiba*' did you say, crazy girl? What is this?"

"That's what my people call those with Naji's abilities—people who can punch holes through dimensional boundaries."

"Yes, the . . . 'poofing.'"

"That's right. Naji's been 'poofing' things for months. For the most part, he's been 'poofing' them into the crawlspace under my house."

"Things? What things?"

"Small appliances, bricks, street signs, a dog."

"A dog?" Mr. El Sayed repeated, his voice almost flat from emotional exhaustion.

"Yes sir. He didn't understand what he was doing at the time. The expert sent by my people will teach Naji how to control his ability so it doesn't happen again."

Mr. El Sayed made his way to the counter, stepped behind the register, and took a seat on his stool. He put his elbows on the counter and pressed his head into his hands. "Who are your people, crazy girl, that they know so much about an impossible thing?"

Rachel leaned on the opposite side of the counter and took a swing of her soda. She felt so bad for Mr. El Sayed. This poor man had been handed a heavy burden today, and she was not in a position to relieve him of it. "There's a complicated answer to that, sir," she told him. "I'd share it with you, but I'm worried how it will sound coming from someone you know as 'crazy girl.' It might be easier to accept if you hear it first from the expert."

"Will the explanation be different from his?" he asked, spreading his hands in a gesture of surrender. "There are Djinn in my home, my son's stories of monsters and 'poofing' are true, and my wife, far from being ill with a mere cold, was in mortal danger. I can no longer separate what is real from what is fantasy. If you can do so, please tell me the truth."

Rachel stared into her plastic soda bottle, her eyes following the delicate dance of fizzing bubbles, as she collected her thoughts. "I don't know that what I have to say will lighten your load at all, sir," she finally said, "but if you'd like me to talk while we wait, I can do that."

"Then talk, crazy girl," he said. "Wait. What is your name?"

"Rachel Wilde, sir."

"Then talk, Miss Wilde. Talk."

STORIES

On any other morning, a knock on the window would have alarmed Safiya, but on this particular morning she could not summon any distress. The blond man, Bach, disappeared down the hall, presumably to investigate the knocking, while she remained in her kitchen and, together with her son, slowly circled the two Djinn, inspecting them. The prisoner, the Ifrit, occasionally glared at her, all four of his eyes red and blazing, but he never made a sound. The captor, the Marid, watched her movements closely, without concern. Even when she came to a stop and leaned close, the blue Djinni viewed her with no more interest than if she were a piece of furniture.

Eaten up with curiosity, Safiya examined the Marid's arm, his skin only inches from her nose.

"You are not as my father describes in his stories," she said at last.

"Stories?" he said. "You have heard stories of us?"

"Yes. All my life, my father has told me stories of the Djinn. But none of his stories describe what I see."

Azraq sighed, a pained and weary expression on his face. "Most likely your father never saw one of my kind. So far removed are we from this world that we are reduced to myth."

"Oh, my father never spoke of you as myth," she told him. "He insisted that you were as real as we are. 'We are all the creations of Allah,' he told me, 'whether we are human, Djinn, angels, or beasts.' He spoke of your kind as elders to humanity, created before the first man, but he also said you were mischievous and sometimes dangerous. For both reasons, he said that the Djinn were never to be trespassed against and always to be treated with respect."

The Djinni watched her from the corner of his vision with a strange expression on his face. Safiya saw a conflict of feeling dancing in his eyes, a waltz of curiosity and doubt. His lips parted as if he meant to speak but then he closed them and looked away.

She squinted at his arm. "Your skin seems to move," she said. "It looks like a slow tide moving in and out." She brought her hand close to his flesh then paused, lifting her eyes. "May I?"

"May you what?"

"Touch your skin. Or," she hastily added, "will it burn me?"

The Djinni flapped his fin-like ears and looked away. "Do as you like."

Safiya pressed one finger to the Djinni's blue forearm. It was warmer than a human arm would be, but not uncomfortably so. The rippling flesh felt solid yet malleable, like sculptor's clay before the kiln. She leaned a bit closer and sniffed. There was a hint of something organic, but no smell of smoke. Though she sniffed several times, she could make no better identification. *Smokeless fire.* That's what her father always said in his stories. Djinn were made of smokeless fire.

Naji watched his mother with hungry eyes. As she touched the Djinni's skin, he reached out to follow her example, but she swatted his hand away. "Naji, do not touch without asking."

The boy looked up at Azraq, the question in his eyes. The Djinni responded by extending the captive Djinni's broken wing. "Touch him, if you must."

Naji reached out and grasped a torn flap of yellow skin that dangled from the wing. His eyes grew wide as he turned it over in his hands and brought it closer to his face. Safiya took the end of the wing-skin and rubbed it between her fingers. It was warm, like the Marid's arm, but it was also textureless, sliding through her fingers without a hint of friction—like weightless silk. Safiya glanced at her boy and Naji grinned at her, a child-reflection of her own excitement.

The thought of her childhood stories being true filled Safiya with sublime excitement. Her eyes absorbed every inch of the blue Djinni, sculpting a duplicate image to hold in her memory forever. Her vision dove into every crease and traced the shape of every muscle from the top of his hairless head to the tips of his webbed toes. She tried to mentally replicate his voice—that deep, rumbling timbre that seemed to speak across time and worlds. A strange feeling washed over her, bringing a smile to her face. She heard her father and grandmother's voices in her soul and found herself wondering how best to tell this story someday.

SENTENCING

Bach returned to the kitchen with Simon on his heels. He felt disquieted that he had assisted with two break-ins at this family's home—first Azraq, now Simon. An intruder himself, he certainly had no right to the authority he had assumed. Hell, those cops downstairs should have arrested him. He really wished he had gone about this business in a non-criminal way. As it stood, he owed this family a thorough apology.

At the sight of yet another stranger in her home, Safiya stiffened and put a hand on Naji's shoulder.

"Mrs. El Sayed," Bach said, "this is Simon Morley, a friend of mine."

"Ma'am," Simon greeted her. "Sorry to come up your fire escape. There are cops in your store."

Safiya nodded and gestured for the two men to enter the room. "Amr is tending to that matter. Are you here to address . . . this?"

Simon looked at the Djinn, his eyes drifting from one to the other, and shook his head. "Rachel just wanted me to bring this thing up here." He withdrew the Djinni's broken box from his coat pocket. As he pulled it clear, a few scraps, wrappers, and a balled-up sheet of paper came up with it and fell to the floor.

Bach stooped to clean up the litter while Simon stepped forward and set the two pieces on the kitchen table.

Azraq sneered at the sight of Simon's delivery. "The box," he said through bared teeth.

"What is this?" Safiya ran her fingers over the two pieces of wood.

"It's a portal to another place," Bach said. "Azraq was locked in there for thousands of years before I let him out."

"The smell of that island is still in my nose," the Djinni muttered, flaring his many nostrils. "Putrid, salty, death-in-life stink. It clings to my organs like a million parasites. Should I live another five thousand years, it will follow me all my days."

Bach stared at him. The intensity of the Djinni's voice struck him as the same sort of voice a crusty old man would use to curse a group of kids trying to retrieve a Frisbee from his lawn. He understood Azraq's hatred of the box and the portal it contained—his resolution to never return to that place reminded Bach of his own determination to avoid ending up under another bridge—but nevertheless, the theatrical flair of his words bordered on absurd.

"Dude," he said, "respectfully, I'm gonna ask you to take it down a notch."

Azraq drew himself up tall and snorted. "What could you know of it?" he shouted. "Paltry though your life may be, it is yours. No chain binds you, now or ever. What stench of imprisonment have you to claim?"

Bach thought of the river stone he had taken from under the bridge. He thought of the rancid odor that clung to it—a smell that made his skin crawl, and yet stirred precious memories of his lost time. It was back at Rachel's house, in his room, tucked away where he didn't have to see or smell it but where it would never be lost.

But no, it wasn't the same.

He had never been shut away from the world by someone else; he had been locked inside his own mind. Still, like Azraq, he'd had only himself for company—and poor company he was. Being a raving lunatic did not make for good conversation, especially when spoken internally. But, in a way, his incoherency had made his imprisonment easier. The time had passed in short bursts for him, with long stretches of nothing in between, unlike Azraq's solitary millennia inside the portal box. Although his experience made him feel a certain connection with the Djinni, he had no doubt that Azraq had suffered more.

Still, there was such a thing as too much drama.

"The fishy stink is gross, yes," he said, "but just chill. You're out and you're not going back in. But, y'know," he added, feeling a twinge of sight-beyond, "somebody else could go in."

Following Bach's gaze, Azraq looked down at his defeated foe and smirked. "That is fitting. My one-time home on that speck of an island is surrounded by endless ocean. I could not take five steps without touching the water. Trapped in that place, this insolent cur's wings will take him nowhere and his flames will not long burn. That will silence his boastful tongue."

"Will that work?" Simon asked, eyeing the box. "The lid's broken."

"The portal is still there," the Djinni said. "The seal is broken but the pocket dimension of my imprisonment is still contained within."

"So we just have to get the Ifrit inside and find a way to keep him in there," Bach said thoughtfully.

The Ifrit snarled, lifted his head, and spat sparks at Bach. He hissed a string of foreign words, his voice full of venom. Shades of red and orange flashed through his skin and waves of heat rolled through the room. Everyone in the room but Azraq backed away from his rage.

The Ifrit lunged toward them, his four eyes blazing, but Azraq held him back. The captive Djinni glowered at Bach and cursed again, but Bach only stared back at him, afraid but uncomprehending.

Within seconds, the Ifrit was panting like an overheated beast, his arms and wings limp in Azraq's hands. The Marid responded to this futile show of strength with a snide smile.

The room became silent, the quiet broken only by a series of gradually loudening thuds that Bach identified as Leda's crutches climbing the stairs.

Though the Ifrit continued to snarl, not another word left his mouth. Bach watched all four of his eyes shift to the portal box, fear emanating from their red depths.

41 LEM

Rachel finished her soda while standing several paces back from the conversation taking place before her. She had walked Mr. El Sayed through only a basic framework of the Arcana when the awaited expert had arrived to take up the narrative, at which point she'd happily yielded the floor to him. Odero Lemath len Odero (who introduced himself as "Lem") had launched quite comfortably into an explanation both detailed and efficient. He was clearly better prepared for this interaction than she was. Under his guidance, Mr. El Sayed seemed to be readily absorbing the information.

"Your child's gift," said Lem, who spoke English with a woolly accent, "helps us construct the passages we use to move from place to place. We can make them by using our technology, but it saves so much time and energy to have someone with his talent make them for us. Imagine," he said with a smile, arms spread wide open, "having the ability to construct a super-high-way hundreds of miles long with just a thought. That is what your son can do for us."

"Wait." Mr. El Sayed held up his hands. "What does this mean? You want to take my son away?"

"No, no, no," Lem said. "Your child belongs with you. That's as it should be. What we want is to prepare him to help us when he's grown—and not until then. Nothing that we offer will take place without your permission and your direct supervision."

"And what is your role in all this?"

"To teach him how to use his gift."

"How?"

Lem set down the satchel he had slung over his shoulder and then held out his hands like a magician preparing for his act. Sensing what was about to happen, Rachel inched closer for a better view.

The *ukiba* fished a penny from the take-one-leave-one tray and then maneuvered Mr. El Sayed's hand into a palm-up position. With the penny pinched between his thumb and forefinger, he held it at eye-level, a foot or so higher than the shop owner's outstretched palm. Lem paused, his eyes gleaming, as he basked in their undivided attention. Then, with a flick of his wrist, he flung the coin across the room.

Mr. El Sayed and Rachel tracked the penny's arc through the air as it soared over the counter and toward the back wall, the light from the street illuminating it like a gem. A second before it should have struck the wall, the coin vanished, its reflected light seemingly swallowed whole. Mr. El Sayed blinked—and the coin materialized in front of his nose and dropped into his open hand. He gasped in surprise.

As Mr. El Sayed inspected the coin and the air from which it had come, Rachel gave Lem a nod. "That's cool to watch," she said in Arcanan.

"Thank you," he replied with a smile. "I understand I'm not the only one here with a rare talent."

"Meaning?"

"Ms. Dokgo tells me you're one of the lucky few who can understand daemon-talk."

"Yeah." She rolled her eyes. "Lucky me."

"You know she wants to keep you in daemon collection past your term of service because of it, don't you?"

"I suspected. It's not going to happen."

Lem snorted. "I said the same thing when she recruited me. Ms. Dokgo tends to get her way."

"Ms. Dokgo can bite me."

Lem chuckled. "She has sharp teeth."

42

LOCKET

Rachel and a man Bach didn't know entered the El Sayed
family home just behind Mr. El Sayed, the two quietly conversing with each other—until he caught sight of the Djinn, at
which point his words seemed to leave him and his eyes popped
open wide.

"This is Lem Odero, everyone," Rachel said. "Our *ukiba* expert."

Lem waved a hello, but his focus remained on the Djinn.
Letting out a low whistle, he circled the pair, scanning them up
and down.

Azraq grumbled under his breath but did not look at the
man. The Ifrit stared at the tiled floor in silence.

"I have never seen such magnificent beings!" Lem exclaimed.

Azraq glanced at Lem and lifted his chin a tad higher.

Rachel took a seat at the kitchen table, which was shoved up
against the wall with its chairs scattered about on one side. Leda
sat to her right while Simon sat on his sister's far side, her braced
leg propped up on the edge of his chair. Bach continued standing,
leaning against the wall near the kitchen entrance. Somehow, it
felt impolite for him to sit down.

Mr. El Sayed brought Lem over to his wife and formally introduced them; she greeted him politely, smiling like a good

hostess, then bombarded her husband with a slew of Arabic while wagging one finger at Lem.

The Arcanan man made no attempt to insert himself into their discussion. Instead, he knelt down and addressed Naji eye to eye.

"It's a pleasure to meet you, young *ukiba*," he said, grasping Naji's hand and nodding grandly with his eyes closed. "I'm Odero Lemath len Odero. You may call me Lem."

"What's *ukiba*?" Naji asked. "That's not my name."

"Of course not." Lem chuckled. "You're Naji El Sayed. That's *who* you are. I call you *ukiba* because that's *what* you are. You are an *ukiba*: one who creates tunnels through worlds."

"Tunnels?" Naji asked, his face scrunched up in doubt. "I don't make tunnels. I poof things."

"Poof," Lem repeated. "Ah. When I was a child, I called it 'blinking.' I would blink my eyes, and things would vanish or appear as I wished them to." He gave Naji a wink. "I often blinked the vegetables from my plate into the ocean when my father's back was turned."

Naji's eyes lit up. "You can poof things, too?"

"Oh yes," Lem said. "We're both *ukiba*."

"Really?"

"Really. I'm here to teach you to use your gift properly. And when I have taught you everything I know, you'll be able to open doors to new worlds. Would you like that?"

Naji's eyes widened and a smile spread over his face. He nodded eagerly.

Lem nodded back. "Good. Then we can begin right away."

"Before you do that," Leda said, "maybe you should do something about *them*." She pointed at the Djinn.

Lem's smile faltered, and his eyes darted about the room. He rose to his feet. "I have neither means nor authority to resolve a

Djinn matter," he said apologetically. "I'm afraid the Central Office gave me no guidance in this issue."

Internally, Bach swore. This revelation didn't surprise him—few things did—but on this occasion, he had hoped that his sight-beyond was wrong. Though he disliked it, the ball was still firmly in his court.

"But the Djinni!" Mr. El Sayed said. "He cannot be released! He attacked my family!"

"We won't release him," Bach said. "We're going to put him in the box."

"Right," Simon said, holding up the lidless portal. He gestured to Azraq with the wooden block. "You can put him in here, can't you?"

"I can force him into the box," Azraq said, "but without a seal, he could easily escape."

"What if we . . . I don't know . . . glue the lid on?" Leda suggested.

"If repairs could be made that easily," Azraq said, "I would not have bothered to break the box in the first place. It is now useless, just as I intended it to be."

Leda tapped a finger on the table. "What if we make a new lid? Would that work?"

"Anything other than the original lid will be a less than perfect fit," Azraq said. "The portal was created around the exact shape of the original box. Even a slight difference in dimensions could create a crack through which this whelp could escape."

"So," Simon said, "the box is a bust?"

"The box is still a portal," Azraq replied, "but now that it is broken, there is no lid that will close the opening it contains."

"Well hell," Leda said, slumping low in her seat, "we may as well smash the damn thing."

"Could we open a new door?" Bach asked.

"We already have an open door through the box," Rachel said. "Why would we want to make a second escape route?"

Feeling the stares of everyone around him, Bach blushed and turned his gaze to the floor. Doubt choked him and he suddenly wished he hadn't spoken. Still, he cleared his throat and pressed on, eyes trained on his feet. "If the box is useless, like Azraq said, then we might as well get rid of it. I assume that if we burn the box or chop it up or something, the doorway inside it won't work anymore, right?"

"Probably not," Lem said. "It's connected to the box, so if the box is gone, it should disappear."

"So, I was thinking we should do that and then open a new door—one we can close. I mean"—he looked at Lem—"you open passages between dimension, right?"

Bach swept his gaze around the room. Rachel opened her mouth, her eyes alight with snark, and he flinched—but she seemed to think better of it and maintained her silence. Relieved, he looked back to Lem, eager for his reaction.

Lem tapped one knuckle on his chin, his eyes sparkling. Encouraged, Bach straightened up. Out of the corner of one eye, he could see Azraq smirking in his direction.

"That is the sort of thing you do, right Mr. Odero?" Bach asked again.

"That is precisely what I do," Lem said.

A flush of confidence rushed through Bach. As he took a moment to enjoy the feeling, a low, rumbling chuckle echoed through Azraq's chest. The alien sound washed over Bach and made the hair on his nape stand on end.

The Ifrit, still held tightly in Azraq's grasp, glared at Bach but the fire in his red eyes was strangely dim and distant, swimming in a sea of fear. A swell of pity rose in Bach but was quickly suppressed by the memory of the creature's crimes against the El Sayed family. Like it or not, this really seemed the best possible option.

"So," he said, "maybe we could pick another box or something—one with a working lid—and use that box as a portal."

He watched as everyone around him exchanged glances, each seeming to wait for another to offer a criticism. When no one spoke up, all expressions gradually shifted from skeptical to accepting, even relieved. Pride bloomed in his chest.

At that exact moment, Azraq's lips parted and his low rumble exploded into a booming laugh. The entire room drew a breath and stared at him, held captive by the unnatural noise.

As the laughter faded, Bach shook off his unease and turned to face the Marid.

"You think I'm wrong?" he asked.

"I am surprised by you," the Djinni said.

"How so?"

"Your solution is lacking in absurdity and inefficiency."

"Oh." Bach's brow furrowed and he squinted at Azraq. "Okay. Thanks?" Keeping one eye on the snickering Djinni, he glanced around the room. "So what now?"

"We'll need a new box," Rachel said. She turned to the El Sayeds. "Do you have something we could use, something you won't miss? Something with a lid on it?"

The two glanced at each other.

"I have a jewelry box that I do not use," Mrs. El Sayed said.

Mr. El Sayed squinted at her. "Which box would that be?"

"The black one."

He frowned at his wife. "My mother gave you that box," he said sternly.

"I know," she replied. "I do not use it."

"It was a gift. You must keep it."

Mrs. El Sayed narrowed her eyes at him and put her hands on her hips. "It is ugly."

"My mother wanted you to have it."

"She bought it at an airport gift shop."

"She will be crushed if you give it away!" he shouted.

"And who is going to tell her?" she shouted back.

As the argument escalated in volume, it shifted from English to Arabic. The couple continued to shout at each other, wagging fingers and gesturing wildly, until Leda slowly waved a crutch in between them.

"Okay now," Leda said, clearly trying to sound pleasant through a tense smile. "I'm sensing that maybe the jewelry box is not the best option. Maybe something else?"

After one final, burning, mutual glare, the couple turned their heads toward their guests.

"I have an emergency cash box that I keep in our closet," Mr. El Sayed said. "It is made of metal and has a lock."

"It also has a dent," Mrs. El Sayed said.

"But the lid is attached."

"The dent loosened the lid."

Mr. El Sayed threw up his hands. "What else is there?"

The group in the kitchen kicked around some ideas for a new portal door, ranging from cabinets to books with hidden compartments cut out of the pages. No suggestion was found satisfactory. Bach tried to think if there was anything in the stuff he'd rescued from his parents' curb that might work. Nothing came to mind. For all the piles of crap he'd reclaimed recently, he was still possession-poor.

"How about that?" Simon pointed at Mrs. El Sayed.

Mrs. El Sayed blinked, glanced around in confusion, and asked, "What?"

Simon pointed again, jabbing his finger toward her chest.

She raised a hand to her breast. "My locket?" She scooped up the circle in her palm and lifted it closer to her face. "But it's so small."

"Looks like it closes up real tight," Simon said. "Does it?"

"It does," she said, nodding. She looked at Azraq, eyebrows raised. "Is this large enough?"

"The size of the door is immaterial," he said. "Any opening will suffice."

"But can a door be opened through such a small thing?" Mr. El Sayed asked, turning to look at Lem.

Lem grinned. "A well-trained *ukiba* can open a passage as large as a battleship or as small as a flea."

Gripping her crutches, Leda stood and swung her way closer to Mrs. El Sayed. She leaned in and examined the necklace.

"It's very pretty," she said. "Are you sure you want to give it up?"

Mrs. El Sayed ran her thumb over its surface. "I am fond of it, but it has no real value. I bought it at a clearance sale and even before the sale it was not expensive." After a moment's hesitation, she clicked it open, removed the tiny photograph within, then snapped it shut again. She lifted it over her head and swept her hair free of the chain. "It is just a necklace," she said. "It is replaceable. This"—she held up the picture, a miniature of her husband and son—"is all I need."

She handed the locket to Lem with one hand while pressing the photo, wrapped in her other hand, to the now empty spot on her chest. A smile crept over Mr. El Sayed's face. He draped his arm around her shoulders and squeezed her.

"I will buy a new locket for you," he said quietly. "Any one you want."

She smiled and leaned her head against his neck. Amr rested his chin against her forehead. As they stood pressed together, Naji grinned at them. Bach felt a twinge of envy for this boy growing up with such loving parents.

Lem opened and closed the locket, holding it out toward Azraq. The Djinni watched this display with a critical eye and then nodded his satisfaction.

The Djinni's approval secured, Lem palmed the locket and knelt next to Naji.

"I think this would be a fine learning opportunity for my new student. Provided"—he inclined his head toward the El Sayeds—"that his parents approve."

"You believe Naji can do this thing?" Mrs. El Sayed asked, looking at Lem slightly askance.

He nodded. "Certainly. With a little guidance."

"Is that wise?"

"There is no danger. I will supervise."

"No." Mrs. El Sayed shook her head. "What I mean to say is, is it wise to encourage Naji to . . . 'poof' things?"

"Yes," Mr. El Sayed jumped in. "Would it not be better to stop him from doing this?"

"No!" Naji cried.

"Hush, Naji," his mother said. "This is a conversation for adults."

"We would rather Naji not do such things," Mr. El Sayed said. "Your skill is fascinating, but I think it is in Naji's best interest to *not* develop his."

"But I want to!" Naji said, only to be shushed again.

"That's not advisable," Lem said. "Your son was born an *uki-*

ba. He will always be an *ukiba.* His power cannot be eliminated or suppressed. If he does not learn to control his ability now, it will become harder to control as he grows. By the time he's a man, if he does not have a grasp on it, the power will overwhelm him and could cause irreparable harm to interdimensional barriers."

Mrs. El Sayed's face crinkled with confusion. "Interdimensional barriers?"

"Essentially," Lem said, "he could open up your world to attack from any number of undesirable life forms."

"That's half the reason we monitor your world for *ukiba,*" Rachel jumped in. "We love them because they're useful to us, but we also fear the damage they're capable of. The last time an *ukiba* wasn't identified while young, he accidentally opened a portal that let something run loose in your world. Whatever it was, it had a taste for human flesh and a huge appetite. It consumed an entire village—Hoer Verde, somewhere in Brazil—before we managed to 'poof' it away." She drew her lips tight and added, her voice grave, "There were no survivors."

The El Sayeds' eyes overflowed with horror—an emotion Bach shared. He had heard of Hoer Verde, though he'd believed it to be a myth: a town of 600 people vanished without a trace. Supposedly, the only clue was a message one inhabitant had written on a chalkboard: "There is no salvation."

"That was a particularly tragic event," Lem said, nodding, "but it was far from isolated. It's fairly common for even a well-trained *ukiba* to make an occasional mistake. In the Arcana, we occasionally find people from your world who have wandered through undocumented portals. I recall a time about one hundred and sixty . . . seventy . . . yes, one hundred and seventy years ago, when an *ukiba* received a nasty head injury and lost partial control of her power. Shortly thereafter, a southern tribe came across a German scientist very excitedly cataloging the vegetation on the plains." Lem chuckled. "He was, apparently, unaware that he had passed into an entirely different world. He assumed he had simply discovered a previously unknown species of plant."

"I remember learning about that," Rachel said, smiling. "Odd man. He stayed in the Arcana to continue his studies. Leichhardt University is named after him."

"At least that sort of mistake is relatively benign," Lem continued. "Several years ago, I passed out after overindulging at a festival. When I woke up, I discovered that I had unintentionally opened a passage to somewhere. My entire town was infested with a colony of small alien animals. Vicious little things. Half of my village bears scars from their teeth and claws, mostly received in the week following their arrival. They very nearly destroyed our farmland. We only stopped them by setting fire to the surrounding areas to keep them contained and then driving them into pens." Lem rolled back one sleeve to show the long, knotted scars that ran the length of his forearm. "A couple of them grabbed me and tore me up. It took me months to heal."

"Ouch," Simon said under his breath.

Seeing the El Sayeds' horrified concern, Lem pushed down his sleeve and waved his hand dismissively. "We got them under control. As it turned out, they're quite tasty. We breed them for their meat now."

Bach saw that this did nothing to ease the couple's worry; Mr. El Sayed's mouth continued to hang open and Mrs. El Sayed kept wringing her hands.

Perhaps hoping for support, Lem glanced at Rachel, but she averted her eyes and took a swig of her soda. He drew a deep breath and spread his hands toward the couple.

"I tell you these things not to frighten you," he said in a soothing tone, "but to make sure you understand the gravity of the situation. Naji was born this way. He cannot be 'cured' of this any more than he could be 'cured' of having brown eyes. As he grows, so will his power. If he is to control it and prevent mishaps, he must learn how to do so now, while he is young. That is why I am here." He smiled kindly as he raised his eyebrows. "Do I have your permission?"

Mrs. El Sayed's eyes fluttered and she brushed her fingers over her lips. She looked to her husband, her expression betraying her doubt, but his eyes met hers evenly. With a sigh, she looked away.

Mr. El Sayed gave Lem a nod. Permission granted, Lem waved Naji closer.

As the boy crossed the small gap between himself and his new mentor, Bach's sight-beyond unleashed a torrent of information, only a tidbit of which he grasped.

Lesson number one, he thought. *The first step in a long journey.*

INSTRUCTION BEGINS

The open locket in Lem's outstretched hand shone under the overhead kitchen light, the links of the attached chain twinkling as it dangled from his fingers. He turned it back and forth for Naji to see.

"If you were to 'poof' this necklace," he said, "where would it go?"

Naji could answer this question with confidence. "To my away place," he said proudly.

"Look closely at it," Lem said to his student. Do you think you could 'poof' just the inside part?"

Naji stared at the open locket. He reached out and tapped the interior compartment with small one finger, stumped. "I dunno. Can *you* do that?"

Lem smiled. He held out his free hand to Simon, indicating the broken box with his eyes. Simon handed it to him and Lem held the box under Naji's nose—and a stench like none he'd ever experienced before filled his nostrils.

Naji gagged and turned his head away.

"Look into the box," Lem told him. "What do you see?"

Pinching his nostrils closed with his fingers, Naji peered inside. "I see . . . sand . . . and water . . . and a tree, I think."

"What you are seeing is the other side of a tunnel—a tunnel that passes from this world, through this box, and into another world," Lem explained. "It is, essentially, a 'poof' without an end. You see, when you 'poof' a thing, you open a tunnel like this one to send that thing to your away place. The way you have taught yourself to 'poof,' the tunnel you create closes as soon as the thing passes through it. The tunnel attached to this box, on the other hand, is a 'poof' that has never closed. The inside of this box was 'poofed' away, sent to that place of sand and water, and left open."

Naji nodded slowly. It made sense . . . sort of.

"This is the very sort of thing that it is my job to teach you." Lem jiggled the necklace. "And we will start with this."

Naji perked up. "How?"

Lem rose and moved to the kitchen table, motioning for Naji to follow him. The boy hurried to his side, climbed into a chair, and perched on his knees to get a good view of the box and open locket, which Lem set on the tabletop. With the exception of the Djinn, the entire room crowded around.

"This is more difficult than you are used to," Lem said, "so I will do most of it. But I want you to understand what's involved." He tilted the box so they could both see the world within it. "The trick to this is to open a tunnel to a certain place. That's easier to do if the first tunnel to that place is nearby." He took Naji's hand in his and pulled it into the box. "Feel the tunnel," he said. "Feel its flow, its edges."

"How do I feel that?" Naji asked.

Lem chuckled. "Perhaps that's too much to start with. Let's try this." He moved Naji's hand to the locket. "In a moment, I will open a tunnel to the same place. When I do that, I will 'poof' the inside of the locket into the sand and water place and I will keep that 'poof' open so that it forms a tunnel. When I do that, I want you to keep your hand on mine and try to feel what I'm doing. Can you do that?"

Naji nodded, vibrating with excitement.

Lem turned his full attention to the tabletop. With Naji's hand resting on top of his own, he ran his fingertips over the lid-less box, his eyes unblinking and fixed on its depths. He let his hand hover over the box for a moment, and then he moved his fingers to the locket. Naji felt a tremor pass through the hand below his—a surge of energy—and suddenly the inside of his mother's locket vanished. In its place, there was a distant glimmer of light on water.

Naji beamed at Lem. "I felt that!" he said. "That's cool!"

Lem gave Naji's shoulder a squeeze. He looked at the El Sayeds and nodded appraisingly. "He's going to learn quickly."

THROUGH THE PORTAL

L em picked up the locket by its chain and held it out toward Bach, who took it and looked inside. Through the opening, he saw a keyhole's worth of sand. A faint sound of waves brushing the shore tickled his ear, as did the sound of a breeze rustling through shrubs. A whiff of rotten fish struck his nose.

"Smells right," he said.

"So now we get rid of the box," Leda said. "Sy, could you stomp it for us?"

"Nah," he replied. "Might hurt my foot. Don't wanna end up on crutches."

Leda glared at her brother. Simon conspicuously ignored her look, grinning. Mr. El Sayed reached over his son's head and picked up the box.

"I can get rid of this," he said. "I have a mallet downstairs. I will smash it into bits."

"Wait." Bach held out his free hand, palm-up, toward Mr. El Sayed, who willingly surrendered the box. Curling his fingers around it, Bach turned it over, his eyes scanning the symbols and markings. His sight-beyond offered glimpses of the little thing's long, checkered history. If this was where its story ended, only one being in the room had the right to close the book.

He offered the box to Azraq. "You were locked inside this little wooden prison for thousands of years. Why don't you do the honors?"

Though his expression remained dignified, the Djinni's large round eyes locked onto the box and began to glow—a cool, green fire that covered his face in an eerie dance of light and shadow. Silent, he released the Ifrit's broken wing and held out his free hand for the box. Bach handed it over.

The moment his limb was unfettered, the Ifrit tried to pull free of the Marid's grasp. Azraq smacked his captive in the back of the head with the box. A corner scratched his scalp and a sputter of sparks leaked from the wound. The Ifrit snarled but fell still.

The locket in Bach's hand caught the light, flashing a golden shine across the Ifrit's four eyes. The Djinni looked at the necklace and cringed, his face so full of fear that Bach felt a stab of pity.

For a few seconds, Azraq cradled the box in his palm; then he wrapped his webbed fingers around the box and squeezed. The wood creaked, straining to maintain its integrity—and then, with one final squeak, the box shattered, reduced to splinters. As slivers of wood rained over the captive Ifrit and littered the floor, a rumble, deep and satisfied, emanated from Azraq's chest. He lifted one foot and stomped on the largest shard, breaking it into several pieces.

Bach felt a flush of empathic satisfaction as Azraq released a slow breath and murmured, "Never again."

The Djinni didn't indulge in emotion for long, however. With a sudden jerk, he yanked his captor to his feet. "Place the gateway on the floor before me," he commanded, "so that it may receive its new occupant."

The Ifrit's eyes grew wide. His skin turned bright yellow and red as a mad rush of flames lit his body. Everyone backed away from the fire—except for Bach. Wary yet confident, he stepped forward and laid the open locket on the tile.

At the sight of the tiny open passage before him, the Ifrit screamed. The shrill pitch of his voice shook the walls, knocking picture frames to the floor and shattering the empty mug on the counter. Mrs. El Sayed gasped and grabbed her husband's arm as he seized their son and pulled them both to the far side of the room. Lem and Rachel clapped their hands over their ears and the Morleys stared in wide-eyed shock at the creature. The shriek ended in a barrage of alien words as the Ifrit launched into a tirade that fell upon largely uncomprehending ears.

Azraq lifted the Ifrit into the air and positioned him above the open locket. With the tiny door beneath him, the Ifrit's panic grew even more frantic. His arms and wings remained trapped in Azraq's hands but his feet, now off the floor, swung in every direction. He kicked a hole in the wall and knocked the kitchen table on its side, and his long-clawed toes sliced a chair in half.

With horror, Bach saw Leda take a step toward the flailing Djinni, eyes fixed on his lips, as if she was trying to absorb the strange words he was issuing. Simon grabbed his sister by the arm, but just as he snatched her back the Djinni kicked in her direction, his claws coming so close to Leda's head that Bach thought she might lose it altogether.

Recoiling, Leda stumbled backward into her brother's chest, dropping one crutch in the process. She looked down at the fallen crutch—and froze.

Bach followed the direction of her stare. There, next to the crutch, was a messy little pile of hair, the color and texture of which looked familiar. His gaze traveled back up to Leda's face, just in time to see her fingers touch the spot where her hair should be but only frayed ends remained.

"Oh, hell no," she said, her face twisted in fury. Hopping on her good leg, she hurled her remaining crutch at the Ifrit. It struck him and clattered to the floor as Simon pulled her away. "I have to be at work later today, asshole!" she yelled over the Ifrit's screaming. "How the hell am I gonna show up with half my hair gone?!"

"At least you've still got your head, baldy," Simon said, holding her tight.

With the Morleys out of range, the Ifrit's flailing could harm nothing but the room itself. His feet shattered tiles on the floor, smashed more holes in the wall, and ripped a light fixture from the ceiling, hurling it across the countertop. The majority of the humans present scampered out of the way, fleeing to the far corners of the room or ducking out of the kitchen altogether, but Bach held steady just out of range, curious to see how Azraq would proceed.

The blue Djinni's muscles tightened and his lips thinned as he slowly brought his hands closer to each other, folding the Ifrit's limbs inward. As the shrieking creature's arms and wings drew closer to its torso, his entire body began to collapse into itself. His limbs shrank, gradually becoming as thin and flimsy as noodles, and his wildly kicking legs shriveled into flapping twigs.

The Ifrit ignited, his skin flaming red and yellow in thick, molten waves even as the edges of his body folded and bent. Still bellowing unintelligibly, the Ifrit's burning torso crumpled in Azraq's hands. Azraq, his four hands still tightly clenched but now reduced to doll-sized fists at the end of his wrists, dropped to one knee and stretched his arms toward the open locket. The voice of the Ifrit had grown thin and high-pitched as his body shrank into a crinkly ragdoll version of itself, but his incoherent words continued to stream forth.

Azraq gave his prisoner a final shake and then plunged his tiny hands, still clutching the shrimpy Ifrit, into the open locket. Seconds later, he withdrew his empty hands, which immediately regained their true size. An echo sounded from within the locket, the distant shout of the watery dimension's new tenant. Azraq chuckled. He scooped up the locket and, before another echo could breach its border, snapped it shut.

All sound died as a shimmery reflection of light danced over the locket's golden surface.

THE PROMISE

The kitchen, though now quiet, was in shambles. As Bach surveyed the mess, he heard Rachel cluck her tongue and Simon let out a low whistle. Large holes in the walls revealed naked timber and electrical wires, and dust and broken drywall was scattered everywhere.

Lem began to pick up pieces of a splintered chair, starting with one leg that had impaled a cabinet door. He yanked it free, creating a splintered hole that opened onto the broken dishes inside.

Mr. El Sayed gingerly walked through the room with his eyes in constant motion, as if he was afraid to look at any one spot of damage for too long. Leda, missing a crutch, sagged against her brother for support as they both swept their gazes over the path of the light fixture, which had flown across the kitchen, carved a labyrinth of scratches on the surface of the countertop, and slammed into the stove.

Bach looked at Azraq. "He's officially stuck in there, right?"

"Yes," Azraq replied in his low rumble.

Naji darted over and, without hesitation, jumped up and grabbed Azraq around his wrist. He hung there, dangling from the blue creature like he was a jungle gym, until the Djinni lowered his arm with a grumble and the boy's feet touched the floor. Naji pulled Azraq's hand even lower until he could see the locket nestled in his palm.

"How long will he stay in there?" the boy asked. "Forever?"

"No," Bach jumped in. "Not forever. He just needs to cool off."

"For how long?" Naji asked.

"I dunno." Bach ran a hand through his hair. "I didn't think beyond getting him into the locket. What do you think, Azraq?"

"The insolent whelp in this locket," the Djinni said, "feels that if he fails to take revenge on the child, he and his family will be dishonored. As long as the boy is alive, the Ifrit will feel compelled to take revenge."

"So he'll need to stay in there until they're gone?" Bach asked.

"At least until the boy has lived out his life," Azraq said. "Once the child has passed, the Ifrit may return home unavenged but with his honor intact."

Bach heard Mrs. El Sayed draw in a sharp breath at the mention of Naji's death.

"Before we worry about that," he said hastily, "we should figure out where to keep this thing. It needs to be kept somewhere safe."

"I can put the necklace back in my jewelry box," Mrs. El Sayed offered.

"No," Mr. El Sayed said. "I do not want to take the chance that someone will open it by accident. It cannot stay in this house."

"We are not going to open it, Amr," his wife said.

"Of course not," he said, "but are you prepared to guard the necklace against every visitor? Suppose the locket falls to the floor and breaks? Suppose we have to move and the locket is lost? A stranger could open it and turn the creature loose. What if one day, when Naji is grown, he comes to visit us with children of his own and one of our grandchildren finds the necklace? Are you prepared to guard against all of that, Safiya?"

The resolve in her expression faltered and a touch of fear drifted through her eyes.

"No," she finally said. "The necklace should not stay here."

"So that's out," Bach said. He turned to Rachel. "Ra, could you maybe—"

"No," she said firmly.

"But—"

"The locket can't go to the Arcana," she told him.

"She's quite right," Lem said. "It would be a breach of inter-dimensional law to keep a Djinn prisoner in the Arcana."

"Then," Bach said, brow furrowed, "won't you be in trouble when someone finds out he's in the locket?"

"We had nothing to do with it," Rachel said. "Lem came here to teach Naji about portal creation; I just watched and drank a soda. You Notans are the ones who shut him in there."

"You're not obligated to stop us?"

"Nope," she said lightly. "Nothing happening here is our problem."

Skeptical, Bach glanced at Lem. "Really?"

"Yes," he said. "This is a matter between Djinn and Notans."

Their mutual lack of concern nibbled at Bach's conscience. He had assumed that they would take charge or at least have a plan to put in place, but they seemed totally unconcerned.

Well, if they weren't going to assist with a resolution, some-one else would have to step up—and Bach supposed that some-one would have to be him. The El Sayeds were fumbling for an idea, Azraq didn't care, and, now that the action was over, the

Morleys didn't seem to be that interested, either. In fact, Leda seemed more concerned with her hair than she was with the Djinn.

Heart thundering, mouth dry, Bach desperately cast about for a solution.

"Well," he finally said, "I don't feel qualified to play warden, but I don't wanna saddle someone else with the responsibility."

"Humans are inherently incapable of handling a responsibility of this magnitude," Azraq said. He tossed the locket in the air, making the entire room gasp in unison, then caught it in another hand. "Not one of you here is reliable enough to bear the weight of this brat's imprisonment."

For a moment, Bach accepted the Djinni's assessment; but then an echoing voice crept through his memory—a voice dripping with contempt yet calling him powerful and beyond ordinary. Suddenly, Bach felt as Azraq had wished him to feel when he'd said those words: like a warrior with a weapon in his hand. A long-lost sense of strength surged in him, a sensation that simultaneously shocked him and brought a realization: Months spent without a roof over his head had left his skin scarred but hardened. Long days between meals had withered his body but made him patient and resourceful. The absence of a lucid mind had made him a pariah but brought him to sharper thoughts and solidified his intent to never lose his grip again. He was now something he had never been before: a man in control of himself, in command of his surroundings, emotions, and life. Moreover, he was a man with a solution.

"You do it."

Azraq blinked. "What?"

"You watch him," Bach said. "You put that locket around your neck and you carry him around until he's ready to go free."

"Ridiculous," he said. "I can easily deposit this portal in some inaccessible location to protect it from human interference. The tallest peak on earth, the deepest chasm, an underwater abyss—"

"No," Bach said. "If no one can reach the locket then the Ifrit will be trapped in there forever."

"What of it?"

"Stop!" Bach said. "Think how you felt when you were trapped in there. Locked away in a pocket dimension, stuck on an island, no one to check up on you. Do you really wanna inflict the same fate on someone else?"

Azraq curled his lip. "You compare this inferior creature to me! Outrageous!"

"He's a living thing, a sentient being. He should be treated like the rest of us would want to be treated."

"Then why bother to imprison him at all?" the Djinni said with a sneer. "If you are so very inclined toward mercy then why not release the little fool immediately?"

"Because he did some bad shit! Oh"—Bach flinched as he remembered Naji, whose big brown eyes were currently staring up at him. He lowered his head toward the El Sayeds. "Sorry about that."

Mr. El Sayed waved away the offense.

Mrs. El Sayed nodded. "I agree with you. The prisoner must remain where he is for the time being. But not forever." She patted her husband's arm, then turned her attention to the Djinni.

Azraq watched her approach him through suspicious eyes. His webbed fingers closed around the locket as she laid her hand over his.

"I do not want him in my home, nor any other place where he could find me or my family again," she said. "But I think of him in that place as you described it—the tiny island with no escape—and I feel badly for him. He is a Djinni, a being of fire and air. He is not meant for such a place."

"I lived in that place," Azraq snarled. "I was there for thousands of years, and no one felt pity for me."

"*I* feel pity for you," Mrs. El Sayed said. "My pity comes too late to free you, but I feel it nonetheless."

"So do I," Bach said. "Solomon did you wrong. Maybe you deserved to be locked up, I don't know . . . but not for millennia. And the same's true for the Ifrit."

"You yourself called him a 'brat,' did you not?" Mrs. El Sayed asked. "You said he was 'young' and 'contemptible.'"

"All true," Azraq said.

"Then while he stays there, waiting to outlive Naji, you can give him some much-needed lessons to help him grow." She smiled up at him. "Surely you would be a good teacher for him."

"Me?" Azraq snatched his hand away from her. "Why do you say so?"

"You're good!" Naji said. "You stopped the bad monster!"

"Yes," Mr. El Sayed nodded. "You saved my family. You must have changed very much since your days on that island."

"My every action since emerging from that damned box has been at *his* behest," Azraq retorted, pointing one finger at Bach.

"Yeah." Bach snorted. "Keep telling yourself that."

The Djinni narrowed his eyes. "What do you mean?"

"You've been calling me weak and stupid and God knows what else from the moment we met," Bach said. "You took one look at me and you knew I was nothing like Solomon. You *knew* I wouldn't be able to control you—and, hey, you were right. That's why you led me here every step of the way."

Azraq shook his head. "I have led no one."

"It was your idea to come here. It was your idea to take

down the Ifrit. It's your idea not to give the locket to a human. It's all been you."

"No."

"Yes." Bach jabbed a finger toward the Djinni. "You. All you."

"Absurd!" Azraq shouted, backing away. "Shut up, you fool!"

"You shut up!" Bach shouted back.

Silence devoured every sound in the room but for the distant rumble of passing cars in the street. Everyone stared at Bach with wide-eyed shock—a look that reflected his own amazement at himself. He swallowed hard, resisting the urge to slink away.

"I mean," he said, "that you made one good decision after another when you saw that I wasn't ready to make them for myself. In my opinion, you're fully rehabilitated—and since I'm your 'master,' I think my opinion counts for something. For all your talk about the inferiority of humans, you've consistently acted as if you have our best interests at heart. I can't think of anyone in a better position to judge the Ifrit's progress than you. I'm totally comfortable putting him in your hands. You keep him in there for the rest of Naji's life and check in on him regularly to see how he's shaping up. When you're confident that he's no longer a threat, let him go."

"Are you saying that you are ordering me to be the keeper of this inbred runt?"

Just an hour ago, Bach would have shrunk from the idea of giving a direct order of any kind, let alone an order that involved the imprisonment of a sentient creature. Now, he felt possessed of a wealth of self-assurance to which he was unaccustomed, and was still a little nervous about embracing. He felt like a whole new man—but he was still coming to terms with who that man was.

"I'm *saying* . . . I trust your judgment." Bach stepped forward and held out his hand.

After one last, suspicious glare, Azraq extended his arm and opened his palm, offering up the locket. Bach took it by the chain and let the golden trinket swing and bounce in the air.

"Even if I knew how," he told Azraq, "I wouldn't brand the Ifrit like Solomon branded you. That means when he gets out of there, he won't be under anyone's control. You're the only one I know who can deal with him." He held up the necklace. "I'm not ordering. I'm asking. Please take this and give me your word that you'll honor my trust in you."

Azraq tilted his head. Bach saw a mélange of emotion roaring through the Djinni's eyes, their green hue taking on peculiar shades as one feeling overshadowed another and then faded behind its replacement.

The Djinni looked absolutely flummoxed.

Sight-beyond taking over his mind's eye, Bach suddenly felt himself in Azraq's place. The Djinni was in a strange sort of limbo, caught in a blank spot where the correct emotion for this moment should reside. Though he would never say so aloud, this was well outside of his experience. He could not remember any time in his life when his assistance had been requested rather than commanded, and he had never known humans to say please. Any responsibility he'd borne had been given only at the end of a leash or—more often—a lash. To see these human eyes on him, holding not fear or contempt but trust, created a paralyzing numbness in his mind.

The feel of that emptiness made Bach's chest ache. Azraq had no idea how to react to kindness.

"It's all right," Bach said gently. He lifted the locket again, holding it out toward the Djinni. "You can do this."

Slowly, almost mechanically, Azraq took the necklace from Bach and placed the chain over his head. "I will take it," he said.

"And you'll watch over the Ifrit?" Bach asked. "You can't just leave him in there forever. You have to look in on him periodically. Eventually, when he's not a threat to Naji's family anymore, he has to be let out. Will you give me your word that you'll do that?"

"Very well," the Djinni said, his eyes unfocused and his gaze distant. "You have my word. I will monitor him during his imprisonment, and when the boy has passed, I will uncork the island dimension and escort him home. He will trouble this world no longer."

Mrs. El Sayed smiled first at Azraq and then at her husband. "Thank God."

"Yes," Mr. El Sayed said, taking her hand in his. He nodded to the Djinni. "Thank you."

Azraq stared at them, silent, as if unsure how to respond. Bach was beginning to wonder if he should reply for him or if that would offend the Djinni when Leda loudly cleared her throat, drawing everyone's attention.

"I gotta go," she announced. She gave Simon a firm yank. "*We* gotta go." She swatted irritably at her shorn hair. "I can't go to work like *this*."

Simon stifled what looked like a laugh and crossed the room to retrieve her missing crutch. "All right, Lee, let's go."

IN THE WAKE of the Morleys' departure, the Arcanans and the El Sayeds chatted among themselves, cleaning and carrying on as if there had not been a chaotic collision of worlds in the kitchen just moments ago.

Watching them, Bach stuck his hands in his pockets and encountered a lump of crumpled papers. He pulled the lump of his pocket and examined it—a rather sizable ball containing some scraps with unfamiliar handwriting on them, a bunch of gum wrappers, and one big wad of paper. He wondered for a moment when he had last chewed a piece of gum and then realized that he was looking at the paraphernalia that had fallen out of Simon's coat pocket when he brought out the Djinni's old box— not knowing where the trashcan was, he'd just shoved it all in his own pockets after picking it up.

Full of sudden curiosity, and a sight-beyond twinge, he unballed the wad of paper—and felt his heart freeze. His mind locked up, threatening to skip away, but he knocked the feeling back and refused to let it touch him. He brought the paper to his chest and drew a breath. This had to be dealt with. *But this is not the place*, he thought, looking around the crowded room.

Flyer in hand, he quietly stepped away.

46
BURDENED

The locket around his neck felt strangely cool
against his fire-forged skin.
He tapped the locket with one webbed finger
and the light danced.

He thought of the Ifrit inside.

Right now, he was either
pacing the island
or beating his fists
against the invisible, sealed doorway.

He might be cursing Azraq, Bach, Naji,
or anyone else he could think of.

Perhaps the reality of the situation
was sinking into his young mind.

He could be wailing,
tearing at his own skin with his claws,
weeping himself into exhaustion,
the first daze of many in the years to come.

All were his own reactions
when he met the island.

He was half-tempted to
crack open the locket
and check on the Ifrit,
but he dashed the impulse.

The brat may as well
get used to his surroundings;
he was going to be on that island
for at least the lifetime of the boy.

If, when Azraq finally opened the door,
the Ifrit was still hungry for blood,
he would shove him back in
and let him stew on the island
for another lifetime.

Whether the Ifrit's imprisonment outlasted
just Naji,
or Naji's grandchildren,
the difference was minimal to Azraq.

After thousands of years on the island,
he had thoroughly absorbed the lesson
of patience.

Perhaps the Ifrit will likewise mature,
he thought, tapping the locket
with one webbed finger.

This locket, he mused.
This burden.
This choice.

In the moment the request was made
he had frozen,
snared by old experiences,
until he saw the scion's gaze
and heard him speak.

Bach had seen something,
learned something about him.

He had seen this happen before.

The king.

It was the way of seers—
that faraway stare,
that unnatural glow in the eyes,
the haunted vibration in the voice.

But this was the first time Azraq
had witnessed it used
to soothe
and not to wound.

Had the king's scion commanded him
to take on this burden,
he would have found some loophole,
avoided the charge.

But when the seer stood before him,
asking instead of ordering,
expressing trust in him—
that had somehow convinced him
to give his word.

Strange man.

The humans scurried around the kitchen,
cleaning up the Ifrit's mess,
looking like ants repairing
a collapsed tunnel.

Azraq's presence had been forgotten
and he was grateful for it.

Thoughts of the near future
drifted into his mind.

Should he travel forth
and see more of this world
and its multitude of changes?

Or return to his own world
and see what had become
of his people?

Each option had its appeal and repulsion.

The balance of them left him unsatisfied.

He did not remember freedom
being so conflicting.

A fear suddenly stung him.

Am I free?

The scion had not said so,
not explicitly.

He turned to address the seer
but saw with a shock
that he had disappeared.

Hungry for the final word
that would break his chains,
he strode from the kitchen
and went room to room,
searching for the only man capable of ending
a millennia-long nightmare.

BARGAINING

N aji stared at the mess in the kitchen. Now that the excitement with the Djinn had passed, he finally felt the full impact of the day's events. Though he was still excited by it all, he also felt heavy and tired. Tears welled up in his eyes before he understood that he was upset, and he began to sob loudly.

Every eye in the room turned toward him.

"I'm sorry I brought the Ifrit here," he said, crying freely now. "I shouldn't have. It was all my fault. I'm sorry. I'm sorry."

His mother rushed to his side and swept him into her arms. "You did nothing wrong," she reassured him.

His father placed a hand on his bowed head. "You are not to blame for the Djinni's crimes. You made a mistake. He made a choice."

"But I poofed him here," Naji wailed into his mother's shoulder. "He tried to hurt you because he was mad at me. It was my fault."

Though his parents continued to assure him that it was just a mistake and no one was angry, Naji keep crying. His mother stroked his hair and whispered softly in his ear as his father rubbed his back, but nothing calmed him—until, eventually, exhaustion dried up his tears.

Naji leaned against his mother, his tear-soaked cheeks clinging to the material of her shirt. He didn't like the coldness of it but he didn't want her to let go.

A face slid into his view, smiling gently. Lem.

"If it bothers you," the *ukiba* said, "the best thing to do is learn to control your ability so it won't happen again." Lem gave Naji's father a knowing look, the sort grownups gave each other and thought he didn't notice. "I'm here to teach you precisely so this won't happen again."

"Just so," said his father encouragingly. "That is excellent advice."

His warm tone gave Naji a boost of energy. "Really?"

"Yes indeed," Lem cheerfully replied. "By the time I've taught you all I know, you will able to build highways from one dimension to another with only the power of your mind."

Naji's eyes brightened and he smiled. Lem sounded so pleased. And he liked the idea of being that strong. His mother, however, tensed up. Tenderly separating herself from Naji, she stood up, cocked her head at Lem, and folded her arms over her chest.

"Where, exactly, is he to build these highways?" she asked.

"Wherever they are needed, ma'am," Lem replied.

"Here? In this city?"

"Oh, no." Lem laughed. "Your world does not employ such technology."

"But yours does?"

"Yes. It is our primary mode of transportation."

"So my child will be expected to go to your world rather than live here?"

The bite of her tone jolted the smile from Lem's face. "We would never expect you to part with your son, ma'am," he said.

"He will remain here, with you, until he is ready to leave home."

"And then you will take him to another world, where I cannot contact him?"

"No! Well, yes, in a manner of speaking, but—"

"My son goes nowhere without me or my husband!"

Lem stared at her, his mouth agape. Naji was used to his mother's shifting tone but he had seen other people caught off guard by it, just like his new teacher was now. He saw him glance at the crazy girl; it looked like he was pleading for help. But the crazy girl just shrugged and went back to collecting broken pieces of tile and cabinets.

His mother grabbed an unbroken kitchen chair and sat down, her arms still crossed, her eyes still ablaze.

Clearing his throat, Lem positioned a second chair in front of her and sat down.

"It would be acceptable to us if you wished to move to the Arcana when Naji is old enough to begin work," he said.

"And if we wish to remain here?"

"Also acceptable."

"And if Naji wishes to remain here as well?"

"Then . . . I'm sure arrangements can be made. The final decision will, of course, be his to make when he is of age."

Naji's mother tossed her head and looked Lem up and down. "I assume he would be well paid for any 'construction' he might perform for your people."

"Well, we are a non-monetary society," Lem said carefully, "but we are prepared to offer Naji an excellent education. We have a number of schools that could provide him with both specialized training and a well-rounded curriculum. I can give you a great deal of information about them, and you can choose whichever one you feel is best."

"These schools are in your world, are they not? Far away from here?"

"Y-yes," he stammered, "but think of it as a boarding school. An elite boarding school. You would be free to visit as often as you like and Naji would come home every few weeks."

"So," she said sharply, "you wish to train and educate Naji in one of your schools so that he can learn about your ways and your society. That will certainly prepare him for a life in your world. How, then, is he to choose to live in this world, if he has only been taught about yours?"

Lem opened his mouth to reply but she backed him down with a glare.

"This arrangement only benefits you," she said. "At best, it will pigeonhole my son into a career that your people have laid out for him."

"No, no!" Lem said. His eyes were huge with panic. "He can choose any career he likes! Our *ukiba* abilities are more of a . . . side job, just something we are called upon to do now and then. I offer my services as an *ukiba* one weekend a month and I accept emergency calls now and then. My career is in technology. The *ukiba* who trained me was a doctor. Naji will not be pigeonholed in the least."

Naji's mother drummed her fingers on her arms. "And what assurances do we have that you will have our family's best interest at heart?" she asked. "How do we know you won't just remove Naji from our care, place him in your school, and poison his mind against us?"

"We will certainly lay it all out in writing."

"That is not enough."

Lem looked perplexed. Naji understood. His mother had that effect.

"What assurances can I give you?" the *ukiba* asked.

The moment she heard Lem utter those words, Naji's mother lifted her chin and fixed him in a calculated gaze.

"I want Naji to have as good a life in this world as you can offer him in yours," she said. "I want him to attend school here. A private school of our choosing."

Lem tapped his foot, clearly thinking. "That could be arranged," he finally said. "Provided, of course, that you allow me to continuing teaching him to use his gift. And my people may also wish to supplement his education with some extra classes. So long as you don't feel it would be too much school for a young boy."

"There is no such thing," Naji's mother replied firmly. "Education is the key to a good future. But a good future is easier to come by when life at home is comfortable. To that end"—she swept a hand in a wide arc—"I want all of this damage repaired."

"Of course."

"And another building for our restaurant."

Lem blinked and drew back. "What?"

"Our restaurant," she repeated. "We always meant to open one but there were monetary complications, so we opened the market instead. I want to keep the market here and open the restaurant in a second building."

Lem stared at her, his jaw slack. From the far end of the kitchen, Naji heard the crazy girl chuckle.

"And," she pressed on, "I want this apartment to be updated. I want a modern kitchen and a new bathroom. I want the patio space on the roof to be prettied up and I want a garden installed beside it." She smiled. "And a piano for the living room."

Lem hemmed and hawed, struggling to explain that he was not authorized to grant such requests, but Naji's mother would hear none of it. She tossed her hair and demanded that Lem either give her what she wanted or let her speak to someone in charge. Naji kept his face turned away from the table to hide his grin as he watched Rachel and his father lift the broken light fixture off the stove and sweep up bits of shattered glass.

"This thing's a lost cause, sir," Naji heard the crazy girl say, inclining her head at the remains of the fixture. "It'll never light up again."

"No matter," Naji's father said, looking at Naji's mother with an expression full of pride. "My wife is well on her way to negotiating a massive redesign of our home. New lighting will no doubt be included."

Naji watched the events that would determine the course of his life unfold in his family's destroyed kitchen. Though he was too young to grasp it all, he instinctively felt safe now that he saw his mother was clearly in control of the discussion. He stood to the side, absorbing it all with a pleasant half-smile on his face.

FREEDOM

He found the seer in the El Sayeds' master bedroom,
gazing out the window overlooking the back alley,
his bony form half lit by the shade-dotted sunlight
peeking through the glass.

"You must release me," he said, standing tall.

The seer's head moved slightly,
his back still to the Djinni.
"What'd you say?" he mumbled.

"You must declare my term of service to you at an end.
I cannot claim to my freedom until you do."

"Oh. Yeah. About that."
A rustle of paper momentarily distracted Azraq
until the next words focused his attention
with laser precision.
"I can't."

The words of betrayal ripped a hole in him
that was quickly filled with fire.

"You swore you would release me
once the Ifrit was no longer a threat!"

"And I will. There's just . . .
there's one thing I need you to do first."

Lips curling back from his sharp teeth in a snarl,
Azraq's glowing green eyes bulged
as he stared at the back of Bach's head.
"I performed your 'one thing' when I defeated the Ifrit.
You promised me freedom!"

"It won't take long."

"Curse you and all your bloodline!" the Djinni roared.
"May your third eye show you nothing but horrors
and bring you nothing but pain until—"

"Whoa," Bach said.
He pivoted around, one hand outstretched.
"Cool it, man. All I need is for you to
find someone for me."

Azraq's jaws opened wide to spew damnation
upon the king's scion
but when he saw the seer's bloodshot eyes
and the trickles of blood dripping from
each nostril and the corner of his mouth
his fury yielded to confusion and distrust.

"What trick is this?" he asked.

"Trick?"

"Your face."

The seer, looking perplexed, walked over to
the mirror hanging from the opposite wall
and, when he saw his ravaged face,
flinched.

"Damn," he said, sounding impressed.
"I look like I got my ass kicked."

"I cannot speak for your ass," Azraq said,
"but the state of your face does imply contact
with someone's boot."

"No one kicked me," Bach said, sighing.
"I think I must have done it to myself.
I was trying to force my 'third eye,'
the one you were cursing,
to tell me something about this."
He tossed Azraq a crinkled piece of paper.

On the paper,
Azraq saw a man's image,
along with some writing.
"Who is this man?" he asked.

"Javier Alvarez," the seer said.

I think the last bit of sight-beyond information I got
before I lost my mind
had something to do with this man
and his daughter.
I was already under a lot of stress
and when the Alvarez short-circuit hit me . . .
I snapped."

Azraq would never understand humans.
"If that is that case," he said,
"Then why trouble yourself now?
You said you know nothing about this man.
Why should his situation be important to you?"

The seer clenched his fists.
"Because it is, dammit,
and I need to know why!"

Azraq drew back in surprise.
There was a fierceness in the seer's expression
to which he was unaccustomed:
his young face hard,
his jaw set,
and those blue eyes
crackling with lightning.

Though the man was a fraction of his size
and had no real authority to his name,
Azraq felt cowed.
For the first time
since reentering the world,

he saw in this young seer
a hint of resemblance to the king.

"There is something about the Alvarez girl,"
the seer said, ranting with the fervor of a lunatic,
"that's connected to me.
Somehow, someday,
her life is gonna be mixed up with mine."
Wild-eyed, he shook his head.
"I just wish I didn't get this feeling of dread
every time I think about helping her.
I'm so drawn to her;
I can't envision a path to take
that doesn't lead her way.
But when I try to step down that path,
I feel broken glass under my feet.
How can both things be true?"
With a quaking sigh, he shook his head.
"If I don't do something,
I really will lose my mind."

Though he did not understand what was happening,
Azraq saw that the seer had only
a tentative grasp on sanity,
which did not bode well
for his impending freedom.

Holding up the paper, he said,
"You want me to find this man."

"No," the seer said. "Javier's dead.

I need you to find Tatiana—
his daughter."

The dusty thirst for freedom clawed at Azraq
more ferociously than it had
in thousands of years of imprisonment.
The promised drink was at his fingertips,
so close it had brought drool to his lips
reviving a craving long ignored—
and yet now he found his full attention
taken up by the seer.

From the moment he had first spied his new jailor,
Azraq had been certain of one thing:
the man was weak.

He was a wretched physical specimen
composed of wasted muscle and scarred, pale skin
and he walked with the slumped shoulders
and shuffling feet
of a downtrodden peasant.

He was indecisive, sycophantic,
and possessed of unreasonable emotional attachments
to useless things.

And yet.

He was single-minded in his kindness.

He was mutable, adaptive, and quick to recover.

He bowed under the weight of his burdens
but managed not to break.

Reluctantly, Azraq admitted to himself that this man was,
perhaps,
not as weak as he had assumed.

"You are strange," he said.

"If that's the worst thing you can think to call me,
I'm cool with it," the seer said.

"What do you require of me?"

"Just find Tatiana Alvarez,
the girl posting these flyers.
I need to know someplace she'll be
in the near future,
maybe someplace she visits regularly.
I have to be able to pinpoint her location
at a definite time.
Can you do that?"

"Yes."
Azraq cocked his head
and looked at him intently.
"Then what?"

"Then . . . nothing.
Find Tatiana, tell me where she'll be,
and then you can go."

Those words! So very close
to the release he needed.
"Go?"

"Yeah," the king's scion said.
"You do this one last thing and then . . ."
His eyes assumed the seer's glow.
"Then shake the dust of your labor
and go your way,"
he recited in a voice not quite his own.
For a moment, Azraq could almost believe
that it was the king himself
speaking through his descendant.
"Find Tatiana," the seer continued,
sounding like himself again,
"and you're free."

The Djinni turned to leave,
but the seer wasn't done.

"I want to tell you, Azraq," he said,
"that in the short time I've known you,
I've learned a lot.
You've said some horrible things to me,
but there's a grain of truth in it all.
I have been depending on Rachel
to make my decisions for me.
I've been trying to get my life back on track,
but I've gotten used to living in survival mode.
I gotta stand on my own two feet.
I just didn't think I was capable of it

until you gave me a push.
Thanks for that."

Azraq shook his head in puzzlement.
From trust to gratitude now, he thought.

The world he had left behind
when thrust into imprisonment
had been warped into something
far more complex in his absence.
This was not a world of clearly defined stations in life,
a world where kings stood above peasants
and humans enslaved Djinn.

This was a world where the scion of a king
lived like a dog but still gave of himself to others.

This was a world where a subjugated Djinni
was hailed as a hero
by a family who had thought him fictional
but yesterday.

In a world so upside-down,
it was hard to put his feet on the ground.

And it was hard to know,
now that the choice was his,
what to do and where to go.

The myriad of prospective paths
held him captive at the crossroads.

No choice seemed correct,
yet no choice seemed overtly wrong.
For the first time in his long life,
he felt incapacitated.

"It's hard not having someone else choose for you,
isn't it?" the seer said.

At a loss for words,
Azraq could only furrow his brow.

"Ever since you were branded,"
the seer went on,
"someone else has been making your choices for you.
And it's weirdly liberating, having no choice.
You never get lost when there's only one road.
It's a lot harder to live under your own power.
But hey—that's what freedom is."
He shrugged and smiled.
"Your time and your life are your own now."

Azraq closed his eyes and nodded.
The endless paths before him
became less intimidating.
The abundance of choices was not a burden
but a liberation.

Every choice was his to make.

Voices in the kitchen drifted through the open door.
He listened without opening his eyes.

He heard the child's parents,
their mutual tone firm but animated.
Their son projected his voice over theirs
as only a child unconscious of his volume could do.
He sounded pleased, excited.

Azraq found himself curious
as to what would become of the family.
He wondered how the father
would adapt to his altered world view.
He wondered if the mother
would tell stories of him
as she had been told stories of his people.
He wondered what the
underdeveloped seedling of a boy
would grow into.
If he accepted the Arcanan's training,
then he would grow up
with a foot in each world,
not unlike Azraq himself.

His heart lurched
as he realized that he had
compared himself, favorably,
to a human.

This world *was* upside-down.
But somehow,
though he had not quite found his footing,
he was beginning to feel grounded.

"You are, perhaps," he said to the seer,
"not as useless as I initially believed."

The seer smiled. "Thanks. Good luck."

"To you as well."

In a shimmer of light and shadow, he was gone.

49

DONE

Bach stepped into the kitchen with his hands in his pockets. The first thing he saw was Lem Odero sitting at the kitchen table with his face in his hands while Mrs. El Sayed, standing over him, chattered into a phone. Her husband stood at her shoulder, listening in and adding a few words to insist on some point or another, but for the most part his wife was steering the conversation.

Bach looked back over his shoulder to see Naji in the living room. The boy had lost interest in the grownup talk and was sitting on the floor by the sofa, playing with some toys.

A few feet from Naji, Rachel sat on the sofa, eyes glued to the phone in her hand.

Bach crossed the floor and took a seat next to her. "What's going on in there?" he asked, gesturing to the kitchen.

"An epic contest of wills," she answered without shifting her gaze. "Ms. Dokgo vs. Mrs. El Sayed. They're negotiating the terms of Naji's education."

"Who's winning?"

"Naji," she said, smirking. "Whether it's in your world or mine, this kid's going to get the best education there is. And he'll learn how to use his gift, which is in everyone's best interests."

Bach looked down at the little boy, still hard at play on the

living room carpet. The smile on his face was sweet and innocent, his expression blissfully self-absorbed. A sudden wash of
memories from his own childhood made Bach wonder if he had
ever been that happy. Most of his childhood memories of his
mother involved her shooing him out of whatever room she was
in. He primarily remembered his father as a three-piece suit
leaving the house early in the morning and returning home after
dark. He'd rarely seen them together. They'd even slept at opposite ends of the house.

For the second time that day, Bach felt a surge of envy for
the boy. A wisp of sight-beyond showed him good things ahead
for Naji.

Some minutes later, the boy raised his head and noticed
Bach. He grinned and looked expectantly across the room. Seeing nothing, he looked from one corner to another. When every
corner proved empty, his smile drooped.

"Where's Azraq?" he asked.

"He left," Bach said.

The boy's face dissolved into abject misery. Tears gathered in
his eyes and his lip trembled. "Why didn't he say goodbye?" the
child wailed.

Caught by Naji's enormous, tear-filled eyes, Bach fumbled
for something to say.

"W-well," he stammered. "I . . . I guess . . ." A rush of sight-
beyond came to him, flooding him with relief. He leaned forward
and smiled. "Don't worry, kid," he said. "You're gonna see him
again."

Naji sniffed and wiped his face with the back of his hand.
"When?"

"I don't know," Bach said, "but I do know for sure that you
will see him again."

"Yeah?" The tears began to dry as the boy gazed up at him. "How do you know?"

Bach made a show of glancing around the room and then leaned down, gesturing with one hand for Naji to come closer.

"You know how you have that special gift that lets you 'poof' things?" he whispered.

A smile emerged through Naji's teary streaks. "I'm an *ukiba*," the boy said proudly.

"Right! Well, I have a gift too. I sometimes know things about other people."

"What kinds of things?"

"All kinds of things. The past, the future, their friends, their family. That's how I know you're gonna see Azraq again. Someday, somewhere, you will see him again."

"It's true," Rachel said without lifting her head. "Bach's an oracle. If he says it'll happen, it will."

Without warning, Naji jumped up and threw his arms around Bach's neck. Bach grunted as the kid accidentally kneed him in the gut, but he put an arm around him and patted him on the back.

"I'm gonna be happy to see Azraq," Naji said. "I hope he comes back soon." With that, he released Bach and went back to his toys.

As Bach fell back into the sofa, rubbing his bruised stomach, Rachel stood up.

"What's up?" he asked.

"I finished," she said.

"Finished what up?"

"My report on this assignment. I just sent it in."

"Really? Must've been a short report."

"Not much to write," she said, looking pleased. "I explained that the dimensional breaches were caused by an *ukiba* and posted references to Ms. Dokgo and Lem Odero for further explanation."

"What about the Djinn?"

"I mentioned them in my report, but I wrote that it was a Notan/Djinn matter that was solved by Notans and Djinn. End of story."

Rachel looked down at Naji. Her expression softened a bit and she stooped down to ruffle his hair. "Seems like it all worked out, huh?"

He flashed her a giant smile. "Thanks, Ms. Crazy Girl."

"You're welcome, kid."

After giving his hair one more tousle, Rachel turned and strode out of the room.

Confused, Bach hurried after her.

"Where are you going?" he asked.

"Back to the house," she said, sounding surprised by the question.

"But"—he gestured around the apartment—"all this . . ."

"All this is done," she said. "For me, at least. I've done what I needed to do. The El Sayeds are being taken care of. I'm leaving." She took another step, paused, and looked back at him. "You coming or staying?"

Slack-jawed, Bach stared at her. He felt an instinctive need to see this series of events to its conclusion and was about to tell her that he would stay. But then he realized that there was nothing for him to do. He wasn't involved in the negotiations for Naji's future, the Djinn were gone, and the Morleys had already left. At this point, he was just loitering.

He had the sudden realization that never in his life had he been this productive in one day. In the last handful of hours he had cut ties with his parents, inherited control of a Djinni, helped save a family from an unearthly intruder, and made progress toward cracking the Alvarez nut. It felt satisfying. Like Rachel, he had done all he could here.

He straightened up and nodded.

"I'm coming."

50
GIRL / REST

Following the human traces
left on the flyer,
Azraq located the girl with ease.

To deliver
what he'd promised,
he followed her
for a short time.

There was little to learn.

The paths she walked
were thick with her footsteps.

The constant,
inescapable rhythm
of the tide
was maddening.

The random rise and set
of the sun—

a sun, not *the* sun—
was frustrating.

The Ifrit screamed at the sky,
at the sea,
at the sand,
but especially at the sealed door.

He screamed for hours,
screamed until his head throbbed,
screamed until his throat
was raw.

Then he fell silent,
curled up in the shade of a tree,
and listened.

All humans looked small to Azraq
but this girl more so.

Though tall she was lean,
hollow, and hungry,
like a lamp nearly empty of oil.

Watching her move,
he got the impression
of wind rustling reeds.

Most humans walked heavily,
as if weighed down
by the earth itself.

ALISON LEVY

Tatiana walked
as if made of clouds,
buoyant and insubstantial,
like she might float into the sky
or be whisked away by a dust devil.

Young, weary, and isolated,
she hardly seemed the sort
to fill a seer's eye.

Occasionally, he heard voices
through the sealed door—
human voices,
a steady stream of nonsense
like the chittering of birds.

But through it all,
underneath every sound,
that leaked through from outside,
there was a thrumming,
like the muffled beat of a drum
played underwater.

It wasn't until
he had screamed himself silent
that he began to realize
where the sound came from.

The locket
that contained the passageway
must be strung around the Marid's neck.

The drumming sound
was the Marid's heartbeat.

He watched her
for only a short while
before looking away.

Whatever it was about her
that upset the scion,
he would not learn it by staring.

"It matters not," he said,
taking the locket in one hand
and giving it a tug.
"She is merely the last step I take
before I am free."

He looked at the locket,
at his distorted reflection
in the gold surface.

"She is the seer's problem,
his burden,
just as you are mine
until the boy has lived out his days."

Until the boy has lived out his days.

He heard the words through the door.
Conflicted, he sat down in the sand
and wrapped himself in his good wing.

ALISON LEVY

Everything was upside-down.

He was trapped here,
unable to fly,
nowhere to fly to.

He was a prisoner.

However, since the boy
would no longer be flinging him through portals,
he would no longer be compelled
to travel long distances to face him again.

The boy and his mother lived
but not by his choice.

The rip in his wing would heal
and the scar it was sure to leave
would be proof that he'd fought
to honor his family name.

Vengeance would not be forthcoming,
but neither would dishonor.

He could rest.

Never had he felt a desire
for anything
as deeply as he desired
a long, long sleep.

He recorded the necessary information
on a piece of paper.

Soon, he would drop the thing
into the seer's hands
and then . . .

Freedom.

He smiled to himself.

Freedom felt closer, lighter, warmer,
and more exceptional
with every passing second.

To have an abundance of choices
was a wealth that he had not known
in such a long time.

BONDING

Leda sat at her desk, quietly fuming. People walking past her office found any pitiful excuse to knock on her door just to sneak a peek at her new hairdo. Their big, dumb eyes soaked up her appearance like sponges. Only for the sake of her job did Leda resist the urge to throw her stapler at them.

"IT'S NO GOOD, honey."

That was all Sarah Marie could say when, immediately after leaving the El Sayeds' home, Leda charged into the salon and presented her mangled hair. All around them, the noisy place turned eerily quiet while Sarah Marie made a close inspection of the damaged side, her perfect pink nails caressing the frayed ends. "Hm, hm, hm!" buzzed through her lips as she turned Leda's head to one side and then another. After a thorough examination, she sighed, closed her eyes, and shook her head. "It's no good, honey."

In that moment, the overwhelming stress of the previous couple of weeks descended upon Leda all at once. Kidnapped, a busted knee, a cut up cheek, and a lifetime's worth of nightmares and panic attacks. Mutilated hair was mild by comparison, but it was still a slap in the face. She had worked so long and so hard to craft a professional persona—one that met the wide assortment of expectations her colleagues held *and* made her look both approachable and commanding. That image—the result of years of careful sculpting—was now ruined, destroyed with one swipe of a Djinni's claw.

It was too much, too damned much.

Against her every instinct, Leda burst into tears. Sarah Marie's maternal instinct seized control; she swept Leda into her arms and whispered, "Hush, now," as Leda cried helplessly into her shoulder. Then, keeping an arm around her, she seated Leda in a chair and directed her attention to the mirror.

"Let's see what I can do, baby," she cooed, smiling.

The result was an ear-length bob, suitable for the office but decidedly unflattering. Leda's features weren't delicate or cutesy enough to make Sarah Marie's creation look right. On a girl with narrower cheeks and a tapered chin, it would look classy and sophisticated; on Leda, with her rectangular face and wide nose, it looked harsh.

WINCING, LEDA SNAPPED her compact shut. *I look like a man in a flapper wig.*

Sarah Marie had warned her this would be the case, but all Leda had been able to think about was maintaining her "office" look. Now, as coworkers wandered into her vicinity to steal a glance at her, she felt hideous.

Her boss spent an unusual amount of time discussing paperwork with her that day. She couldn't help but feel his little piggy eyes scanning her hair as the slight inflection of his voice implied repressed chuckles. By the time he departed, leaving her with a mountain of work (half of it his own), she was ready to punch him.

She shut her door and worked through lunch so she could leave early and beat the end-of-day rush. Late afternoon, before the other employees, she hobbled out of her office, out of the department, and out of the museum without saying a word.

Starving from her skipped meal, she bought a sandwich at the deli down the block. She found a seat on a nearby park bench and inhaled her early dinner. As she swallowed the last bite, she felt an urge to talk about her day and unload some lingering emotions. She tried to call her mother, but it went straight to voicemail.

Rather than leave a message she knew her mother wouldn't get until bedtime—she never remembered to turn her phone on —Leda considered calling one of her girlfriends. But how could she? She couldn't tell any of them about the Djinn or the Arcana or anything else that had happened to her recently.

That left her with one option.

Nervous and unsure, she dialed Rachel. The phone rang only twice before she answered.

"Leda?"

Immediately, Leda launched into a narrative about her day, from the salon to her office and everything in between. With her voice rising and falling, she poured out her anger, her heartbreak, and her frustration. And then she stopped and waited, expecting to hear some bizarre Arcanan interpretation of it all.

"What happened to your hair," Rachel said, "that sucks."

The tension in her stomach unknotted and Leda exhaled. *That sucks.* This, at least, was familiar ground. "It really does," she said.

"You obviously take a lot of pride in your appearance," Rachel said. "It must be so hard to have to make a change like this."

Leda felt her body lighten. "Yeah. Thanks."

"What did you tell your stylist about how your hair got cut?"

"Oh, I told her some freak show on the bus snuck up and chopped off my hair from the seat behind me."

"And she believed it?"

"Girl." Leda snorted. "We were on a bus together not long ago. Do you really think that kind of thing doesn't happen?"

"Hmm," Rachel said thoughtfully. "I see your point. I have had strangers touch me on the bus. Why is that? Is that a Notan thing? I was always taught not to retaliate against Notan strangers unless I feel I'm in danger, but it really pisses me off that they think it's okay to put their hands on me. One time, a guy on the subway grabbed my breast."

"Been there."

"I punched him in the face. I think I knocked out his tooth. When I looked around, everyone nearby acted like I was the one with the problem."

"Yeah," Leda said, "that's what usually happens. If you fight back, it's your fault for making a scene. If you don't fight back, you were asking for it."

"I'd never even heard of 'asking for it' until I came here," Rachel grumbled into the phone. "Part of my training involved dressing to be inconspicuous. The instructor repeatedly told us that women should always try to stay 'at least somewhat covered' in public."

"Yeah," Leda said, equally irritated, "cause men can't be expected to control themselves if they see cleavage. But Arcanans probably don't have that idea."

"No, we do," Rachel said, catching Leda by surprise. "The idea that men can't be expected to control their primal impulses is a very old, very ingrained notion in my world. For thousands of years, it was used to justify keeping men out of positions of power. After all, if they can't control their basic urges, they can't be trusted to act in the best interest of the people."

Leda opened her mouth to respond but then paused. Actually, that did seem like the more logical end to that stereotype. How the hell had Notans taken it to the opposite extreme?

Rachel sighed, her breath so laden with repressed emotion that it seemed to make the phone heavier in Leda's hand. "I never got touched in public in the Arcana. I miss home."

"Yeah," Leda said. "I kinda miss your home, and I've never even been there."

They laughed together, a robust, feminine harmony.

"Oh, hey," Rachel said, still chuckling, "I've got all that software you wanted. I know you wanted the history and language programs but there's some other stuff in this box, too. When I told Creed what I wanted the programs for, he got some ideas of his own, so there's also cultural information and some stuff on daemonic theory. Don't know how much it'll interest you, but Creed seemed excited to have a non-collector for a student. He said you could contact him directly if there was anything else you wanted."

Leda's heart leaped, all the pain of that day forgotten. "Great, I'll take a look at all of it! Aah . . . I can't wait to get started! If I jump into it tonight, I think I'll have a basic understanding of your common language in a few days."

"Wow, that's quick," Rachel said, sounding impressed—a response Leda was accustomed to getting when it came to her language skills. "It took me months to learn English and that was using sleep manipulation techniques to speed up the learning process."

Though grinning, Leda resisted the urge to brag. Whether inspired by daemons or not, pride was still a sin. "Sleep manipulation?" she said instead. "Sounds exhausting. I need my sleep."

"It wears you down a little toward the end, but it really is faster. In less than a year, I learned three Notan languages. Sounds like you're a lot faster than that, though. I'm a little jealous."

All thoughts of her hair had fled. Leda smiled and laughed into her phone, chattering on with Rachel as she would have with any other girlfriend and—for the moment—forgetting the job she would return to in the morning.

52
ASK, AND YE SHALL RECEIVE

Bach approached the church that evening while turning over the events of the morning in his head. Djinn, *ukiba,* and his entire childhood dumped on a curb. Though just hours had passed, he felt years older. He climbed the church steps, wrapped his fingers around the door handle, drew a slow breath, and pulled.

Even before he opened the door, he heard a ruckus of voices filling the nave. Upon entering, the voices boomed with the power of multiple echoes bouncing back to their source.

An assembly of people was gathered at the far end of the floor, rustling paper in their hands and talking to their neighbors. They were standing in three rows, each in front of the other. One man stood at the front, facing them, and he was holding up his hands for attention as he attempted to raise his voice above theirs.

Choir practice, Bach realized. Not wanting to interrupt, he stayed close to the wall as he made his way up the nave and toward the sacristy.

The moment he turned his back to them, the choir burst into song, making him jump. He chuckled to himself, steadied his nerves, and stepped through the sacristy door.

The song of the choir rumbled in the walls as he walked down a hallway lined with doors. Unsure which room he wanted, he knocked on each door he passed. At the fourth knock, he heard a response, opened the door a crack, and peeked inside. A wall of bookshelves lit by drape-filtered sunlight met his eye; the room had a homey vibe. He pushed the door all the way open.

A pair of chairs stood side by side on a woven rug at the center of the room. Opposite the chairs was a desk, its top overflowing with papers and open books. Hunched over those papers was a man in a white collar.

"Father Nathaniel?"

The wiry priest looked up from his desk and his eyes, magnified by his glasses, lit on Bach. His eyebrows twitching with recognition, he waved the young man inside. "Come in, come in! Please have a seat."

"Thanks." Bach plopped down in a chair. Despite its rigid appearance, it was surprisingly cushy. "Do you remember me?"

"Yes, yes!" he said. "The young man with the special talent. I remember very well."

The word "talent" still sounded odd to Bach. It suggested that his sight-beyond was a skill he had honed, rather than it being a fluke. Having a quirky brain didn't seem like the equivalent of studying and training for years.

He shook off the thought and focused. "Sorry to come unannounced."

"Not at all, not at all." Father Nathaniel set aside the book and papers he had been reading and leaned forward, fingers knitted together. "Such a pleasant surprise! What can I do for you?"

"Well . . ." Bach fingered the piece of paper in his pocket. "There's this thing my . . . 'talent' keeps telling me I need to do, and I need a little help to do it."

The priest's eyes sparkled. "Is this a, um, a vision you had, son?" he asked eagerly. "Some particular dream or intuition?"

"It's just something that's been pecking at me for a long time," Bach said. "But there's a problem."

"And what's that?"

"Every time I try to . . . engage this problem, it shorts out my mind. I want to help, but I just . . . I can't."

"Shorts out your mind," the priest repeated, his mouth shaping the words carefully. "I'm afraid I don't understand."

"I ended up under that bridge where you met me because my mind short-circuited and wouldn't function correctly," Bach said. "I think this issue may have been the cause."

"I see, I see." Father Nathaniel tapped one knuckle to his chin.

"Which is why I'm here," Bach continued. "I hate to ask, but I need someone's help. I, uh, I don't have many friends left . . . and the ones I do have aren't really equipped for this sort of thing. So I'm hoping you might be willing."

The priest's enlarged eyes widened even further and he grinned. "Of course, of course," he said. "Nothing happens that is against God's plan. Perhaps this favor you came to ask me is the reason God steered us toward each other. If I can help you, son, I will. Now, what is it that you need?"

"What I need," Bach said, "is for you to lend a hand to the girl who's been putting up these flyers." He removed the crumpled sheet of paper from his pocket and passed it to the priest.

Father Nathaniel unfolded it and adjusted his glasses as he read. "Javier Alvarez."

"The flyers were made by his daughter Tatiana."

"I see, I see," the priest murmured. "And this man and his daughter are the source of your . . . vision?"

"That's about the sum of it."

"Well, what sort of help does the young lady require?"

"I don't really know." Bach sighed. "The only thing I know for sure is that her father's dead."

Sympathy flashed through the priest's eyes. "Oh no, no," he muttered. He stared at the photograph on the paper and shook his head. "The poor man. What happened?"

"I don't know. But I *do* know that his body wasn't identified. It's been labeled as a John Doe and left in the city morgue. She needs someone to take her there to claim it. So . . . could you . . ."

The priest's expression eased. "Oh yes, yes!" Father Nathaniel exclaimed. "Yes, I've performed a similar service for members of my congregation. I can certainly take her. When does she wish to go?"

"Well, that's part of the problem. You see, she's posting these flyers everywhere because she doesn't know he's dead. She just knows he's missing."

"Oh dear," he said, brow furrowed. "The poor child! She must be so worried!" His face fell, the weight of this knowledge dragging it down. He looked at the flyer again and licked his lips. "It does complicate the matter, doesn't it?"

"I don't know what to tell her," Bach said. He rubbed his face with his hands. "She doesn't know he's dead and there's no legitimate way I could know about it. I can't very well explain how I got the information, so . . . what to say?"

Father Nathaniel squinted at the flyer. After swimming in thought for a moment, he tapped the paper with one finger. "I know a young man who was employed by the city morgue until recently. Perhaps if I speak with him about the missing gentleman, he can confirm that the body is there. Once he's told me, then I can simply tell the girl that someone from the morgue recognized him as the man in her flyer, and I offered to be the intermediary to her. That way, your talent need not be mentioned and I can tell her the truth. Would that be satisfactory?"

Bach exhaled, the knot in his stomach loosening at last. This was good. He could let someone else take control of this situation and help Tatiana at the same time. He nodded and smiled. "I knew there had to be a reason I felt I should bring this to you. Yes sir, that sounds ideal."

"Well then!" The priest set the flyer down on his desk. "How do I find Miss Alvarez?"

"A, um, friend of mine told me where to find her. There, on the back of the flyer, he wrote down her address and some places she goes regularly."

Father Nathaniel flipped the paper and scanned the information. Bach knew the writing was unusual, as Azraq's looping script ran top to bottom rather than left to right, but at least it was in English.

The priest gave the handwriting a curious look, but if he had questions about it, he didn't voice them. "I recognize this intersection," he said. "It's another church. If she visits regularly, someone there will know her. I'll give them a call and find out how best to get in touch with her." He looked at Bach and held him in a level gaze. "The young lady will not have to face her father's death alone, son. You have my word."

It was meant to be reassuring and to a certain degree it was. But the feeling Bach had carried with him for months, that nagging sense of having taken a wrong turn despite being on the right road, refused to be appeased. He pushed the feeling aside and smiled at the priest. If he continued to dwell on the feeling, he risked losing control of his mind again.

"Thank you," he said. "I'm really glad to know she'll be in good hands."

Father Nathaniel nodded. He tilted his head and looked carefully at Bach, his magnified eyes penetrating. "Was there something else, my son? You seem troubled."

"Yeah." Bach sank deeper into the chair. All the worries he carried about Tatiana and her father were knocking on the door, just begging to be heard, and here was a good, kind man ready to listen. He threw open the door and let his worries rush out.

"I just don't get it. There have to be dozens of people in this city who've lost loved ones without ever knowing what happened to them. Why is my sight-beyond fixated on this one girl?" He bent forward and hung his arms over his knees. "There's something special about her. She's tied up with my future in some way that I can't see. But why can't I see it? I've never met anyone who was so integral to my life that just thinking about them unhinged me. I don't understand."

"God often asks things of us that we don't understand," Father Nathaniel said. "We have to trust that He has a plan for us all."

"I don't know that my sight-beyond came from God, Father," Bach said. "I don't even know that there *is* a God. My sight-beyond doesn't extend that far."

"Okay, okay," the priest said. "Putting aside questions of the Lord, do you feel that you've done the best you can with what you have? By that I mean, do you feel that you've acted on your visions in a way that will help the people involved?"

"I hope so."

"That's what matters, then. Don't you see, son? Your first instinct is to use to your talent to help people. You're trying your best to do the right thing. Not everyone in your position would do the same." He locked eyes with Bach. "You're a good man."

Bach squirmed, doubt still gnawing at his gut. "And if Tatiana gets hurt because of a choice I made?"

"That's a risk we all take with each and every choice we make. It's the price of living in this world."

The price of living in this world. Was that supposed to comfort him?

"In life, we all risk hurting those around us," Father Nathaniel repeated. "All we can do is try our best to do the right thing."

With great effort, Bach quieted his worries and let Father Nathaniel's words soak in. *We all risk hurting those around us. All we can do is try our best to do the right thing.* He didn't quite believe it today, but he'd carry the words with him and maybe someday they would get past his doubts.

"Thanks, Father," he said. "For everything."

53

HOME

Rachel lay with one foot slung over the arm of the couch, her shoe dangling from her toe, and the other buried in the depths of the cushions, and scrolled through options on the wall screen as she chatted with Leda on the phone. Page after page of Arcanan news rolled by on the wall.

The daemon passed by the sofa, its coat dragging behind. It suddenly stopped dead in its tracks inches from Rachel's face, blocking her view of the screen. Though she didn't have her glasses, she felt certain that the thing was staring at her again. She gave the creature a shove and it shuffled off without a sound.

"I gotta go," Leda said. "I'm gonna head home."

"Okay," replied Rachel. "Talk to you later."

"Bye."

Ending the call, Rachel felt a sense of comfort that she hadn't expected. Talking to Leda had never been this easy before. The woman's intellect was intimidating, and because she had a curiosity to match it, her well of complex questions seemed bottomless. This conversation was the first time Rachel had felt no anxiety at all about not having answers. There were no scribbles in a notebook, no linguistic examinations, no attention to minutia—just two women commiserating over a difficult day. It had actually been fun.

Still lounging and staring at the wall screen, Rachel read through the top headlines. The first one she saw was about the dramatic increase in daemonic activity. As a collector, she was already familiar with the problem; she and her colleagues dealt with it every day. No one seemed to know why daemonic malfunctions had increased across the board, though she'd heard plenty of theories. Frankly, she didn't care why it was happening. She just wanted it to stop so she could get back to a regular work schedule.

Another headline trumpeted a theft in the Central Office. Someone had stolen several bottles of *woz dawl*—a popular and potent alcoholic drink which a few officials always snuck through customs to get them through the year-long audit—along with a bunch of personnel files. The *woz dawl* Rachel understood, but as far as she knew, everything in the personnel files was also in the public records. She sighed and rolled her eyes. Probably whoever stole the files had indulged in the *woz dawl* while still in the Central Office and then stolen the files while drunk. Just once, she'd had a glass of that pink sludge. She remembered only snippets of that night—what she did remember she'd love to forget—and she'd woken up the next day with one eyebrow inexplicably shaved.

She scrolled on, looking for something more interesting to read.

A sudden flash lit up the screen, temporarily blinding her. Blinking rapidly to clear her vision, she looked at the screen again—and when she saw the breaking story headline, her stomach leaped into her chest, strangling her heart.

There was the photo of her kidnapper again, his soulless

eyes boring into her just like they had that night in his basement, but this time there was a banner across the corner of the picture saying, "UPDATE." So tense she could hardly breathe, Rachel leaned in to read the short, freshly posted paragraph.

THE SERIAL MURDERER known as the Breach Killer—so named for his intended purpose of opening a breach into the daemon wastelands—has been tracked to another location. The killer managed to avoid authorities, but he left behind a grisly scene. Two victims, young Notan women, have been found, both murdered in ritual fashion just like the killer's previous victims. Damage to dimensional barriers was minimal. Authorities credit diligent monitoring of dimensional breaches for the killer's failure to make good on his intentions, but questions remain as to how the Breach Killer continues to elude capture. Allegations of an Arcanan conspiracy have dogged this investigation from the beginning but, to date, no solid evidence has been found.

NO SOLID EVIDENCE. That phrase was starting to leave a bad taste in Rachel's mouth. The killer had said things to her that had punched a hole in her view of her people, her home world, but until now she had clung to the fact that his claims were totally unsubstantiated. Now, two more women were dead and he was still free.

Staring into the killer's frozen eyes on the screen, she chewed on her lip and scraped her fingernails on the sofa arm. "No solid evidence" was getting to be a thinner and thinner thread to hold on to.

The front door opened, startling her. Quickly, she closed the news feed and turned off the sound on her phone, just as a message from Suarez lit up the screen.

Did you see it? the text said. *What do you think?*

Rachel didn't think. Instead, she shoved all her troubled thoughts into a mental box, making a note to open that box again the next time she talked to Suarez in person but to keep it closed around Leda; it had not escaped her attention that her new friend was struggling to cope with her emotions related to their abduction. She wanted to keep her informed, but she didn't want to cause her distress.

Both of us are having to readjust our view of the world we thought we knew. I guess we're both having some trouble with it.

The pitter-patter of puppy feet racing through the house, back and forth, back and forth, resounded as Bach strode into the living room.

"I'm back," he said.

"I see that."

"What're you doing?"

"As little as possible." She shrugged. "I'm back to a full work schedule next week and my ribs are still sore. I gotta rest up while I can."

"Okay." He sat down on the edge of the sofa arm nearest her head. "I walked Blue up and down that street with all the restaurants."

"You walked what?"

"Blue," Bach repeated. "That's what I named my dog."

Rachel squinted up at him. "Why Blue?"

"It's what the homeless folks called me when they didn't know my name and it's what Azraq called himself so he could keep his real name private. I passed the name on to the dog because Azraq's free and I don't need it anymore, but I can't afford to forget." He looked down at her and smiled strangely. "I'm not the same person I used to be, and I need to remember why." He looked up at the blank wall screen, but his eyes didn't seem to focus on it. "Maybe that sounds weird, I don't know."

Rachel shook her head. "No, I get it. My mother always says that our experiences should be treated like meals, not photographs; we need to digest them, not carry them around. That way they become part of us and help us grow instead of just becoming stagnant moments from the past. And," she added, "as dog names go, I've heard worse."

"Yeah?"

"Sure. When I was a kid, one of the neighboring clans had a dog named 'Cat.'"

The faraway look on Bach's face vanished as he started laughing. "'Cat?' Wow, that's something! Did a kid give it that name?"

"No, it was a grown man, a neighbor of ours. We could hear him in the evenings, standing on his porch, screaming, 'Cat! Come home, Cat!' Every time he heard it, my grandfather would roll his eyes and go inside, mumbling under his breath about what an idiot that guy was. It went on for seven years, until the dog died. Grandpa was relieved that he wouldn't have to hear about Cat the dog anymore. Then the guy got another dog and named it 'Tree.'" Rachel grinned at the memory. "You should've seen Grandpa the first time we heard, 'Tree! Come home, Tree!'"

Laughter shook Bach's body so heartily that he slipped from the sofa arm and slid to the floor. From another room, Blue came running, jumped into his lap, and licked his master's face with enthusiasm. Rachel smiled, the memory of her grandfather's exasperated expression stirring up a pleasant homeland feeling.

Bach continued chuckling madly as he rubbed the dog's ears. "You have dogs on your family's farm?" he asked.

"Three," she said. "Two herders and one hunter."

"Herders, huh? Nokis?"

"No. S'vahs. And the hunter's an allee."

"What are their names?"

"Vena, Dromi, and Custo. That would translate to . . ." She thought for a moment. "Swifty, Smartass, and Tough Guy."

"I like the names," Bach said. "I should've let you name Blue."

"Just as well you didn't. I'd have named him *Tulira*."

Bach frowned. "I still don't know what that means, but I know it's not good."

"It means . . . 'useless,' more or less," Rachel said.

"'Useless,' huh?" Bach shook his head and scratched the dog's chin. "Don't sell him short. You never know what he'll grow into."

The puppy looked up at Rachel, wagging his tail. She rolled her eyes. He was kind of cute, but that didn't change the fact that with no livestock to herd, he served no useful purpose.

"Listen," Bach said, cuddling Blue, "when we were out on our walk, I picked up a few job applications from restaurants. I'm gonna look for a more permanent job, too, but in the meantime I'll wait tables, bartend, wash dishes . . . I'll take whatever I can get. So I might be out of the house at odd hours. Just wanted you to know."

"Okay," she said. "Do what you need to do."

"Is it okay if I leave Blue here when I'm gone?"

"So long as he doesn't destroy anything of mine."

"Got it." He hugged the wiggling puppy to his chest and kissed the top of his head. "I won't stay here forever, Ra. I promise. As soon as I find a long-term job, I'll go."

"No rush. So far, you've been a fairly useful houseguest."

She glanced up at the ceiling. "And you're decent company, too."

"Thanks. You too."

Blue fixed his eyes on Rachel again and, wagging his tail, lunged toward her. Bach pulled him away and rose to his feet.

"Want some dinner?" he asked. "I've got a shitload of chicken in the fridge."

"Sure." She pulled herself up and started to lead the way to the kitchen.

"Y'know something, Ra?"

She stopped and glanced back at him. "What?"

"I feel good," he said, wearing a more relaxed expression than she was used to seeing on his face. "My life's not perfect—whose is?—but that's okay. I'm starting to feel like myself again. In fact, I feel more like myself now than when I was living in my parents' house or the apartment they paid for. This time, I'm not hiding parts of me or juggling different masks for different people. I feel honest . . . I feel real. Things are hard, but I feel good." He smiled, the electric glow of his eyes warming her. "Thanks for being part of it."

After a moment's hesitation, Rachel returned a slight smile. Things were happening in her life that bothered her and made her worry for the future. A man who'd tried to kill her, who had killed many women, was still free, and there was a very real chance that her own people were responsible. She was divided from her family and her world and still had months to wait before she could go home. But she had made new friends here and was finding the experience of knowing them rewarding. She would be sad to say goodbye to Leda and Bach one day, something she never would have guessed when she first came to the Nota.

Unlike Bach, she didn't feel good . . . but she didn't feel bad.

On balance, she was okay. And there was nothing wrong with that.

Nodding, she smiled at him again, a little wider this time. "You're welcome."

54

GOLD

A teenage boy slouched down the street, his sandy hair hanging in his eyes and his hands jammed in his pockets. As he turned the corner, he pulled a folded-up cap from his back pocket and slipped it on his head just a few steps before crossing into view of the security camera across the street.

Halfway up the block, he subtly moved to his right to avoid the buttery glow of the streetlights. Securely wrapped in shadow, he continued on his way, pulling his jacket tight under his chin. He glanced over his shoulder, quickly ducked into an alley, and jogged toward the back of the building.

There, sitting behind the dumpster, out of sight of the back windows, was another boy also with his jacket collar turned up and wearing a cap.

The younger teen jumped to his feet when he saw the newcomer. "Hey!"

"Hey."

The younger boy trotted over, his dark curls bouncing around his ears. "Did ya bring it?"

"Uh, yeah," said the older boy in a voice soaked with disdain. "Of course."

"Don't be a dick, Michael. You've forgotten before."

"Once, Ian," Michael said through a snarl. "Just that one time I forgot." He scanned the back alley from underneath the visor of his cap. "Where the hell's Freddie?"

"He's coming."

"Anybody notice you?"

"No way." Ian snorted. "I've been watching that Arab family since dinner. I think they closed the market early. They've got a visitor or something upstairs."

"Well, that'll make this easier."

"Hey"—Ian pulled a cell phone from his coat pocket—"did Dad call you? I got, like, four messages from him."

"What about?"

"The first message was to ask if we knew where the fish from the fridge had gone. Then he texted to say that if we had the fish, we better bring it back, 'cause we're having it for dinner. Then he texted to tell me that we better not be using the fish for anything weird. The last message said that since we'd stolen our dinner, he was going out to eat and we're on our own."

"Whatever." Michael spat on the ground. "So, where's the fish?"

"Here." Ian snatched up a bag from beside the dumpster and held it out toward his brother.

"Good." Michael took the bag and peeked inside. "Four pieces."

"One for each corner of the market."

Michael scowled at Ian. "That's stupid. "If we just put 'em in the corners, the Arabs'll find 'em too quick."

Ian's cupid-bow lips grew taunt. "So where do you wanna put 'em, genius?"

"In the vents, dumbass. That's where ya put 'em so nobody finds 'em. When they're in the vents the stink gets spread all over, and it's harder for people to figure out where the smell's coming from."

Ian's eyes widened and he grinned, his face beaming respect. "Yeah!" he crowed. "That's a good idea!"

"Shut up, moron! They'll hear you!" Michael grabbed Ian and yanked him deeper into the shadows behind the building.

Together, they stared up at the second-story windows, the light behind the blinds outlining vague shapes moving within the apartment. Their eyes drifted lower, to the market, which was locked up for the night, empty and dark. The boys flashed identical impish expressions.

"Come on, let's do it," Michael said.

"What about Freddie?" Ian asked. "He wanted to be here for this."

"Then he shoulda got here on time," Michael replied. "I don't wanna sit in this shithole all night. Let's go."

Clutching the bag of fish close to his side, Michael looked all around the alley for any possible witness, then pulled his cap a little lower over his eyes and headed for the market's back door. Ian copied his brother's actions before falling into step behind him.

From the pocket of his coat, Michael removed two thin strips of metal. He shoved the bag at his brother, knelt by the back door, inserted one piece into the lock, and jimmied it into place. Just as he was about to insert the second piece, the sound of approaching footsteps made him jump to his feet. Heart pounding, he snagged Ian by the arm and dragged him toward the dumpster.

No sooner had they ducked out of sight than the owner of the footsteps appeared. Short, skinny, all knees and elbows, he spun in a circle as he searched the alley.

"Michael?" he shouted. "Ian?"

The pair rushed their youngest brother, racing to clap a hand over his mouth.

"Freddie, shut the hell up!" Ian said.

"What the fuck are you shouting like that for?" Michael hissed. "Someone's gonna see us!"

"I'm sorry," Freddie mumbled from behind their hands. "I forgot. But look, I remembered to wear my hat this time."

"Won't do any good if someone catches us in the act." Michael turned his back on his brothers. "Forget it. Let's just do it." He kneeled on the back step and resumed picking the lock while Ian stood behind him, keeping watch.

Freddie ducked around Ian and poked Michael in the shoulder. "I brought something!"

Michael shot a glare at him and pushed him back. "You're in the way."

"But look what I brought." Freddie fished a cardboard box out of his coat pocket. "I got it at the pet store. I thought it'd be good for tonight." He shoved the box under Michael's nose.

Without looking down, Michael pushed him away again. Undeterred, his youngest brother popped open the lid of the box just a hair and showed it to him again.

To get him out of his face, Michael took a peek inside. "Crickets?"

"*Crickets?*" Ian echoed.

"Don't you remember how nuts it made Dad when that cricket was in the house last month?" Freddie said. "I thought it would be great to turn a bunch of crickets loose in somebody's house. Think how crazy everyone'll get when they all start chirping."

Freddie's face practically hummed with hopeful excitement.

The metal strips still pinched in his fingers, Michael stared at the box for a moment—and then chuckled. "That's pretty smart." He gave his little brother a smile and a nod, causing Freddie to grin from ear to ear. "It's funny as hell. Let's do it."

"Tonight?" Freddie asked, eyes all aglow.

"Yeah, tonight. We'll hide the fish in the vents and then you can sneak your crickets under the door to their apartment." He smirked at Freddie. "Okay?"

Freddie puffed out his chest. "Hell yeah!"

"Keep it down," Ian hissed, lightly smacking the boy upside the head. "Michael, come on. Get the door open already. I thought you didn't wanna be stuck out here all night."

"Yeah, yeah, yeah," Michael said, returning his attention to the lock. "Don't get your panties in a bunch."

Minutes passed, the quiet broken only by the gentle click of the picks in the lock. Then there was another click, louder than the others, and Michael, with a light touch to the knob, opened the door. He clucked his tongue, stood tall, and straightened his coat. "We're good to go."

The two younger brothers moved to his sides and the three of them advanced on the market. Michael was one step shy of the threshold when the door, without so much as a squeak, slammed itself shut.

The brothers stopped short, gasping as one. Michael grabbed the knob and tried to turn it. It didn't budge.

"What the fuck?" he mumbled. He whipped the two picks from his pocket and, his face scrunched up with impatience, stooped to the lock again. "I just opened this."

Before he could place the first one inside the lock, the metal pieces were ripped from his hands as if seized by a tornado. Before their shocked eyes, the picks zig-zagged between the boys, hovered in their midst, and then flew across the alley and embedded to half their length in a brick wall. Chips of brick sprinkling the ground like rain, the metal sang with vibration until it came to rest. The boys stared at the picks with mouths agape.

Suddenly the cricket box was knocked from Freddie's hands, making the boy yelp. The box struck the ground and the lid flipped off, freeing the crickets to scatter in all directions. An eerie groan wafted through the air.

Freddie whimpered, clutching at Ian, whose hands shook so badly that the bag of fish slipped from his grasp and landed near his feet. Ian stared at Michael, shaking his head while slowly backing away.

With an effort, Michael swallowed his fear and reached for the doorknob again. Before he could make contact, something hot grabbed his wrist in an iron grip. A second later, he felt a sledgehammer's worth of force strike him in the chest and hurl him backward. He soared a full three yards into the alley and landed hard on his backside.

Gasping, he crab-walked backward, eyes frantically searching for whatever had hit him, until he collided with the dumpster.

Ian dashed to his elder brother, Freddie on his heels. "Michael, let's go!"

"Wha—?" Michael panted. "Wha—?"

"Dad says ghosts probably aren't real," said Freddie from behind Ian, "but that if they are, everybody should leave them the hell alone."

When Michael remained frozen where he was, Ian and Freddie shuffled up the alley without him, edging away from the door. Michael felt paralyzed in place, capable only of listening to his own breath and feeling his own heartbeat. Then a scraping sound broke the air, startling him.

His eyes darted about the alley. Aside from his retreating

brothers, it was empty. Yet the sound drew closer and closer.

A low growl thundered so close to his ear that he could feel the breath of whatever had made it. A primitive instinct suddenly engaged: he leaped to his feet, dashed up the alley, grabbed each younger boy by one arm, and propelled them out to the street.

Together, the three Bell brothers raced away from the El Sayeds' market and ran for home.

SAFIYA OPENED THE hallway window and looked out into the alley. There were some unusual noises outside this evening, but she saw nothing. After another quick scan, she shrugged and closed the blinds.

"Wait, Mama!" Naji called. He jogged down the hallway from the kitchen, a plate in his hands. "I wanna put this outside!"

"Naji, don't run in the house," she scolded. "What do you have there?"

He held the plate up for her to see. It contained the carcass of the roast chicken they had eaten for dinner—its bones, gristle, and fat. Safiya squinted at the plate and then at her son.

"What on earth are you doing with this?" she asked.

"It's for Azraq," he said.

"The Djinni?"

"He eats bones. Mr. Bach said so."

"Azraq left," she said. "He has gone his own way."

"Mr. Bach promised I would see him again."

She smiled and knelt beside him. "I cannot speak for what Mr. Bach knows," she said, smoothing his hair, "but Azraq was trapped in the box a long time. After being alone for so long, I'm sure he must be eager to see other Djinn. Perhaps he will come again one day, but surely not so soon." She kissed his cheek. "Do you understand?"

Naji nodded but his hopeful expression was unchanged. He smiled at his mother and held out the plate to her.

"I want to leave the plate for him," he said. "Just in case he comes back, I want him to know that it's okay for him to stay. Can I put it outside?"

Safiya sighed. She had no objection to her boy's request—aside from the concern that the bones would attract rodents—but she didn't want to give him false hope. Seeing his optimistic face, she worried that his little heart would break if the Marid did not return soon. *But who am I to say what a Djinni will do and where he will go?* she thought. *Perhaps he will come back sooner rather than later. And if he never returns, well . . . every broken heart in the world continues to beat.*

She smiled at her son and nodded. "Very well."

Naji's smile widened, and without hesitation he fixed his eyes on the landing of the fire escape outside and tightened his muscles, intensifying his focus.

A kick in her gut warned Safiya what he was up to and she quickly broke into his concentration. "Do not 'poof' the plate!"

Naji pouted. "But—"

"No!" she said. "I have seen you make that face with Mr. Odero. You will not 'poof' that plate through the window. I will open it and you will set it outside. With your hands."

Naji scowled. "Okay, fine."

Safiya sighed. It was going to take some getting used to, having a son with an otherworldly talent. As much as Naji had to learn about his gift, there was just as much for her to understand. They would both have to come to terms with it, each in their own way.

She drew the blinds, unlocked the window, and shimmied the sticky pane up. Naji leaned out as far as he could go and set the plate of chicken remains on the fire escape next to her potted herbs. The cool breeze of the evening stirred the plants, blending the rich scent of the herbs with the fading aroma of their dinner. Safiya checked her son's face and smiled at how pleased he clearly was with his work. She closed the window, and put an arm around his shoulders.

"Let's go back to the kitchen," she said.

"But what if he comes tonight?" he asked.

"Then we should let him enjoy his meal in peace," she said. "Come, let's have some hot chocolate."

The offer of chocolate was a sufficient distraction; Naji hurried down the hall to the kitchen.

About to follow her son, Safiya glanced back at the window. A tiny glitter of gold flashed through the blinds, catching her eye. She paused, pushed up one blind slat with her fingers, and looked again. All she saw was her own reflection in the glass staring back at her.

She chuckled, shook her head, and turned away. As she walked on to catch up with Naji, she caught herself wondering if the bones would still be there in the morning.

THE BAG OF fish was torn, chunks of the filets strewn about the alley for the stray cats to find. The bones and scales were gone. Up on the fire escape, one bone snapped from the chicken carcass and disappeared. A glint of gold—the glint of a locket swinging on its chain—flashed briefly in the shadows, and then vanished to the crunch of another chicken bone.

ACKNOWLEDGMENTS

Thank you to my husband, Matt. His love and encouragement keep me going.

Thank you to my son, Eric. Watching him grow keeps my imagination engaged.

Thank you to Eileen McFalls, Barbara Levin, and the Women Writers of the Triad critique group. I continue to grow as a writer because of their time and effort.

Thank you to the staff of SparkPress for polishing this book into its final form.

Thank you.

ABOUT THE AUTHOR

Credit: Ivan Saul Cutler

ALISON LEVY lives in Greensboro, North Carolina, with her husband, son, and variety of pets. When she's not writing or doing mom things, she crochets, gardens, walks her collies, and works on home improvement projects.

SELECTED TITLES FROM SPARKPRESS

SparkPress is an independent boutique publisher delivering high-quality, entertaining, and engaging content that enhances readers' lives, with a special focus on female-driven work. www.gosparkpress.com

Gatekeeper: Book One in the Daemon Collecting Series, Alison Levy, $16.95, 978-1-68463-057-8. Rachel Wilde—sent from another dimension to bring defective daemons in for repair—needs to locate two people: a woman whose ancestors held a destructive daemon at bay and a criminal trying to break dimensional barriers. Helped by a homeless man with unusual powers, she uncovers a rising shadow organization that's changing her world forever.

Ocean's Fire: Book One in the Equal Night Trilogy, Stacey L. Tucker. $16.95, 978-1-943006-28-1. Once the Greeks forced their male gods upon the world, the belief in the power of women was severed. For centuries it has been thought that the wisdom of the high priestesses perished at the hand of the patriarchs—but now the ancient Book of Sophia has surfaced. Its pages contain the truths hidden by history, and the sacred knowledge for the coming age. And it is looking for Skylar Southmartin.

Alchemy's Air: Book Two of the Equal Night Trilogy, Stacey L. Tucker. $16.95, 978-1-943006-84-7. Now that she's passed her trial by fire, Skylar Southmartin has been entrusted with the ancient secrets of the Book of Sophia. Ahead is her greatest mission to date: a journey to the Underworld to restore a vital memory to the Akashic Library that will bring her face to face with the darkness within.

Sky of Water: Book Three of the Equal Night Trilogy, Stacey L. Tucker. $16.95, 978-1-68463-040-0. Having emerged triumphant from her trials in the Underworld, Skylar Southmartin is stronger and gutsier, and can handle anything that comes her way. In the gripping climax of the Equal Night Trilogy, she uncovers one last secret no one saw coming—one that Vivienne, the Great Mother of Water, hoped would stay buried for another 13,000 years.